Sammy Rambles
and the
Angel of 'El Horidore

J T SCOTT

Sammy Rambles and the Angel of 'El Horidore

www.sammyrambles.com

For Ari & Sam

J T SCOTT

J T Scott lives in Devon with Ari and Sam surrounded by open countryside, lots of castles, pens, paper and a vivid imagination.

Also available in the Sammy Rambles series:

Sammy Rambles and the Floating Circus
Sammy Rambles and the Land of the Pharaohs
Sammy Rambles and the Angel of 'El Horidore
* Sammy Rambles and the Fires of Karmandor
* Sammy Rambles and the Knights of the Stone Cross

* Awaiting publication.

More information about Sammy, Dixie and Darius can be found on the Sammy Rambles website.

www.sammyrambles.com

Sammy Rambles and the Angel of 'El Horidore

Chapter List:

CHAPTER 1

DARIUS ARRIVES

A bright purple, orange and lime green minibus full of people trundled past Sammy Rambles's living room window and stopped abruptly outside his green front door.

Loud dance music was blaring from the radio, the booming of drum beats breaking the silence in the otherwise peaceful village street.

Children of all ages were singing along to the music and shouting at each other. They were standing on the seats and rocking the minibus from side to side.

Large blue letters printed on the side of the minibus said "Murphy Family Dragon Healers – Looking After Your Dragons Since 1980".

Above the brightly coloured minibus, there were several large dragons circling around the nearby houses. They were huffing impatiently at the interruption to their journey.

The dragons cast huge, dark, aeroplane shaped shadows through the living room window.

Seeing the shadows, Sammy threw down the magazine he had been reading, leaped up from his chair and dashed out of the room.

'Darius is here!' Sammy yelled to his parents. 'Come down quickly! His parents are dropping him off! Darius is finally here!'

Sammy raced along the hallway and threw open the front door. He charged out onto the pavement.

'Hi Darius!' Sammy shouted, tapping his hand on the glass window of the minibus. 'I've been waiting all morning for you!'

A dark skinned, dark haired boy pushed his way to the front of the minibus and dragged open the sliding side door.

'Hi Sammy!' yelled the boy. He dragged a brown and black suitcase with the initials "D.M." embossed on the straps out of the minibus and threw it on to the pavement, narrowly missing Sammy's feet.

Sammy jumped out of the way as Darius leaped out of the minibus after his suitcase, landing awkwardly and falling over into a heap on the ground.

With a huge grin on his face Darius got to his feet. 'I'm here!' he said triumphantly.

Someone inside the minibus shut the brightly coloured door with a bang and within seconds the purple, orange and lime green minibus was being driven off down the street at top speed.

Hands waved out of every window and above the drums and electric guitars on the radio they heard Darius's family shouting goodbye and telling him to be good at school.

The large dragons followed the minibus, their wings creating the familiar black aeroplane shaped shadows all the way down the road.

Sammy and Darius waved vigorously until the minibus turned the corner and was out of sight. The music faded and Sammy picked up Darius's brown and black suitcase. It was surprisingly heavy.

'Come on,' said Sammy, heaving the suitcase, 'let's go inside.'

'Sorry I'm late,' said Darius, giving Sammy a hand pushing the suitcase through the doorway. 'It was because of all that lot. We stopped eight times, "can we stop for food", "can we stop for the toilet", and then,' Darius waved his arms in the air, 'then we had to stop for petrol!' He frowned, 'then we stopped for…dragons.'

Sammy nodded, knowing that Darius's parents were Healers who helped sick dragons. They travelled all over the country in the family minibus, stopping every time someone needed help.

Sometimes Darius's parents were called to help with something simple, like a stone or thorn caught in a dragon's paw, or to give a dragon medication to cure a cold. Other times they performed on the spot surgery, helping to mend broken bones or broken wings.

'There was one dragon with its draconite stone half in, half out,' Darius continued, 'but we fixed him.'

'That's awful,' said Sammy, thinking about the precious, sparkling, shimmering stone, called draconite, found inside the dragon's brain that enables a dragon to breathe fire and to fly. Without draconite, a dragon cannot breathe at all and would die instantly. 'Do you think it was the Shape?'

Darius nodded. 'I think it was the Shape. Who else could it be?'

'Is that Darius, honey?' a voice belonging to Julia Rambles, Sammy's mother, called down the hallway.

'Yeah, he's just arrived,' shouted Sammy.

Julia Rambles appeared in the kitchen doorway. She had the same blonde hair and blue eyes as Sammy and was about the same height as her son, now that Sammy had grown a few inches over the summer. She was wearing a green apron over her white blouse and three quarter length denim jeans and her hands were covered in flour.

'Hello Darius,' said Julia. 'I hope you had a good journey. It's lovely having you to stay. Sammy, please take his suitcase upstairs and call your father. Dinner is nearly ready.'

Sammy led Darius through the hallway, heaving the suitcase, which weighed a ton, up the narrow twisting staircase on to the landing. He knocked on his parents' bedroom door. He could hear the shower running in the en-suite bathroom.

'Dinner's ready Dad!' Sammy yelled.

Not waiting for a reply, Sammy and Darius ran to the door that led into the airing cupboard. Behind the wooden slatted door were rails of his father's shirts and his mother's skirts and another smaller, wooden staircase that led up into the attic flat.

They thundered up the steps into the fully furnished, two-bedroom flat above the house. The flat had been given to Sammy to use after his uncle, who owned the house and jewellery shop downstairs, admitted that he was the "P" in the Shape and had been arrested and detained for further questioning.

At the end of Sammy's first year at school, his uncle had admitted that he wanted to kill all the dragons in the world and steal their draconite. Sammy had learnt that by having draconite, this might give his uncle control of the elements of earth, air, fire and water, invincibility and immortality.

Sammy's uncle, his mother's brother, Peter Pickering, had signed both the house and jewellery shop over to his sister, Sammy's mother, Julia Rambles, when he had been taken prisoner two months ago by the Snorgcadell.

The Snorgcadell, also known as the Dragon Cells, are the organisation in the dragon world which was set up to fight the Shape and stop the Shape from killing all the dragons.

Using his belongings, which had been delivered from his parents' old house in Ratisbury, Sammy had tried to make the flat more like home.

Although the boxes had been in the flat for just over six weeks since the Ratisbury house was sold, Sammy hadn't finished unpacking and many of his books and toys were still in cardboard boxes.

Sammy had found the process of unpacking his things rather tricky since he was sharing the flat with three fully grown dragons, his own dragon, Kyrillan, and now Darius and his dragon, Nelson, who had stuck his navy blue head out of the top of Darius's suitcase.

'You put your dragon in your suitcase?' exclaimed Sammy. 'No wonder it was so heavy! How did you do it?'

Darius let out one of his famous explosive giggles and held out his hand to his dragon. 'Come here Nelson. Did you sleep on our way to Sammy's house?'

Ignoring Darius, Nelson looked around the room, his black eyes taking in his new surroundings. He stretched his navy blue body and crawled out of the top of Darius's brown and black suitcase. His sharp claws gripped the side and he stood up tall on his hind legs. Tiny wings expanded and grew wide as he spread them to their full span. Nelson opened his mouth and yawned loudly, showing two rows of sharp white teeth.

The dragons were being kept in the flat in secret and Sammy's parents knew nothing about any of them. They couldn't see them or hear them and as far as they were concerned, dragons did not exist.

'How did you get him into your suitcase?' repeated Sammy, but Darius just laughed even harder and he could get no sense out of his friend at all.

'Where's Kyrillan?' asked Darius when he finally stopped laughing.

'Probably in my bedroom,' said Sammy, puffing slightly as he lifted Nelson's heavy spiky tail away from the small television on the sideboard. 'Gerrup!'

Nelson obliged, flicking his tail and scattering a tub of jelly beans in every direction. Darius let off another of his famous giggles as he clonked heads with Sammy as they bent down to pick them up.

As they straightened themselves, Sammy noticed a puff of pale orange smoke wafting from the second bedroom towards them.

'Do you remember Cyngard, Jovah and Paprika?' asked Sammy.

'Your parents and your uncle's dragons, yes, of course,' whispered Darius nervously.

Sammy didn't blame Darius for being scared. All of the dragons had grown steadily over the summer. He had fed them a varied diet of hay, mice, sweets and, when he felt it safe to smuggle it up, a variety of cooked and fresh meat he had bought with his pocket money from the butcher in the village.

When Sammy had told the butcher why his parents weren't able to collect the meat themselves, the butcher had frowned, then smiled, then from that day onwards he had given Sammy double servings at half price.

'Shall I call them?' asked Sammy. 'You can see how much they've grown.'

Darius nodded. 'Go on.'

'Cyngard! Jovah! Paprika!' called Sammy, pronouncing their names "Sin-guard", "Yo-vah" and "Pa-pree-car".

There was a scuffling noise in the second bedroom and the clinking of scales as the three adult dragons marched into the lounge area.

Paprika, Peter Pickering's dragon, was first to emerge from the bedroom. She was a large, orange dragon, the size of a medium sized van, with streaks of pink, yellow and red on her tummy. She marched into the middle of the room and stared at the new occupants with her dark black eyes.

Cyngard and Jovah followed Paprika into the lounge. Their footsteps sounded like thunder and their scales made a loud clinking sound as they walked into the lounge.

They were the same size as the orange dragon, however Cyngard, Charles Rambles's dragon, had jet black scales and enormous amber eyes. Julia Rambles's dragon, Jovah, was forest green in colour with a pattern of gold streaks on her back and all the way down her tail.

Darius took a step backwards. 'They've got enormous,' he whispered.

'It's ok,' said Sammy. 'They should remember you from when you stayed at Christmas.'

Darius nodded and stepped forwards, going up close to Paprika, Peter Pickering's dragon, to inspect her.

'Paprika could do with some fresh air,' said Darius. 'She's missing your uncle. Her scales are dull.'

'I know,' said Sammy, 'but I can't ride her. She's gone wild without Uncle Peter here. I've had to buy loads of green pellets to keep her quiet at night.'

'Can I try getting on her back and take her flying?' asked Darius, his eyes gleaming, his fears forgotten. 'I've always wanted to ride a fully grown dragon.'

'Um,' started Sammy. He was sure his parents wouldn't approve. 'Maybe after tea? How are you going to get outside?'

Darius grinned and tapped his nose. 'Wait and see.'

CHAPTER 2

TELEPORTING

Downstairs, Sammy and Darius found that Charles and Julia Rambles had already started eating the home cooked Chinese banquet Sammy's mother had prepared.

There were four oval plates with a mother of pearl rim on the dining room table. Each plate had a mountain of delicious smelling chicken and sauce. Silver chopsticks were laid beside each plate and there were side dishes of noodles, beansprouts, chestnuts and brightly coloured yellow, pink and orange rice.

Sammy and Darius sat opposite each other and helped themselves to the mountain of food. Julia poured a glass of red wine for herself and Sammy's father and glasses of cola for Sammy and Darius.

'I've had a letter from Uncle Peter, Sammy,' said Julia. 'He says we are to make use of the whole house and its residents for as long as he is away at the Snorgcadell.'

'The Snorgcadell?' interrupted Charles. 'Does the letter say that is where he has gone?'

'Snorg-cad-ell?' repeated Julia. 'It sounds vaguely familiar. Didn't we use to…'

Sammy leaned forward, accidentally elbowing his drink and knocking the contents into the last of the beansprouts. Charles Rambles tutted and a wail came from upstairs.

'Clumsy,' said Charles.

'Be more careful honey,' soothed Julia. 'I'll go upstairs this time.'

Sammy and Darius helped mop up the spilt drink and rescue the drowning beansprouts.

'She said that "Snorgcadell" sounds familiar,' Sammy whispered as his mother returned with a powder pink baby wrapped in an emerald green towel.

'She needs changing,' said Julia, smiling at the baby.

'Darius, meet Eliza, my baby sister,' said Sammy.

Darius gawped at the baby.

'Trying to be a fish Darren?' Charles laughed. 'Have you never seen a baby before?'

'It's Dar-i-us, Charles,' said Julia frowning. 'I do wish you would pay more attention to Sammy's friends.' She turned to Darius, patting the back of the green towel. 'Sammy has been playing at the home of the little girl with green hair these past few weeks, haven't you darling.'

Sammy pulled a face at Darius. 'Please can we leave the table?'

'It's "may" Sam, please "may" we leave the table,' sighed Charles.

Sammy nodded at his father. 'Please may we leave the table?'

'Of course honey,' said Julia, 'just use the downstairs lounge for now. Your father and I would like to see you without you tearing up to your room.'

Sammy and Darius helped clear the table and take the dirty dishes out into the kitchen. Then they settled down in the comfy chairs in the lounge and turned on the television.

Dr Livitupadup's chat show was on and Sammy and Darius roared with laughter as the host played pranks on his guests and set them impossible challenges. Just at the end of the show, Sammy's father came into the lounge.

Charles looked at the television and shook his head. 'We must get the television people out,' he grumbled. 'Where's BBC1?'

'Board games anyone?' asked Julia, returning with baby Eliza covered from head to toe in a green jumpsuit. Specks of talcum powder rose in a wisping cloud as Julia sat down.

'Not for me,' said Charles, switching the television off. 'I have letters to write, then the books for Peter's jewellers to do.'

'He's doing both jobs,' explained Julia. 'By day he runs Sammy's uncle's jewellery shop. Would you believe it? Charles has a natural skill with the gemstones. He knows so much about them all. An undiscovered talent,' she laughed, 'and then by night he works as a solicitor for his London clients, helping with their legal cases and once a week he also does the accounts for the shop.'

'Oh,' said Darius. 'He sounds as busy as my parents. They work all day and all night too. What games have you got that we can play?'

Julia pointed at the bookcase behind the television. 'Have a look. There are some games up there.'

'Hey cool!' said Darius, examining the shelf. 'You've got Castle Rocks! Can we play that?'

'Of course we can,' said Julia, patting Eliza on the back.

More talcum powder erupted into a cloud above her head. Eliza gave a little cough and Julia patted her again.

'It's one of Peter's games,' said Julia. 'You'll have to explain the rules to me. I haven't played it before.'

Darius picked the square cardboard box off the bookcase shelf and unpacked the game on the coffee table. He unfolded the playing board, which was round with a three dimensional plastic castle shaped tower in the middle. The tower had numerous windows at regular intervals up its walls.

Narrow paths made from different coloured squares painted on the board led in different directions to get to the castle tower and the tower itself was filled to the top with small grey plastic rocks.

Darius unpacked piles of coloured coins, two large white dice with black spots and four different playing tokens. There was a silver knight, a white horse, a black shield and a bag of golden treasure.

'Can I be the knight?' asked Darius, picking up the shiny silver swordsman.

'I want to be the horse,' said Sammy. 'Mum, do you want to be the shield or the treasure?'

'I don't mind,' said Julia. 'Do we have to collect the coins?'

'Yes,' said Darius. 'I've played this loads of times. You start with ten coins. Then you throw the dice and move around the board. If you land on these squares,' he pointed to the black squares, 'then the castle drops a rock on you and you lose a coin. Whoever gets to the castle with the most coins wins. Can I go first?'

Julia laughed and nodded. 'Of course Darius honey, you're our guest. You may go first. Good luck!'

Darius shook the two white dice and rolled them onto the table.

'Double six!' exclaimed Darius, moving his silver swordsman twelve squares around the board. 'It's a double so I get to go again!'

On his second roll of the dice, Darius scored three and his swordsman landed on a black square. There was a click and a small window opened in the plastic castle. A small grey plastic rock rolled to the edge of the window and fell down onto the playing board. The plastic rock landed on Darius's swordsman's head and knocked him over.

'Oh no! I lose a coin!' Darius groaned and took one of his ten coins and tossed it back into the cardboard box.

He put the plastic rock back into the top of the castle tower and stood his swordsman back upright.

'Sammy, you go next,' said Darius, handing over the two white dice. 'Just don't land on the black squares!'

Several hours later, Sammy fell asleep dreaming of the grey rocks falling from the grey tower as the playing tokens moved around the board. He dreamed he was riding on the white horse, galloping around the paths as rocks fell all around him.

He awoke to the sound of Kyrillan snoring softly at the bottom of his bed. Relieved it wasn't rocks falling through the ceiling, Sammy got out of bed and dressed in his favourite blue and green striped t-shirt and denim jeans.

Sammy went into the kitchen area in the attic flat. Darius was already up and was feeding Paprika a bundle of hay at the breakfast table. Sammy picked up his homemade "Countdown to Dragamas" calendar and crossed off a new day.

'Morning,' said Darius.

'Hi,' said Sammy, rubbing sleep from his eyes. 'Help yourself to breakfast. There should be some Sugarcorn Flakes in the cupboard.'

Darius looked guiltily at Sammy. 'I've just given them all to Paprika.'

'She doesn't normally eat them,' said Sammy.

Darius shrugged. 'She ate the whole lot this morning.'

'The whole lot?' Sammy tipped up the Sugarcorn Flakes box. A few crumbly flakes and a green plastic toy dragon fell out onto the kitchen work surface.

Sammy threw the box into the pedal bin and moved the plastic dragon onto the shelf next to the fruit bowl, where there were three other plastic toy dragons. There was a red dragon, a blue one and a yellow one. He poured himself a glass of cold milk from the fridge and went into the lounge area.

'Sorry,' Darius apologised. 'She wants to eat everything in sight!'

Sammy took a step back as his parents' dragons, Cyngard and Jovah ambled into the lounge. With a puff of grey smoke, Cyngard flopped onto the floor, resting his large black head on the two seat sofa.

'Off,' said Sammy half-heartedly. He turned to Darius. 'So, do you want to see if Paprika will fly?'

Darius nodded vigorously. 'I'll get my boots and Nelson's harness.'

He returned a moment later armed with a pair of elbow length dragon hide gloves, a pair of shiny black leather boots, which he tugged over his jeans up to his knees, and a jangling metal harness slung over his left shoulder.

'Come on girl!' shouted Darius, leaping onto Paprika's scaly orange back.

Sammy watched open mouthed as Darius slung the harness over the dragon's neck. Paprika reared up onto her hind legs, her tail swishing angrily. Sammy hastily tossed some green pellets into her mouth.

Paprika calmed down instantly. She lowered herself onto her four clawed paws and breathed a faint wisp of smoke.

'Thanks,' grinned Darius. 'Hop on behind me!'

Gingerly, Sammy hoisted himself up, hitching his leg around Paprika's tail for balance.

'Outside!' shouted Darius.

'Outside!' shouted Sammy.

'Hurrumphide!' roared Paprika. Her dragonish voice was so loud that the other dragons scuttled for cover.

Sammy felt a cool breeze wash across his face and the room slid out of focus. He closed his eyes, bracing himself.

When he opened his eyes, he and Darius were outside in the sunshine. They were perched on top of his uncle's garden shed. His mother and father were sitting with Eliza on a blanket on the patio, playing with plastic bricks.

Charles stood up when he saw them. 'Get down from there Sam!' barked Charles. 'What on earth do you think you're doing playing games like that?'

'I didn't see them come through the door,' said Julia, scratching her head.

'Dixie's garden,' Darius whispered in Sammy's ear and gave the sign for teleporting, scrunching and flexing his fingers into a fist.

'Dixie's garden,' echoed Sammy, closing his eyes and feeling Paprika jolt beneath him.

The cool breeze washed over them and they landed behind the large rhododendron bushes and vegetable patch at the bottom of their best friend Dixie Deane's garden on the other side of the village. The leafy bushes were in full flower with large pink blossoms hiding them from the view of the house.

'Are you sure this is Dixie's house?' whispered Darius, sliding down off Paprika's scaly back. 'Do you think she's home?'

Sammy jumped down to the ground and pointed to the three chimneys on the roof of the house and then to the tallest tree in the garden where a red and white mushroom shaped treehouse was nestled in amongst the topmost branches.

'This is definitely Dixie's house. It's called Three Chimneys,' said Sammy, pointing at the three red brick chimneys with terracotta chimney pots on the rooftop.

One of the chimneys had wisps of smoke coming out of the vent at the top. Someone was definitely home.

'Hey! Can you stop Paprika eating those potatoes!' said Sammy. He hurried over to the orange dragon who had put her front paws into the large vegetable patch and was digging things out of the ground at lightning speed.

'She's hungry,' retorted Darius. 'Maybe you should feed her more.'

'When did you learn to teleport?' asked Sammy. 'You couldn't do it before.'

'Mum showed me how to do it over the summer,' said Darius. 'It's actually quite easy once you get the hang of it. We went everywhere!'

'I wish my mum could teleport,' said Sammy.

'She probably could, once…' said Darius, stepping back as a blur of blue and green flung past him and uncurled into a girl almost as tall as they were. She was dressed in navy jeans and a dark green t-shirt that clashed with her bright green hair.

'Hey Dixie!' said Sammy as he received a bear hug from their genetically green haired friend, Dixie Deane, who was in their year and house at school.

'Hi Sammy! Hi Darius!' shrieked Dixie. 'How did you get Paprika here? You know I've been trying to teleport on Kiridor all summer.'

At the mention of his name, a blue-green dragon the size of a dining room table stomped over to them, his tail thumping excitedly and shaking the ground.

'Darius did it,' said Sammy. 'His Mum taught him over the summer. He's been practising and he is really good at it now.'

'I saw some pretty messed up dragons too,' added Darius. 'Sammy's Uncle Peter probably taught Paprika how to teleport and made her run errands for the Shape.'

'Paprika's scales are dull,' said Dixie, stroking the enormous belly of the orange dragon.

'I know,' snapped Sammy, his anger surprising himself. 'It's all right for you growing up in a dragon family. I'm only just learning how to take care of Kyrillan, let alone the other three grown up dragons all by myself.'

'Bring them over here if you like,' said Dixie, who didn't seem to have noticed Sammy snapping at her.

'Thanks anyway,' said Sammy, a little huffily, his anger subsiding, 'but my uncle left them in my care.'

'I'm helping,' said Darius. 'My parents always have loads of dragons around. Anything I don't already know, I can ask them.'

'Especially if they're ill,' said Dixie. 'Anyway, come inside. Mum's been cooking all morning. We can probably get something to eat.'

Leaving the dragons outside, Sammy, Dixie and Darius ran through the garden and burst through the back door that led into the kitchen.

As usual, all the work surfaces were covered with ceramic pots and copper pans, decorative quirky ornaments and well-read cookbooks. The walls were filled with family photographs and the floor was littered with toys and games.

Mrs Deane was dressed in her usual denim skirt and striped blouse and was standing beside the kitchen stove adding ingredients into a bubbling saucepan.

'Hello boys,' said Sylvia Deane, Dixie's green haired mother. 'I didn't hear you arrive.'

'Mum!' sighed Dixie. 'They teleported here!'

'And how did that enormous orange dragon get here?' asked Mrs Deane, peering out of the kitchen window.

'Teleported,' said Sammy, Dixie and Darius together.

Mrs Deane nodded, twisting the plaster she wore underneath her wedding ring on her left hand. 'Keep her away from Jacob's potatoes please,' she said staring into the distance as though she was thinking of something else.

'I'll do it!' said Darius. 'Outside!' he shouted and vanished in a shimmering grey mist.

'Darius really,' reproved Mrs Deane, snapping out of her trance and giggling, despite trying to frown with some disapproval at Dixie and Sammy. 'Outside, all of you.'

'Outside!' shouted Sammy, reaching for Dixie's arm to bring her with him.

A gold mist surrounded Sammy and Dixie and they landed outside the kitchen door, only a few feet from where they had started.

'Have you been taught how to do that safely?' asked Mrs Deane, who had teleported herself outside right next to them.

Dixie looked down at her shoes. 'Commander Altair said it was ok,' she mumbled, sounding a little guilty.

Sammy knew she was stretching the truth a little bit, because actually Commander Altair had said it was ok to teleport as long as he was with them.

Mrs Deane smiled. 'That's ok then,' she said and teleported herself back into the kitchen.

'That wasn't quite what he said to us,' said Sammy.

Dixie giggled. 'As long as you know where you'll end up, it's ok. Come on, let's go up into the treehouse.' She ran to the rope ladder and swung herself up amongst the branches.

Sammy and Darius left Paprika and Kiridor in the garden away from the potatoes and followed Dixie up into the mushroom shaped treehouse.

Dixie took three plastic glasses off the shelf and a bottle of lemonade out of one of the small cupboards inside the treehouse.

They sat on green and purple patchwork beanbags inside the tiny room and Dixie poured glasses of lemonade for herself and Sammy.

As she poured the last glass of lemonade and handed it to Darius, there was a roar from Mrs Deane that didn't sound good.

'Dixie! Down here! Now! Use the ladder!'

Sammy peered out of the tiny window. Mrs Deane was standing with her legs astride. Her cheeks were flushed pink and she had her hands on her hips. She looked absolutely livid.

'Teleporting without permission!' squawked Mrs Deane.

Behind her was a tall, good looking man with sandy hair and piercing cornflower blue eyes with a steely glint. He wore a black shirt and black jeans which were tied at the waist with a large black belt studded with three silver stars.

Dixie gulped down her lemonade and swung herself back down the ladder. Sammy followed Darius, holding tightly to each wooden rung as he felt for the next rung with his feet.

'Commander Altair has a message for you,' said Mrs Deane, relaxing a little as her cheeks returned to their normal colour.

'Didn't know you knew him this well,' Sammy whispered in Dixie's ear.

Dixie nodded. 'He's not just our Armoury teacher at Dragamas. He often comes around. He's a friend of my Dad's and he helps me loads at school.'

Commander Altair smiled as they stood among the flowerpots. He didn't mention anything about teleporting and simply reached into his shirt pocket and held out three green envelopes.

'These are from Sir Ragnarok,' said Commander Altair. 'Your headmaster, Sir Lok Ragnarok, has set a challenge for Dragamas students this year.'

Dixie tore open her envelope with her teeth. 'The Dragamas Quest for The Angel of 'El Horidore,' she read out loud.

'The what?' demanded Darius as he struggled to open his envelope.

'The Angel of 'El Horidore,' whispered Sammy. 'We know what that is. It's the whistle that will call all dragons.'

'In the wrong hands, it would spell the end of all dragons,' said Commander Altair sombrely. 'My father, General Aldebaran Altair, and the Guardians of the Snorgcadell agree that it is time the Angel of 'El Horidore was found.'

'Better for us to find it than for the Shape to find it,' said Mrs Deane nervously. 'Now who would like a cup of tea and some of my special homemade biscuits and cake?'

CHAPTER 3

THE ANGEL OF 'EL HORIDORE

Everyone nodded and Mrs Deane ushered them all inside and put the kettle on.

Within minutes they were all sitting in the Deane's lounge, either on the sofas or on the floor. Mrs Deane made everyone feel very welcome by serving cups of hot tea and plates piled high with strawberry jam sponge cake and homemade chocolate chip cookies.

Sammy, Dixie and Darius bombarded Commander Altair with questions about the Angel of 'El Horidore, trying to learn as much as possible.

'What exactly is the Angel of 'El Horidore?' asked Darius. 'We know it's a whistle that will call dragons.'

Commander Altair nodded. 'Angel whistles got their name because they are like a guardian angel for a dragon owner to bring their dragon back to them, no matter how far away they may have flown.'

'Angel whistles can call one dragon or lots of dragons, can't they,' said Sammy. 'Gavin and Toby share an Angel whistle that calls their dragons, Syren and Puttee.'

'Yes, but the Angel we are looking for will call all dragons, living or dead. It is the most powerful Angel whistle ever created,' said Commander Altair. 'That is why it is so important that we find it.'

'There's a story about that in my book,' added Dixie, skipping out of the room and returning with her well-read copy of "Dragon Tales for Seven Year Olds".

Sammy recognised the battered book as the one Dixie said she had been given by her father before he left to fight the Shape and which she stored up in the treehouse.

'Here it is,' said Dixie, flicking enthusiastically through the pages. 'King Serberon wanted to give his future wife an amazing wedding present, so he got all his dwarves to mine the very best diamonds from the mine under his castle.'

'Dragamas,' whispered Sammy and Darius together.

'The dwarves mined day and night to find the prettiest diamonds with the brightest sparkle and put them into a half-moon shaped whistle made of pure gold. He got his finest court musician to finish the whistle so it made the purest sound,' Dixie paused, her eyes sparkling.

'And then the story finishes with King Serberon programming this particular Angel whistle so that it will call all dragons, living, dead and those yet to be born, to the location of wherever the whistle was blown,' finished Commander Altair. 'Quite a spectacular wedding present don't you think?'

Sammy nodded. 'A Queen who could call all dragons would be the most powerful Queen in the world.'

'Anyone who could call all dragons would be the most powerful person in the world,' said Commander Altair. 'But don't forget, the Shape want to call all the dragons together so they can kill them and take their draconite which they will put into the Stone Cross. They believe this will give them control of the elements, invincibility and immortality.'

'When they finish building the Stone Cross with draconite,' said Sammy, thinking back to his visions in the past. He wondered how many more pieces of draconite the Shape needed to finish their task.

'That's right,' said Commander Altair. 'Having all the dragons under your power is one thing, however if the rumour is true, then that is only the beginning of the destruction the Shape will cause.'

Mrs Deane brought in a fresh tray of tea and more of her homemade chocolate chip cookies. Dixie's triplet older brothers, Serberon, Mikhael and Jason returned from a friend's house, said hello quickly, took handfuls of cookies and headed straight upstairs to play Dragon Questers on their computer.

Commander Altair checked his watch. It was nearly nine o'clock and starting to get dark.

'It's getting late,' said Commander Altair. 'I'll head off. Thank you Sylvia for the tea, cookies and your company.'

Without moving his lips or making any sound at all, Commander Altair vanished in a red teleporting mist.

As Mrs Deane stacked up the dirty plates and empty tea cups onto a tray, the grandfather clock started chiming nine times in the hallway.

Despite chatting with Commander Altair all evening, Sammy still had a million and one questions and, other than the contents of Sir Ragnarok's letter inviting them on the quest to search for the Angel of 'El Horidore, he had very few answers.

'You'd best get back before it gets too late,' Mrs Deane said to Sammy and Darius. 'Will your dragon know her way home?'

Sammy nodded. 'I think so,' he said, even though he really had no idea whether his uncle's dragon would know how to teleport home or not.

'Of course Paprika will know the way home!' Darius laughed and tugged Sammy's shoulder. 'Or if you want, we can fly home instead and then we'll definitely know where we're going. Come on! Let's go!'

They ran outside to where Paprika was two steps away from Jacob Deane's potatoes. She plodded forward, her mouth open, ready to take a bite out of the plant stalks sticking out of the ground.

'Oi!' shouted Dixie. 'Stop that!' She flapped her arms and Paprika stepped back onto the path with a rather disgruntled look in her eyes.

Darius leaped onto Paprika's back and took the reins. Sammy reached for one of her orange spikes and hoisted himself up behind Darius and gripped the dragon tightly with his knees.

'Up!' shouted Darius. 'Take us back to Sammy's house!'

With a swish of her tail, Paprika surged forward, trampling through the vegetable bed, digging up dozens of potatoes with her sharp claws.

She burst open her magnificent speckled orange and gold wings and suddenly Sammy and Darius were up in the air, high above Three Chimneys.

Mrs Deane and Dixie were just tiny specks far below on the ground. Dixie's mother was on her hands and knees replanting the potatoes and Dixie was jumping up and down and waving at them. Sammy could hear her shouting very faintly.

'See you at Dragamas!'

Sammy tapped Darius on the shoulder. 'We're on a quest!' he shouted above the noise of the wind. 'We have to find the Angel of 'El Horidore before the Shape find it.'

Darius nodded without turning around. He pulled on Paprika's harness to turn her towards home and they descended gradually until they landed quietly in the back garden beside the shed.

Leaving Paprika in the garden, out of sight of the house windows, Sammy and Darius walked quietly to the back door.

'How am I supposed to take the dragons back to Dragamas?' asked Sammy. 'They can't stay here. They'll die if I can't give them food and water.'

'My parents could take them,' said Darius. 'If they were here.'

'Actually, it's ok,' said Sammy, re-reading the letter from Sir Ragnarok. 'If I can get them to Dragamas then the Snorgcadell will look after them. It says so at the bottom of my quest letter.'

'It's where they belong,' said Darius, pushing open the back door. 'When your parents were Dragon Knights they would have kept their dragons at Dragamas. It will be like your dragons are going home…kind of.'

'Yeah,' said Sammy, kicking off his shoes and putting them away tidily in the shoe rack. He wished now more than ever that his parents could see dragons.

As Sammy stood up, he stopped in his tracks. His mother was talking on the telephone with baby Eliza in her arms.

This didn't bother him as much as the fact that his sister was staring straight at a blue-green dragon who was perched on the stairs, its body spanning from the top step right down to the bottom step.

'Kyrillan!' exclaimed Sammy.

'What's that honey?' asked Julia Rambles, covering the mouthpiece. 'I'm on the telephone to Mrs Weedlock. She's asking about the village fete.'

'Uh, nothing,' said Sammy, hastily ushering Kyrillan backwards up the stairs. He didn't like the way baby Eliza cricked her neck, following him with her baby blue eyes.

'She can see dragons,' hissed Darius as they squashed into the airing cupboard and up the wooden steps into the attic.

'I know,' said Sammy. 'She's always like that. It's like she can sense them or something.'

'She can see them,' said Darius, 'I mean like, she can really see them. I saw my first dragons almost the second I was born,' he added proudly. 'Apparently, my mum and my aunt flew me home from the hospital in a cradle harnessed between two dragons!'

'That's really cool!' said Sammy, wondering how on earth they were going to get Paprika indoors and upstairs without anyone noticing.

'It was really cold!' Darius giggled. 'It was midnight in the middle of March when I was born.'

'How are we going to get Paprika inside?' asked Sammy.

Darius shrugged. 'I expect she'll teleport or fly in by herself.'

Unconvinced, Sammy looked out of the attic lounge window. He could see the garden shed but not his uncle's orange dragon.

'She's gone somewhere,' said Sammy. 'Do you think we should go and look for her? We could try teleporting her inside.'

'She'll turn up,' said Darius and went into his room.

'We're going back to school tomorrow,' said Sammy, giving one last look for Paprika out of the window. 'Are you packing tonight or in the morning?'

'Tomorrow,' said Darius. 'I wish I could have come and stayed with you sooner. We could have gone flying loads more over the summer holiday.'

'At least there will be people who can see dragons,' grumbled Sammy. 'If we can get five dragons out of here without my parents noticing then I'll give up any hope they'll ever be able to see me fly on Kyrillan.'

At the sound of his name, Kyrillan blew a large grey smoke ring. It wafted around the room and came to rest on a large orange shape that was shimmering into view.

'Paprika! You're back!' exclaimed Sammy, a wave of relief washing over him. 'How did you do that?'

'She's teleported herself in!' said Darius poking his head around the bedroom door. 'I told you she would come back.'

The smoke ring made the large orange dragon sneeze and Paprika stamped her foot.

'Keep it down up there Sam!' Charles Rambles shouted from downstairs.

'There's hope for your dad knowing about dragons again if he can hear that.' Darius grinned. 'Night then.'

'Night,' said Sammy, going into his bedroom for the last time. He pulled his duvet on to the floor so he could sleep with his back against Kyrillan's side and his feet tucked into the coil of his dragon's tail.

CHAPTER 4

BACK TO DRAGAMAS

The next day Sammy had never known such hustle and bustle. First Paprika woke him at the crack of dawn blowing smoke rings into his bedroom. The thick grey smoke made both Sammy and Kyrillan sneeze and Sammy shooed the older dragon out into the lounge.

Then just as he was going back to sleep, his mother came into the attic with steaming plates of sausages, bacon, fried bread, hash browns and homemade onion rings.

'Your breakfast is ready Sammy,' called Julia Rambles. 'Good morning Darius, did you sleep well?'

Smelling the delicious fried food and hearing the sound of voices, Sammy got up and found Darius alone in the lounge. He was helping himself to the cooked breakfast whilst simultaneously throwing his belongings haphazardly into his suitcase.

'It won't all fit!' grumbled Darius, tipping everything out and starting again. 'How am I going to pack my stuff?'

'It'll all fit in,' said Sammy. He grinned and picked up a couple of text books and Darius's school jumper.

'Oi!' shouted Darius as his dragon, Nelson, picked up a pair of black socks and stomped off with them.

Sammy laughed. He wasn't sure if Nelson was hungry and trying to eat the socks or if the navy blue dragon was trying to help with the packing. He helped Darius cram everything in and sat on the suitcase so Darius could fasten the straps.

They ate almost everything on the plates Julia had brought for them and fed some of the food to the dragons. Kyrillan seemed to like the taste of the fried bread so Sammy gave him two slices and some onion rings.

Downstairs, the doorbell rang six times. Sammy heard his mother open the door and he recognized the voices of Commander Altair, Mrs Deane, Dixie, Serberon, Mikhael and Jason, who had come to collect him and Darius and take them back to school.

Sammy nearly jumped out of his skin when Commander Altair teleported into the attic, arriving in a gold mist in the middle of the lounge area.

'I have come for the dragons,' said Commander Altair. 'Bring them together quickly. I don't have much time.'

'Paprika,' said Sammy, pointing to the swishing orange tail that was all that could be seen of his uncle's dragon as she nosed in Darius's room looking for sweets dropped under the bed.

'Cyngard and Jovah,' said Commander Altair, pointing to the forest green dragon and the jet black dragon, who were both looking suspiciously at him with their watchful eyes.

Sammy stared. 'How do you know their names?' he asked in surprise.

Commander Altair smiled at Sammy. 'My father taught me the names and markings of every dragon that belonged to every Dragon Knight in the Snorgcadell. I didn't know your parents personally, but my father spoke highly of them, before, well you know…'

Sammy lowered his head. 'I know,' he said quietly. 'I really do want them to see dragons again.'

Commander Altair leaned close to Sammy. 'What seems wrong to you may be right for another reason,' he whispered.

Sammy looked up, his blue eyes staring at his Armoury teacher. 'I want my parents to see dragons,' said Sammy stoutly, not hearing his father come into the attic lounge.

'Is it you filling my son's head with dragon nonsense and imaginary friends?' roared Charles Rambles, his eyes blazing and bulging as if they might pop out of his head.

Commander Altair took a step backwards. 'You did not see me,' said Commander Altair, pointing at Sammy's father with his staff.

He turned and pointed to the three adult dragons who were looking at him expectantly.

'Dragamas,' said Commander Altair and he disappeared in a shimmering gold mist.

Sammy looked around. 'He's gone.'

'Who's gone?' demanded Charles Rambles. 'Your imaginary friend? Come on Samuel. It's time to go.'

'They've all gone,' said Sammy, seeing that it was just him, his father and Kyrillan in the room.

'Good,' said Charles Rambles. 'Now, if you have finished packing, I will help you take your suitcase downstairs and into that rust-bucket of a car your friend's mother sees fit to escort you back to school.'

'Only because you can't see Dragamas,' Sammy muttered under his breath as he threw the last of his clothes into his already-full suitcase and slammed the top shut.

'They should put these things on wheels,' grumbled Charles Rambles as he picked up one end of the suitcase. 'Come on Samuel, show your strength.'

Sammy picked up his staff from behind the wardrobe, stuffed a few remaining toffees into his jeans pocket for the journey and beckoned to Kyrillan to follow him downstairs.

'What do you want that stick for?' demanded Charles Rambles, spotting it when they were halfway down the stairs. 'That's a funny shape for a hockey stick.'

'It's a staff,' corrected Sammy. 'I use it at school to...' he paused, his confidence wavering at what his father's response might be if he told him the staff was used, among other things, to create fire out of thin air, and for sending green sparks down secret passageways after the Shape.

'To give someone a clout, eh?' puffed Charles. 'It was done with fists in my day.'

Sammy didn't have the chance to explain as his father suddenly let go of the suitcase and fell head over heels down the last three steps. Sammy clapped his hand over his mouth in horror as he saw that not only had his father fallen over Kyrillan but that baby Eliza had crawled out of the kitchen and was staring eye to eye with his dragon.

Oblivious to the chaos he had caused, Kyrillan yawned, bearing his teeth.

'No!' shouted Sammy, running forward.

'What now?' Charles Rambles scowled and dusted himself off.

Mrs Deane came to the rescue. She picked Eliza up off the floor, pulling a button off her shirt at the same time.

'That's better,' cooed Mrs Deane as Eliza started howling. 'Just a pretty button your brother stopped you from eating.' She held up the shiny mother of pearl button.

'Well spotted Sam,' said Charles. He turned to Mrs Deane. 'It looks like it might be one of yours,' he said, holding the button up to her shirt.

'Why so it is,' said Mrs Deane, taking back the button. 'I'll sew it on as soon as I get back from dropping the children off to school.'

'Very good,' said Charles. 'I hope they teach those skills to the girls at Drabblers.'

'The boys too,' said Mrs Deane. 'No, all Dixie talks about is Nitron Dark, Firesticks and Dragonball.'

'Aaargh!' squealed Charles. 'Dragons!'

Mrs Deane chuckled and picked up both Sammy's suitcase and Darius's suitcase and lugged them into the back of her blue Land Rover.

'Good woman that,' said Charles Rambles approvingly. 'Even if she does talk your dragon nonsense!'

Sammy grinned. It was no use telling his father anything about dragons in case he wasn't allowed to go back to school.

Julia appeared from the kitchen and Sammy cringed as his mother gave him a kiss on the cheek in front of everyone.

'Be good honey,' said Julia. 'We'll miss you.'

His father shook hands with Sammy and Darius. Mrs Deane handed Eliza back to Julia and with a flurry of "goodbyes" and "be good" speeches, Sammy and Darius bundled into the back of the Land Rover with Dixie's brothers.

Nelson and Kyrillan squeezed out of the front door without bumping into anyone and took flight. They circled over the top of the Land Rover, impatient to get going.

Julia thrust a bag of freshly cooked iced buns and cream cakes to share through the passenger window into Dixie's hands. Mrs Deane started the car and then they were off.

'Dragamas here we come!' shouted Darius, stuffing a whole iced bun into his mouth as the Land Rover sped away, creaking worse than ever under the weight of all its many passengers.

Sammy waved until his parents were out of sight. He had butterflies in his stomach but they were butterflies of excitement and not nerves.

As they drove along, Sammy thought about Dragamas. In the coming Spring, he would be halfway through his life at the school. He felt like he really belonged there. All his friends were at Dragamas and he was actually quite good at some of the lessons.

Sammy leaned out of the open back of the Land Rover, pleased to see Kyrillan flying above them with Nelson and Dixie's blue-green dragon, Kiridor, whose scales were the same shimmering colour as his dragon's scales.

Serberon, Mikhael and Jason's dragons were flying protectively around them. Then, suddenly, all of the dragons broke away and flew off in a diagonal direction.

'They've gone,' exclaimed Sammy, leaning further out of the car. 'Where are they going?'

Serberon pulled Sammy back into the cabin. 'They always take the short cut,' he explained. 'Why would they want to follow the road when it's so much slower?'

Mikhael held up a purple plastic crescent moon shaped whistle. 'We can always call our dragons back with this Angel whistle at any time.'

Sammy sat back in his seat. Everyone seemed to have Angel whistles for calling their dragons. Everyone except him.

As they rumbled through the country lanes, Sammy thought hard about the Angel whistles. They were simple, half-moon shaped whistles that would call back whichever dragon had been programmed to respond to that particular whistle.

Sammy re-read the letter from Sir Ragnarok about the quest to find the Angel of 'El Horidore. He could see why this particular Angel whistle was so powerful because it had been programmed to call all dragons, living or dead, to the very spot where the whistle was blown. In the hands of the Shape it would be devastating as they would use it to call all dragons together and then slaughter them to obtain their magical draconite stones.

'It will self-destruct if you read it again,' teased Mikhael. 'Honestly, you haven't been listening at all!'

Sammy looked up. Everyone was laughing at him. He looked out of the window and laughed. They had arrived at the layby opposite the gates of Dragamas Castle, also known as Old Samagard Farm to those who could only see a ruined farmhouse. Sitting at the back of the car, Sammy was expected to get out first.

CHAPTER 5

COMMANDER ALTAIR IS THE "A"

Sammy flung open the back door of Mrs Deane's rusty blue Land Rover and leaped out. He looked up at the magnificent grey stone castle with its nine coned towers, each flying the black Dragamas flag emblazoned with the golden twin-tailed "D" emblem.

Just as he remembered, there were two tall towers on each of the four corners of the castle. The towers were named after the compass points, North, South, East and West.

Each tower was five storeys high and contained the separate boys' and girl's dormitories. The first year students slept in rooms at the top of the tower and moved down a level each year they were at the school.

This year, Sammy's third year, he would be sleeping in the dormitory right in the middle of the North tower and he was looking forward to it very much.

The tallest tower in the middle of the castle was reserved for the school headmaster, Sir Lok Ragnarok and Lariston, his smokey grey cat.

Above the castle, the familiar gold bubble shimmered, hiding the castle from anyone who couldn't see dragons and protecting the school from outsiders.

On the opposite side of the layby, a prickly hawthorn hedge gave way to the tall Dragamas gates, which were being heaved open by two dwarfs dressed in blue dungarees, white shirts with red and white spotted neckerchiefs tied loosely around their necks, and black mining boots fastened with shiny silver buckles.

The only difference between the two dwarfs was the colour of their hair and their chest length beards. One dwarf had bright reddish-orange hair and a fiery orange beard. He was called Captain Avensis Firebreath and the second dwarf was called Captain Duke Stronghammer and his hair and beard was the colour of midnight black.

The dwarves had real names as well and Captain Duke Stronghammer was also known as Fignus Hubar, or Figgy to his wife, Mrs Hubar, who taught Gemology at Dragamas.

The students were supposed to address him as Captain Stronghammer but Dixie's brothers were a little less formal.

'Hi Dukey! Hi Firey!' shouted Serberon, Mikhael and Jason together.

The dwarves grinned at the boys and saluted them, raising their right hands to their forehead.

'Dukey and Firey,' giggled Darius. 'Hey, that must mean Jock's already here. Captain Stronghammer is his dad.'

Sammy nodded. He was worried at the back of his mind about how his friends, the twins Gavin and Toby Reed, who shared their dormitory would act around Jock this year. Gavin in particular could be quite a bully around new people and had fallen out with at least one of their housemates in the last two years.

'Alright Sammy?' growled the red haired dwarf. 'You need any help with those?' he pointed to the pile of suitcases.

Sammy reached for his staff, focusing on lifting his suitcase using his mind. The suitcase quivered and slid along the ground scratching on the gravel. With a lot of determination, Sammy managed to lift the suitcase two inches above the ground.

'Good un,' growled Captain Firebreath. 'That'll be one less to carry.'

Mrs Deane whizzed round hugging everyone and waited only until the last bag was taken out of the Land Rover before shooting away in a cloud of country lane dirt and dust.

Serberon coughed loudly and flapped his arms to clear the air. 'I wish she'd wait until we're inside before doing that,' he grumbled.

'She doesn't like goodbyes,' said Jason flatly.

'She'll see us again at Christmas,' said Dixie. 'That'll be your last Christmas at Dragamas.'

'Good,' snapped Serberon. 'Without Mary-Beth, there's no point coming really.'

Darius put his arm around Dixie's shoulders. 'When they're gone next year, we'll look after you.'

Mikhael laughed. 'Yeah, you look after her or we'll break your legs!' he joked.

'We have to find the Angel of 'El Horidore,' said Sammy, quickly changing the subject from broken legs.

'Don't get your hopes up,' said dark haired Captain Stronghammer, stroking his beard. 'There's plenty who've looked and nought that's found it.'

Captain Firebreath held up his hand in an "O" shape. 'Nought,' said Captain Firebreath. 'Sir Ragnarok says it's better to look for it now while there's more of us who want to stop the Shape than them who follow the Shape and don't care if the dragons live or die.'

'Murderers,' said Darius. He spat on the ground. 'There was this dragon on holiday that we had to stitch it's brain up to stop the draconite falling out.'

Jason gave a fake yawn. 'Are we using the Shute?'

Captain Stronghammer nodded. 'Aye, and best get going as the next lot of students will be here soon.'

Sammy led the way to the archway with the stone steps that led down into the underground passage, known as the Shute, which led from the school gates up to the castle courtyard. He had to duck to get inside and realized he must have grown an inch or two taller since last year.

Inside the dim, candlelit passage, students could walk along a narrow path next to an underground stream and put their suitcases on a moving conveyor belt that pulled their luggage towards the castle.

The stream was filled with tiny shards of precious gemstones washed down from the treasure mine the dwarves worked in under the castle. As they walked, they played Dixie's "Find the Biggest Gemstone" competition, stopping every so often to pick a loose rock out of the stream that could be worth a small amount of money.

At the end of the Shute, they met Astronomics teacher Professor John Burlay and school secretary and nurse, Mrs Grock. They were holding hands at the mouth of the tunnel.

'He wants to marry her,' hissed Serberon, giving Professor Burlay and Mrs Grock a black look. 'Her husband left her and went to fight the Shape.'

'Oh,' said Sammy as he lugged his suitcase up the steep stone steps to the surface.

At the top of the steps, school headmaster, Sir Lok Ragnarok, was welcoming the Griffin family back to

Dragamas. Sir Ragnarok shook hands with the girls and directed them and their dragons towards the castle.

One of the dragons, a large green dragon with yellow spikes, broke loose from its harness and started charging around in circles, breathing thick grey smoke everywhere.

The dragon started running away and Sir Ragnarok started running after it. After a few quick steps, he caught up with the dragon and pulled on its metal harness to bring it to a standstill.

Captain Firebreath was right behind them and took the harness out of Sir Ragnarok's hands.

'Feisty one, that one,' growled Captain Firebreath, stroking the dragon's scaly neck.

The youngest Griffin girl came running over to Captain Firebreath, her blonde hair streaming behind her.

'I'm so sorry,' said the Griffin girl. 'My dragon just got away from me!'

Sir Ragnarok nodded. 'Must be the excitement of coming back to school.'

Sammy helped Serberon and Mikhael lift their suitcases out of the Shute and went to stand with Dixie in the middle of the courtyard with the other students who were waiting to be allowed inside. It was cold and he rubbed his hands together to keep warm.

'Simon Sanchez is here,' said Dixie, pointing to a tall thin boy with deep grey eyes and jet black hair. Her eyes glazed over. 'He's changed a bit,' she whispered.

'He's East,' said Mikhael, grinning at his sister. 'And he's Professor Sanchez's son.'

Dixie shrugged as if being in the East house didn't worry her in the slightest. She stared at him for another fifteen seconds while Sir Ragnarok ticked their names off his list.

'We are just waiting for Gavin and Toby Reed,' said Sir Ragnarok. 'If I'm not mistaken, they will lose house stars for being late before the term even starts.' He put away his clipboard of names. 'Would you follow me please. I think I heard the bell for dinner.'

The students filed towards the large oak and iron castle door. Sammy wasn't surprised when Sir Ragnarok held his coat sleeve as the others went inside. They locked eyes.

'Can I trust you with something?' asked Sir Ragnarok quietly and seriously. 'Something I feel will be rumoured and disputed for many moons to come.'

Sammy nodded, wondering what Sir Ragnarok could possibly say to him that his headmaster couldn't say to anyone else.

Sir Ragnarok paused and his blue eyes looked sad. 'It has come to my attention that Commander Altair is working for the Shape.'

Sammy felt his jaw drop. He stared at Sir Ragnarok. 'Commander Altair? Working for the Shape? He's got my dragons…' Sammy stammered. 'Commander Altair has got my parents' dragons. He's on our side. He can't. No. It's not true.'

Sir Ragnarok's eyes opened wide. 'What do you mean he's got your parents' dragons? Did you not read my note? I told you explicitly that the Snorgcadell would collect your parents' dragons from your parents' house this morning.'

'I…I thought you'd sent Altair,' Sammy whispered, tears prickling in the corner of his eyes. 'He's in the Snorgcadell.'

'Commander Altair,' reproved Sir Ragnarok. 'Well, I suppose he won't be "Commander" for much longer. Titles are important. They are a mark of respect given to someone when they have obtained them.'

'Sir Ragnarok,' started Sammy, his lip quivering and his heart pounding, 'Commander Altair won't kill them, will he? I've only just got them and if...if my parents can see dragons again one day...' he stammered fighting back tears.

Sir Ragnarok leaned close, his blue eyes cloudy and strained. 'We have to trust that Commander Altair is keeping them safe. Your uncle, for all his sins against dragons, for every piece of draconite he stole, he kept your parents' dragons alive whilst they were in his care. Maybe for sentimental reasons, who knows? I'm sure they have a part to play. Maybe Peter Pickering feels guilty? Perhaps he was hoping that one day you will be able to help your parents see dragons again. Perhaps Commander Altair will feel the same.'

'So it can be done?' asked Dixie, stepping out with Darius from behind a stone carving of a Dragon Knight in a suit of armour where they had been hiding.

'One must keep hoping.' Sir Ragnarok sighed, not seeming to care his private conversation had been eavesdropped. 'There may be many more people who would like to see dragons again.'

'Even if they don't know it,' grumbled Sammy, thinking about his parents. 'I wish...'

'Careful,' said Sir Ragnarok with a smile. 'Didn't your parents tell you to be careful what you wish for?'

He turned suddenly at a rustle in the bushes behind them. 'My office,' said Sir Ragnarok suddenly. He reached for Sammy's shoulder and gripped tightly.

CHAPTER 6

NEW TEACHERS

A cold mist swept around him and Sammy opened his eyes. He was alone with Sir Ragnarok in the headmaster's office inside the central tower inside the castle.

The room was circular with a thick green carpet and a woollen rug depicting the four house logos in the shape of a compass in the centre of the room. There was a small curved table with Sir Ragnarok's familiar bowl of multi-coloured sweets next to the curved purple sofa with its purple cushions.

Sir Ragnarok's solid wooden desk was still in the same position, opposite a large blank screen. There were no windows, but the screen allowed the Dragamas headmaster to see anything going on in any of the rooms and anywhere in the grounds of the school.

Sammy smiled. He had spotted at the edge of the room, on the last step of the metal spiral staircase that led up into the headmaster's rooftop bedroom, Sir Ragnarok's purple slippers were still there.

'I have something to show you Sammy. Then you may join the others at lunch,' said Sir Ragnarok.

Sammy put his hands deep into his jeans pockets and watched as Sir Ragnarok reached for a blue crayon from a pot of pens on his desk and pointed to a gilt framed picture on his wall next to a large blank screen.

The picture was of the Stone Cross, a Celtic wheel shaped cross filled with tiny blue-green dots. Sammy knew from the last time he had seen a similar drawing that every time the Shape killed a dragon, they would add another blue-green draconite stone to the Stone Cross.

When the Stone Cross was full of draconite it was said to give power over Earth, Air, Fire and Water, to the person who lay the final stone. It seemed that Sir Ragnarok had been keeping track of how many draconite stones were missing and he had created the picture of the Stone Cross to monitor the Shape's progress.

'It seems they have almost completed their task,' said Sir Ragnarok. 'If they find the Angel of 'El Horidore and blow the whistle, they will call every dragon, living or dead, to the Valley of the Stone Cross and then they will slaughter all the dragons. It will make the massacre that took place in my castle look like a children's picnic. With the Stone Cross in their power, they will control all beings, all elements and the laws of time and gravity. They will become invincible and immortal.'

Sammy gulped. 'We will find the Angel, won't we?'

Sir Ragnarok frowned. 'We will find it, if it wants to be found.' He rummaged in his desk drawer and pulled out a small black and white photograph. 'This is the last known picture of what we are looking for.'

Sammy stared at the half moon shaped object. Even in the black and white photograph he could see the whistle was sparkling.

Sir Ragnarok stared at the grainy photograph. Then as if waking from a trance, Sir Ragnarok shook himself. 'What am I thinking?' he said. 'You'll want to unpack your belongings in your new tower room, see your friends, meet the new teachers and have lunch, I presume.'

Sammy nodded. Despite eating several cream cakes and iced buns on the way to Dragamas, he was feeling rather hungry. 'We will find the Angel of 'El Horidore first,' said Sammy as he followed his headmaster out of his office and down the stone spiral staircase, through the tapestry and into the Main Hall.

A deafening noise greeted them as they stepped into the Main Hall. Large chandeliers hung from the ceiling and the four long house tables faced the teachers' table at the front. Wooden chairs with the Dragamas twin-tailed "D" logo emblazoned on the back were filled with students all talking and shouting at the top of their voices.

They sat in rows, the first years', who were the youngest, sat at the front of the hall, nearest the teachers' table. Further up each table were the second, third and fourth years, with the fifth year students, who were making the most noise, right at the back near the double doors, which was the official entrance to the Main Hall.

Sammy looked around the hall, trying to find his friends on the North house table. He caught sight of Dixie and Darius in the middle of the table.

'We saved you a seat!' yelled Darius, leaping in the air and waving.

Sammy made his way into the middle of the hall. He passed Nigel Ashford, the boy he was supposed to be mentoring, offering advice and generally watching out for him during the school term time.

Nigel was now in his second year at Dragamas. Even though he wasn't related to the twins in Sammy's year,

Nigel was the spitting image of Gavin and Toby with tanned skin, freckles on his face and spiky jet black hair.

Nigel was balancing a glass of water on his chin and waving the toy lion Sammy had given him. Sammy smiled. At least Nigel was a bit more confident than he had been in his first year.

Looking further down the table, this year's first year students were huddled together. They looked terrified as the older students arrived and filled up the seats at the tables. The room hushed as Sir Ragnarok made his way to join the teachers at the teachers' table at the front.

Sammy slipped into the seat between Dixie and Darius, opposite Milly Brooks, Jock Hubar, Gavin and Toby Reed and the other North third year students.

He noticed there was a large gap between Professor Burlay and Professor Sanchez at the teachers' table. It was the empty seat where Commander Altair should have been sitting. There also seemed to be some new teachers as well.

Despite thinking Commander Altair had been kind to Dixie and her family, Sammy couldn't stop himself thinking he was glad Commander Altair was missing. He was also really afraid for the safety of his parents' dragons. Where had Commander Altair taken them? Were they still alive?

Sir Ragnarok raised his staff to frighten a group of South students into silence so he could speak and have everyone's attention.

'I have three announcements,' shouted Sir Ragnarok, ensuring his voice carried right to the back of the Main Hall. 'One good, one bad and one you must decide for yourselves,' he raised his staff with a flourish.

The coloured gemstones at the tip of his staff cast rainbows on to the wall behind him.

Sammy exchanged looks with Dixie and Darius. All around them the students were silent. They were all facing Sir Ragnarok, hooked on what he was about to tell them.

'Firstly,' said Sir Ragnarok, 'we have new faces at the first years' table. Please make them welcome and look after them because they will be here long after you are gone.'

'He's only saying that because the daughter of someone in the Snorgcadell is starting,' said Milly. 'Daddy says her whole family is drippy.'

Gavin sniggered. 'Like you! You're drippy!'

Milly glared at Gavin. 'No I'm not,' she said indignantly. 'Mummy says it's a terrible thing to be drippy.'

Gavin snorted. 'Pah, who cares what Mummy says?'

'Is she over there? The one with the face like the scales of a dragon,' whispered Toby, pulling his cheeks into an ugly face.

Milly nodded. 'She's called Amelia Hodge.'

'Denver Hodge's daughter?' whispered Darius. 'My Mum knows him. He's one of the Guardians of the Snorgcadell.'

'Shh,' interrupted Dixie. 'We've missed the bad news.'

'Probably about Commander Altair,' said Sammy, scowling. 'He's the "A" in the Shape and he's got my parents' dragons.'

Toby nodded sympathetically. 'Sorry about that. Darius told us.'

'He made me say where you'd gone,' said Darius, rubbing a spot of dirt off his knife carefully and not meeting Sammy's eyes. 'Sorry.'

Sammy shrugged and turned to listen to Sir Ragnarok.

'And so, Mr Stephen Synclair-Smythe will be taking over all Armoury lessons,' continued Sir Ragnarok.

There was a loud murmur and all the students turned towards the new Armoury teacher.

'Can't you cancel the lessons?' asked a cocky fourth year boy from the South house.

Sir Ragnarok smiled, shaking his head. 'I can assure you that Mr Synclair-Smythe will teach you everything there is to know about Armoury and much more besides.'

Sammy looked closer at Mr Synclair-Smythe. He was sitting at the far end of the teachers' table next to Gemology teacher, Mrs Hubar. He had a large round face and thick grey hair. He was dressed in a green and grey tartan suit with a white handkerchief in his breast pocket.

'All the people in the Shape so far have the same letter in their first name and last name so why on earth would Sir Ragnarok give the Armoury job to Mr S-S?' asked Sammy in amazement.

'I wanted to meet you Sammy,' came a hoarse whisper from nowhere. No one else noticed the voice and carried on talking.

Sammy scratched his head, sure the whisper had been projected to him, and only him, from someone sitting at the teachers' table.

'Mr Stephen Synclair-Smythe. Mr S-S-S,' whispered Dixie.

'Like you,' snickered Gavin. 'S for Sammy.'

'It's not the same,' whispered Darius. 'The others were all pairs of initials. Eliza Elungwen, Peter Pickering.'

'Arion Altair,' said Dixie sadly.

'Arion is it?' sniggered Jock. 'I hear you had private lessons.'

'He's a friend of our family,' snapped Dixie. 'He knows about my Dad.'

'He "was" a friend,' said Darius. 'Anyway, shut up. I want to hear about what we have to decide.'

'I don't think it's Commander Altair,' said Dixie, rubbing green tears away from her cheeks. 'He wouldn't. It can't be. I'll prove it.' She stood up and challenged Jock with her staff. 'Put wrongs to right,' she whispered so quietly Sammy was sure it was meant just for him to hear.

Jock stood up and raised his staff as well. He shook his fist and then sat down very quickly as he caught an angry stare from his mother.

Gemology teacher Mrs Hubar would not stand for any nonsense from her son that might embarrass her in front of Sir Ragnarok or the other teachers.

Sir Ragnarok stood, for the first time Sammy could remember, right up on the seat of his chair, his black cloak touching the ground and his staff, with all the coloured gemstones on the end, pointed towards the sea of students.

'Before we start our feast,' Sir Ragnarok roared, his voice reverberating around the hall, 'each and every one of you must make a decision.'

The whole school turned to face Sir Ragnarok in silence. It was so quiet Sammy could hear his heart beating in his chest.

'You have each received a letter from me,' continued Sir Ragnarok. 'This letter is an invitation to a quest organised by the Guardians of the Snorgcadell. These are the great people who protect us and guard the dragon cells where we send our criminals like Eliza Elungwen and Peter Pickering to be punished.'

Sammy felt his stomach lurch as Sir Ragnarok spoke his uncle's name.

'My Dad is a Guardian,' said Amelia Hodge proudly.

'If you decide to join this quest, you must agree to divulge all that you find. You must agree to search everywhere that you know and you must agree that you shall hand over all information to myself or to General Aldebaran Altair,' Sir Ragnarok pointed to the empty space in front of him.

A golden mist filled the space in front of the teachers table and a man appeared out of thin air. Sammy recognised him immediately. It was General Aldebaran Altair, one of the most senior men in the Snorgcadell.

General Altair was tall and dressed in gunmetal armour from his neck down to his boots. He had a head full of sandy blond hair that was greying at the edges and eyes as piercing blue as his son, Commander Altair's eyes.

'Good morning students of Dragamas,' said General Aldebaran Altair, his sonorous voice booming loudly and commanding authority.

'Good morning!' shouted Gavin.

General Altair raised his staff. It was a thick branch of an old tree at least seven feet tall and carved into a spear shape with a blazing diamond crystal at the tip.

'Sir Ragnarok has informed you that we are searching for the Angel of 'El Horidore. This Angel is the most powerful whistle ever created. It will call all dragons living and dead together. In the hands of the Shape it would have devastating consequences.'

General Altair paused, his eyes scanning the room, checking every student was holding their breath, waiting for his next words.

'The latest information that we have been given is that Charles and Julia Rambles were the last people to hold the Angel of 'El Horidore.'

Sammy choked on his glass of water, he was sure General Altair had mentioned his parents by name.

'Their son is at this school,' said General Altair.

'Here!' yelled Gavin. 'Sammy's here!'

Sammy felt his cheeks explode in crimson red as the whole school, and in particular Mr Synclair-Smythe, stood up to take a good look at him.

'Do not ask their son where to find the Angel,' said General Altair. 'His parents were betrayed by the Shape and they have lost their ability to see dragons. They lost their sight and their son has suffered an unimaginable loss…'

'Poor Sammy,' sniggered Gavin. 'The Shape are after you and your family.'

'…coupled with the fact that the Shape may believe their son to be the key to finding the Angel. His life may be in danger.'

Gavin's jaw dropped. 'I didn't mean it,' he said as the whole school of students gasped in horror.

Sammy shrugged. 'I don't know any more than you do.'

'Anyone who wishes to take part in the quest must pick up a form from the teachers' table. On the first day of each month I will return to Dragamas and hold an assembly to discuss your findings. That will be all. Good day.'

General Aldebaran Altair disappeared in a shimmer of gold mist, leaving a flurry of conversation and activity behind him. Food appeared on the table. Giant platters of sandwiches filled with ham and cheese, chicken and cucumber, egg and cress and many more. There were piles of sausage rolls, towers of cupcakes and bowls of chocolate mousse.

'We'll sign up,' said Dixie, reaching for a chicken and cucumber sandwich. 'We can use our den as a meeting place.'

'Great,' groaned Darius. 'All I want to do is learn enough so I can be a teacher. I use the den to study in.'

'Boring,' sniggered Gavin. 'Who needs teachers?'

Sammy jumped as two hands were placed on his shoulders. He looked around. Professor Burlay was behind him.

'We all need teachers,' said Professor Burlay, smiling. 'Eat up and you'll find your timetables under your plates as usual. Then I'll take you to your new tower rooms.'

'How come Dr Shivers isn't taking us to our rooms this year?' asked Dixie. 'He did last year.'

'Odd and even numbers,' explained Professor Burlay. 'I will be your Head of the North House in your first, third and fifth years and Dr Shivers will be your Head of the North House in your second and fourth years. Professor Sanchez has Sir Ragnarok's permission to follow her son through his school years and she will be his Head of the East House for the full five years.'

'That's really confusing,' said Gavin. 'I wish I was in East.'

'Really? With Amos Leech?' asked Toby, grinning at his brother.

Gavin pulled a face. 'Eugh! No! I forgot about Amos. I'll stay in North, thank you very much.'

'Just one last thing,' said Professor Burlay. 'There is the matter of who will be this year's Dragon Minders.'

Professor Burlay opened his palm and revealed two silver dragon shaped pins with emerald green eyes.

'Last year, Sammy, Dixie and Milly were Dragon Minders,' said Professor Burlay. 'I would like to choose different students this year to give other people a chance to look after your dragons.'

Jock stuck his hand in the air. 'I'll be one,' he said enthusiastically. 'My Dad is Fignus Hubar. Captain Duke Stronghammer.'

'Very well,' said Professor Burlay. He handed Jock one of the silver dragon shaped pins. 'Who else?'

Jock's eyes lit up and he clipped the silver Dragon Minder pin onto his school jumper. The green dragon eyes sparkled and Sammy felt a twinge of sadness. If he wasn't a

Dragon Minder anymore then he wouldn't be able to visit Kyrillan in the Dragon Chambers as often as last year.

Naomi Fairweather and Holly Banks both looked at each other and put their hands up almost at the same time. Dixie dragged Sammy and Darius's arms in the air as well.

'You three have already had access to the Dragon Chambers,' said Professor Burlay, smiling at their enthusiasm. 'Naomi was first. She shall be the other third year North Dragon Minder,' he said, handing the second silver pin to Naomi.

Naomi clipped the silver Dragon Minder pin onto her shirt collar. She grinned at Darius and he grinned back at her.

'We did it last year,' said Sammy. 'If we're not Dragon Minders this year then it will give us more time to spend on the quest to find the Angel of 'El Horidore.'

'Yeah,' agreed Dixie. 'We'll find the Angel.'

'I hope you do,' said Professor Burlay, smiling broadly as he turned to go up to the fifth year table to hand out his remaining Dragon Minder pins.

CHAPTER 7

MR SYNCLAIR-SMYTHE

Sammy found it strange at first waking up in the circular boys' tower room dormitory surrounded by his green velvet curtain.

He had the same bed as last year with the same chest of drawers, moved down from the floor above where he had slept last year. At the foot of the bed, his name plaque still read:

North House
Samuel R. Rambles
5 years

The only difference was the morning light, which now shone lower through the window as the room was only on the third floor now, two floors lower than his first year dormitory on the top floor with the coned turret ceiling.

Sammy yawned and stretched. Above him, written in small green chalk letters on the ceiling were the initials "S.D" and he guessed this was where Dixie's brother

Serberon had slept in his third year. Now Serberon would be two floors further down the tower, in the fifth year dormitory, the last floor before he would leave Dragamas forever.

Sammy pushed back his green duvet and shivered. One of his roommates must have left a window open and it was sending a cold draught whirling around the room. He reached for a pair of socks and put them on before putting his feet down onto the stone floor.

Just like last year, Darius was sleeping in the bed on Sammy's right. Darius was snoring as usual. Gavin was on Sammy's left, then Toby, then Jock. The tower door separated Darius and Jock.

Sammy thought it was probably Jock who had left a window open as he had complained that the room was stuffy. Also, being a dwarf, Jock didn't seem to feel the cold as his skin was slightly thicker than everyone else's.

Sammy stood up properly and stretched his arms above his head. Through a chink in the curtain he caught sight of Jock's Dragon Minder pin on his chest of drawers. He felt a pang of jealousy that he wouldn't be able to duck under the radiator in the corridor next to the painting of Karmandor Castle and go down the stone steps into the Dragon Chambers.

He wouldn't be able to catch up with the castle news from the dwarves, Captain Stronghammer and Captain Firebreath, or learn more about caring for fully grown dragons.

Although, Sammy thought to himself, with Commander Altair kidnapping his parents' dragons, he supposed it probably didn't matter any more. Now that Kyrillan had been descaled and he could fly as well as the fifth years' dragons, it didn't seem to matter as much as it had.

Above the tower door, the copper bell quivered and chimed loudly. It was eight thirty and time to get up. Sammy checked his timetable. The first lesson was Armoury, with the new teacher Mr Synclair-Smythe.

'Armoury first,' said Sammy.

'Mr Synclair-Smythe,' giggled Darius, pulling back the curtain between their beds.

Sammy laughed. Darius had his white shirt and black trousers on, but instead of wearing his tie properly, he had tied it around his neck in a bow.

'What do you think?' asked Darius, pulling the ends of the bow and dancing on the spot.

'Very good,' said Sammy, laughing and reaching into his chest of drawers for his clothes. He loved the first day back with home-washed clothes, freshly ironed shirts and socks without holes neatly divided into matching pairs with his initials sewn into the inside tops.

Sammy pulled out a pair of black trousers and a crisp white long-sleeved shirt with green lines on the pocket illustrating the "North" compass point logo. Each house had the same logo but rotated with the compass point facing the direction of the house name.

'I'll do your tie like mine, if you like Sammy,' said Darius, disappearing behind the green curtains with one of his famous giggles.

'Morning all,' called Jock from the other side of the room.

'Morning dwarf-breath,' sniggered Gavin. 'You were snoring like an old dragon last night.'

'Liar,' snapped Jock. 'I'll tell my Dad of you.'

'Tell-tale,' snickered Gavin. 'You tell on me and Sammy will thump you. Right Sammy?'

Sammy held his hands up. 'No, it's your fight,' he said, shutting his curtain to get dressed.

'Wimp!' snorted Gavin, flexing his arm. 'Both of you, complete wimps,' he muttered and stormed off out of the tower. He was still dressed in his pyjamas and had an emerald green towel draped over his arm.

'I don't know why he's like that,' said Toby, emerging tousle headed from behind his curtain. 'Ever since our Mum's dragon was murdered, he's gone a bit...'

'Loopy,' finished Jock. 'I don't care. It's a nice challenge for me after all the girls at St. Elderberries. I had to fight them off. I could have had the pick of any one of them you know.'

'Lucky,' said Darius. 'Lisa-Mo is the only girl for me.'

'Who?' asked Sammy.

'She's on TV,' said Jock, but Sammy was none the wiser.

Toby shrugged. 'I think Dragonball is much better than girls. Shall we try out for the school squad? I reckon we could take on the fifth years.'

Sammy nodded. 'I'd do anything to fly on Kyrillan all the time.' He held up the timetable. 'We've got Dragonball later this morning.'

'Armoury's first,' said Jock.

'We've got that new teacher, Mr Synclair-Smythe,' said Darius. 'He sounds really posh.'

'I hope he's all right,' said Sammy.

'Well, he can't be worse than Commander Altair,' said Darius, 'unless he's the "S" in the Shape.'

A cold chill flew up Sammy's spine and he shivered. 'I hope he's not.'

'Well, we'll find out soon enough,' said Darius, heaving his rucksack onto his shoulder. 'Come on, let's go.'

Up in Commander Altair's old classroom, Mr Synclair-Smythe was busy making himself at home. The classroom was neater than ever with four symmetrical rows of ten desks, separated with a gangway making eight groups of five desks.

Mr Synclair-Smythe was wearing the same tartan suit as yesterday with highly polished brown shoes. He had his back to the classroom door and was writing his name in yellow chalk on the blackboard.

He turned around as the students filed into the classroom, taking the time to shake each student's hand as they said their names to him and he ticked their names off on the register.

'Mr Rambles.'

Sammy froze, his right hand locked in Mr Synclair-Smythe's double handed handshake.

'I have been looking forward to meet you,' said Mr Synclair-Smythe.

'Sammy's been dying to meet you too,' shouted Gavin from the back of the classroom.

'Interesting,' said Mr Synclair-Smythe, letting go of Sammy's hand. 'Perhaps you would sit at the front Sammy, so that I can teach you about Armoury rather than have you gossip about Sir Ragnarok's silly quest. You do know where the Angel of 'El Horidore is, don't you?'

Sammy shook his head and went to sit in one of the seats by the window in the second row next to Dixie.

Mr Synclair-Smythe shook his head. 'Mr Rambles,' said Mr Synclair-Smythe sugar sweetly, 'unless I am very much mistaken, I believe I asked you to sit in the front row.'

Reluctantly, Sammy moved his rucksack to the row in front. Dixie got out of her seat to follow him but Mr Synclair-Smythe cut in front of her.

'Trolls, even those as pretty as yourself, must stay in their seats,' said Mr Synclair-Smythe in his sickly sweet voice. 'I have a class plan so I can keep my eyes on the troublemakers.'

Sammy closed his eyes in despair as Mr Synclair-Smythe ushered Gavin, Toby, Simon Sanchez, Jock and Amos together on the back row, where they immediately began a three against two paper fight that started with Jock stuffing a crumpled ball of paper into Gavin's shirt collar.

Oblivious, Mr Synclair-Smythe carried on shaking hands and directing students to their seats. Milly, Holly and Naomi sat on Sammy's row, giggling at a girls' magazine that seemed to be called SuperWoman and had the latest advice about how to put on the perfect coat of nail polish.

Sammy shook his head. As if Milly could put on any more jewellery, bangles, bracelets or polish on her. That was what he liked about Dixie, her simple tomboyishness, unafraid of danger or sports.

The only pieces of jewellery Dixie wore were the pretty blue-green dragon scale she wore on a black cord necklace that she had been given at the Floating Circus and a Nitron Dark wristwatch with a half chewed strap.

'Day dreaming Mr Rambles?' enquired Mr Synclair-Smythe, raising his right eyebrow. 'That will cost you three stars.'

The North students groaned as Mr Synclair-Smythe picked up his staff which, by the colour of the wood, seemed to be made from the branch of a silver birch tree and he tapped it hard on his desk.

Three black stars spat themselves from the end of the crystals on the end of the staff and flew out of the door towards the noticeboard in the Main Hall.

Mr Synclair-Smythe smiled. 'Now, if I have your undivided attention, I have your third year gemstones to distribute.'

Sammy found he was disliking Mr Synclair-Smythe more and more every second. The new Armoury teacher delved his hand into a large brown sack beside his desk and pulled out a handful of yellow stones.

'I shall award three stars to anyone who can tell me what these are.'

Sammy raised his hand. He had seen yellow stones like these in his uncle's jewellery shop. Simon Sanchez also raised his hand.

Mr Synclair-Smythe ignored Sammy and Simon and pointed to Peter Grayling from the West house.

'Are they amethyst, Sir?' asked Peter Grayling.

Mr Synclair-Smythe smiled, showing very white teeth. 'That's close Peter, but it's not the right answer.' He looked to the back of the room. 'I know you will know the answer Simon, so, let's give Mr Rambles a chance, eh?'

'Amber,' said Sammy.

Mr Synclair-Smythe looked shocked. 'Well, yes,' he gasped. 'How, did you know? Have you cheated? Did you look at my notes?'

'My uncle is a jeweller,' said Sammy, scowling. 'He has lots of stones like that in his shop.'

'Sammy's uncle is in the Shape,' shouted Gavin.

'I see,' said Mr Synclair-Smythe. 'How very interesting. Perhaps that is why you have not told Sir Ragnarok where the Angel of 'El Horidore is hidden. Perhaps you want the Shape to have it?'

'Sammy's in the Shape,' sniggered Gavin.

'I don't know where the Angel of 'El Horidore is hidden,' said Sammy folding his arms tightly across his chest. 'I don't even really know what it looks like.'

'But you do know it belonged to Helena Horidore,' Mr Synclair-Smythe smiled. 'Dr Shivers tells me you have seen Angel whistles before,' he added, uncurling his palm and showing a yellow plastic crescent moon shaped whistle.

Everyone in the class leaned forward to see the yellow whistle. It was a tiny device, but it had the power to call a dragon from the other side of the world.

'This one will call my dragon,' said Mr Synclair-Smythe, looking as though he was enjoying the attention from the class. 'The Angel of 'El Horidore will call all dragons, living or dead. I believe you have already been in possession of a powerful Angel whistle, one that will call all of the dragons living at Dragamas.'

'It was an accident,' whispered Sammy. 'I destroyed it so it could never be used. Dr Shivers knows I smashed it into tiny pieces.'

Mr Synclair-Smythe locked eyes with Sammy. 'I do not like your backchat and I do not want you in my class any longer this morning Mr Rambles. Please take your amber and attach it to your staff on your way to Sir Ragnarok's office. I imagine you have been there many times before.'

Bright red at being dismissed from class, Sammy nodded, collecting his staff and rucksack. Mr Synclair-Smythe pressed a warm amber stone into Sammy's hand.

Sammy looked at his amber. It was a pale translucent gemstone, yellow-orange in colour, larger than a golf ball, smaller than a tennis ball and had a rough, irregular surface.

There was a stunned silence followed by whispering as Sammy left the classroom and marched down the corridor.

He received a disapproving look from caretaker Tom Sweep who was mopping the stone floor.

'Are you in trouble again?' asked Tom Sweep.

Sammy didn't reply. He crossed into the Main Hall and passed through the tapestry into Sir Ragnarok's spiral staircase. He climbed round and round until he reached the top and knocked on the door.

Although he knocked five times, Sir Ragnarok's office door remained firmly shut. There was no sign of him, or his smokey grey cat, Lariston.

Sammy sat on the top step and attached the amber stone to the top of his staff. The yellow rock fused with the black onyx he had received in his first year and the red ruby he had received in his second year. Sammy spun the staff in his hands and knocked again on Sir Ragnarok's door.

There was still no answer, so Sammy went back down the spiral stairs, hoping the Armoury lesson would have finished and it was time to play Dragonball with Mr Cross in their Sports lesson. He hoped there would be time to play some games, instead of endless warm-up drills.

Sammy put his rucksack beside his chest of drawers in the North third year dormitory. He found his tracksuit with leather thigh padding, white t-shirt and trainers for Dragonball and sprinted over to the Gymnasium to change.

Dixie and Darius were waiting for him in the Gymnasium foyer by the drinks machine. The secondary Sports teacher, Mr Horatio Ockay, was collecting items of jewellery and watches that students weren't allowed to wear during Sports lessons. Sammy took off his Casino watch and threw it in the tin.

'What did Sir Ragnarok say?' asked Dixie.

'He was out,' said Sammy. 'I didn't see him.'

'You lost three more stars for not coming back to the Armoury lesson,' said Darius. 'Mr Synclair-Smythe is horrible. I reckon he's got to be in the Shape.'

'Probably,' said Sammy gloomily. He would have to work three times harder at Dragonball to earn gold stars to cancel out the black stars.

They went upstairs to the changing rooms and returned back downstairs in the foyer dressed in their leather padded trousers, trainers and white t-shirts. It was chilly and Sammy wished he'd thought to bring his jumper.

After just a few minutes, Jock and Naomi arrived outside the double glass doors with the other Dragon Minders and forty large dragons.

The forty dragons were every shape, size and colour. They all seemed very excited to be back on the Dragonball pitch and ready to fly. The noise of the dragons clinking scales and thumping their huge feet was deafening.

All of the other third year students arrived in twos and threes. They filed into the Gymnasium foyer and thundered up the stairs to get changed.

Sammy's first day got worse when Mr Synclair-Smythe turned up at the Gymnasium with Mr Cross. Both teachers gave him frosty looks.

'Thought you'd skip your meeting with Sir Ragnarok, did you?' asked Mr Synclair-Smythe, stepping back as the third years thundered back down the stairs.

'Good, you're all changed. I hope you're ready to play some Dragonball,' said Mr Cross. 'We're only doing warm-ups and a practice game in this lesson. Trials for our first match against the Nitromen will be later this week.'

'I'm not sure Mr Rambles should play Dragonball or Firesticks until he has divulged to us the whereabouts of the Angel of 'El Horidore,' said Mr Synclair-Smythe.

'I don't know where the stupid Angel is,' snapped Sammy. 'You can't stop me playing Dragonball.'

'Oh, I think you'll find I can,' said Mr Synclair-Smythe. 'There's more to life than Dragonball. Now go to Sir Ragnarok's office!'

'Don't bother getting changed Sammy,' said Mr Cross, running a weathered hand through his sandy hair. 'You mustn't keep Sir Ragnarok waiting. If everything works out,

I'm sure you'll be on the Dragamas team. You're a natural Dragon Rider.'

'Sammy's in trouble,' sniggered Gavin, springing up behind Sammy and making him jump. 'Look at my new tracksuit. Mum bought me and Toby new kit from Excelsior Sports.'

Toby cringed. 'I hate it when he shows off like that.'

Mr Synclair-Smythe however seemed impressed and began chatting with Gavin about the quality of Excelsior sportswear. This gave Sammy the opportunity to collect his clothes and watch and make his way back to the castle.

Holding his staff tightly, he was tempted to fire green sparks towards Mr Synclair-Smythe's back. To ease his frustration, Sammy decided to teleport to Sir Ragnarok's office. If he could get there quickly, he could explain to Sir Ragnarok what had happened earlier.

'Sir Ragnarok's office,' said Sammy.

The familiar mist engulfed him but, to Sammy's surprise, he watched his feet melting and reappearing on the grass. He was still outside and near the Dragonball pitch.

'Sir Ragnarok's office,' repeated Sammy, frustrated as nothing happened. 'Outside Sir Ragnarok's office,' he tried again, wondering if the office was somehow protected and you were only allowed to teleport onto the stairs outside the door.

This time it worked. The ground disappeared beneath his feet and Sammy reappeared at the top of the staircase outside Sir Ragnarok's oak office door.

'Deja-vu,' whispered Sammy, spotting his footprints in the dust from earlier.

Sir Ragnarok opened the door himself, without waiting for Sammy to knock or for Lariston to greet his guest for him.

'Inside please Sammy, now,' said Sir Ragnarok.

Sammy did as he was told. He shut the outer office door as a gold shimmering mist appeared on the stairs.

There was a loud knocking on the office door but Sir Ragnarok made no move to answer it.

'I fear I have made a bad employment decision,' said Sir Ragnarok, 'but I promised to try him out for the term.'

'Mr Synclair-Smythe?' asked Sammy.

Sir Ragnarok nodded. 'At the time, I thought he was interested in finding the Angel of 'El Horidore, to prevent the Shape from finding it and using it.'

Sammy stared open mouthed. 'But…'

'I am telling you this,' Sir Ragnarok seemed to read Sammy's mind, 'because you are mature enough to handle my expectations. I expect you to find the Angel of 'El Horidore and so does the whole of the Snorgcadell.'

'I don't know where it is,' started Sammy. He felt anxious as Sir Ragnarok rested his head in his hands. 'I'd tell you if I did,' stammered Sammy. 'I don't think my parents know where it is either. They don't know anything about dragons. The can't even see Dragamas.'

Sir Ragnarok lifted his head and smiled. 'Your uncle may have done you a favour in this instance. Knowledge in the wrong hands is a worrying thing.'

'Mr Synclair-Smythe thinks…'

'No doubt he is listening outside,' interrupted Sir Ragnarok, waving a hand to Lariston.

The grey cat wove between Sammy's legs and made his way to the door.

'I want you to go back to your Sports lesson and play Dragonball,' said Sir Ragnarok. 'I will explain the situation with your parents to Mr Synclair-Smythe and hopefully we will see you join the school Dragonball team. Being able to fly on a sure and steady dragon is an essential skill if you wish to become a Dragon Knight.'

Sammy nodded. He walked over to Sir Ragnarok's door as a fuming Mr Synclair-Smythe barged into the office, ushered in by Sir Ragnarok's smokey grey cat.

'I'm here to make sure Mr Rambles actually came this time,' said Mr Synclair-Smythe.

'Oh, Sammy was here earlier. I was busy and just didn't answer.' Sir Ragnarok laughed. 'Go back to Dragonball Sammy. Exercise is good for you and Mr Cross tells me you are quite good at Dragonball and Firesticks.'

'Cats in your office! Students teleporting! What is this circus you run Lockyear?' said Mr Synclair-Smythe, taking his white handkerchief out of his tartan jacket pocket and mopping beads of sweat off his forehead.

'Locksmith,' snapped Sir Ragnarok, 'Lockswood! My name is just Lok! Can't you remember a name? I am Lok Ragnarok!'

Sammy closed the office door quietly behind him. He walked down the stone stairs, not daring to teleport himself back to the Gymnasium in case he aroused any more attention. He felt he'd got himself into quite enough trouble for one morning.

CHAPTER 8

THE DRAGONBALL TEAM

Three days later, Sammy was sitting at the breakfast table in the Main Hall with the other third year North students. He was looking forward to tucking into his favourite breakfast of sausages, eggs and fried bread when Dixie came running up to Sammy bursting with excitement.

'You're in the team!' squealed Dixie, sliding into the seat beside Sammy. 'It's on the noticeboard!'

'There's going to be five students from each house on the Dragamas team,' said Gavin, sitting down next to Dixie and helping himself to a large glass of orange juice. 'Even if we get in the team there will still be some useless Westies.'

'Won't matter to you,' snorted Jock. 'You're not in.'

'What?' shouted Gavin. 'Says who? My passing is the best! Better than Nitron Dark!'

Dixie shook her head. 'No one is better than Nitron Dark,' she said dreamily.

'Who else is in?' asked Toby. 'Is it one person from each year?'

Jock stood up to read the noticeboard. 'There are no first year students because either their dragons haven't hatched yet or if they have hatched then they're not big enough to ride. No fifth years' either. It says they're going to play in a separate match.'

'That means Serberon, Mikhael and Jason won't be in,' groaned Dixie. 'Hey, wait! Did you say they're playing separately? That's not fair.'

Jock nodded. 'From North, it's...'

Gavin thumped his fists on the table in a drumroll. Everyone looked up expectantly.

'...Sammy, Toby, Dixie, Clive and me!' finished Jock.

'What!' shouted Gavin standing up and elbowing Jock out of the way. 'Let me see! How come Toby got in and I didn't!'

'Four people from our year,' said Sammy thoughtfully. 'There are no other girls from North.'

Dixie nodded at Sammy, her green eyes shining. 'This is so cool! We can talk tactics in the den.'

'Who's Clive?' demanded Gavin. 'I want to play.'

Hearing his name, Clive Roebank from the fourth year stood up. He was six feet tall with a solid body and strong, thick arms, which he folded over his chest. He flexed his muscles and his arms bulged even bigger.

'Someone say my name?' asked Clive, looking directly at Gavin. 'Was it you? What do you want?'

Gavin shook his head and sat down hurriedly. He had suddenly changed his mind about wanting to play.

As more students filed into the hall for their breakfast, they all stopped to look at the notice board. Mass hysteria broke out and there was lots of pointing and murmuring.

All the North students looked over at the third year North table to catch sight of the players who had been chosen.

Serberon, Mikhael and Jason came up to the third year table and gave Dixie a hug.

'Congratulations making the team, Dixie,' said Mikhael.

'Yeah, really good,' said Jason.

'It's the first time the Nitromen have played Dragonball at Dragamas,' added Serberon.

Sammy nodded, his eyes wide with excitement. He had only ever seen Nitron Dark play Firesticks, but now it seemed as though the whole Nitromen team were coming with their own fire breathing dragons to play Dragonball at the school on Bonfire Night. It was very exciting.

After breakfast, Sammy checked the noticeboard. He wanted to see with his own eyes who else Mr Cross had chosen to play for the Dragamas team.

As well as himself, Dixie, Toby and Jock from North, there weren't many other third year students. Simon and Amos from East and Peter Grayling and Samantha Trowt from West had been chosen and the others, like Clive Roebank, were students from the second and fourth years.

As the match day drew closer everyone huddled in corners discussing who was playing and different tactics. The teachers watched them scrupulously to make sure lessons were being given at least eighty percent attention.

The North Dragon Minders Jock and Naomi skipped as many lessons as possible to prepare the dragons for the match. They spent hours washing and polishing all of the dragons until their scales were bright and shiny. They made sure every dragon had plenty of food, water and rest before the big day.

Sammy always tried to leave the Dragon Studies lessons early to avoid Dr Shivers holding him back at the end of the class and trying to give him a Dragon Minder pin.

After last year, Sammy didn't want to be responsible for anyone dying just so he could have access to the dragons in the Dragon Chambers.

He still knew where most of the passages and entrances were from the map Dr Shivers had given him, but Sammy carefully avoided them.

This was partly because he felt bad about not being able to use the passages as these required the Dragon Minder pin to gain entry. It was also partly so that he pushed himself to explore other areas of the castle and explore the grounds. He was taking the quest to find the Angel of 'El Horidore very seriously.

So far, Sammy thought the best place to plan the search was inside the den he, Dixie, Darius and Serberon had created by the treestump in the clearing in the woods. They had stacked tall branches in a wigwam shape at the end of last year and used the den as a secret meeting place. It was also somewhere peaceful to write up any homework or revise for a test.

Serberon had helped protect the den with a spell of protection using his sapphire gemstone to prevent anyone else from going inside or finding the den.

Darius took up the position of the unofficial Dragamas Dragonball coach. He spent hours with Sammy and Dixie in the den, drawing up charts of possible attack and defence positions. These charts were shared amongst the Dragamas players at mealtimes and everyone agreed that Darius had some really good ideas.

The last lesson on the day before the Dragonball match, was Astronomics. Up in room 37, Professor Burlay had prepared a session studying the Dragamas Constellation using the telescopes outside on the classroom balcony.

'Organise yourselves in groups of four please,' said Professor Burlay, opening up the balcony doors.

Sammy shuffled forward and joined a group with Dixie, Darius and Jock. They stood by one of the telescope stands and Dixie took the first go looking through the lens.

'It would be nice to see the stars a little better,' said Professor Burlay. 'The sky is far too bright at the moment.'

'Make it dark, Sir,' Gavin shouted out from the back of the class. 'Turn off the sunshine!'

Professor Burlay nodded and using his staff, he pointed the crystal end towards the sky. Sammy looked up expectantly. He had seen Professor Burlay do this before.

Without making a sound, a shimmer rippled through the clouds. Daylight slowly vanished as though disappearing down a giant plughole. The sky dimmed to dusk and then darkness. Thousands of sparkling stars started twinkling above them.

In their groups of four, Sammy took his turn looking through the large telescope lens. He shifted the telescope to the right and then to the left, searching for the Dragamas Constellation.

Eventually he saw it. The four coloured stars with the white star in the middle. They were surrounded by what looked like a red circle made from hundreds of tiny dots.

'Ah yes, Sammy,' said Professor Burlay, when Sammy pointed at the circle. 'Those red dots represent the people who have turned their backs on dragons. People the Shape have paid handsomely to buy their draconite. They have swapped their dragons for money.'

'Blood money,' whispered Sammy, feeling suddenly sick.

Professor Burlay nodded. 'There are many people in the world who would rather have extra money in their bank account and who do not care about the consequences of their actions.'

'We have to stop them,' said Sammy. 'We have to make them want to keep their dragons.'

'My parents are always talking to people about their dragons,' said Darius, leaning forward to take his turn looking through the telescope. 'There are a lot of red stars up there, aren't there Professor.'

'I know,' said Professor Burlay. 'It is very sad. Every time I look at the sky there are more red stars. More people who have lost their dragons.'

'Well the Shape are not taking my dragon,' said Sammy firmly. 'Even if they have got my parents' dragons.'

'We don't know that for sure,' said Professor Burlay, resting his hand on Sammy's shoulder. 'I think Commander Altair is a good man.'

'Me too,' said Dixie quietly.

'We have to keep hoping for the best,' said Professor Burlay. 'Good luck with your game tomorrow. I have examined the stars and I am predicting a convincing win for the Dragamas team.'

CHAPTER 9

NITRON DARK

Sammy found it very difficult to fall asleep that night. Professor Burlay's rather optimistic prediction that the Dragamas team would win against the Nitromen was putting extra pressure on him to score lots of goals.

It kept Sammy awake for a long time, thinking about flying on Kyrillan and all the tactics he had discussed with Dixie and Darius. Eventually, sometime after midnight, he finally drifted off into a deep sleep full of dreams about dragons and Dragonball matches.

In the dream Dragonball match, Nitron Dark and the Nitromen were chasing the black leather balls and scoring goal after goal. No matter how hard he tried, Sammy couldn't kick a ball anywhere near the goal.

When he woke he was drenched in sweat from tossing and turning, practicing dives and loop the loops in his sleep.

Sammy didn't think it wouldn't be a fair match between the Dragamas students and the Nitromen. All twenty

Nitromen were older, larger, much stronger and far more experienced than anyone at Dragamas.

Sammy also had a strong feeling that Dixie wouldn't be able to concentrate on the game with her hero, Nitron Dark, as life-size as her bedroom poster, within touching distance.

'Get up sleepy,' Gavin called from the other side of the room. 'You're needed downstairs. Or have you forgotten it's the Dragonball match day today?'

Sammy laughed. 'Of course I remember!'

'Jock's already getting our dragons,' said Toby.

'I wish it wasn't Saturday,' said Gavin. 'If the match was during the week we could have missed some lessons!'

'I think they thought of that,' said Toby.

Sammy heard the twins stand up on their beds and predicted a pillow fight was about to start. He jumped out of his bed and picked up his pillow ready to join in.

As he pulled back the green velvet dividing curtain he froze on the spot. He jerked his arm but he could hardly move. Everything was in slow motion.

Sammy looked around the room. Gavin was in front of him, rock solid, pillow in mid swing. Mr Synclair-Smythe was standing in the tower doorway with a ruby glowing in his palm.

'Good to see some of my students can resist the power of the ruby,' said Mr Synclair-Smythe. 'I have just come here to warn you Sammy, the Nitromen may use this against you on the pitch.'

'I'm..fi..i..ine,' said Sammy, disturbed to find that the ruby had slowed him down and his feet felt like lead. He'd got badly out of practice of deflecting the effects of the ruby gemstone over the summer.

'Good,' said Mr Synclair-Smythe. 'I will be cheering for you and the Dragamas team,' he added, making his way back down the tower stairs.

'Like he'd cheer for the Nitromen,' said Darius, when Mr Synclair-Smythe was safely out of earshot. 'Are you all right Sammy?'

Sammy nodded slowly. 'Bit...out...of...practice.' He grinned and threw his pillow at Darius's head.

Gavin threw his pillow at Toby and the pillow fight broke out in earnest. Soon all the pillows were destroyed and feathers were flying around the room. Sammy announced he was the winner and lay back on his bed exhausted.

He had barely caught his breath when Dixie appeared at the tower room door. She was dressed in her leather padded tracksuit with a crisp white t-shirt that looked suspiciously as though she was wearing her Nitromen black and gold t-shirt underneath. She wore black leather gloves and wrist guards and her green hair was tied back in a simple ponytail.

'Come on boys!' she shouted, banging her fist on the door. 'Let's play Dragonball!'

Sammy leaped up and shooed her out of the bedroom. 'We'll see you downstairs,' he shouted, grabbing his own tracksuit and white t-shirt.

He dressed quickly and put on his dragon hide gloves which would protect his hands when he was holding onto Kyrillan's metal harness. Sammy put the harness over his shoulder and his green gum shield into his mouth. He marched down the stairs with Darius and the twins in hot pursuit.

Outside, they found the Dragonball pitch was buzzing with activity. Sammy ran with Toby to join the rest of the

Dragamas team who were huddled together in a circle and talking about last minute tactics.

In the corner of the pitch near the Gymnasium, school caretaker, Tom Sweep, was packing away an enormous orange lawnmower. The grass pitch was looking very green and in immaculate pristine condition with neatly mown vertical stripes, alternating between light green and dark green due to the change in mowing direction, running up and down the pitch.

Students from all the four houses had turned up to watch. They were busy laying out lots of wooden benches at the side of the pitch and putting up the black Dragamas flags with the golden twin-tailed "D" logo and brightly coloured bunting.

At the far end of the pitch, there was a large black coach with gold doors and gold stripes zig-zagging down the side.

'It's the Nitrobus!' squealed Dixie. 'Look!'

Sammy looked at the gigantic coach. The gold doors opened and men dressed in black leather trousers and black and gold shirts stepped out.

'There's Nitron Dark!' shouted Dixie jumping up and down and grabbing Sammy's arm. 'Look! It's Nitron Dark!'

'You're wearing a Nitromen shirt under your t-shirt,' said Sammy. 'I thought you were.'

'I'm going to ask him to sign it at the end of the game,' said Dixie, her green eyes shining.

'It might be worth some money one day,' said Mr Cross. 'As long as you put these balls in this goal,' he pointed to the black leather Dragonballs and the goal at the far end of the pitch, 'there won't be a problem.'

Dixie stared into space. 'This goal,' she murmured, facing the Dragamas end.

Sammy turned her around. 'No, we need to shoot at this goal,' he said, grinning at her. 'Come on, Jock and Naomi are here with our dragons.'

Dixie stared dreamily into the distance as the twenty Dragamas dragons approached the Gymnasium. There was a sudden stampede as the dragons recognised their owners and broke away from the pack. Sammy ran over to his blue-green dragon.

'Hi Kyrillan,' said Sammy, pleased that his dragon stopped obediently in front of his feet.

Kyrillan knelt on the grass, his scaly knees clinking as he bent down to the floor. Without being asked, he tucked his scaly head into the metal harness that Sammy held in front of him.

Mr Cross called all the players back into a circle. The Dragamas students lined up next to their dragons, each student making last minute preparations and checking all the last details before the game.

Some of the fourth year students had proper saddles for their dragons and they checked the clips and clasps to make sure everything was in place.

'This won't be an easy game,' warned Mr Cross, 'but I want you all to play your very best and see if you can score a few goals for Dragamas.'

Sammy nodded, taking in every word. He nudged Dixie who was still staring at the Nitrobus. She nodded, without taking her eyes off the men in gold and black shirts who were making their way towards them.

'He's coming over,' Dixie breathed. 'Nitron Dark is coming over here.'

'He's only a Dragonball player,' whispered Sammy, trying to listen as Mr Cross gave advice on which tactics to use to defend their goal.

'Don't look at the rider, keep your eyes on which way their dragon is facing,' said Mr Cross. 'Watch which arm they're using to throw the Dragonball and follow…Dixie, listen to me please.'

The Nitromen got closer and Sammy saw Nitron Dark reach under his shirt collar and take out a gold and black half-moon shaped whistle. He put the whistle to his lips and even though no sound came out, Sammy knew the whistle would be calling all of the Nitromen's dragons to Dragamas.

Sammy knew the Nitromen's dragons wouldn't be far behind the Nitrobus and they would be flying a lot faster than the bus because they didn't need to follow the road or stop for traffic lights.

Even before the Nitromen's dragons came into sight, Sammy could hear the thunderous beating of wings high up in the sky. Then the dragons appeared. Large majestic black shapes weaving amongst the clouds.

Gradually, the black shapes became outlines of dragons with large bodies the size of camper vans, huge widespread wings and long snaking tails that they used to guide them down to the school.

The Nitromen reached the circle of Dragamas students. They were all dressed identically in black and gold shirts with black leather trousers and boots.

'Hello Dragamas,' said Nitron Dark, flashing a perfectly white camera-ready smile on his tanned face. He turned to Dixie. 'Alright gorgeous?' he said, grinning at her.

Each of the Nitromen shook Mr Cross's hand and then they marched back towards the Nitrobus, where twenty enormous, jet black, dragons were landing in neat rows.

'Focus please,' groaned Mr Cross as Dixie's jaw remained open long after Nitron Dark had gone.

'He called me gorgeous,' said Dixie, her voice quavering.

'And so you are,' said Mr Cross exasperatedly, 'more so if we win.' He tapped his pink games whistle. 'Let's get started. Mount your dragons please.'

'Gorgeous,' said Dixie, redoing her ponytail. 'Do you think he meant it?'

'He was probably just trying to put you off,' grumbled Sammy. 'Looks like it worked.'

Dixie stumbled over Kiridor's tail and caught her balance. 'I do not fancy Nitron Dark,' she sniffed.

CHAPTER 10

THE DRAGONBALL MATCH

Sammy nodded obediently and fastened the leather and metal straps around Kyrillan's body. Resting his left hand against his dragon's neck for support, he swung his right leg over the spikes on his dragon's back so he was facing forward, his feet swinging in front of the webbed wings, his hands gripping the harness tightly, butterflies swarming in his stomach.

'Right! Good luck all of you!' said Mr Cross and he ran across the pitch to Mr Ockay, who was waiting by the golden dragon statue in the middle of the pitch.

On Sammy's command, Kyrillan took ten quick steps forward, then launched himself into the air. Sammy took one hand off the harness and waved to the crowd. Everyone cheered as the Dragamas students took flight on the backs of their multi-coloured dragons.

'Dixie, you're in goal!' shouted Clive, waving for her to fly downwards towards the large netted goal at the Dragamas end of the pitch. 'Amos, Simon, you need to defend the goal! Don't let anything in!'

Sammy did a double-take as Dixie lined herself up in goal. Sitting astride her blue-green shimmering dragon, she reminded him of Mary-Beth, Serberon's former girlfriend.

Sammy saw Serberon in the crowd. Dixie's brother had obviously thought the same thing as he shouted "Good luck Mary-Beth!" and then Sammy saw Serberon shake his head as he realised it was his sister.

Dixie stretched her arms and put her green gum guard into her mouth. She set Kiridor on a pattern of walking up and down the goal.

Following Clive's instructions, Simon and Amos flew in circles over the top of the goal to help defend against the Nitromen attack.

'Phee-phip!' Mr Cross blew his whistle to start the game. Everyone cheered louder and started clapping.

In the centre of the pitch, the golden dragon statue came to life, spinning around and around. The familiar black leather football sized balls were released from its mouth and flew high into the air. Sammy lost count of how many there were as the balls spun away in every direction.

Toby flew past on his grey-green dragon, Puttee, and caught a black ball. He threw it wildly and Nitron Dark intercepted the pass. In a single motion, Nitron Dark turned his black dragon around and belted the ball with his fist high above Dixie's head and into the goal.

As soon as the ball touched the back of the net it disappeared, making its way through the underground passage to the golden dragon statue. Seconds later it flew out of the golden dragon's mouth and was back in play.

Down on the ground, the Dragamas crowd groaned and booed. They waved their black flags with the twin-tailed Dragamas "D" emblem and started chanting "Dragamas, Dragamas, Dragamas", faster and faster, louder and louder.

Sammy swooped low across the pitch on Kyrillan. He was chasing another ball. Nitron Dark blew him a kiss as he swerved past and stole the ball.

'Give them a chance!' shouted Mr Cross.

Nitron Dark grinned and lobbed the ball between Toby and Clive making them clash together as they both went for the ball in mid-air.

'Foul!' shouted Sammy, surging forward on Kyrillan to collect the ball. He caught it and took Kyrillan high into the clouds. Out of sight, Sammy flew towards the Nitromen's goal. As he got closer, he caught sight of a dark shadow above him.

'Oi! Troll-lover, show us your stuff!'

Sammy looked up. Nitron Dark's jet black dragon was directly above him. Nitron Dark was smiling, holding his arm out, teasing Sammy to shoot.

'I'm going to score!' shouted Sammy. He swooped down, dodging a blond Nitromen defender. He swerved within kicking distance of the goal and threw the ball lightly in front of him as more defenders swarmed around him on every side.

On cue, Kyrillan spun round and thumped the ball with the tip of his tail into the goal. The Dragamas crowd stood up and whooped and cheered "Dragamas! Dragamas!".

Nitron Dark rubbed his eyes in disbelief. 'Good shot kid. Your father must have been like mine. Taught you to fly before you could walk.'

'He doesn't know about dragons...' started Sammy as Nitron Dark loop-the-looped over him.

'Well someone sure did,' shouted Nitron Dark. 'That goal was world class. Only someone with dragon blood could do that kid.'

Sammy nodded blankly, not taking "dragon blood" seriously, but giving it enough thought to miss a heavy pass from Clive. Sammy's world spun as one of the leather balls hit him on the head and he regained his balance.

'Catch it, stupid,' groaned Clive, swooping down to the ground on his green dragon to collect the ball.

'Half time!' yelled Mr Cross, blowing his whistle five times. 'Thirty-six points to the Nitromen. One point to Dragamas. Well done Sammy!'

Wedged between Dixie, Toby and their dragons, Sammy flew to the ground. As the only fourth year on the team, Clive had appointed himself as a Dragonball expert and was getting on Sammy's nerves by repeating Mr Cross's pep-talk word for word.

'This is no good,' moaned Simon Sanchez. 'Even my mother can play better than our team.'

'She'd blast them out of the sky,' said Toby.

'Turn them into gold,' added Sammy.

Simon scowled. 'This is no joke. We must win.'

'Against the best team in the league?' scoffed Jock. 'Even if they were being nice, which they're not, we wouldn't have a chance.'

'Nitron Dark let me take a shot,' said Sammy. 'I scored a goal.'

'Only because he saw all those defenders and he thought you'd miss,' retorted Jock. 'We're going to lose and we're going to lose badly. Really badly.'

'Easy boys,' said Mr Cross, coming over to consult with them, 'and Dixie,' he added at her not-so-discrete cough. 'I'm going to rotate the team. Dixie, you and Sammy will defend from each side of the goal. Jock, you will go in goal. Everyone else, I want you all to defend and let past as few goals as you possibly can.'

Mr Cross reached for his notebook and flipped through the pages. 'Yes, everyone else can defend from midfield, except Clive, who I want to try and score. I want you to all help Clive to get the balls and fight the Nitromen. I want the Dragamas score to be in double figures!'

'Even getting two goals would be nice,' said Sammy to Dixie and Jock as they set off into the new positions.

'I hate the way Mr Cross won't let me play further up the field,' grumbled Dixie.

The way the Nitromen were playing and in particular how Nitron Dark had called him a "Troll-lover", Sammy thought privately it was just as well Mr Cross had kept Dixie at the Dragamas end.

'I guess,' Sammy said out loud.

'No more goals,' said Dixie resolutely. 'Get up Kiridor. Jock's going in goal now.'

Dixie's blue-green dragon, the spitting image of Sammy's dragon Kyrillan, spread his blue-green wings like a giant bat and took off effortlessly.

'Let's save some goals,' Sammy leaned down to Kyrillan's head and whispered in his dragon's ears. He clutched Kyrillan's harness and kicked off the ground.

The crowd got to their feet again. They all cheered and waved black Dragamas flags with the golden twin-tailed "D" logo as the game started again.

Twenty minutes later Sammy was exhausted. Kyrillan was exhausted and half the Dragamas team had dropped out. Thanks to Mr Cross's changes at half time, the score was forty-seven to eleven. Dragamas had broken double figures and, with Dixie helping defend the goal from outside, very few balls had reached Jock and even fewer had been let inside the Dragamas goal.

Nitron Dark was circling over the Dragamas goal, his jet black dragon casting a fearsome shadow over the net that Sammy, Dixie and Jock were guarding. He waved his arm in a circle, sending a signal to the Nitromen.

Four Nitromen hurtled towards the Dragamas goal, lobbing ball after ball in synchronised overarm passes between themselves.

'It's their grand finale!' shrieked Dixie. 'Take cover!'

Sammy spun around. Fifteen other Nitromen were curving around the goal in a wide arc. They had all the balls and were on a course heading straight for the Dragamas goal. All of the dragons were breathing fire.

Clouds of black smoke and tongues of orange and yellow flames surged forward. It was a terrifying sight, let alone the noise of the flames crackling and the sound of the dragons roaring.

In the crowd, the Dragamas students got up from their seats on the wooden benches and backed away from the pitch, scurrying away to safety. Simon and Amos were sent flying backwards through the pack of Nitromen and fell, tumbling and somersaulting off their dragons, down to the ground.

'Pheeeee!' Mr Cross blew violently on his whistle. 'Stop! Stop the match!'

The Nitromen swarmed like a black and gold cloud of angry wasps.

'Move!' shrieked Dixie.

Sammy and Jock fled, getting caught in a tangle of black dragons. Jock screamed as he fell off his dragon. He fell past Sammy to the ground with a thump.

Sammy felt himself thrown off Kyrillan's back as the Nitromen whizzed past. He held on tightly to his dragon's spiky tail and with a flick of Kyrillan's muscles he found himself back in the saddle with only minor scratches.

'Your dragon's looking after you, Troll-lover.'

It took Sammy a second to realise it was Nitron Dark speaking to him from upside down above him. Nitron

Dark had a nasty smile and was carrying four balls, two under each of his arms.

'Another four points for the Nitromen,' said Nitron Dark, grinning, and throwing the four leather balls into the empty goal.

Sammy followed Nitron Dark down to the ground. Mr Cross came running over with Mr Ockay closely behind him. They both carried large green suitcases with medical supplies.

'My leg hurts,' said Jock, with tears in his eyes. 'I think it's broken.'

'Hold still please,' said Mr Ockay. With a decided air of experience, he opened the first green suitcase and whipped out a tight green scarf bandage. He wound it around Jock's left leg from his ankle to his thigh.

Mr Ockay opened the second suitcase and it expanded into a full size green stretcher. He rolled Jock on to the stretcher and elevated it with his staff.

'To Mrs Grock's house,' said Mr Ockay, pointing towards the gingerbread style cottage on the outskirts of the pitch.

'Look after my dragons,' whispered Jock hoarsely. He pressed something metal into Sammy's hand as he floated past.

'I can't,' said Sammy, closing his fist on the Dragon Minder pin. 'I'll give it to Professor Burlay.'

'Not to keep, stupid,' hissed Jock. 'Just until I get out of Mrs Grock's.'

'Oh,' said Sammy, a wave of relief flooding through him. 'Dr Shivers, last year, he...'

'Barmy,' said Jock. 'Make sure Dixie's dragon stays away from mine. They don't always get on.'

Sammy grinned. 'Sure.' He looked up. The Nitromen were standing in a line, shaking hands with the Dragamas players. Sammy sprinted up the pitch and stood next to Dixie to shake the players' hands.

'Sorry about your friend,' said Nitron Dark, grinning and moving up the line. 'Well, hello again, darling,' he picked up Dixie's hand and kissed it.

Dixie went bright pink. 'Please may I have your autograph?'

'Sure,' said Nitron Dark, 'and take these tickets to come and watch my next game.'

Dixie went even pinker, making Sammy feel rather uncomfortable. Nitron Dark let go of her hand and shook Sammy's hand firmly.

'Good luck kid,' he said to Sammy and walked off to see Mr Cross.

'He kissed my hand!' squealed Dixie when Nitron Dark and the Nitromen were out of earshot.

'Don't use any soap,' said Simon Sanchez, grinning at her.

'Or you'll wash it off,' sniggered Toby. 'Honestly, he's only a Dragonball player.'

'The best Dragonball player,' said Dixie dreamily.

'Who nearly killed us,' snapped Sammy. He couldn't shake off the feeling that Nitron Dark was only being nice to Dixie's face.

'What's your problem?' snapped Dixie.

'I'm going to put our dragons away,' said Sammy, changing the subject. He held his palm open showing the Dragon Minder pin. The green stones in the eyes of the dragon seemed to mock him. He walked off as Milly and Darius arrived.

'Sammy's got a Dragon Minder pin,' said Dixie. 'Do you reckon it's from Dr Shivers again?'

Even though they weren't speaking to him, it made Sammy's blood run cold and shivers run down his back.

Naomi was in a bad mood when she helped Sammy round up the dragons. Apparently she had been looking forward to hearing about Dixie's kiss from Nitron Dark and was disgruntled that she had to help put the dragons away when she hadn't even been playing.

'It was on her hand,' said Sammy, feeling even more exasperated when Naomi giggled at him.

CHAPTER 11

COMMANDER ALTAIR RETURNS

Sammy used Jock's green-eyed Dragon Minder pin to open the door that led into the Dragon Chambers. The twenty Dragamas dragons followed him obediently inside.

Sammy saw Naomi hanging back and he had a feeling she wasn't staying. Apparently none of the official Dragon Minders had bothered to stay either.

'I'll see you later Sammy,' said Naomi, turning on her heels, 'I want to hear about the kiss!'

'Go on then,' said Sammy, knowing she was already miles away from hearing him. 'I'll do it all by myself.'

Sammy struggled with Simon Sanchez's bulky black dragon, feeling glad he wasn't an official Dragon Minder this year. All of the dragons seemed bigger and more awkward than last year. They each had a mind of their own and walked this way and that way, eventually arriving in the underground sleeping chambers.

In the distance, Sammy could hear singing and guessed some of the dwarves were nearby. As he approached the underground office, he saw Captain Stronghammer and

Captain Firebreath slumped in their chairs next to a barrel of cider.

Each dwarf had a long straw which they were using to drink from the barrel. Captain Firebreath was singing about losing a battle with Captain Stronghammer joining in, out of tune, in some sort of chorus. It sounded interesting and Sammy stopped to listen.

'Oh the battle is too big to be won. All of our dragons are dead and gone,' sang Captain Firebreath.

'Roll em, roll em. Call em, call em. Call on the dragons of old,' sang Captain Stronghammer.

'Oh the battle is nearly done. All of our dragons are saved by one,' sang Captain Firebreath, pausing to take a swig of cider up the long straw.

'Roll em, roll em. Call em, call em. Call on the dragons of old, hic,' sang Captain Stronghammer, finishing the song with a large burp.

Sammy slipped past the dwarves and ducked between the pillars of the underground chamber. The dwarves barely noticed as Sammy led the twenty dragons quietly into their individual quarters.

Spotting that the food basins were empty, Sammy decided to refill the four baths of oats for the third year dragons. He checked the water supplies and filled twelve buckets of ice cold water to pour into each of the twelve water basins to top them up.

If none of the other Dragon Minders could be bothered to help, then he was going to see to it that all the dragons were all being taken care of himself.

It also helped having time away from everyone else so he could go back over the excitement of the Dragonball match and have the time to put Nitron Dark calling him a "Troll-lover" into perspective.

As Sammy shovelled oats from the sacks into the metal baths using the grey plastic scoop, Nitron Dark meant less and less and Sammy got carried away in a fantasy that he was a Dragon Knight responsible for all of the dragons at Dragamas.

A stone scuttling across the Dragon Chambers made him stop and look around. A tall black shadow was facing him. Sammy felt his heart stop beating. The shadow had its hand on Kyrillan.

'Who's there?' asked Sammy, taking a step back as the figure stepped into the light. 'You?' he gasped. 'What have you done with my dragons,' he demanded as he saw the sandy hair and slept-in clothes of Commander Altair, his black belt with the three silver stars dividing a sagging grey jumper and well-worn jeans.

Commander Altair put a finger to his lips. 'Hush, please let me explain.'

'Tell me where you've taken my parents' dragons,' demanded Sammy.

Commander Altair nodded. 'They're safe. Trust me.'

Sammy leaned on one of the cold marble pillars for support. 'Trust you?' he asked.

'I am innocent,' said Commander Altair. 'Please believe me. Trust me. I have kept your dragons safe.'

'So you can kill them?' asked Sammy, putting his hands on his hips. 'Sir Ragnarok says you're in the Shape with my Uncle Peter Pickering.'

Commander Altair held up his hands. 'I admit I was there over the summer. Has Darius told you what happened to the dragons?'

Sammy nodded. 'He said his mother tried to save some of them by the roadside.'

'It was a mass murder, similar to what happened to our fifth year dragons,' said Commander Altair quietly. 'I had information on the attack. I was supposed to be there to stop it from happening,' his voice cracked. 'But I arrived late and the Snorgcadell, my father and Sir Ragnarok, they arrived after me and caught me with my hand inside a dragon skull. I was checking if the stone had gone but, they believe I am, what you would call, the "A" in the Shape.'

Sammy stood still. He could hear footsteps in the shadows. It sounded as though Captain Firebreath and Captain Stronghammer had stopped drinking and started doing their checks on all the dragons.

'Let me prove to you that I am not the "A" in the Shape,' said Commander Altair hurriedly. 'I will bring your parents' dragons to your house on Bonfire Night. You can check them and decide if you want me to carry on looking after them or take them somewhere else, to Dixie's house perhaps?'

'You'll bring them to my uncle's house?' asked Sammy.

'On Bonfire Night. Use the underground passage when the fireworks start,' said Commander Altair.

'Do you promise you'll bring them?' asked Sammy.

Commander Altair nodded. 'Yes, I will definitely bring them. Thank you Sammy,' he said and evaporated in a silver mist.

Sammy shook himself. This was crazy. Sir Ragnarok had been so sure Commander Altair was in the Shape that he had fired him and replaced him with Mr Synclair-Smythe to teach Armoury this year. It didn't make any sense.

Sammy badly wanted to trust both Commander Altair and Sir Ragnarok but both of them could not be right.

'I'll wait until Bonfire Night,' Sammy muttered, dodging out of the way of one of the second year dragons. He made his way over to one of the secret inside doorways into the Dragon Chamber and walked up the stone steps.

Sammy inserted Jock's Dragon Minder pin into the groove at the top of the steps. There was a small mirror at the top of the steps which Sammy to check the coast was clear. No one was around so he pushed open the hidden door behind the radiator in the corridor and made his way to the Main Hall to find the others.

When Sammy arrived at the Main Hall, he found it had been transformed into a black and gold themed party to celebrate the Nitromen coming to the school and playing the Dragonball match.

The wooden dinner tables were covered in black and gold striped tablecloths with black and gold serviettes and black and gold decorations.

Everywhere he looked, Sammy could see black and gold flags, banners and stickers all matching the Nitromen's team colours.

Sammy slipped into the empty seat next to Dixie and Darius at the third year North table just as Sir Ragnarok announced the start of the feast. In whispers, Sammy relayed what had happened in the Dragon Chambers to his best friends.

Dixie's green eyes were gleaming. 'I told you he was innocent.'

Sammy nodded. 'That's what he said. He said he will definitely show me my parents' dragons on Bonfire Night.'

'You don't have any proof at all,' whispered Darius dismissively. 'For all you know, it could be a trap.'

Dixie scowled. 'So, he must have jinxed the Nitromen to knock Jock off his dragon, so Jock gave Sammy his Dragon Minder pin, and then he made Naomi and all the other Dragon Minders disappear? Are you honestly saying Commander Altair made sure Sammy went into the Dragon Chambers on his own?'

Darius gave Dixie a dark look. 'That's the stupidest thing I've ever heard. But there must have been some sort of spell going on to make Nitron Dark kiss you.'

'Troll Princess,' sniggered Gavin, overhearing them.

Dixie raised her fork at Gavin. 'What did you call me?' she demanded.

'You heard,' snapped Gavin, picking up his fork and lunging at Dixie.

The silver five pronged forks clashed together. Dixie twisted her wrist, wrenching Gavin's fork out of his hand. It landed with a clatter on the table and Dixie picked it up, holding it in an iron grip.

'Apologise,' said Dixie, bending Gavin's fork with her fingers.

'Whatever,' snapped Gavin, taking Toby's fork instead. 'I can't see why you want to find secret passages anyway. What's wrong with stairs and corridors?'

CHAPTER 12

ANCIENT AND MODERN LANGUAGES

A few weeks later, Sammy was fully back into the school routine and enjoying most of his lessons. He enjoyed Alchemistry with Professor Sanchez and Astronomics with Professor Burlay. His favourite lesson was still Sports, especially the weekend games-only sessions, where he could fly on Kyrillan for a whole afternoon.

Since Commander Altair had been suspended, Sammy found Mr Synclair-Smythe's Armoury lessons unbearable as he was under constant scrutiny about the location of the Angel of 'El Horidore.

However, if he was finding Mr Synclair-Smythe's Armoury lessons dire, it was nothing compared with how bad Sammy was finding the new Ancient and Modern Languages lessons.

The subject was taught to the third years and above by Miss Angela Amoratti, who had taken over teaching Ancient and Modern languages after Professor Hilltop's retirement last year.

Miss Amoratti was at least a foot taller than all of the third year students. She had jet black hair with electric blue streaks, which matched the black and blue tunic she always wore and contrasted sharply with her icy white skin and coal black eyes.

Miss Amoratti's eyes were quicker than a bird's and expertly tuned into spotting trouble in the class and finding any mistakes in their work.

Sammy soon found out that Miss Amoratti was a stickler for both the school rules and the rules of grammar. She had a large wooden ruler that she liked to tap on her desk and she especially seemed to liked flicking the end of her ruler on the knuckles of anyone speaking out of turn.

Miss Amoratti took an instant dislike to Dixie because of her green hair. Perhaps because she dyed her own hair, she refused to accept that Dixie had no choice about the colour of her hair and insisted that she washed the colour out at least once a week.

Despite Dixie explaining time and time again that her green hair was genetic, Miss Amoratti wouldn't believe her and told her she was just making a statement and going through a phase copying her brothers. The rest of the North house had stuck by Dixie and as a result they were all out of favour.

'Birds of a feather,' said Miss Amoratti one Wednesday afternoon, 'you are all the same. You are all troublemakers.'

To make matters worse, Miss Amoratti had decided to commandeer half of the Sports lessons and half of Professor Sanchez's Alchemistry lessons.

'You need to study hard,' said Miss Amoratti. 'I will give the best grades to students who study my subject through their lunchbreaks and on Sundays.'

Sammy's dislike of the new teacher intensified when Miss Amoratti punished Dixie, who had unfortunately commented that Miss Amoratti had repeating initials and so she could be the "A" in the Shape.

Dixie had bleeding bandages on her knuckles from her caning and bruises on her wrists from where Miss Amoratti had missed her mark.

To make matters even worse, Miss Amoratti had taken a liking to Gavin and Toby, calling them "my twins" and unintentionally egging Gavin on in his merciless taunts about anyone and anything that disturbed his one-man universe.

'Are you attentive Samuel?' asked Miss Amoratti, running a hand through her blue tinged hair.

Sammy glared. He hated being called "Samuel" at the best of times and especially by a teacher he hated and especially in front of the whole class.

'In dwarven,' continued Miss Amoratti, 'please tell me what your parents do with their dragons. I will write up your answer on the blackboard.'

Jock's hand shot up, whisking past Sammy's ear. It wasn't even a fair question as Sammy was sure Miss Amoratti knew his parents couldn't see dragons, let alone do anything with them.

'Dearie me Samuel,' said Miss Amoratti patronisingly before Sammy had a chance to speak. 'Perhaps you could tell me in Elvish? Or Goblin? Did I tell you I can speak fifty-five different languages? I used to be secretary to Old Heisenburger in my twenties, then I was Senior Vice President of Translation at...'

Gavin yawned loudly. 'Miss Amoratti,' he called out, deliberately extending the "Amoratti" into "Amoratti-Catcher" under his breath.

It was his favourite joke as he knew it wound Sammy up reminding him of the bullies at his old school in Ratisbury.

Miss Amoratti fluffed up her blue tinged hair. 'What is it Gavin?'

'I'm bored,' said Gavin, yawning again.

Sammy shook his head. He couldn't understand why Miss Amoratti didn't discipline Gavin like she did with everyone else. In that situation, even Professor Burlay would have at least deducted some stars.

'What would you like to do instead, Gavin?' asked Miss Amoratti smiling sweetly at the dark haired twin.

'Hunt for treasure!' shouted Gavin, without a moment of hesitation.

Sammy was sure this was the first thing that had popped into Gavin's brain but it seemed to take Miss Amoratti's fancy and she carried on smiling at Gavin.

'Do you mean the Quest? To search for the Angel of 'El Horidore?' asked Miss Amoratti. 'How wonderful of you! What a super idea! I will organise a trip to the Land of the Pharaohs with Sir Ragnarok to look for it…but only if you're good.'

For the first time in any of her lessons, Gavin got his Ancient and Modern Languages textbook, his pen and lined notepaper out of his rucksack and began to work, not just in that lesson, but in every single one.

CHAPTER 13

A DRAGON IS DEAD

Summer turned quickly to autumn, with a taste of the winter weather yet to come. Multi-coloured leaves fell like confetti from most of the trees in the forest. The weather turned colder and it rained, lots.

Caretaker, Tom Sweep, complained constantly about the never ending muddy footprints in the corridors.

He also complained about the Dragon Minders, telling anyone who would listen that they kept forgetting to close the secret passage doors into the Dragon Chambers and he was forever closing the doors after them.

As promised, Miss Amoratti signed up the entire third year for Sir Ragnarok's quest to find the Angel of 'El Horidore, whether they wanted to join the quest or not.

Students in the West house complained vehemently that it was too cold for searching for something that may not exist. They complained the quest was too hard and told her Sir Ragnarok had set an impossible task.

General Aldebaran Altair had teleported into Dragamas one morning and he had written down the names of all students participating in the quest.

A day later, Sir Ragnarok announced that General Aldebaran Altair had assigned the students into small groups of three. Sammy was pleased he had been assigned to a group with his best friends, Dixie and Darius.

For Halloween, Sir Ragnarok turned the Main Hall into a giant pumpkin again and he provided the most enormous feast for all the Dragamas students.

Sammy and Darius were sitting with Gavin and Toby on green velvet beanbags in the North common room eating leftover sweets from the party. The door burst open and Dixie danced in waving a copy of "The Metro" newspaper.

'Have you seen this!' Dixie shrieked, jumping up and down. 'Nitron Dark's coming here on Bonfire Night!'

'They're all coming!' shouted Naomi Fairweather, following Dixie into the common room. 'They're putting on a Fire Show with their dragons. That's probably instead of having fireworks this year!'

'No fireworks?' asked Sammy.

'Who needs fireworks when they've got fire breathing dragons?' shouted Gavin, leaping up and scattering the bowl of sweets. 'This is going to be great!'

'Our dragons don't breathe fire, do they?' asked Sammy, feeling his cheeks go crimson as he asked. Why didn't he know enough about dragons? It wasn't fair his parents didn't know dragons existed. They could have taught him so much.

Dixie leaped over the study tables and rapped the side of Sammy's head with her newspaper.

'You wouldn't think you know anything about dragons,' said Dixie reprovingly. 'Of course our dragons will breathe fire when they're older. Lots of fire!'

'Oh,' said Sammy. 'Kyrillan breathes smoke,' he added, trying to redeem himself.

'Really? That's advanced too.'

Sammy turned his head to see who had spoken. He saw Dixie's green haired brother, Serberon, had teleported himself out of a grey mist and was sitting on the study table, where only cups and magazines had been there a moment ago.

Sammy nodded. 'I wish Kyrillan could breathe fire.'

'I wish my dragon could breathe fire too!' shouted Gavin, picking up a cushion and hurling it towards the common room door. 'Let's have a cushion fight!'

Unfortunately, it was at that very moment Professor Burlay opened the door. He was carrying a tray of half-moon shaped biscuits and was accompanied by Jock and Dr Shivers. With acrobatic skills, Professor Burlay dodged the cushion and kept all of the biscuits securely on the tray.

'Bed, please, all of you,' said Professor Burlay, helping himself to a biscuit as he passed the tray to Serberon.

'Take one and pass them on,' Professor Burlay said to Serberon, motioning for him to hand out half-moon shaped biscuits to the remaining students on their way to the dormitories.

Sammy didn't like the way Dr Shivers looked at Jock as he pushed past holding his Dragon Minder pin. Sammy looked away as Dr Shivers mouthed "You should be a Dragon Minder Sammy" at him.

Jock refused to take a biscuit and went upstairs without saying a word to anyone. Sammy, Darius, Gavin and Toby followed him up the tower stairs, each carrying a couple of the half-moon biscuits to eat in bed.

Inside the boys' dormitory, Jock drew his curtains tightly shut and didn't even say good night. Sammy stayed awake, eating his half-moon shaped biscuits and looking through his Gemology text book for a few minutes.

At the end of the chapter on Amber, Sammy felt his eyes closing. He put the book down and rolled over on to his side so he could look out of the window until he fell asleep.

Sammy tossed and turned during the night, his dreams filled with dragons. He dreamed of his parents' dragons and his uncle's dragon. He saw Cyngard, Jovah and Paprika again and again. He desperately hoped they were alive and he could see them again.

In the dream, he had to decide whether he should trust Commander Altair or whether he should ask for the dragons to go and live with Mrs Deane while he was at Dragamas. These were decisions he would need to make when he was awake.

The copper bell above the boys' dormitory door rang loudly but Sammy was already awake. He had heard footsteps since six o'clock from the floors above. He guessed it was the second years coming down for an early Dragonball practice. Or maybe it was the first years coming down for a dawn Astronomics lesson with Professor Burlay. He wasn't sure.

Sammy was bothered however by the growing number of red dots appearing in the sky around the Dragamas constellation. Each dot represented someone who had been bribed or blackmailed by the Shape to give up their dragon's draconite stone, killing the dragon and helping the Shape. No one else seemed to notice the dots as much as he did.

Dixie was preoccupied with Nitron Dark, drawing little "ND" initials in the margins of her work and lowering her marks due to her lack of interest. In Dragon Studies, Dr

Shivers asked her to sit right at the front to improve her concentration.

Darius was no better. His nose was permanently in one Gemology book or another. He was extremely snappy if anyone tried to prise him away from it and told them in no uncertain terms not to interrupt his studies.

Sammy couldn't shake the feeling that if anyone was going to stop the Shape, then it would have to be him and he would have to do it alone.

'Wake up!' shouted Gavin, slinging open the green velvet curtains and leaping from bed to bed armed with a large jug of orange juice. 'Who wants a drink?' he demanded.

Sammy opened his eyes. Gavin had stopped by Jock's bed, the jug poised, dangerously close to spilling the juice.

'Gotcha!' shouted Gavin, tipping the jug of orange liquid all over the duvet. 'Wake up Jock! Go and mind some dragons, you dwarf-breath Dragon Minder!'

'I think he's already minding the dragons,' said Darius, yawning. 'He got up an hour ago.'

The tower door opened slowly. Jock was standing in the doorway, his face paler than gaunt, ghost-like Dr Shivers. Blood was dripping from scratches on his arms.

'Dragon's dead,' Jock whispered, falling face first into his soggy duvet and orange juice soaked pillow.

'What?' said Sammy, sitting bolt upright.

'How many dragons? Where?' demanded Darius. 'What happened?'

'Who cares?' snapped Gavin, throwing the empty jug on the floor where it broke into two pieces. 'Just more meat for sausages on Bonfire Night.'

'Our Mum's dragon died,' explained Toby. 'Come on Gavin, let's go. I don't want to hear this,' he said, dragging his brother out of the tower room.

'What happened?' repeated Darius. 'Is Nelson ok?'

'Just mine,' came a muffled whimper from beneath Jock's pillow. 'Stone cut out.'

Sammy got out of bed and went over to Jock. He rested his hand on Jock's shoulder.

'But your dragon wasn't very old,' said Sammy. 'Why would they take her stone?'

'She was twelve years old,' sniffed Jock. 'My Dad brought her home one day. I've been flying longer than I've been walking.'

'Who did it?' asked Darius. 'Did they take any others?'

Jock rolled over and sat up in his bed. He wiped the orange juice off his face with his jumper sleeve. 'I'm sorry. I shouldn't get upset. It's only a dragon.'

'She was your dragon,' said Sammy. 'We would be the same if it was ours.'

'I found out last night. That's why I didn't want the stupid biscuits and didn't want to speak to anyone,' said Jock. 'Dad says it was the Shape. They must have done it a few weeks ago. Maybe after the match against the Nitromen.' Jock stared at Sammy. 'You put her away, didn't you?'

Sammy nodded slowly. 'I put all of them away. Your Dad and Captain Firebreath were drinking in their office. They didn't see me, but I got all the dragons inside the Dragon Chambers. Naomi was supposed to help but she went off to hear about Nitron Dark kissing Dixie's hand.'

'So, you put them away by yourself?' asked Jock.

'Yes,' said Sammy. 'I put out food and water and…'

'What?' asked Jock.

'Nothing,' said Sammy.

'Commander Altair was there,' said Darius excitedly. 'You said you saw Commander Altair in the Dragon Chambers. Maybe he did it.'

'He said he was looking after my parents' dragons,' said Sammy. 'Commander Altair said I could see my parents' dragons and he can prove to me that he isn't in the Shape.'

'It's a trap,' said Jock, wiping his eyes with the back of his hand. 'He'll lure you in so you can't stop him. He killed my dragon on his way out, didn't he?'

'No!' exclaimed Sammy. 'He wouldn't...'

'You sure about that?' Jock snapped icily. 'I'll tell my Mum he was in there. She can tell Sir Ragnarok.'

'Fine,' said Sammy. 'You think what you like. I believe what Commander Altair said to me.'

'There's blood on his hands,' said Jock. 'I'm going to kill him if it's the last thing I do.'

Sammy exchanged a worried glance with Darius. The idea of killing Commander Altair seemed to have put some energy back into Jock. He stood up, stripped his bed and threw the damp, orange stained, covers into the washing pile. He splashed a glass of cold water over his eyes and slicked back his hair.

'Room 7, Gemology classroom, North table' said Jock resolutely and he disappeared in a shimmering silver mist.

'He won't kill Commander Altair, will he?' Sammy asked Darius. 'I believe Commander Altair was telling the truth.'

Darius shrugged. 'Jock's pretty upset at losing Giselle, even if that's not what he said. You can tell.'

Sammy nodded and got dressed. He checked his timetable and packed the books he'd need for the morning's lessons into his rucksack. Within a few minutes, he and Darius and headed off towards the Gemology classroom.

CHAPTER 14

IT'S MY DRACONITE

When Sammy and Darius reached the underground classroom, Mrs Hubar seemed to be suffering from shock that her son's dragon had been murdered.

'The writing is on the wall,' muttered Mrs Hubar as they walked in. 'Another one down. Soon the Shape will have all the dragons.'

'Sorry we're late,' said Darius, slinking into an empty seat at the North table.

Sammy sat next to him, thinking it was unusual for Mrs Hubar not to notice late comers to her lessons. He was glad not to lose any stars.

Jock looked better than he had in the tower room. He was sitting next to Dixie and showing her how to attach her amber gemstone to the tip of her staff.

'Today we are studying amber,' said Mrs Hubar, showing the class her staff with many brightly coloured gemstones at the top. 'I would like you to write an essay for me about amber. It must be two or three thousand words long and you may use the diagrams on the blackboard to help you. I would like your essays handed in to me by this time next week.'

Everyone groaned and started taking notes and copying the complex diagrams Mrs Hubar had drawn in yellow chalk on the blackboard.

As they wrote about amber, Mrs Hubar walked around the four tables, helping students fix their amber into the tip of their staffs.

'Simply unclick each stone if you want to concentrate on a particular spell,' said Mrs Hubar, demonstrating with her own staff.

Sammy stared at the assortment of coloured gemstones. There must have been at least ten different coloured stones packed together at the top of her staff.

Mrs Hubar plucked out the ruby and held it in her palm. 'Let's start with the ruby gemstone. I hope by now that you all know how to counter the effect of the ruby from a short distance, don't you?'

She rotated the stone and it gave off a faint red mist that started swirling towards the class.

'Gavin, please tell me three things about the ruby gemstone,' said Mrs Hubar, guiding the mist towards the North table.

'It's red, hard and you shouldn't eat it,' said Gavin to a volley of giggles from the girls at the East table.

Mrs Hubar raised her hand holding the ruby. It gave off a darker red misty cloud that wafted towards Gavin.

Instinctively, Sammy picked up his staff, focussing his thoughts in an attempt to block the mist. Across the classroom, on the East table, Simon Sanchez was doing the same.

The mist evaporated and Gavin wobbled, trying to regain his balance. He steadied himself with his hands gripping the North table very tightly.

'You would be wise to study these two,' said Mrs Hubar, pointing at Sammy and Simon. 'Both of them have the makings of being Dragon Knights.' She sniffed loudly. 'My poor Jock has lost his chance.'

Jock went crimson. 'Mum!' he snorted, exasperatedly shaking his head. 'I can still be a Dragon Knight if I want to be one. All I need is another dragon and there are plenty of those in Rescue Centres, aren't there Darius. Your parents find abandoned dragons all the time, don't they?'

Darius nodded without looking up from his notes. He was scribbling at a hundred miles an hour. Sammy looked over his shoulder at Darius's paper.

Darius was already halfway through creating a perfect replica of Mrs Hubar's drawings on the blackboard. He was copying her detailed diagrams and annotating them with labels in capital letters using his distinctive, neat and tiny writing.

'Amber,' sniffed Mrs Hubar, ignoring her son and writing left handed with a piece of purple chalk on the blackboard, 'is known as one of the healing stones. It has powerful organic energy.'

'My amber has got bugs in it!' shouted Gavin, standing up and showing the class his stone, which as Gavin's hand swung close to Sammy's head, the amber gemstone did indeed have many tiny bugs inside the yellow stone.

Just as everyone stood up to take a look at the bugs in Gavin's amber, the two chief mining dwarves, Captain Stronghammer and Captain Firebreath, appeared around the corner into the classroom each pushing a wheelbarrow filled with gemstones.

'Sir Ragnarok's asked for more stones from the mine,' explained Captain Firebreath, stroking his red beard. 'Like we haven't got enough to do.'

'Is he expecting to pay more money to the Shape?' asked Mrs Hubar, abandoning her diagram momentarily.

'Aye,' said Captain Firebreath, 'and more money to the fools who's thinking about taking their bribes.'

'Please come back after my lesson has finished so you don't disrupt the students learning about amber this morning,' said Mrs Hubar, allowing herself the brief indiscretion to blow her husband, Captain Stronghammer, a kiss.

Captain Stronghammer touched his cap. 'Come on Firey, there's a good pint o' your rum back in the office.'

Captain Firebreath nodded and backed the wheelbarrow out of the Gemology classroom. 'Yes M'am,' he growled.

'Oh an' there's a piece o' your draconite here an' all,' said Captain Stronghammer, taking a shimmering stone out of his dungarees pocket. 'It came from our Jock's dragon. It's draconite from Giselle.'

Jock stared first at his mother, then at his father. His cheeks turned a pale crimson and he clenched his fists.

'It is a sign,' said Mrs Hubar, accepting the shimmering stone from her husband.

'It's mine!' shouted Jock, standing up and kicking back his chair. 'I want it! It was from my dragon! It's my draconite! Give it to me!'

'Your father has given it to me,' said Mrs Hubar firmly. 'It belongs to me now and we shall study it in class at a later date.'

'It's mine! It should be buried with her!' screeched Jock, thumping his fists on the North table.

Mrs Hubar remained very calm. 'You should be proud to share your draconite stone with the class. It will be excellent first-hand experience for you to learn about the magic stone. Perhaps we shall learn how dragons fly, how they breathe fire, how they fly through walls,' she added, giving Sammy a knowing look. 'Jock, you will share your draconite with the class and that is the end of the matter.'

'If we ever see it again,' muttered Jock darkly, slumping defeatedly back in his chair. He started writing with a thick black pen, pressing really hard on the paper.

Sammy looked over Jock's shoulder at his essay on amber and gasped. In really heavy writing were the chilling words "Commander Altair kills dragons and he should die". Jock had scratched out the words "should die" and replaced it with "will die".

Although Sammy didn't believe Jock would carry out his threat, he had to make sure nothing bad happened before Bonfire Night. Sammy was still planning to slip away from the Nitromen's Fire Show and go into the passage under the treestump in the clearing in the forest and make his way underground to his Uncle Peter's house, assuming the path was clear.

The other option was to fly there on Kyrillan. However, if Dixie and Darius were coming as well, and the possibility that they would not come with him was so unlikely it wasn't worth considering, it would mean they would need to squeeze not one, but three large dragons out of the Dragon Chambers and past the eagle eyes of Captain Stronghammer and Captain Firebreath.

Also, Sir Ragnarok had increased security around the Dragon Chambers even more than ever before. Sammy decided they would have to take their chances in the underground passage and hope they didn't get caught.

'If you want to stare into space, then please do it in Professor Burlay's lessons please Sammy,' said Mrs Hubar. She rapped her hand on the desk next to Sammy and dragged him back to reality. It was an old joke, but funny none the less.

'Yes Mrs Hubar,' said Sammy meekly. He was glad the end of the lesson bell had started chiming.

'Please also take a copy of your third year Gemology textbooks with you,' said Mrs Hubar, pointing to a pile of yellow books on her desk. 'This year, we are studying from a book called "An Aeon of Amber", written by the acclaimed author, Ron Pirate.'

'I've already read this book from cover to cover,' said Darius, picking up his copy of the Gemology textbook.

'Swot,' said Dixie, picking up a book for herself and one which she passed to Sammy.

Sammy looked at the bright yellow textbook with amusement. 'Do you think it's a yellow book because it's about amber?' he asked Darius.

'Who cares!' interrupted Gavin, linking arms with Milly and Naomi. 'We're having cheeseburgers and chips for lunch. That's my favourite dinner ever!

Sammy compressed his staff and packed it into his rucksack behind the unused Gemology textbook and his file of notes. He noticed Simon Sanchez lurking near the North table. All of the other students had gone to lunch and Mrs Hubar had disappeared into the mining tunnel.

'Sammy,' said Simon, projecting his voice without making a sound or moving his lips. 'My mother has asked us to organise the fireworks display on Bonfire Night. We will have fireworks as well as the fire breathing dragon display from the Nitromen. She has decided this.'

'What about you? Why do you need me?' Sammy projected back, impressed he hadn't lost the skill when Simon answered his question. It was hard work using projection and Sammy felt a little faint doing it.

'She wants us both to do it,' Simon replied, still not making a sound. 'Apparently it will be her biggest firework display ever and she would like our help.'

'I can't,' said Sammy out loud. 'I'm going to be somewhere else.'

Sammy tried very hard to focus on the cheeseburgers and chips they were having for lunch, knowing Simon would be trying to read his mind and find out where he was going and why. For some reason, Sammy found thinking obsessively about food kept his mind absolutely clear of all other thoughts that he wanted to protect.

'You are good,' said Simon out loud. He lowered his stare and extended his hand. 'We will both be Dragon Knights one day.'

Sammy shook Simon's hand. It was as cold as ice and rather slimy and slippery.

'I will ask Jock instead,' said Simon. 'He has had a very bad time. It is so sad his dragon is dead.'

As privately as he could, Sammy couldn't help thinking that organising a firework display would be the last thing Jock would feel like doing after losing his dragon.

'Or perhaps Toby,' said Simon thoughtfully. 'Gavin is irresponsible and Darius is weak.'

Sammy grinned. 'Thanks for asking me anyway,' he said, picking up his rucksack and heading off for lunch.

CHAPTER 16

IF YOU CAN'T BEAT THEM

Overnight, the excitement of it finally being Bonfire Night rose to a higher level with the arrival of a freak flurry of snow and icy temperatures. Snowflakes fell to the ground like pure white flakes of confetti, and the castle windows were permanently misty with condensation.

Jock, Naomi and the other Dragon Minders were frequently missing from class to tend to the dragons. Rumours quickly circulated that the younger dragons were suffering from the sudden change in the weather.

As the younger dragons weren't able to breathe smoke or fire to keep themselves warm, at Sir Ragnarok's instructions, the third year Dragon Minders were given the extra responsibility of ensuring the smallest dragons were kept warm by feeding them hot oats and wrapping them up in extra blankets.

Sammy woke early, his thoughts entirely focussed on the meeting he had scheduled with Commander Altair at his uncle's house later that evening. He desperately wanted to see his parents' dragons and his uncle's dragon again and most of all, he wanted to make sure they were safe and being taken good care of.

'Bang!' shouted Gavin from behind his curtain. 'Fizz! Pop! Bang!'

'Shut it Gavin,' said Toby sleepily as tiny green and red sparks flew up over the curtain poles.

'Stop it,' moaned Darius. 'I didn't finish my essay on amber until midnight.'

'Oooooh!' shouted Gavin, whipping open all the curtains. 'Morning Sammy! Morning Jock…where's Jock?'

'He's gone to the Dragon Chambers,' said Toby, patient as always with his brother. 'Like he does every morning.'

'Good morning Gavin,' Sammy grinned and raised his staff. He fired one large green spark that exploded with a thunderous BANG that shook the room and erupted into hundreds of tiny green flames.

'Sammy!' groaned Darius. 'I'm trying to sleep!'

'That's so cool!' shouted Gavin. 'Do another one! You should be getting up anyway Darius. Lazy bones.'

Getting somewhat carried away, Sammy let off another two green sparks, aiming his staff towards the ceiling. The sparks rocked the tower and sent the beds and chests of drawers crashing together. Hundreds more green flames appeared, clinging to the walls, the curtains, some were even stuck on the ceiling.

'We're in so much trouble!' said Darius, throwing a white t-shirt and black school trousers over his pyjamas. 'We have to get out of here!'

'Why don't you show Professor Sanchez those green sparks?' said Gavin. 'She can use that in her firework display. It would be awesome!'

'I'm helping with the fireworks,' said Toby indignantly. 'Simon asked me to help. I'll show her some green sparks,' he said, trying the same manoeuvre as Sammy, but only a dribble of feeble, pale, washed out green sparks fell out of the end of his staff to the floor.

'I don't expect the green sparks are supposed to be used for that,' said Sammy, a little embarrassed at his success and Toby's failure. 'I think they're some kind of weapon. That's why we learn about the ruby first, so we have some self-defence.'

'No, Sammy, they're not supposed to be used for fireworks displays,' said Toby, a little nastily, 'I expect when you're a Dragon Knight you'll probably use green sparks for something far more important.'

Sammy shrugged. 'I guess so.'

'You'll never be a Dragon Knight,' continued Toby. 'Your parents haven't got any dragons and even if they had, they can't see them,' he added spitefully.

Feeling angrier than he had in his entire life, Sammy felt tears prickle at the corners of his eyes. He scooped up his green dragon shaped soap and put it in his pocket. He slung his emerald green towel over his shoulder and marched out of the tower room, almost knocking a group of first year boys flying head first down the staircase.

'You've been crying,' taunted one of the boys.

'Cry baby,' said another of the boys.

Sammy snapped. He grabbed the collars of both boys at once. 'My uncle is in the Shape. If I call him, he'll get you.'

'So what?' said the boy caught in Sammy's left hand. 'My parents sold their draconite. They paid off our mortgage and bought two new cars.'

'I'm going to sell my draconite when my dragon's old enough,' said the boy in Sammy's right hand. 'That's what all the fifth years are doing. They'll all be rich when they leave school.'

Sammy gasped took a step backwards. 'They can't do that,' he whispered.

'Says you!' the first year boys laughed and pushed Sammy against the wall to get past and marched down the stairs.

In the shared bathroom, Sammy took his longest time ever getting ready. He nearly didn't notice that he'd used his soap on his toothbrush instead of toothpaste and spat out the frothy liquid. He was so distracted wondering how people could treat their dragons so badly.

The shift in attitudes towards dragons was terrible. The Shape were forcing people with fully grown dragons to give up their draconite and then encouraging their sons and their daughters to do the same.

Sammy felt he was responsible for this. He had helped Sir Ragnarok raise the ransom money two years ago. The Shape had taken the money and were now using it to buy draconite.

The Shape seemed to be encouraging dragon owners to give up their dragons, bribing them with money in return for the precious draconite gemstones which the Shape were using to rebuild the Stone Cross and gain their immortality.

In Sammy's opinion, it didn't matter who killed the dragons. It was the Shape who were ultimately responsible for destroying the dragons and stealing the draconite.

'People must stop giving their draconite to the Shape,' Sammy said out loud.

'If you can't beat 'em, join em, eh?'

Sammy spun round. Dixie's brother, Serberon Deane, had come out of the showers and was combing his hair into hedgehog spikes. He was painfully thin with rib bones showing through his white t-shirt.

'Oh, it's you,' said Serberon, lighting a cigarette with his staff.

'What are you doing?' asked Sammy.

Serberon raised his hand. 'Smoking. You want one?'

Sammy shook his head. 'What about trying to save all the dragons?'

'Lost cause,' said Serberon, blowing a heart shaped smoke ring. 'I'm going to sell mine and join the Navy. You don't need a dragon when you've got a boat.'

'What about becoming a Dragon Knight? Or a Dragonball player?' asked Sammy.

'Who cares?' Serberon shrugged and blew the letters "M" and "B" through the dissolving wispy heart.

'I do,' said Sammy. 'We have to stop the Shape.'

'You'll never do it,' said Serberon.

'I will!' shouted Sammy, thumping his hand on the washbasin. 'I have to,' he whispered.

Serberon burst out laughing and Sammy stomped out of the bathroom. He marched back to the third year dormitory and swung the green velvet curtains back around his bed so vigorously that they unhooked and tumbled to the floor.

After a moment, there was a quiet voice from Darius's side. 'Are you ok Sammy?'

Sammy leaned over. Darius was studying hard using his Gemology book and taking notes. He was writing so fast and clutching his pen so tightly that his knuckles were shaking as he wrote furiously.

'Everyone's turning against dragons,' said Sammy.

Darius stopped writing and looked up. 'Funny, isn't it?'

'What?' asked Sammy.

'Two years ago, you couldn't care less about dragons,' said Darius.

'I didn't know they existed,' corrected Sammy.

'Now you want to save them all?' asked Darius.

Sammy crossed his arms. 'So?'

'It's too big,' said Darius. 'You'll never do it.'

'That's what Serberon just said to me,' said Sammy. 'But you'll help save the dragons, won't you? Dixie will help and Sir Ragnarok. We have to save them.'

'You can't even save your parents' dragons!' said Darius, letting out one of his giggles.

'We're going there tonight,' said Sammy. 'You, me and Dixie. We're going to my uncle's house to see my parents' dragons.'

Darius shrugged. 'So what? You'll find your parents' dragons, but how are you going to get them out?'

'We'll do it your way,' said Sammy, making the teleport sign, squashing his thumb and fingers together. 'You'll show me, won't you?'

'Sure,' said Darius, putting down his pen and looking so thoughtful that Sammy knew his friend was coming round to the idea. 'But I haven't done it with three adult dragons before.'

'Dixie will help,' said Sammy enthusiastically.

Darius nodded. 'We'll have to have one dragon each. It will be very tricky. I've only just learnt how to do it.'

'I can't wait to see them,' Sammy grinned and picked up his rucksack.

They ran to the Ancient and Modern Languages classroom and arrived just as Miss Amoratti teleported herself into the classroom. Luckily she didn't notice that Sammy and Darius were a couple of minutes late. However, she did notice Sammy fidgeting throughout the lesson.

'Samuel Rambles, are you listening?' demanded Miss Amoratti. 'I am very angry at your lack of attention. Fifteen stars from North!'

Sammy held out his hands on auto-pilot, waiting for her to strike him with her ruler.

Things worsened in Mr Synclair-Smythe's Armoury lesson, where the steely eyed professor wasted no time telling the class that Sammy's parents' dragons were almost certainly dead. Sammy lost both his temper and another fifteen stars.

CHAPTER 16

INDOOR FIRESTICKS

All in all, Sammy was glad to stop for lunch. Even then he was disappointed when he read the noticeboard and found out the afternoon playing Dragonball outside in the Sports lesson had been cancelled due to the Nitromen wanting to practice their fire breathing loop the loops on the Dragonball pitch.

Instead, Mr Cross wanted the third years to play Firesticks in the Main Hall. Sammy supposed they were lucky to play anything indoors at all.

Although they sometimes played Dragonball indoors, it was so much better when it was played outside as dragons weren't allowed indoors. Even though it had once been new and exciting, Sammy found any game of Dragonball without Kyrillan was very tame and boring. He quite enjoyed Firesticks, especially when they were allowed to play with the Invisiballs.

Sammy was also surprised Miss Amoratti hadn't seized the opportunity of taking over the Sports lesson, replacing it with another Ancient and Modern Languages lesson.

As they were finishing lunch, Mr Cross arrived in the Main Hall dressed in his usual navy tracksuit with white stripes. He was carrying his clipboard and ticked the names off the register.

'I have left the usual house coloured bibs back in the Gymnasium,' Mr Cross apologised. 'However, so that we can easily tell who is in which team, we will play Firesticks with the girls against the boys.'

'Yeah!' shouted Gavin, punching the air.

'Boys, please start at this end,' Mr Cross pointed towards the double entrance doors, 'and girls, please start by Sir Ragnarok's table. Today you may use your staff or you may go and fetch your Firestick from your rooms.'

There was a flurry of activity as the third years raced back to their tower rooms to collect their Firesticks, the long thin sticks, like a hockey stick, but with a double hook at the end. The bottom of a Firestick looked like a "W" and the design made it easier for the players to control the balls.

When everyone was back, Mr Cross divided up the teams, separating the boys and girls. He held out seven small pink, cricket ball sized, hard plastic balls.

Mr Cross bent to the floor and rolled the balls out into the open area in the Main Hall. He blew his whistle.

'Let the game begin!' shouted Mr Cross.

Sammy ran forward, holding tightly to his Excelsior Sports Firestick, the one he had been given as a Christmas present by his uncle. He hurtled towards one of the nearest pink balls.

He reached the ball first, beating Darius and Gavin who were hot on his heels. Sammy swung his Firestick at the ball and hit it as hard as he could. The Firestick connected with the ball with a loud "crack" and the ball flew through the air. It ricocheted off the wall and bounced through the makeshift goal posts at the girls' end.

'Goal!' yelled Sammy, throwing his fist in the air to celebrate. He turned on his heels and headed back into the game, intercepting a pass Dixie had aimed at Naomi.

'Oi!' shouted Dixie, abandoning the ball Sammy had stolen and running off to the next nearest ball. 'Goal!' she shouted as she hit the ball hard with her Firestick and it sailed over Jock's head into the boys' goal.

'Goal!' shouted Toby as he thumped one of the balls past Rachel Burns, who was trying to defend the girls' goal.

'Goal!' shouted Peter Grayling as he flicked one of the other balls over Rachel's head.

Rachel picked up one of the pink balls and threw it back into the middle of the Main Hall. Dixie and Naomi both dived for the ball, their Firesticks clashed together and both girls filled the hall with their laughter.

Using some of the Dragonball tactics, Sammy teamed up with Jock and Toby to circle around the Main Hall. They watched for wild passes and intercepted the pink balls that came near them.

'Good play!' shouted Mr Cross. 'Stay wide, keep your stick low on the ground.'

Sammy weaved his way through the players with one of the pink balls almost touching the end of his Firestick. It took a lot of concentration but it was worth it to hear the resounding crack as he hit the ball straight into the goal.

'Good play Sammy!' shouted Mr Cross. 'I think we'll make this harder and I'll add some Invisiballs.'

'Invisiballs!' shouted Gavin, holding his Firestick over his head. 'Come on!'

Sammy heard Milly grumbling as Mr Cross threw seven black balls into the game arena. She really didn't like Sports lessons at all.

As usual, the Invisiballs started out jet black, then they flickered and completely disappeared. Then, moments later, they reappeared and vanished again.

With fourteen balls in play, the goals came thick and fast. Sammy found he preferred looking for the Invisiballs, trying to predict how far they would roll when they vanished so he could hit them as soon as they reappeared.

Also, the Invisiballs were worth more points than the pink balls so it made sense to chase them, especially as the scores for the boys' team and the girls' team were level.

After just five minutes of playing with the Invisiballs Sammy dived for a ball but got tangled up with Peter Grayling from the West house. Peter tried to hit the Invisiball but hit Sammy's ankle with his Firestick instead.

'Ouch!' said Sammy, dropping his own Firestick on the floor in the collision.

'Sorry, Sammy,' said Peter. 'Are you ok?'

Sammy nodded, but Mr Cross came running over with a first aid kit.

'I'm ok,' said Sammy, but Mr Cross disagreed.

'Sit out for the rest of the game, Sammy,' said Mr Cross. 'You're on the Dragonball team and I can't afford any injuries. You can keep the score.'

Sammy scowled and picked up his Firestick. However, as he walked over to the house dinner tables that had been pushed to the side of the room, he was glad to perch on the table. His right ankle was throbbing and hurt a bit more than he would care to admit.

Mr Cross gave him a large board and a pen to keep track of which team won the most goals. With the fourteen balls in play, the game was very fast paced and there was a goal every two or three seconds to record.

Sammy counted thirty-two goals that Dixie had scored by herself. Even with this impressive score, the girls were still thirteen goals behind. He added goal after goal to the total and soon the girls' team was only two goals behind.

Dixie had one of the pink balls, worth one point. She weaved in and out of the players, breaking into a run as she approached the goal.

'Come on Dixie!' shouted Sammy, clutching the large scoreboard tightly as she got past Peter Grayling. He held his breath as out of nowhere Simon Sanchez, Amos Leech and Jock teleported in front of Dixie.

With a loud crash they flattened Dixie to the ground. Gavin and Toby piled in and soon there was a mountain of players piled up in front of the boys' goal.

'Stop!' shouted Mr Cross, blowing his whistle and running over. 'Stop the game! You're not allowed to teleport in Firesticks! Get up! Is everyone all right?'

When the mountain of people untangled their arms and legs from each other, Dixie emerged from the bottom of the pile. Hair askew, blood smeared on her arms and her Firestick in pieces, she stood up triumphantly. With the ball in her right hand, she threw it with all her might straight into the goal.

'Foul!' shrieked Gavin. 'Mr Cross blew the whistle.'

Dixie stuck her tongue out. 'You didn't get the ball,' she taunted.

'You still lost,' Mr Cross looked at the scoreboard and smiled, 'but only by one point in the end. Gather round please and we can review the game.'

Mr Cross gathered the class into the middle of the room. They naturally split from being in groups of boys and girls to stand in groups according to their house.

Sammy noticed they had even managed to stand in a circle in the correct order of the compass points for North, East, South and West.

'Let's forget Firesticks for a moment. As you all know, I have been watching you play Dragonball for two years and I have seen how well you play as a team,' said Mr Cross. 'I have seen who the weak players are and who among you could have a career in the world of Dragonball,' he added, handing out leaflets for Excelsior Sports. 'On page five, dragon hide gloves are on special offer and on page twelve, Firesticks are buy one, get one free.'

'Me and Toby are world class players!' shouted Gavin. 'We've got the best Firesticks in the catalogue.'

Mr Cross smiled again. 'No shouting out please Gavin.'

'Yes Sir!' shouted Gavin. The class snickered.

'Make sure you keep trying one hundred percent in every game,' said Mr Cross, his voice drowned out by the chimes of the end of lesson bell.

The double entrance doors burst open and Captain Firebreath and three other dwarves, all similarly dressed in white shirts, blue dungarees and shiny black boots, danced into the Main Hall singing a painfully high rendition of "We Wish You A Merry Christmas".

'It's a bit early for that,' said Mr Cross dryly.

Captain Firebreath checked his watch. 'We're right on time, as always, Mr Cross. Sir Ragnarok wants the tables set for five o'clock on the nose.'

'Very well. Class dismissed. You may go and change out of your sports clothes,' said Mr Cross. 'Enjoy your Bonfire Night, but don't play with fireworks.'

'Like we would,' scoffed Simon Sanchez. 'He thinks we are babies.'

Captain Firebreath pointed a gnarled hand towards the dwarves, directing them towards the house tables with instructions to pull the four long wooden tables back into their usual positions.

As the tables were being moved, the Main Hall suddenly filled with a cloud of black and gold mist.

'It's Nitron Dark!' shrieked Dixie, as a swarm of men wearing black and gold Nitromen shirts suddenly appeared in front of them.

The teleporting mist faded quickly and Sammy saw Nitron Dark turn a scowl into a forced smile as he took Dixie's hand and kissed it.

'Cut yourself love?' said Nitron Dark, looking at the blood on Dixie's arm from the Firesticks game, his dark brown eyes flashing in his tanned face.

Milly and Naomi pushed past Sammy to get to Dixie.

'He called you "love",' gushed Milly.

'Wow,' said Sammy sarcastically, watching as Nitron Dark strutted over to Mr Cross and shook his hand.

Sammy turned away and walked out of the Main Hall to go back to the North Tower to change. As he walked down the corridor he met Dixie's brothers. To his surprise, the green haired triplets were really angry.

'We told you to look out for her,' said Mikhael and he thumped Sammy in the stomach.

'Protect her from Nitron Darkness,' said Jason, grinning and punching Sammy's shoulder.

'You let her down,' said Serberon. 'He's sick.'

'Hates trolls,' added Jason.

Sammy doubled over under the blows. 'I'm sorry,' he gasped. 'I'll find her and put it right.'

'Too late,' said Serberon, taking out his staff.

'No!' Sammy felt his knees buckle as a swarm of tiny green sparks hit him from behind.

'You stay out of her way,' threatened Mikhael.

'We're going to sort it out, right now,' said Serberon, giving Sammy a final kick on the shin before the brothers left him and ran down the corridor towards the Main Hall.

Sammy closed his eyes, whispering "third year North tower room" and let the golden teleporting mist sweep him back to his bedroom.

CHAPTER 17

ALFIE'S BACK

When Sammy opened his eyes, he was standing in the third year boys' tower room and it was pitch black. It took him a moment to realise where he was.

He rubbed his ankle which was still sore from Firesticks and his bruised shin from Serberon's kick. He examined his skin where the green sparks had touched him. Even though he had been hit multiple times, the sparks didn't seem to have broken his skin or caused any damage at all.

Sammy stood up and pulled aside the green velvet curtain to look out of the window. This year, the view of the Dragonball pitch was partially obscured by trees. It hadn't been a problem last year as the second year dormitory was higher up and even less of a problem seeing the pitch out of the first year dormitory window which was right at the top of the tower.

Sammy stood on tiptoe to see better. Down on the Dragonball pitch dozens of people were lined up on the grass to watch the Nitromen perform their fire breathing routine with their blaze of matching black dragons.

A scuffle broke out in the middle of the crowd of supporters. Sammy saw a flash of green hair and wondered whether it was Serberon, Mikhael or Jason, or all three, as they tussled and tumbled.

Sammy picked up his staff and put his cross for bravery necklace over his head and under his t-shirt. The silver metal felt cold next to his skin and it reminded him of his forthcoming task to meet Commander Altair that he had agreed to do.

'Here goes,' Sammy said to himself and he set off down the tower stairs.

The corridors were completely deserted. Hollowed out pumpkins left over from Halloween were starting to rot on the windowsills. Each pumpkin held a tiny scented candle. The faint musky smell wafted in the air from the incense burning inside.

Through the ground floor windows, Sammy could see the smokey spire from the fenced off bonfire at the far end of the Dragonball pitch. He ran towards the castle door.

Tom Sweep was brushing up leaves from the doorway. Sammy almost bumped into the caretaker as he ran past him out into the cold, dark night.

A buzz of excitement swamped Sammy as the first person he met was a small first year who handed him a gold sparkler that fired gold star shaped sparks into the darkness. The first year wrote her name, "Marianne" in gold stars.

Not wanting to disappoint her, Sammy amicably wrote "Sammy" in gold shimmering stars, even though he knew he could have used his staff to write his name in flames in any colour of his choice.

'Aren't they pretty,' gushed Marianne. 'Marianne and Sunny.'

'It's supposed to say "Sammy",' said Sammy. 'My name is Sammy Rambles.'

'Oooh,' said Marianne, her brown eyes as wide as saucers. 'You're the one whose parents were eaten by the Shape.'

Sammy left in despair, bumping into Professor Burlay who was leading a teary-eyed Mrs Grock to her house on the school grounds. Professor Burlay looked pale and as though he might have shed a few tears of his own.

'All good things must come to an end,' he muttered to Sammy.

'Alfie's back,' sniffed Mrs Grock, by way of explanation.

Sammy nodded, not really understanding. 'Have you seen Dixie, or Darius?'

'Dixie is with my sister Molly at the caravan,' said Professor Burlay, smiling briefly. 'Sir Ragnarok invited her and Mum to come and do hotdogs for the Bonfire Night party.'

'Ooch and I saw Darius and young Jock leave with Helena,' said Mrs Grock.

'Helena Hubar, Jock's mother, Mrs Hubar to you,' Professor Burlay added helpfully.

'Ooch yes, Mrs Hubar was a friend of my Alfie's a while back, before he left.'

'Let's not talk about him,' said Professor Burlay. 'Least said…'

'…is soonest mended,' finished Mrs Grock. 'Ooch go on with you John,' she giggled, putting her hand in his hand.

Sammy shook his head and left them to it. He could see Molly's pink and white caravan poking out from the trees and he walked towards it, dropping his used sparkler in one of the buckets of water at the side of the Dragonball pitch.

He arrived at the caravan just as Molly was opening the pink and white awning ready to serve hotdogs.

'Hello lovvie,' said Molly, grinning at him. 'Dixie's around the back helping Mum with some candy floss. We're diversifying after last year. There's not much demand for ice cream when it's so cold already.'

Sammy nodded. 'Professor Burlay can arrange the weather. If you ask him, he could make it warmer.'

Molly looked thoughtful. 'Such a shame about Alfie coming home. I believe John and Elsie were meant for each other after all.'

'My Dad's coming home too!' shouted Dixie, her green haired head appearing at the serving hatch. 'They all are!' She vaulted through the hatch, landing nimbly on her feet. 'They went off to fight the Shape, but the Shape are here now.'

'So they're coming back,' said Sammy nervously.

'Aye,' said Molly, wrestling with a pink and white umbrella. 'The whole of the Snorgcadell, all the Dragon Knights, they're all coming home. Mum's so pleased. Here Sammy, would you help with this?'

Sammy obliged, yanking the umbrella so hard that a piece of cake that had apparently wedged it shut popped out and hit Dixie in the eye.

'Oi!' Dixie grinned, her green hair clashing with her crimson cheeks.

Sammy understood her excitement. This was the news she had been waiting for since she was seven years old.

'Your Dad's coming home,' Sammy grinned and wrapped his arm over Dixie's shoulder.

'I know,' she whispered, her green eyes sparkling with more than Milly's glitter mascara that she had borrowed.

'Are you ready to go down the secret passage to my uncle's house and see my parents' dragons?' asked Sammy.

Dixie's cheeks flushed pink again. 'Um, I've promised Molly I'd help here.'

'Oh,' said Sammy, his heart sinking.

'You go on lovvie,' said Molly. 'I'm sure I'll manage.'

'You said you'd tell me all about my Dad and the Snorgcadell,' pleaded Dixie. 'I'm sorry Sammy, I have to know everything Molly can tell me.'

Sammy wrestled desperately with his thoughts. He really wanted Dixie to go down the underground passage with him. But he also wanted her to hear the news about her father. Also, there was quite a large part of him where he secretly wanted to see Paprika, Cyngard and Jovah alone.

'I suppose it might come in useful to learn all about them if we want to become Dragon Knights,' Sammy conceded.

'So you'll stay?' asked Dixie, looking up at him, her green eyes shining and bright.

'I can't. I have to know if my parents' dragons are alive,' said Sammy. 'You can tell me all about it later.'

Dixie nodded. 'I'm sorry.'

'It's ok, I'll catch up with you later,' said Sammy.

'You're not going alone, are you?' asked Dixie.

Sammy shook his head. 'No, I'll go and find Darius. He promised he'd come with me.'

'You come and find us when you get back,' said Molly. 'Otherwise, I'll send John to find you.'

'I will come straight back here, Molly,' Sammy reassured her. 'See you later.'

Dixie gave him a fresh bag of pink and blue candy floss. 'It's a long way down there,' she grinned.

Sammy took the red lipstick out of his pocket and Dixie giggled.

'It's a straight passage!' said Dixie.

Sammy laughed. 'Maybe if there's time, Darius and I could explore what's inside the second trapdoor.'

'You need a Dragon Minder pin for that,' said Dixie, 'and to get through the treestump in the first place. How are you going to get inside the passage?'

'Where do you think Darius has gone?' Sammy grinned, backing away from the caravan. 'He's getting Jock's Dragon Minder pin.'

Sammy found Darius sitting with Jock and Mrs Hubar at a picnic bench watching a display of giant flames put on by the Nitromen and their fire breathing dragons. Jock and Mrs Hubar stood up to applaud the display.

'Here,' whispered Darius, pressing the emerald eyed silver dragon pin into Sammy's hand. 'Mrs Hubar's teaching me and Jock about draconite.'

Sammy peered over Darius's shoulder. On the wooden picnic bench was a sheet of green velvet with six blue-green crystal gemstones laid out in two neat lines.

'Has she found some more draconite?' asked Sammy, looking at the gemstones and feeling sick.

Darius nodded. 'She's promised to tell me everything about draconite. It comes up in this year's exam.'

'So you're not coming down the underground passage with me either?' exclaimed Sammy.

'You know how important the stones are to me,' whispered Darius. 'I'm going to be a Healer one day. I have to know everything about them. Dixie will go with you.'

Sammy shook his head. 'Molly's telling her about her dad. He's coming home.'

'Oh,' said Darius, a little apologetically. 'Can we go tomorrow instead? You can't go alone.'

'I'll have to go on my own, won't I,' said Sammy, feeling hurt and angry his best friends were abandoning him at this most important time. He'd do it alone if he had to. He had to know if his parents' dragons were alive. Then he would have to figure out a way to move them.

'Tomorrow,' grinned Darius.

Sammy backed away into the dark shadows. On his way to the treestump, he passed Professor Burlay and Mrs Grock. They were sitting together on a swinging hammock in her garden.

'Make a wish,' called Mrs Grock.

'It will come true,' called Professor Burlay.

Sammy ignored them, ducking behind a tree as Professor Sanchez, Toby and Simon stumbled past him, each holding two giant sacks of fireworks.

'This will be the biggest fireworks display Dragamas has ever seen!' Professor Sanchez cackled. 'Providing Professor Burlay can hold off the rain for us.'

Sammy let them pass and then made his way across the Dragonball pitch, mingling amongst his classmates and other Dragamas students. He ducked through some bushes into the woodland and into the clearing where he had found the branch that had become his staff.

It was the same clearing where he, Dixie, Darius and Serberon had made their protected den on top of the special treestump that was the entrance to the secret passage that led from Dragamas to his uncle's house in the village.

'Right,' whispered Sammy, walking into the den and kneeling beside the treestump. He took the silver Dragon Minder pin with the emerald green eyes out of his pocket and inserted it into the groove. 'Here goes,' he muttered, touching his cross for bravery necklace to give him extra confidence.

The Dragon Minder pin snapped into place with a quiet click. Sammy pulled open the mossy top of the treestump, revealing the dark passage and the metal ladder rungs that led downwards. He noticed that the inside of the dragon shaped lock was shiny, as though someone may have used it recently.

Sammy lowered himself backwards, feeling blindly for the ladder rungs. He took two extra steps by mistake at the bottom of the ladder, jarring his ankles on the rough floor. He felt for his staff in the pitch black tunnel and assembled it to full length.

'Fire,' whispered Sammy, his confidence growing as the familiar warm glow of the orange flames immersed the passage.

He took two paces down the passage and stopped. On the earthy floor in front of him, there was a rolled up rug, a sandwich box and a mug with the initials "AA". There was also a silver Dragon Minder pin, the same dragon shape as the one he had "borrowed" from Jock, except that this one had red rubies for eyes.

'Commander Altair?' whispered Sammy. 'Are you there?'

There was a scuffling noise further down the passage that made Sammy's heart turn in a somersault. As quietly as he could, he pressed himself close to the passage wall and side-stepped forward.

Using his mind, he turned down the flames at the end of his staff until they were just a glowing ember. The scuffling stopped and there was a muffled cough.

'Who's there?' asked Sammy, his voice trembling.

'Who's where?' said a loud voice and Sammy's heart froze altogether.

He remembered that voice from the Great Pyramid at the Land of the Pharaohs. Whoever was just a few steps ahead of him was someone in the Shape. They were responsible for his parents losing their ability to see dragons and they thought he was the key to finding the way to kill all dragons so they could become immortal.

'Um, wrong turn,' said Sammy, backing up the passage to the ladder. 'I'll go back.'

'Good,' hissed the voice. 'Don't want the likes of you here anyway, least of all tonight when there's work to do.'

'What work?' Sammy bit his tongue. What was he thinking getting into a conversation when he should be getting away?

'Killing dragons,' said the voice matter of factly. 'Show yourself if you want to help.'

'If this is Commander Altair, I trusted you!' shouted Sammy. 'It's a long walk to my uncle's house. The Snorgcadell will get you first!'

'What do you mean "my uncle"?' shouted the voice. 'You must be Sammy Rambles! What a very good day this is! Join us! Join the Shape!'

Sammy fumbled with the ladder, snatching the "AA" mug as proof. He climbed the rungs as quickly as possible in the darkness.

'Never! I will never, ever, join the Shape!' Sammy shouted, throwing back the lid of the treestump and sitting on it. He burst into a flood of unwanted tears that he dragged away angrily with the back of his hand.

CHAPTER 18

ORION

Moments later, out of the darkness, a voice called out his name.

'Sammy?'

Sammy blinked. Through his teary, blurred eyes he could see three figures. He stood up.

'Get away from me!' Sammy shouted and charged forwards. He slapped straight into the warm solid chest of Professor Burlay. He blinked. 'You're real?' asked Sammy in surprise. 'You're not the Shape?'

'Of course we're not,' snapped a male voice beside him. 'Professor Burlay and I were coming after you.'

'Altair?'

'Commander Altair, please show respect Sammy. I called tonight off. Dixie and Darius were diverted and you were supposed to stop at Mrs Grock's house.'

'Ooch, make a wish dearie,' said the third figure. 'You were supposed to take one of my wishing well coins and make a wish to see your parents' dragons.'

'Then I would appear and take you to the underground chamber beneath Mrs Grock's house, where I'm keeping your parents' dragons,' said Commander Altair.

'They're here?' asked Sammy, dumbstruck.

'Your parents' dragons are safe and well,' Professor Burlay reassured him. 'Safe and well.'

'Come,' said Commander Altair, smiling. 'I'll show you your dragons.'

Sammy thrust the mug he had retrieved from the passage under the treestump into Commander Altair's hands. 'This is yours.'

Commander Altair stopped in his tracks and looked at the mug. 'Where did you get this?' he demanded.

'In the tunnel,' said Sammy. 'You left it with your things, the rug, the lunchbox and Dragon Minder pin.'

'It's not mine,' said Commander Altair firmly. He dropped the mug on to the ground. 'Come, I will show you your parents' dragons.'

Sammy allowed himself to be led away, sandwiched between Professor Burlay and Commander Altair. Mrs Grock stood alone in the clearing, staring in the darkness at the mug.

'It was your mug,' insisted Sammy as they reached the wishing well in Mrs Grock's garden. 'The initials were "AA" for Arion Altair.'

'Commander Altair, please Sammy,' said Professor Burlay. 'He will be returning to the Snorgcadell when we have the chance to explain everything to Sir Ragnarok.'

'That's my name Sammy, Orion Altair. I was named after the stars,' said Commander Altair, pointing to the three star studs on his jeans belt. 'Orion's belt,' he laughed.

'Arion's not a star,' said Sammy.

'It's "O" Sammy, "Orion",' said Commander Altair.

'Dixie said...' started Sammy.

Commander Altair laughed harder. 'That's my fault. I should have corrected her when she was five years old and we first met. She called me Arion and I thought it had a nice ring to it. She had trouble pronouncing her "O"s.'

'Oh,' said Sammy.

Commander Altair nodded. 'Oh indeed. I assume you will now believe me if Professor Burlay says I am returning to the Snorgcadell. Everything is being re-instated.'

'Yes Sir,' Sammy nodded vigorously. 'We thought you were the "A" in the Shape.'

Commander Altair laughed. 'You thought it was me? Never,' he shook his head vigorously. 'I would never join the Shape. Neither would I allow you to join them.'

'Ooch go on with you. Let the laddie see his dragons,' said Mrs Grock, returning to the cottage.

Sammy noticed she was holding the mug with the "AA" initials. She was running her fingers over the letters, turning the mug in her weathered hands as if it was troubling her. Professor Burlay seemed to be on edge as well.

'Quickly Sammy,' said Commander Altair, 'then you must go back to the fireworks.'

Professor Burlay and Mrs Grock paused at the wishing well. They each threw a coin into the well and waited for the splash.

'A fool's folly,' Commander Altair muttered under his breath. 'No prizes for guessing what they're wishing for.'

'I don't know,' whispered Sammy.

'It'll never work. Not now the Dragon Knights are returning,' said Commander Altair. 'Even though he left her, Alfie will want her back.'

'Dixie's Dad's coming home as well,' said Sammy.

'Yes he is,' said Commander Altair, holding open Mrs Grock's green front door.

144

Commander Altair led the way to the store room. He heaved aside the heavy sacks of grain to reveal the trapdoor. As he knelt down to pull the iron ring to open the trapdoor, Commander Altair looked up, a concerned expression on his usually relaxed face.

'Sammy.'

'Yes Sir,' said Sammy.

'I would prefer you not to mention that you have seen me or your parents' dragons, or that I am staying at Mrs Grock's house to anyone.'

'Ok,' said Sammy.

'Including Sir Ragnarok.'

Sammy paused. 'Doesn't Sir Ragnarok know you're here?'

'That shouldn't concern you Sammy. Trust me, he will be told when the time is right.' Commander Altair lit a storm lantern and passed it to Sammy. 'There are six fully grown dragons down there, but they're expecting you.'

Sammy gulped. 'Ok,' he said nervously.

Leaning on the handrail for support, Sammy took the storm lantern and used the stone steps to go into the circular underground chamber beneath Mrs Grock's house.

As he descended, a pungent odour overwhelmed him and he held his nose as the smell washed over him. It was a combination of straw and dragon dung. Sammy took a big step to go over a fresh mound of dragon dung and fell over the last step. He landed on Paprika.

'Hello girl,' he whispered, holding up the lantern.

Sammy just stopped himself yelling out in fright as a large purple dragon yawned inches from his right foot, spraying him with dragon spit.

'That's Mrs Grock's dragon, Xenon,' said Commander Altair from the top of the steps. 'She's docile unless you provoke her or you feed her rotten eggs or mushrooms.'

'She's beautiful,' Sammy whispered, wiping the spit off his arm and taking in the saucer sized golden eyes which were firmly focussed on him.

He saw gold streaks running down the purple wing lines and touches of gold on the peaks of the spikes that trailed down from her neck and disappearing into the passage along her pure gold coloured tail.

'The red dragon is mine and the green one belongs to Professor Burlay,' said Commander Altair.

'Wow,' said Sammy, looking at the six dragons, wondering how they all fit into the chamber. Each fully grown adult dragon ranged in size from a small van to a double decker bus.

'We've made a few minor modifications to this room,' said Commander Altair, reading Sammy's thoughts.

Sammy looked at the perfectly circular walls and guessed Commander Altair had used other means than widening the room with a digger or spade.

'Magic Sammy,' said Commander Altair. 'I trust in my absence you have kept up with your studies?' He held out his palm, which was holding a glowing ruby the size of a tennis ball.

Red light flooded the chamber and Sammy staggered forward, his feet like lead.

'You are weak!' stormed Commander Altair. 'How do you expect to be a Knight when you act like a Pawn?'

With effort, Sammy shook his head, gathering his thoughts. He had a ruby of his own on his staff. Could he reach it and play Commander Altair at his own game? He reached for his staff, each joint on his arm resisting any movement.

Commander Altair smiled at him. 'You need to try harder.'

'I…am…trying,' Sammy shouted inside his head, his hand grasping at the stones on his staff. 'Try…this!'

A bolt of red lightning burnt a hole in his jumper and struck the ceiling above Commander Altair. Paint, plaster and stone cascaded down in a shining curtain of silt and gravel.

The six dragons in the chamber leaped to their feet, snarling and hurrumphing as they were covered in dust.

'Dragon smoke!' moaned Commander Altair, rubbing his eyes.

Sammy stepped forward. 'I'm sorry!'

'Turn…it…off!'

Sammy found he could move freely. He rubbed his hand over the ruby on his staff and the red light faded to nothing. 'I'm sorry,' he repeated. 'Are you ok?'

Commander Altair clapped. 'At thirteen, I only dreamed of creating this weapon.'

'I'm not thirteen for three weeks,' said Sammy quietly.

'Holy dragon! You must be exactly what the Shape need.'

Sammy climbed the steps and faced Commander Altair. 'I know the Shape want me to join them. That's what he said down in the passage.'

'What! Who was down the passage?' asked Commander Altair. 'You said there was a rug, a lunchbox, a Dragon Minder pin and a cup down there. You never said you saw someone down there!'

'So what?' asked Sammy.

Commander Altair looked coldly at Sammy. 'Had you told us this at the treestump, we could have followed him. We could have caught another member of the Shape.'

'He knew me,' said Sammy flatly.

'Of course he did,' said Commander Altair. 'They all know you. They were going to your uncle's house tonight. I knew that. Why do you think I called it off?'

Sammy gulped. 'You thought they were going to kill my dragons...'

Commander Altair took Sammy's shoulders in an iron grip. 'Your parents' dragons are safe. You have seen them. Find Dixie and Darius and enjoy the rest of the evening. Professor Burlay and I will go back and deal with whoever we find down there.'

'Thank you,' Sammy forced the words past the lump in his throat. 'Thank you for saving them.'

'I just wish I'd stopped you going down there in the first place,' said Commander Altair, his voice softer. 'I never thought you'd have the courage to go there alone.'

'Are you ready?' asked Professor Burlay appearing at the top of the stone steps wearing a thick navy coat over his grey linen suit. He was carrying his staff and had a very determined expression on his face, his brown eyes bright and alert.

On another occasion Sammy would have laughed at Commander Altair but tonight he let himself be guided out of Mrs Grock's house, where he met Darius and Jock who were leaning on the garden gate.

Jock held out his hand and Sammy pressed the Dragon Minder pin with the emerald eyes into his friend's hand.

'Let's go!' said Jock enthusiastically. 'Darius told me all about it.'

'He's already been,' said Commander Altair. 'Next time Darius, you go with him and make sure he doesn't get into any trouble.'

Darius looked sheepish. 'I said we should go tomorrow.'

Commander Altair raised his staff. 'Come on John, let's go.'

'They're going after the Shape,' said Sammy.

'Cool!' said Jock. 'We'll come too.'

'Ooch no boys, you can come with me. I have to patch a few loose ends with Molly.' Mrs Grock kissed both Professor Burlay and Commander Altair on the cheek. 'Find him for me,' she whispered.

Sammy, Darius and Jock watched as Commander Altair and Professor Burlay marched towards the trees.

'Come on,' said Sammy. 'Let's find Dixie and Molly.'

CHAPTER 19

THAT'S MY DRAGON

Back at the Molly and Megan's ice cream van, Dixie was serving an enormous cloud of pink candy floss to three boys from the second year.

Sammy recognised Nigel Ashford, the first-now-second-year boy he was supposed to be mentoring. Nigel turned around as Sammy arrived with Darius, Jock and Mrs Grock.

'Hi Sammy!' said Nigel enthusiastically. 'We were just talking about you! Try some of this!' Nigel thrust a wadge of pink cotton candy in Sammy's hand.

'Thanks,' said Sammy, wondering what they had been saying.

Nigel turned to Jock. 'Oi dwarf breath, do you want some candy floss from the greenhair?'

'Watch it squirt!' said Dixie and Jock together, catching each other's eye and ginning.

Sammy overheard some of their projected conversation. He pulled Darius away just in time as Dixie threw a can of cola to Jock who fizzed it up and sprayed it in Nigel's face.

'Hey!' shouted Nigel, rubbing the cola out of his eyes. 'I'll get you dwarf breath!'

'Another time dearie,' said Mrs Grock appearing from behind the caravan looking rather pleased with herself. 'I showed her.'

Seconds later, Molly appeared with a bag of peas pressed against her left eye. Her right eye opened wide when she saw Nigel was drenched.

'What on earth happened here?' demanded Molly.

'We were helping,' said Dixie, grinning.

'That kind of help I could do without,' said Molly, adjusting the peas. 'Here Nigel, try some of my new caramel popcorn. Have a free bag and don't tell your Mum about this.'

Nigel took the bag of popcorn and left with his friends without looking back.

'Oops,' said Jock, grinning at Dixie. 'Hey let's go and see the fireworks!'

A loud explosion on the horizon shook the ground. Sammy stumbled and reached for Dixie's shoulder to keep his balance.

'Whoopee! It's starting!' screeched Jock. 'Wish I could have let that firework off.'

'Me too,' agreed Sammy checking his watch. 'The Nitromen's display must be nearly over. Professor Sanchez must be starting early.

A second explosion vaulted through the stratosphere erupting in a psychedelic display of green and blue, a beautiful waterfall of colour that finished with Dixie's brothers' trademark initials "SMJ".

'That's so cool,' said Dixie, looking up at the sky as the embers and remnants of the firework fluttered and fell to the ground.

A girl wrapped up in so many scarves that only her eyes were showing came up to them handing out coloured sparklers.

Sammy took one and wrote his name twice. Dixie wrote "Dixie and Kiridor forever", then the initials "ND". Jock wrote "Altair must die" and Darius wrote a complicated Gemology structure that to his annoyance perished before he could complete it.

'Darn it,' groaned Darius as the swirls faded and disappeared. He wrestled unsuccessfully with Dixie to use her sparkler but she was busy drawing a heart around the "ND" initials and wouldn't give it up.

Sammy pushed through the crowd to the edge of the Dragonball pitch, which was now off limits due to the bonfire. The bonfire was giving off an unusual blue gold smoke. He craned his neck to see any sign of Professor Burlay and Commander Altair returning. He jolted as he was pushed forward, over the line and on to the pitch.

'What do you think you're doing?' Sammy snapped at Jock who had appeared behind him and was the reason for him falling forward.

'That's my dragon,' croaked Jock. 'They're burning her.'

Sammy choked, putting his arm on Jock's shoulder. 'Are you sure?'

Jock ran forward but was restrained instantly by Serberon and Mikhael who were helping to police the bonfire and keep students from getting too close.

'Stand back,' said Mikhael firmly.

'Jock's dragon is burning!' yelled Sammy. He was still angry with the green haired brothers for fighting with him earlier in the evening. 'Let him through!'

'Dragon steaks,' said Serberon coldly.

Mikhael shoved his brother. 'Shut it Serberon. You wouldn't like it if it was Valcor on there.'

'Better her than Mary-Beth,' snapped Serberon. 'I'd burn the lot of dragons if it was up to me.'

'You don't mean that!' Dixie stepped forward and thumped Serberon.

'Leave it sis,' snapped Mikhael. 'Of course he doesn't mean it.'

'I do!' shouted Serberon pushing Jock forward. 'Go and see your dead dragon.' He stormed off.

Jock stepped forward towards the bonfire. Sammy heard him talking to himself as he approached the flames.

'Dragon in life, dragon in death, may we meet again, when the time is right,' Jock cracked, falling on his knees as the brittle body of Giselle fell through the flames sending up a shower of scales that the first years' gathered greedily.

'Leave them!' shouted Sammy.

'Dr Shivers told us to collect as many scales as we can,' said one of the first years.

'Come on,' said Darius. 'I don't feel like celebrating Bonfire Night anymore.'

More rockets launched into the sky. Even amongst the brightly coloured fireworks Sammy could make out the all-to-familiar red dots circling the Dragamas constellation.

'At least your parents' dragons are here and they're safe,' said Dixie. She leaned close to Sammy, 'Molly told me what Commander Altair organised for tonight. I think she fancies him,' she whispered conspiratorially.

'I went down there by myself,' snapped Sammy. 'I nearly got caught by the Shape.'

'You were supposed to stop at Mrs Grock's house. Commander Altair planned it with Molly and Professor Burlay. He arranged it all so I could find out more about my Dad, Darius could find out about gemstones and you could see your parents' dragons.'

'Well I did, didn't I,' said Sammy, still feeling out of sorts. 'I went down the passage all by myself.'

'You met the Shape again.'

'I found the mug with "AA" on it. It has to belong to someone in the Shape.'

'I know what you think,' said Dixie. 'The "AA" is "Arion Altair", but he's not, he wouldn't…'

Sammy grinned. 'It's Orion Altair, spelt with an "O", not an "A". I know he's on our side.'

'Orion?' asked Dixie. 'What do you mean?'

Sammy nodded. 'You know that belt he wears with the three star studs? Well that's who he is, Orion, wearing Orion's belt.'

'Oh,' Dixie blinked hard and slapped her forehead. 'Of course, that makes so much sense. Oh, so if it's not him…'

'Who is it?' finished Sammy.

'Who is it,' echoed Darius, scratching his head. 'It really could be anyone.'

Sammy held the door open as they reached the North Tower common room. The room was completely empty as the rest of the school was still watching the fireworks display. On one of the tables a set of fifty or so dice were stacked in hexagonal towers, abandoned by the players.

'Dragon Dice anyone?' asked Darius, deliberately knocking over one of the towers.

'Not for me,' said Sammy. 'I'm going to get up early to see my parents' dragons tomorrow before lessons.'

'I'm going to find Serberon,' said Dixie. She blew them both a kiss and teleported out of the common room.

'I'm going to study for a bit,' said Darius, picking up a Gemology textbook.

'Night,' called Sammy and he closed his eyes. 'Third floor, North Tower boys' room,' he said and he teleported himself upstairs, a golden mist surrounding him.

CHAPTER 20

A LUCKY ESCAPE

Sammy opened his eyes in the tower room. All of the curtains had been drawn back and a single green candle had been lit on a wooden stand on each boy's chest of drawers. Reflecting in the clear windows, it looked as though ten candles were burning.

Dr Shivers was sitting at the foot of Sammy's bed reading a magazine. When he saw Sammy, he stopped reading and put the magazine down.

'Good evening Sammy,' Dr Shivers spoke in a low gravelly voice and Sammy had the feeling something was wrong. 'I'm afraid I have some bad news for you?'

'What news?' asked Sammy, a million things running through his mind at once. 'What's happened?'

'You must leave Dragamas at once,' said Dr Shivers.

Sammy sat on the edge of his bed, resting his head in his hands, preparing himself for some impending doom.

'Sir Ragnarok asked me to wait until after this evenings fireworks display before telling you but since you are here early, you might as well know now.'

'Know what?' asked Sammy. 'I know the Shape are at the school and I know they want me to join them.'

'It's worse than that I'm afraid,' Dr Shivers smiled, 'far worse, I'm afraid. Sir Ragnarok can take care of the Shape, but it is no longer your problem.'

Sammy looked up, his heart in his mouth. 'Why not?'

Dr Shivers looked him in the eye and spoke slowly and kindly. 'There has been an accident...a fire at your uncle's house...your parents are safe and so is your sister...house is in ruins...no longer inhabitable...and,' Dr Shivers paused, 'you are to meet them at once. They are to fly to Switzerland from Heathrow in a matter of hours. Your parents still have their property there. Hard to sell apparently.'

'A fire?' whispered Sammy. 'At my uncle's house?'

Dr Shivers nodded solemnly. 'I am so sorry.'

'No,' whispered Sammy. 'It's not true. I can't go. I'm not...'

'I'm sorry Sammy. Even after your descaling fiasco last year, I had high hopes for your achievements here.'

'Then tell Sir Ragnarok I want to stay. Please tell him I want to stay here,' begged Sammy.

A rustle came from behind the curtains and Sir Ragnarok appeared. Sammy wondered if the headmaster had been there all along.

'I cannot force your parents to reconsider,' said Sir Ragnarok quietly, 'but I can give you the opportunity to ask them.' Sir Ragnarok clicked his fingers and the dormitory and Dr Shivers disappeared.

They were replaced by the smell of burning bricks. Bright red fire engines were dousing the charred and burnt out remains of Pickering and Co Jewellers.

Sir Ragnarok gripped Sammy's shoulder. 'I'm sorry,' he said.

'The Shape did this,' said Sammy.

Sir Ragnarok leaned close. 'If you want the chance to put wrongs to right then you will need to reassure your parents that you are grown up enough to manage on your own. They will be…'

Sir Ragnarok didn't have time to explain more as Sammy was engulfed in a breath-taking hug from his mother with baby Eliza tucked into a charred green blanket strapped to Julia Rambles' shoulder.

'Thank goodness you're safe!' exclaimed Julia. 'How did you get here so quickly?'

'Teleport,' said Sir Ragnarok with a wink.

'How enchanting,' said Julia, looking beyond the fire engines for a car. 'Next you'll tell me you flew here on the back of one of those dragons you keep talking about.'

'We teleported,' said Sammy matter of factly.

'So you didn't ride on the back of your dragon?' asked Julia with a smile.

'No, he's in the Dragon Chambers under the North Tower,' said Sammy.

'I see,' Julia winked to Sir Ragnarok above Sammy's head. 'Would you like some hamburgers to take back for him?'

'As long as they don't have mustard,' said Sir Ragnarok. 'Gives dragons terrible bouts of flaming cough.'

'Oh,' Julia looked taken aback. 'Sammy, come over to your father. He's with the firemen collecting our things.'

Sammy looked over at the pile of charred rubble. A group of neighbours were coiled around his possessions like bees around a honey pot, or a dragon egg, Sammy thought wryly.

'Be strong Sammy,' reassured Sir Ragnarok. 'If it doesn't kill you…'

'...it will make you stronger,' finished Julia. 'That's funny, someone said that to me just this morning. A man dressed in black with a belt with stars on it said that to me when he gave me the tickets to the show tonight. Such a bit of luck that he called by, otherwise we would have been in the house when it blew up.'

'A man dressed in black with a belt with stars on it,' repeated Sammy, the pieces of the jigsaw slotting into place.

Somehow, Commander Altair had known the Shape were going to blow up his uncle's house, killing his parents' dragons, and he had come here specially to save Sammy's parents and baby sister. It was his job to do things like that. Commander Altair was a Dragon Commander in the Snorgcadell. A large lump formed in Sammy's throat. He was so grateful his family was still alive.

Sammy walked over to the remains of the house alone. In the distance, he could hear Sir Ragnarok talking about cups of tea and asking how it happened. He pulled rags of what used to be his striped duvet cover out of the rubble.

'You don't want that muck,' said a middle aged woman, sifting through the pile of rubble with two small boys. She took the ragged duvet out of Sammy's hands, folded it up tightly and put it in her handbag.

Spying something else, the woman bent down and pulled out the board game Sammy had played with Darius only a few months ago. The two boys eyed the Castle Rocks board game eagerly.

'How about this game, boys? Do you want it?'

The two boys nodded and Castle Rocks went into her handbag as well.

'Keep it,' Sammy scowled, angry that his personal possessions were being rifled through. He stomped off, looking for his father and found him in what once had been the back garden.

'Hi Samuel,' said Charles Rambles.

'Dad!' Sammy rushed forward into his father's awkward arms.

'Bit of luck we weren't in the house when she blew,' said Charles Rambles. 'The fireman over there said it was a substance leak from something in the cellar. Can't think what Peter might have had down there.'

'Dragon poison. The Shape stored dragon poison in there,' said Sammy, thinking of the small brown glass bottles with the skull and crossbones on the labels.

'Not in much shape any more,' said Charles, taking a fountain pen and spiral bound notebook out of his pocket. 'Still, at least we can go back to Switzerland. Did your mother tell you she's been given her job back after her maternity leave? The house where we lived is still on the market so we'll just take down the "for sale" signs and move back in.'

'How do you know?' snapped Sammy, watching as the woman and her sons tossed some books and his racing car alarm clock into a bin liner they had brought with them.

'Your mother has friends in high places,' said Charles. 'She works with Big Al, well, his real name is Aldebaran Altair. He's helped us with everything.'

'General Aldebaran Altair?' asked Sammy.

Charles laughed. 'General of the Snorgcadell you'll be saying next! Why, he was two years above us at school when…' Sammy's father stopped mid-sentence.

Sammy stared open mouthed. 'You know about the Snorgcadell?'

His father chuckled. 'Did I say Snorgcadell? What a funny name! I heard it once, I remember it from somewhere.'

'Where?' Sammy asked eagerly.

Charles scratched his head. 'Television perhaps, or maybe a customer in Peter's jewellery shop. It's not the sort of thing my clients would talk about in court.'

'You must remember, the dragons, the Snorgcadell, Orion Altair and his father Aldebaran?' asked Sammy, desperately clutching at straws.

'I'm sorry Samuel. You must have a touch of the heat from the fire. You're in shock, it's too much to take in. Your things can be replaced of course,' Charles added, surveying the burnt remains. 'This should make quite an insurance claim here.' He nodded and started writing in his notebook.

'I'm not going,' said Sammy quietly.

Charles didn't look up. 'What's that? We will need passports, driver's licence, money. What else do we need Julia?'

'I said, I'm not going,' Sammy repeated, a little louder. 'I want to stay at Dragamas.'

'Dragons? Nonsense Samuel, we'll go by aeroplane. Too much to carry,' his father carried on writing the checklist in his notebook, completely oblivious to anything Sammy was saying.

'Please Dad, Mum, I want to stay. I want to be with my friends. It will be easier for me to cope,' said Sammy. 'I don't want to ruin my education.'

Julia laughed. 'How can we resist that?'

'He should come with us,' said Charles. 'We should keep the family together. He can get to know his sister.'

'But you wanted me to go to boarding school,' said Sammy. 'You told me it gave you your confidence.'

'I've changed my mind,' Charles snapped the notebook shut. 'You're coming with us. Your school can pack your things and send them on to Switzerland.'

'No!' yelled Sammy, kicking the remains of the television. 'You can't make me!'

'Don't you dare embarrass us in front of the neighbours,' said Charles, his face boiling with anger.

'If you move house they won't be your neighbours any more,' retorted Sammy.

'In front of your headmaster? What must he think of you?' demanded Charles.

'Quite a lot actually,' said Sir Ragnarok calmly. 'Sammy shows excellent promise and I believe it would be quite a mistake to move him in this crucial year.'

'Crucial year?' enquired Julia.

'Why yes, this year they have the competition set by your friend Aldebaran Altair.'

'Aldebaran? Big Al?' asked Julia.

'Yes,' continued Sir Ragnarok. 'He has set my students a task to find the Angel.'

'The Angel?' asked Julia.

'Of 'El Horidore,' said Charles, clapping his hand to his mouth. 'Oh! I didn't say that. More dragon nonsense. It must be the stress. Do what you want Samuel. We fly tomorrow at one thirty, check in is at ten o'clock so you'll need to meet us at seven o'clock so we can drive there.'

Sammy frowned, making the hardest choice of his life. On the one hand it sounded as though his parents were starting to remember about the dragon world.

Perhaps with his uncle being held prisoner by the Snorgcadell it was stripping Peter Pickering of his powers and the spell binding his parents was weakening. If he stayed with his parents maybe he would learn more about the past.

'What if they are only remembering because they are here and the house is gone?' Sir Ragnarok projected silently into Sammy's head without moving his lips.

Or, Sammy thought hard, should he go back to Dragamas, back to Dixie and Darius and they could continue to try and find the Angel of 'El Horidore.

'Your parents were the last to hold the Angel,' projected Sir Ragnarok. 'Choose wisely.'

Sammy nodded, his mind was made up. 'I don't want to change schools,' Sammy decided out loud. 'I'm happy at Dragamas. I can always fly out at Christmas.'

'Oh Sammy,' he was squashed by another hug from his mother.

'That's my boy,' beamed Charles. 'Work hard and you'll be a Dragon Knight like me.'

Sir Ragnarok raised an eyebrow.

Sammy stared open mouthed. 'A Dragon Knight!'

'No more dragon nonsense,' snapped Charles, shaking his head. 'Whatever next? Teleporting?'

Sammy stared even harder. 'Teleporting,' he whispered. 'You know about teleporting?'

'Your mother and I know all sorts of things,' said Charles Rambles. 'That's why we send you to a dragon school. So you can learn things as well. A dragon school,' Charles laughed nervously. 'Whatever will I say next!'

'Take care Sammy,' said Julia, wiping her eyes and adjusting the blanket covering baby Eliza. 'Be good.'

Sammy looked away, embarrassed at his mother's tears.

'See you at Christmas Samuel,' said Charles.

With his mouth still wide open, Sammy waved goodbye to his parents and Eliza.

Sir Ragnarok put his hand gently on Sammy's shoulder. The gold teleporting mist surrounded them, taking them back to Dragamas.

CHAPTER 21

MRS GROCK'S

Sammy was still waving in Sir Ragnarok's office as the shimmering gold mist evaporated.

Sir Ragnarok's smokey grey cat, Lariston, came down the spiral stairs from Sir Ragnarok's bedroom to see who had arrived.

Recognising Sir Ragnarok and Sammy, Lariston leaped on to the office sofa and curled up into a ball on one of the soft purple cushions.

'I'd like you to go to Mrs Grock's house, Sammy, just for a few days' rest,' said Sir Ragnarok. 'It's always a shock when something terrible like this happens at home. It will give you time to think things through and decide what is best for yourself. If you do want to leave Dragamas and go to Switzerland, then we will arrange that for you.'

Sammy sat on the sofa next to Lariston. 'Sir Ragnarok?'

'Yes Sammy?'

'Do you think my parents are remembering about dragons because my uncle is being held in the Snorgcadell, or because the house blew up?'

Sir Ragnarok sighed and shuffled some papers on his desk. 'It makes no sense to burn down your uncle's house. Almost certainly your uncle is being questioned by General Aldebaran Altair's Dragon Knights. They may well have reversing techniques that will help your parents see dragons again. However, you must be prepared that even though your parents may start to remember that dragon exist, they still may not believe it to be true.'

'They will believe in dragons again,' said Sammy stoutly. 'Please may I teleport to Mrs Grock's house?'

Sir Ragnarok nodded. 'As a one-off you may teleport. But do it from outside my front door. Teleporting inside my quarters is reserved for myself and for my trusted advisors.'

'So not Mr Synclair-Smythe,' Sammy grinned.

'Certainly not,' Sir Ragnarok chuckled. 'He has not been here long enough to prove himself.'

'But he might prove himself?' asked Sammy.

Sir Ragnarok smiled and gave nothing away. 'Go to Mrs Grock's house please Sammy. At the moment there are many more questions than answers.'

Lariston uncurled himself and jumped down from the sofa. He escorted Sammy to the door, his warm amber eyes glowing. It was almost as if he knew the questions Sammy wanted to ask.

'Mrs Grock's front room,' said Sammy, closing his eyes.

The gold mist swirled around and carried Sammy from Sir Ragnarok's tower, out of the castle, and landed him, as requested, in Mrs Grock's front room.

Mrs Grock was kneeling on the hearth by the fire, which was roaring in the grate with bright purple flames.

Professor Burlay and Commander Altair were studying sparkling stars that were circling around a globe on the dining table. All three looked around as Sammy arrived in the gold mist.

'Hello Sammy,' said Professor Burlay. 'What can we do for you?'

'Sir Ragnarok sent me,' said Sammy. 'He said I need rest after what's happened. My house has burnt down.'

'Ooch, dearie me, how terrible, young Dragon Knight,' said Mrs Grock, standing up from the hearth. She gave Sammy a hug. 'Of course you canna stay here for as long as you like.'

'We'll look after you,' said Commander Altair, waving his hand across the globe so the stars faded and disappeared. 'You were right, Sammy. It was someone from the Shape you saw down the passage earlier. As far as we can tell, after setting fire to the poison in your uncle's cellar they escaped up the second tunnel.'

Professor Burlay looked a little embarrassed, his cheeks a faint shade of crimson. 'Unfortunately a shot from my staff brought down the tunnel roof between us and them,' Professor Burlay apologised. 'Now we'll never know where it goes or where they went.'

'My house burnt down,' said Sammy hollowly.

'Ooch, come and sit here,' soothed Mrs Grock. She went into the kitchen and returned holding out a mug of steaming hot chocolate with marshmallows and a plate of freshly baked chocolate chip cookies which she placed on the coffee table.

'People were looking through our stuff like vultures. They were stealing everything,' said Sammy, picking one of the marshmallows off the top of the hot chocolate.

Commander Altair came up so close Sammy could smell his stale breath and see the stubble of the unkempt beard he had grown recently. Apparently there weren't any razors or access to washing facilities while he had been in isolation underground, sleeping covertly with the dragons.

'You must focus on the task to find the Angel of 'El Horidore,' Commander Altair informed Sammy. 'All of your property can be replaced in time. Remember, you still have many of your belongings here at Dragamas.'

Sammy nodded and took a sip of the hot chocolate. It was just the right temperature and he took a large swig from the mug.

'Did your parents say anything about the Angel of 'El Horidore?' asked Commander Altair. 'Anything at all?'

Sammy took another swig of the hot chocolate and helped himself to two cookies. He curled up on the sofa in front of the purple flames and retold everything that had happened.

'They started to remember about dragons,' said Sammy, gripping his mug tightly. 'They know your father and they talked about teleporting and the Snorgcadell. I know they will remember everything eventually.'

Commander Altair nodded. 'Hopefully, in time, they will remember more.'

Outside, Sammy could hear the Bonfire Night fireworks and celebrations continuing. Rainbows of coloured sparks flew up into the sky followed by fizzing and loud bangs.

Through the windows, Sammy could just make out men dressed in gold and black flying on huge black dragons. He stood up and took his mug of hot chocolate over to the window to watch.

The Nitromen were continuing the jaw-dropping display of their extraordinary talents, doing loop the loops and daring stunts on their fire breathing dragons. Sammy shook his head, thinking back to how Nitron Dark had been so two-faced, being nice to Dixie's face and horrible about her behind her back.

Sir Ragnarok arrived two days later carrying a large wooden crate. Dixie and Darius were with him, pushing noisily past each other, racing to be the first to the front door. Sammy heard them as they ran up the stairs and he sat up in bed.

Dixie was first to arrive in his room, her green haired head appearing at the door, followed by the rest of her, then Darius, then Sir Ragnarok.

'Hi Sammy!' shouted Dixie, running into the hospital style upstairs room with the row of beds for patients. She vaulted over one of the beds and landed on the end of Sammy's bed.

'Hi Dixie! Hi Darius!' Sammy moved up so his friends could sit on the edge of the bed.

'Are you here on your own?' asked Darius, poking at the Astronomics magazines on the bedside table.

'Professor Burlay, Mrs Grock and…are downstairs,' Sammy bit his tongue, remembering just in time not to mention Commander Altair was living under the house.

Sir Ragnarok winked. 'It's ok Sammy. I have been informed Commander Altair is here at Mrs Grock's house. Some rather interesting developments have taken place at the Snorgcadell and his name has been cleared. He is no longer under suspicion of being the "A" in the Shape.'

Sammy opened his eyes wide. 'Since when?'

Sir Ragnarok put a finger to his lips and rested the wooden crate down on the floor. Sammy looked at the bulging contents.

'Everyone's put some stuff in,' said Dixie, pointing to the crate. 'I put in the Nitromen keyring. Nitron Dark gave it to me on Bonfire Night.'

'I put in the chocolate,' added Darius. 'My wish from the first year is wearing off, but I get a couple of bars under my pillow occasionally.'

Sammy felt suddenly hot and found he was sweating. 'Thank you so much for all of this,' he said, wiping his forehead.

'Your parents have arrived safely back at their home in Switzerland,' said Sir Ragnarok. 'General Aldebaran Altair has sorted things out taking their house off the market and settled them in. They will have a live-in nanny who will look after Eliza during the day and enable your parents to return to their jobs.'

Sammy nodded, taking it all in, glad his parents and baby sister, Eliza, were safe.

'There's two sorts of chocolate,' interrupted Darius, looking hungrily at the bars. 'Mint caramel and one with nuts and raisins.'

'Thank you,' said Sammy, taking the chocolate out of the crate. He snapped the chocolate bars into small pieces and shared them around.

'Oh, and Dr Shivers sent you this,' said Dixie, passing Sammy a grey envelope. 'He said it was an early birthday present.'

Sir Ragnarok eyed the envelope then stood up and stretched. 'You may return to the castle when you're ready Sammy. I'm sure you'll have some school work to catch up on and worried friends to reassure that you are alright.'

'Thank you Sir,' said Sammy, clutching the envelope. He hadn't liked the way Sir Ragnarok had frowned over Dixie's head as she had given the grey envelope to him.

Sir Ragnarok nodded and vanished in the familiar gold shimmering mist.

'He might have let you off lessons and homework,' Darius grumbled. 'Like you haven't got enough to deal with.'

'What's in the envelope Sammy?' asked Dixie.

Sammy squeezed the grey paper. 'It feels heavy.'

'Open it!'

At Dixie's instruction, Sammy pulled the seal open and tipped out the contents of the envelope. A silver pin in the shape of a dragon fell into his palm with a small piece of paper.

'No,' whispered Dixie. 'I'm sorry. If I'd known it was that, I wouldn't have let him give it to me to give to you.'

'Why not?' asked Darius, helping himself to more of the mint caramel chocolate.

'It's from the Shape,' said Dixie. 'Dr Shivers must be working for them. He wants to kidnap you down one of the passages and put draconite from your brain into the Stone Cross!'

Sammy coughed back a laugh at Dixie's sincere face. Darius let out one of his explosive giggles.

'Dr Shivers isn't in the Shape and this isn't a Dragon Minder pin. Look, it has clear eyes,' said Sammy. 'The Dragon Minder pins have eyes the same colour as each Dragamas house. Green emeralds for North, yellow amber for East, red rubies for South and blue sapphires for West.'

'They're real diamonds,' said Darius, touching the eyes. He let out a low whistle. 'Let's read the note that came with it.'

Sammy passed Darius the piece of paper. He held the dragon shaped pin up to the light so that the eyes glinted at him. Darius could be right. The tiny eyes could be made from diamonds.

'Dear Mr Rambles,' Darius read out loud. 'It has come to our attention that the Angel of 'El Horidore, last seen by Mr Charles Rambles and Mrs Julia Rambles, formerly Miss Julia Pickering, was stored in the Great Pyramid at the Land of the Pharaohs and sealed with a DNA strand and diamond magic.'

'What!' Sammy sat bolt upright. 'Diamond magic?'

'There's more,' said Darius, 'shall I read on?'

'I'll read it,' said Sammy, taking the paper out of Darius's hands. 'In current circumstances, where they are no longer able to see dragon related material, you are the only living organism with the ability to pass their seal. You will need the diamond eyed dragon pin to access the chamber and provide a sample of blood to prove your heritage.'

'Holy smoke,' whispered Darius.

'Let me read it,' squealed Dixie. 'The Shape really do need you.'

Darius nodded. 'I guess this explains a few things.'

'The Shape must be so mad with you,' said Dixie. 'You were in the Great Pyramid probably inches from it last year.'

'Sammy didn't have the diamond dragon pin last year,' said Darius.

'It says the pin is for the second entrance at the back,' said Sammy weakly. 'The entrance Serberon pushed me through. All I'll need to do this time is to stab myself with the pin. What?' Sammy looked across at Dixie and Darius. They were silent, open mouthed, speechless with horror.

'The Shape were so close to the Angel of 'El Horidore,' whispered Dixie after a long pause. 'Imagine if they'd found it last year.'

Sammy nodded, a shiver running up his spine. 'Come on. I want to go back to the North tower,' he said, packing up the crate of gifts. He put the letter and the diamond eyed dragon pin back into the envelope and into his trouser pocket.

Back in the third year boys' tower room, Sammy tucked the envelope securely at the back of the top drawer of his chest of drawers and forgot all about it.

Less than three weeks later, in a school assembly, General Aldebaran Altair arrived in a cloud of shimmering gold mist behind Sir Ragnarok at the teachers' table. After a brief word with Sir Ragnarok, he disappeared. Sir Ragnarok pushed his chair back and stood up gravely.

'Students of Dragamas,' said Sir Ragnarok, his voice carrying all the way through the Main Hall from the first year table right to the back at the fifth year table. 'We have been called to our challenge. On the last day of November, we will take our studies to the Land of the Pharaohs'

There was a loud gasp from the students, except for the students on the third year tables, who, thanks to Gavin, already knew the visit to the Land of the Pharaohs was on the cards.

'We are to assist the Snorgcadell further in the search for Queen Helena Horidore's Angel whistle, which is believed to have the power to call all dragons, living and dead, to the location of the person who has used the whistle. The Snorgcadell believe it has been lost for long enough and must be found before the Shape and those now working for the Shape lay their evil hands upon it!'

'We're going to the Land of the Pharaohs!' yelled Gavin, standing up and clapping his hands. 'Miss Amoratti has arranged this for us!'

The whole school started clapping and shouting. Some students stood on their chairs and others drummed their hands on the tables.

'It's on my birthday,' said Sammy, sinking his head into his hands.

'Your thirteenth birthday,' added Dixie.

'It's only in two weeks,' said Darius, grinning. 'What have you asked your parents to get you?'

Sammy lifted his head. 'I asked to stay at Dragamas and for a new Dragonball set. Not that they'll have a clue what it is,' said Sammy. 'I knew I should have brought the one Sir Ragnarok gave me back to school at the beginning of term. It got ruined when the Shape blew up my house.'

CHAPTER 22

SAMMY'S BIRTHDAY TRIP

The 30th of November finally arrived. Sammy jerked his eyes open, remembering where he was and what day it was. He sat up in bed and noticed a few things were different from last night when he had gone to sleep.

A large parcel had arrived at some time during the night and was staring temptingly at him from the bottom of his bed.

Next to the parcel was a bobbing green helium balloon that definitely hadn't been there last night with the number "13" written in large gold numbers.

Something else caught Sammy's eye. It was another helium balloon, bobbing in through the tower door. The balloon was pink this time with "Happy Birthday Sammy" in silver writing. Pulled along behind it were the third year North girls, with Dixie at the front holding the string.

'Hi Sammy!' said Dixie. 'Happy birthday!'

'Happy birthday!' said Milly, coming into the tower room followed closely by Holly, Helena and Naomi.

'Milly wanted the pink balloon,' Dixie apologised and sat at the end of Sammy's bed. She let go of the string and the balloon floated up to the ceiling where it bobbed in circles.

'Cool,' said Sammy, pulling his duvet up to his chin.

'Got him any lipstick this year Dixie,' teased Darius, swinging back the green velvet curtains and opening up the tower dormitory so the girls could find space to sit down.

Dixie shook her head laughing. 'You know we all clubbed together to get him "that",' she pointed at the large parcel.

Sammy leaned closer to get a better look at "that". It was a large rectangular box that weighed a ton. The box was wrapped in green foil paper with a repeating pattern of silver dragons facing head to tail in horizontal lines. He wrenched open the paper and unravelled several metres of sticky tape.

He paused as the name on the box appeared under the green foil paper. The box was silver and in large gold letters it said "Excelsior Sports – Limited Edition Draconis Plus with Invisiballs".

A large lump got stuck in Sammy's throat. 'Thank you,' he mumbled.

'Sammy's gonna cry!' taunted Gavin.

'Wouldn't you, if your stuff got burned?' snapped Dixie.

'Sammy's got a girl...' Gavin stopped as Dixie launched herself at him, sending Gavin falling back on his bed in hysterics.

'Thank you for this. Thank you, all of you,' said Sammy, his voice sounding not quite its normal pitch. 'Who wants to play Dragonball?'

Holding his breath, Sammy opened the silver briefcase and it clicked smoothly, releasing the silver metal clasps and giving off a low humming as he touched the coloured spheres.

There were fifty balls in total. Twenty pink balls, like the ones they played with in Sports lessons. Twenty purple balls, which were slightly smaller and harder to hit. Then there were ten Invisiballs which one moment they were black and the next moment they had vanished. Sammy stared as they hovered in and out of sight.

'It's awesome,' said Sammy, picking up one of the Invisiballs.

Just like the Invisiballs they played with in the Sports lessons, it was heavy in his hand when it was black, then it vanished and there was no weight. Then a second later, it was back to black and heavy again.

'It was really, really, really expensive,' said Gavin. 'Like, loads of money.'

'Shut up Gavin!'

At everyone's request, Gavin shut up, although he was unable to stop himself staring at the silver briefcase and the exciting, exclusive, Dragonball set.

There were heavy footsteps on the stairs and Professor Burlay appeared around the door.

'Morning boys!' Professor Burlay called jauntily. He was wearing a pair of knee length khaki shorts and a lime green t-shirt under his normal grey suit jacket.

Under one arm was his register, a green clipboard with a pencil tied to a piece of string dangling freely. Under his other arm he clutched a wad of papers that he handed round.

'These are your instructions from General Aldebaran Altair,' Professor Burlay explained. 'The Snorgcadell are telling you where not to look for the Angel of 'El Horidore and also who not to ask as not everyone will be your friend up there. Oh, and a very happy birthday to you Sammy,'

Professor Burlay smiled and handed Sammy a small parcel. 'It's only a pencil set but it might come in handy.'

'Me and Toby didn't get any birthday presents from the teachers!' exclaimed Gavin.

'That's because you weren't here,' said Professor Burlay.

'Yeah, your birthday's over the summer,' said Jock. 'You only get presents from the teachers if you're at school for your birthday. I got a sack of dragon feed for Giselle.'

'That's not much use to you now,' scoffed Gavin. 'Your dragon's dead.'

'Enough! Stop it!' said Professor Burlay. 'Or I shall recommend to Sir Ragnarok that you stay behind,' he snapped. 'You must remember you are representing Dragamas up there. We are there to find the Angel of 'El Horidore, not to advertise ourselves as hooligans.'

'What about lessons?' demanded Gavin.

Sammy knew Gavin couldn't care less about lessons, as long as he was having fun, but he wanted to put Professor Burlay on the spot.

'No changes,' Professor Burlay grinned broadly and ticked names off the register. 'We will be studying Astronomics as usual. Of course we will be closer to the stars and so we will see much more of the night sky than we will from down here.'

'What about...' started Gavin.

'All will be revealed,' interrupted Professor Burlay. 'This is most exciting. It's the first time the entire school has been mobilised for a field trip since we went to...'

'Who cares!' shouted Gavin. 'We're going to see the Pyramids!'

Professor Burlay closed the register with a click. 'Be ready by the time I come back please. The first and fifth years are downstairs. Dr Shivers already has the second and fourth years ready.'

'Oversleep did you, Sir,' chirped Gavin.

Sammy looked out of the window. A steady stream of Dragamas students carrying their staffs and rucksacks were marching from the courtyard across the castle lawns towards the forest. Dixie's green haired brothers were among the group waiting in the courtyard for Professor Burlay.

Dixie, Naomi, Milly, Holly and Helena all followed Professor Burlay out of the boys' tower room, hurrying back to the girls' tower to pack their bags for the trip.

Sammy tipped his rucksack upside down to remove everything and then repacked it, copying Darius, putting in the lightest of each subject textbook and enough clothes to last a week in on top. Darius threw Sammy a packet of boiled sweets.

'They're for emergencies,' said Darius.

Sammy packed the sweets and his diamond eyed dragon pin as well. He smiled as he saw Darius pack a torch into his rucksack when he thought no one was looking.

Outside it was bitterly cold. Sammy put on his dragon hide gloves and wrapped his scarf around his neck. Even though it was only the start of winter the wind blew icily around them as they met up with all of the girls from the third year North house.

Dixie was wearing her Nitromen shirt under her school jumper. With a bitter memory of Nitron Dark hating trolls, Sammy was glad his Nitromen shirt had burnt in the fire.

'Hey Sammy!' Dixie leaped over to him and put her arm over his shoulder. 'Milly's got a new camera. She's taking lots of pictures!'

A light flashed in Sammy's eyes blinding him for a second. Milly was giggling with Holly and Naomi who both shrieked "say cheese".

Professor Burlay came over to Sammy. 'Your parents' dragons will be safe while we're away,' he projected silently at Sammy, then went over to Gavin to reprimand him with a tap on the shoulder for doing a bad impression of mocking Dr Shivers.

'Let's get going,' said Professor Burlay, checking his watch. 'Our slot in the lift is in about half an hour.'

They walked through the woods to where the trees opened out into a small grassy clearing. The familiar grey rock face with the large black opening towered above them.

The dark mouth of the cave entrance loomed large even before they reached the clearing. More rocks had fallen from the cave mouth and the pointed pearl white stones Dixie called "teeth" looked eerie in the dim light.

'Keep close to me,' ordered Dr Shivers. 'North first, then East, then South and West last.'

'North first!' shouted Serberon, pushing a boy from the West house out of the way.

A scuffle broke out and Serberon, Jason and Mikhael stormed up the roughly hewn steps. The boy from the West house sent a volley of multi-coloured sparks up after them but no one got hurt. Dixie's brothers vanished inside the cave, followed by their fifth year classmates.

Sammy, Dixie and Darius sat down on the grass while waiting for their turn to use the lift. Milly, Gavin and Toby joined them and, after taking lots of photos, Milly got out her set of Dragon Dice and insisted everyone played.

Forty minutes later, Captain Firebreath appeared at the cave entrance.

'Mornin' all,' said Captain Firebreath, mopping his forehead with a red and white spotted handkerchief.

'It's afternoon now,' grumbled Gavin.

Captain Firebreath shot Gavin a dirty look. 'Well, good afternoon to yer an' all. C'mon, this way. Hurry up.'

Sammy followed Gavin and Toby up the stone steps and into the dark cave. He felt his way to the back and into the small square lift. As they all piled in like sardines, he ended up sandwiched awkwardly between Dixie and Milly as the cubicle filled up with students.

'See you up there,' called Professor Burlay as Captain Firebreath closed the doors with a loud bang.

Captain Firebreath pulled the red lever inside the lift and Sammy felt his stomach lurch as the lift took off, hurtling at an unbearable speed up the swaying pearlescent tube that connected Dragamas with the land above the school.

Sammy closed his eyes and tried to block out the swaying motion which was making him feel slightly sick.

Eventually he opened his eyes and the first thing he saw was Dixie grinning at him.

'Don't chuck up on me,' said Dixie, her face nearly as green as her hair. 'We're there.'

Sammy wobbled on his feet and laughed. 'I think you're going to be sick before me!'

CHAPTER 23

THE LAND OF DARKNESS

The lift doors creaked open and Sammy took a wobbly step forward. His legs felt like they were made of jelly. They seemed to have arrived in dusky darkness and could hardly see a single step in front of them.

When the last student had stepped out of the lift cubicle, Captain Firebreath raised his hand in a salute. He closed the door with a bang and made the descent back to Dragamas alone.

Sammy looked around. The square lift hole was pitch black and unguarded by any railings. He could hear the cubicle humming as it swayed from side to side, whooshing back to Dragamas to collect more students.

'Chuck buckets over there,' barked a cloaked figure stepping out of the shadows. 'You're not the first and I dare say there's more to come.'

'I'm ok, thank you,' said Sammy. 'Dixie might need it though.'

The man looked closely at him. 'I think I recognise you. Are you Sammy Rambles? Dixie's friend?'

'Yes Sir,' said Sammy.

'Interesting,' said the cloaked man. 'Welcome Sammy Rambles. Welcome to my Land of Darkness.'

Dixie stumbled over to the plastic bucket and knelt down, leaning her head deep inside the bucket. She made strange gurgling noises followed by retching and sloshing as she was violently sick into the bucket.

Sammy didn't like the way the cloaked man held Dixie's head in the bucket as she threw up, her stomach unsettled from the long ride in the lift.

'It took nineteen minutes and three seconds,' Darius informed Sammy. 'Ever since you timed the lift rides, I have too.'

'It's the longest lift ride ever,' said Sammy, looking over at Dixie and the bucket. 'Hey are you ok Dixie?'

Dixie looked up and wiped her face on a black towel conveniently placed next to the bucket.

'I'm fine now,' Dixie grinned. 'Better out than in. I must have lost at least three pounds!'

'Make your own way through the Land of Darkness,' said the cloaked figure, raising his arm and pointing to a dim speck of light in the distance. 'There are many rooms to travel through and each room will try to defeat you.'

Darius let out an explosive giggle. 'What do you mean? How will they defeat us?'

'We call this room the Forest of Darkness where there is no ceiling, no walls and no floor,' said the cloaked man, pointing a cloaked arm in a circle around him. 'It is quite easy to get lost in a forest and never be seen again.'

'Like Karmandor,' Sammy whispered to himself. He gasped. The cloaked man was right. For as far as he could see there were rows and rows of dark trees immersed in pitch darkness. Even the floor was black. If you looked up, the sky was pitch black and there were no stars to see.

'There are many other rooms to encounter before you reach your crossing point,' said the cloaked man. 'You are to meet your school headmaster at the edge of the Land of Darkness and he will personally escort you onwards to the Land of the Pharaohs.'

Darius raised his hand. 'Why haven't we just arrived at the Land of the Pharaohs like normal?' he asked.

The cloaked man laughed. 'Surely that is obvious?' he asked sarcastically. 'You have not been able to go there directly this time, because the Land of the Pharaohs is not currently over your school. You will have to make a crossing to the next land going through my land first.'

The cloaked man reached inside his cape and pulled out a silver box. He opened the box and Sammy saw that it was filled with hundreds of green bracelets with the gold Dragamas twin tailed "D" logo embossed on the outside. The cloaked man handed out the green bracelets, one to each student.

'Wear these at all times,' instructed the cloaked man.

'Free stuff!' yelled Gavin. 'Like at the Floating Circus!'

'Free passage,' said the cloaked man. He pointed his hand down towards the black floor. A narrow path became illuminated, but it seemed to lead just into more darkness.

'He means you won't get killed if you show anyone that bracelet,' said Dixie.

'Correct,' said the cloaked man ominously. 'You may go first Dixie. Enjoy your time here and let your nightmares commence! Boo!' he added, making everyone jump.

Milly shrieked and clutched Gavin's arm.

'That's so tacky,' scoffed Darius. 'Next he'll whip out some ghosts and a banshee. He's probably from Palm Café.'

Dixie led the way down the narrow path. Behind them, the lift rumbled into sight and more Dragamas students spilled out. Sammy heard Professor Burlay ushering the students into the Land of Darkness.

'You? What are you doing up here?'

Sammy heard Professor Burlay utter the words at the cloaked man, but there was no time to look back as he was holding on to the back of Dixie's t-shirt and had Darius hot on his heels.

Dixie and Darius chaperoned Sammy along the narrow path surrounded either side by long black grass stretching into black forest woodland. Sammy noticed the others had stayed back in the clearing, waiting for Professor Burlay.

'Who was that man in the cloak?' asked Sammy.

'I don't know,' said Darius, 'but Professor Burlay didn't seem too pleased to see him.'

'Come on,' grumbled Dixie. 'I hate the dark and if we have to go across this horrible Land of Darkness then I'm not going on my own!'

Sammy felt a shiver run up his spine as the black grass swayed. He'd thought he'd seen eyes in the black forest beyond the grass and there was the sudden odd sound that spooked him. He held his wrist with the green bracelet high in the air so whatever it was could see he was protected.

The eyes saw the green bracelet and sank back into the darkness. With his heart beating a little faster than normal, Sammy was glad when the path opened out into a clearing with an open archway made of white stones. The arch was enormous but it didn't seem to go anywhere.

'Do we go through it?' asked Darius, walking all around the stone arch. 'It doesn't look like it goes anywhere.'

'Maybe it's a transporter,' suggested Dixie, her voice quavering. 'Maybe it will take us to another part of this horrible land.'

Sammy followed Darius completing a circle around the stone arch. 'There's nowhere else to go,' he concluded. 'Shall we go through the arch?'

Darius shrugged. 'Maybe we should wait for Professor Burlay.'

'I hate the dark,' said Dixie firmly and without any warning, she grabbed Darius's arm with one hand and Sammy's arm with the other and dragged them towards the arch at full pelt.

'Dixiiiieee,' Sammy felt his body being pulled in all directions as they fell into the archway. It was like nothing he'd ever experienced, not even when teleporting. It felt like all the worst fairground rides and rollercoasters he'd ever been on rolled into one excruciatingly painful ride.

After a few seconds, although it could have been minutes or hours, Sammy felt the ride was ending and braced himself. His ears felt like they were about to explode and there was a high pitched whistling and deep rumbling all around him.

Just as he was getting used to the noise, it stopped suddenly and he, Dixie and Darius were thrown forwards out of the archway and landed with a bump on a hard surface. Dixie screamed and clutched at Sammy's arm, drawing blood as her fingers gripped him extremely tightly.

'What?' hissed Sammy, pulling his arm free and rubbing it vigorously to restore the circulation.

'People,' said Dixie, sounding close to hysterics. 'Look! They're all looking at us!'

It took nerves of steel to stop Sammy from screaming as well. Dixie was right, everywhere he looked, hundreds of faces were looking at him. He held his wrist with the green bracelet in front of him, showing whoever it was that they must leave them alone.

'It's just mirrors,' said Darius, letting out a shaky giggle. 'The people are us. Lots of us.'

'Broken mirrors,' said Sammy, laughing nervously. 'That's really bad luck isn't it?' Now that the people and the strange faces had been explained, it wasn't so scary. Even so, it took some time for his heart to stop beating faster than normal and even longer for his hands to stop shaking.

'It's a room of mirrors,' said Darius. 'Probably a maze that we have to get through. I've done this hundreds of times. Follow me.'

Sammy looked at the hall of mirrors. Each mirror was chipped and broken. The jagged edges reflected hundreds of copies of himself. It looked completely impossible to know which way to go.

Darius bent down and started tapping the mirrors. Just by Sammy's feet he stopped.

'This is the right way,' said Darius. 'Look, we aren't reflected here, but we are everywhere else. It's this way.'

Dixie clung to Sammy as he bent down to his hands and knees and followed Darius crawling through the hole in the mirror. It was cold on his bare skin. His hands touched the broken glass gingerly and he crept forward.

'We can stand up now,' said Darius, getting to his feet. 'We have to hoist ourselves up and then there's another of those small passages to go through.'

Sammy and Dixie followed Darius, crawling along the mirror pathway and standing up when they reached the end of the passage.

'Oh my...' Darius muffled a scream with his hands and Sammy squeezed forward to see what had happened.

Sammy clamped his hands over his mouth. It was a horrible sight in front of them.

Dripping from floor to ceiling behind the chippings of mirror were millions of disembodied eyes, all different colours, black eyes, brown eyes, blue eyes and green eyes all twisting and turning, following them, dripping with dark red blood and yellow ooze and slime.

Dixie screamed. 'Look! They're all looking at us!'

Sammy could see the eyes and looking beyond them, further down the corridor, he could see their path was littered with thousands of fragments of scales, bones and toothless skulls. There were hundreds of tiny rats scurrying and nibbling the bones trying to find the last pieces of meat.

'Were they humans?' asked Sammy, holding his nose as the horrible smell threatened to make him sick.

'They were dragons,' hissed Dixie. 'Look at all these scales. How many dragons have been murdered here?'

Sammy bent down and flicked a rat away from a skull by his foot. He picked up the skull and turned it over. Then he picked up another and another. Each skull was sparkling white, completely stripped of all its flesh. But there was something missing.

'There's no draconite,' whispered Sammy. 'It's all gone.'

'The Shape have been here,' said Darius. 'We have to tell Professor Burlay.' He turned and started walking back down the corridor the way they had come.

Sammy stood up. 'No, let's keep going and get to Sir Ragnarok. He'll know what to do.'

'Will he bring the dragons back to life?' asked Darius sniffing loudly and rubbing his eyes. 'This is really bad. My parents are Healers. They would hate to see this.'

'The Shape must be close to finishing the Stone Cross,' said Dixie thoughtfully. 'They need all the draconite from all the dragons and then their work is done. They'll be immortal and have power over earth, air, fire and water. They'll be unstoppable.'

'Let's keep going,' said Sammy, changing the subject

quickly. He was afraid what else might happen if they stayed still too long. He slung his rucksack over his shoulder and marched ahead.

Once they figured out how it worked, the mirror maze seemed fairly straightforward. If they saw reflections of themselves facing forward, then it was a dead end. Or if their reflection seemed to be a bit further in the distance then there would be a narrow opening which they could slide through and move on.

Sometimes the mirrors would move and they became revolving doors that spun you around and around until you were dizzy. Then they would release you and you would be back on the right path again.

Some of the mirrors were misleading, showing distorted and elongated reflections. In one mirror, Sammy found he looked as short as Captain Stronghammer. In another mirror, he was as tall as Commander Altair.

Eventually, after a few wrong turns, dead ends and double backing on themselves, Dixie spun through one of the revolving mirrors and shouted back to Sammy and Darius from the other side.

'I think this is the end,' she shouted, her voice echoing through the mirror.

Sammy and Darius waited for the mirror to stop rotating and they crossed through the gap to meet Dixie again. The "end" that Dixie described was an opening into a small mirrored room.

At the far end of the room, there was a flight of steps made from broken mirrors. Sammy counted twenty-five steps before the mirror turned into cobbled stone and they were outside in the dark forest again.

Sammy looked up, although it was very dark, there were now stars in the sky. It was a very starry night and Professor Burlay was right, being so high up, the stars seemed even brighter now they were closer.

In amongst the dark trees, Sir Ragnarok sat with Mrs Hubar and Jock on a wooden bench next to a small rope bridge. They were each holding a steaming mug of hot chocolate and were clearly expecting more students to arrive.

'Greetings,' smiled Sir Ragnarok raising his mug and peering into the darkness to see who had arrived. 'We have a fine starry sky tonight. Very good tidings indeed.'

'There's dead dragons down there!' exploded Darius. 'Blood and scales! The Shape have been here! It's not good tidings at all!'

Sir Ragnarok stood up towering over them. He smiled kindly. 'And many more dragons may die before the Shape are stopped. Be pleased that we are so close to finding that which we seek.'

'The Angel of 'El Horidore?' asked Sammy, his eyes wide. 'Is it definitely here?'

Sir Ragnarok nodded. 'We have information to suggest that the Angel of 'El Horidore has been hidden in a pit, deep underground inside one of the pyramids, but we don't know which pyramid.'

'Is it inside the Great Pyramid?' asked Sammy.

'Do not choose the most obvious solution,' warned Sir Ragnarok. 'Please remember that the Great Pyramid is still off limits to everyone below the fourth year. There are many other pyramids to explore. Above all, have fun and enjoy yourselves.'

Sir Ragnarok waved them on to the small, narrow, rope bridge as the other students caught them up.

'Greetings and welcome,' said Sir Ragnarok, turning to face the newcomers.

'What's the point if it's in the one pyramid we aren't allowed to go in?' moaned Dixie. 'I really wanted to find it.'

'Sir Ragnarok said we can still have fun,' said Darius, taking his first step onto the rope bridge, which wobbled under his weight. 'We can go swimming in the Oasis.'

'In winter? You're mad!' said Sammy, following Darius onto the rope bridge.

The bridge took their weight perfectly fine, but Sammy held tightly to the guide ropes as he crossed the wooden slats. He didn't know what was underneath them or how high up they were. Probably best not to know, he thought to himself.

'It'll be hot,' insisted Darius. 'You wait and see.'

Sure enough, at the top of the bridge when they started on the rickety downward slope that was almost like a slide, the temperature forced them to abandon their heavy winter coats and jumpers.

Grains of sand started appearing on the bridge and soon it felt like walking on a beach, except that the path was still thin and rickety and you needed to keep holding tightly to the hand ropes so you didn't fall off.

'See,' grinned Darius. 'I told you it would be boiling hot. Hey, isn't that Antonio?'

CHAPTER 24

THE LAND OF THE PHARAOHS

Sammy steadied himself on the thin rope bridge and followed Darius's outstretched hand. On the other side of the bridge, he could see a tall balding man with thick set shoulders and a twirling jet black moustache. The man was dressed in a full-length white robe tied at the waist with a wooden beaded belt.

Sammy instantly recognised the man. He was Antonio Havercastle, their friend from the previous school trip to the Land of the Pharaohs last year.

Antonio's brother, Andradore Havercastle, was the circus ringmaster at the Floating Circus and a great friend of Sir Lok Ragnarok.

When Sammy had saved Andradore Havercastle's lion, Rolaan, from being poisoned, both Andradore and his brother, Antonio, had been so grateful they had promised Sammy they would do anything for him.

Antonio was a very successful businessman. He owned the Oasis Café with the Oasis pool that Sammy, Dixie and Darius liked to dangle their feet in the cool water and then jump in and swim when it got too hot.

Antonio also owned one of the prestigious hotels at the Land of the Pharaohs, called Hotel de la Pyramid, and he was a stakeholder in several businesses, particularly those businesses who sold goods in the stalls in the local market.

Antonio lived in his hotel's penthouse apartment with his friend Vigor, who sold rugs and camel blankets at one of the market stalls. Sammy liked both Antonio and Vigor and was looking forward to seeing his friends again.

As they got nearer, they could see Antonio was carrying a large blue crate, with the word "ICE" stamped on the side, just ahead of them. The crate appeared to be leaking and was leaving a trail of water behind him.

Darius cupped his hands. 'Antonio!' he called out and the man stopped, rubbed his eyes and came striding over to the bottom of the rope bridge.

'Well hello again you three,' said Antonio, in the same deep, rich, voice they remembered. 'Welcome to the Land of the Pharaohs. I thought I'd probably be seeing you again before too long.'

Antonio held out his hand and Sammy was grateful for the help jumping down off the swinging bridge. His legs felt like jelly and he could hardly stand up straight.

'Hi Antonio!' said Dixie enthusiastically. She jumped nimbly off the bridge, landing neatly on the sand, without any help. 'We're here to find the Angel of 'El Horidore.'

'Aren't we all,' said Antonio, smiling kindly at her. 'Many have sought, yet nought have found. I trust you will be staying with myself and Vigor?'

'At your hotel? Hotel de la Pyramid?' asked Darius, his eyes gleaming.

'Of course,' said Antonio, reaching into one of the many deep pockets on his white robe. He took out three gold VIP invitation scrolls. 'Come to my hotel when you've finished exploring. Tea will be served between five and eight. Vigor's doing camel stew today.'

'Mm,' grinned Darius, rolling his eyes. 'My favourite.'

'If you come to the Oasis Café I will give you all free drinks. Please excuse me, I must get on,' said Antonio, taking his blue crate of melting ice, which was still leaking behind him, through the arches of palm trees and out of sight.

'He knew you were making fun of him,' Dixie hissed.

'I'm not eating camel stew,' retorted Darius grabbing Dixie's hair. 'It's disgusting! You can eat it all!'

Sammy stepped in to prevent the inevitable squabble. 'Come on, let's go to the Great Pyramid first. We can always try sneaking in past Professor Burlay and Mrs Grock.'

'Do you really think the Angel of 'El Horidore is in there Sammy?' asked Darius. He looked worried and stopped pulling Dixie's ponytail.

'Are you sure you want to go back in after last time?' asked Dixie, her eyes wide. 'After what Serberon did to you?'

Sammy nodded. 'I think we have to do it. I know it's very dark and really scary, but we have to find the Angel of 'El Horidore for the Snorgcadell.'

'Do you really believe you can find it?' asked Darius. 'Honestly, it could be anywhere in the whole wide world.'

'I have to find it,' Sammy said firmly. 'I think it's the key to making my parents see dragons again.'

'Yeah right,' said Darius.

Sammy could tell from the sarcastic tone of Darius's voice that his friend didn't believe a word of it.

'I want my parents to see dragons again,' said Sammy resolutely.

Dixie coughed impatiently and tapped Darius on the

shoulder. 'So, are we going to the Great Pyramid or not?'

'Fine,' said Darius, giving in. 'I still don't think we'll find it but...'

'But it would be good if we did,' interrupted Sammy.

'There are supposed to be giant rubies hidden in one of the pyramids. Rubies as big as cars,' said Darius, suddenly coming around to the idea. 'Imagine if we found one of those. The power from an enormous ruby like that would be phenomenal.'

'Imagine if a ruby that size got activated,' said Dixie thoughtfully. 'Anyone trying to get past it would be frozen in time. There's no way anyone could protect themselves from a ruby that size. Also, no one would be able to get near them to save them.'

'Then the Angel of 'El Horidore has to be hidden there,' said Sammy excitedly. 'It would be the perfect hiding place to put the Angel of 'El Horidore in a place where anyone who tried to come near it or take it away would be trapped forever.'

'King Serberon would probably have thought of that. After all it was his Angel whistle,' said Dixie.

'Don't be stupid. King Serberon was never here,' said Darius. 'Why would he put it here?'

'Maybe he moved it,' suggested Sammy, ducking under a low palm tree. 'Maybe my parents put it there.'

'Yeah right!' laughed Darius. 'I want your parents to be able to see dragons just as much as you do, but there's nothing to say that they had anything to do with the Angel of 'El Horidore.'

'But General Aldebaran Altair said...' started Sammy.

'So what? It was a long time ago,' said Darius. 'Let's stop for something to eat first.'

'You're always hungry Darius,' said Dixie. 'Such a pig!'

Darius laughed. 'I like eating! So what!'

'I'm want to see if we can get into the Great Pyramid and explore inside it. Imagine if the giant rubies and the Angel of 'El Horidore are there,' said Sammy, feeling a little nervous, just in case the giant rubies were there and the Shape turned them on and trapped them. But he kept those thoughts to himself.

'Fine,' grumbled Darius, 'just let me fill up my flask with water if we're going in.'

'We'll probably have to go in using the South entrance at the back like last time,' said Dixie, holding back some bushy ferns so that Darius could dunk his water bottle under the crystal clear fountain that led into the Oasis pool.

Beyond the fountain, the cool blue Oasis pool was full of people cooling off in the intense heat. The sun was almost directly overhead and it was very hot.

Gavin and Toby were showing off and diving into the pool to retrieve shoes that had been thrown in by Milly and a group of third year girls.

Most of the Dragamas students had arrived. Sammy could spot people from Dragamas amongst the Land of the Pharaohs native inhabitants by the bright fluorescent green bracelets they'd received from the cloaked man at the Land of Darkness jangling on their wrists.

No one paid any attention to Sammy, Dixie and Darius as they walked along the outskirts of the pool and out into the narrow streets that were filled with the hustle and bustle of brightly coloured market stalls, selling everything under the sun.

No one stopped them as they walked right through the market and out into the desert where the pyramids loomed on the horizon. The enormous yellow sand dunes were still there, rising and falling for miles around.

As they reached the array of imposing triangular pyramid structures, Sammy, Dixie and Darius found

Professor Burlay and Mrs Grock sitting together on a wooden bench under a red and yellow parasol outside the entrance of the Great Pyramid. It seemed they had found some shade out of the bright sunshine and were happy sipping a sludgy green cocktail in a triangular shaped glass with two straws.

Since last year, there were tall wooden boards advertising various hotels and shops outside the Great Pyramid. In behind the boards, wooden fences had smaller signs in the rubble advising people to keep within the area accessible to tourists.

Sammy ducked behind one of the wooden boards and pulled Dixie and Darius out of sight. The last thing they needed was a lecture from Professor Burlay about not going inside the Great Pyramid.

They crept along the inside of the boards and Sammy led the way to the back of the Great Pyramid. He remembered it so clearly from last year. Two of the four sides of the pyramid had collapsed. Tons of rubble and rocks spilled out of the pyramid creating handy footholds for them to use to climb up the decaying wall.

Behind the Great Pyramid, the noise from the Oasis Café and the busy market streets had subsided and the only sounds were the faint rustle of birds foraging in the palm trees and the louder rustle of the leaves of the low bushes blowing in the wind.

Dixie threw her rucksack on to a ledge jutting out from the pyramid at shoulder height and hoisted herself up.

'Catch!' Sammy called, throwing his rucksack up towards the ledge for Dixie to catch. He tried to remember which footholds she had used so that he could copy her path to the South entrance.

There were more boulders than he remembered at the foot of the pyramid and the opening seemed harder to reach than before.

'It's miles to climb up there!' complained Darius, taking a swig from his bottle. 'Ooh, the water's cold.'

Sammy took a swig from the bottle and threw it up to Dixie, who had already slung his and her rucksacks one over each shoulder and climbed up to the next ledge.

'How did you get up there?' asked Sammy.

'Easy!' called Dixie. 'I'll show you.'

Sammy shielded his eyes from the sun. Dixie raised her staff and fired tiny green sparks that bounced lightly off the pyramid to show the safe footholds she had used.

Sammy climbed up the jagged pyramid wall very slowly. After just a few steps, he put his right foot on a loose stone. The stone slipped away from him and scattered loose sand and gravel showering down below.

'Oi!' shouted Darius, as the gravel rained down on him.

'Sorry!' Sammy called down to Darius. 'Are you ok?'

'Yes!' shouted Darius. 'Just don't do it again!'

Moments later, Sammy reached what was left of the platform by the South entrance. He hauled himself up onto the ledge.

The black marble plaque was still there with the white text informing anyone brave enough to climb up that there was a shaft from the South entrance leading into the centre of the Great Pyramid.

Dixie was sitting on the marble plaque, drinking sips of water to keep hydrated. She offered the bottle to Sammy and he took a large swig, the ice cold water refreshing him.

Sammy held out his hand to Darius, who crawled up on to the ledge. Sammy didn't like to look, but he knew it was an awfully long way down. He turned instead to the dark opening next to the plaque that was inviting them inside.

'We're up high,' puffed Darius. 'Is this where Serberon pushed you in, Sammy?'

'That's my brother you're talking about!' retorted Dixie. 'I know he was totally in the wrong but he's still my brother and I'll push you inside the pyramid if you say that again.'

Sammy shuddered, remembering falling head first into the Great Pyramid. Dixie's brother, Serberon, had wanted to see his girlfriend so badly he had been tricked by the Shape to lure Sammy into the Great Pyramid so they could ask him to join them.

Dixie knelt down by the dark square entrance. A few more slabs of the pyramid wall had fallen since last time and it was now only just big enough to crawl through.

'Inside, there's a long slope that goes right down to the ground,' said Sammy, kneeling next to Dixie. 'We should be able to light the way with our staffs.'

'I'll use my torch,' said Darius. 'I still haven't got the hang of creating fire with my staff.'

Darius grinned and took out his black cylinder torch. He switched it on and the white beam shone brightly into the pyramid entrance.

'It's easy,' said Sammy. 'You hold your staff like this and say "fire". It's really simple,' he added, holding his staff upright with the small flames shining brightly at the top.

Dixie lit a small fire at the end of her staff and the flames flickered against the rock walls as they descended into the Great Pyramid. The passage floor was sprinkled with sand and loose rocks and disappeared into the darkness.

Sammy felt Dixie press close behind him, holding his rucksack. A bright white light shone ahead of them. Sammy felt his stomach lurch, then he laughed as the light made "D" shapes in a repeating pattern in the middle of the stone passage wall.

'You scared me,' moaned Dixie, 'I hate the dark.'

'Woooh!' Darius grinned, holding the torch up to his

chin. 'I'm so scary!'

'Shut up!' snapped Dixie.

'Come on,' said Sammy, intervening to prevent another squabble. 'We go down in a zig zag, right into the middle of the Great Pyramid.'

'Woooh!' shouted Darius making an eerie echo "woo-ooo-oooh" and a few rocks and gravel fell from the ceiling whizzing past them in the dark.

'Shut up Darius!' shouted Dixie.

Sammy felt something grab his arm. 'Ug, Dixie, you made me jump.'

'Did you hear that?' Dixie whispered.

'What?' asked Sammy.

'Voices,' said Darius, swinging his torch around.

'Shut up Darius! You're scaring me. I don't like the dark and you're making it worse.'

CHAPTER 25

THE RUBY CAVE

Sammy found his feet scuffing and he bent down to touch the floor.

'It's sand. We're at the bottom,' said Sammy, letting the fine grains slip through his fingers.

'Spookeee!' shouted Darius, listening as the echo came round and round "spookee-ee-ee".

Sammy squeezed past Darius to explore the room inside the Great Pyramid. 'That's the platform where Serberon was,' said Sammy, pointing his staff into the middle of the room.

'Where?' demanded Dixie, sending a volley of flames across the cavern. 'Hey there's something there. It's a platform or something.'

Before Sammy could say "stop", Dixie bounded up on to the ledge and down on to the platform. A creaking, groaning sounded overhead and chains banged and clanked together.

'It worked,' said a voice in the darkness.

Sammy spun round to Darius. 'Did you say something?'

Darius shook his head. 'The sunlight's affected you. Come on.'

The banging, creaking and groaning grew louder and Dixie disappeared from sight.

'Hey Dixie! How did you do that?' asked Darius. 'You must be really heavy to make the platform go down.'

'I pressed the rock here. It's some sort of lever,' said Dixie sounding indignant. 'Your left foot weighs more than I do!'

'Come back up,' Sammy called to Dixie, 'then we can all go on the platform together.'

Dixie pushed the rock beside her and the platform raised back to the floor level.

'It's a lift,' she said triumphantly as she returned. 'I wasn't scared at all.'

'Liar,' Sammy grinned and jumped up onto the platform beside Dixie.

Darius jumped on as well. 'Let me press the rock! I want to do it!'

Dixie pushed Darius aside and reached the lever first. She pulled the lever towards her and the platform creaked and started to lower into the shaft. The chains rattled and clanked and they started descending into the depths of the Great Pyramid.

Sammy was sure he heard a bump beside him but nothing was there when he moved his staff and the flames lit up the corners of the lift.

'We must be going down a long way,' said Sammy after a minute.

'We're going very slowly,' said Darius. 'You can't go very far when you're going very slow.'

Just then, the rock lever jutted back out into its original position and the platform lift stopped suddenly.

'Who pressed it?' demanded Darius. 'I was just getting

used to the ride.'

'No-one pressed it,' said Dixie, a twinge of fear in her voice. 'It did it all by itself.'

'Levers don't just do that,' said Sammy trying to be reasonable. 'Who pressed it? Did you press it Darius? Dixie?'

Sammy pushed the rock lever again but nothing happened. 'Ouch!' he cried out as the lever burnt his hand.

Blood trickled out of his palm and he kicked the lever. 'It's stopped. It won't move.'

'We must be there then,' said Darius flashing his torch upwards and around. 'Cool!'

'No, I mean it's stopped,' said Sammy. 'Properly stopped. We can't go up or down.'

'What!' squeaked Dixie. 'Push it again!'

Sammy kicked the rock lever twice more but nothing happened. 'I guess we can teleport,' he said helpfully.

'You can,' moaned Darius.

'So can you,' said Sammy. 'You teleported before.'

'He did it using the power of dragon scales,' said Dixie quietly. 'He knew you wouldn't know about it and made me promise not to tell you.'

'Fine,' snapped Darius. 'Now you know. Apart from the stones, I'm useless at everything else.'

'He uses the power of draconite in dragon's brains to do things,' explained Dixie. 'In living dragons, obviously. It's nothing like how the Shape are stealing draconite and killing the dragons.'

'I can do anything with the stones, onyx, ruby, amber, any stone you can think of. Anything at all,' said Darius.

'But not...' started Sammy.

'No,' said Darius, 'and no-one else needs to know, ok?' he added firmly.

'I suppose,' said Sammy, 'so how come...'

'I'm at Dragamas to learn how to be a Healer, that's it,' said Darius. 'All I want to do is save the lives of dragons using the stones. I couldn't care less about the rest of it.'

'There's a passage here,' said Dixie, breaking the awkward pause. 'We can go down there and maybe it'll lead back up into the chamber.'

'Or back to the surface,' added Sammy hopefully.

'Yeah right, then Professor Burlay will know we've been in here,' said Darius. 'Imagine how many stars we would lose for breaking the rules and coming in here.'

'We have to go somewhere,' Sammy looked around thoughtfully. 'We can't go back up, but also we can't wait here forever.'

'Come on,' said Dixie, grabbing Sammy's hand, which made his stomach jolt. It was clammy and strong and she was leading him down the passage.

'Wow!' said Darius from behind them. 'Look at that!'

Sammy looked up and gasped. The passage extended into a giant underground cavern stretching the entire length and breadth under the Great Pyramid. From the floor to the distant ceiling, the walls were covered in a ruby red iridescent glow.

'It's beautiful,' whispered Darius.

'We're in a ruby cave,' said Dixie walking in. 'A whole cave made entirely of ruby gemstones. Do you have any idea how valuable this would be?'

'Wait!' started Sammy. 'It's dangerous. You know what rubies can do.'

'So what?' Darius marched in after her. 'These aren't active. You should know that from our Gemology lessons.'

Feeling uneasy, Sammy followed. 'How do you know they're not active?'

'The colour,' said Darius, his voice muffled by him bending down with his torch in his mouth, scraping the glowing surface with his fingernails. 'When they glow pink and then bright red, they're active and everything slows down. You must remember that from our lessons.'

Dixie and Darius wandered deeper into the cave and Sammy nodded, a sound distracting him.

Above them there was a faint humming and the clanking of chains. Sammy looked backwards. The lift was going back up and in its place stood a cloaked figure.

The figure was wearing a long black cape which covered its body from head to toe.

'Good evening Samuel Rambles,' said the cloaked figure.

'No!' Sammy stumbled backwards.

'Thank you for finding this chamber for me,' said the cloaked figure. 'Give me the Angel of 'El Horidore.'

From the depths of the cavern, Darius called out. 'It's not here. There's a smashed up box where it might have been at one time. It looks like would have needed the Dragon Minder pin.'

'Who's that?' demanded Dixie running back towards Sammy. 'Who are you? What are you doing here?'

'Give me the Angel of 'El Horidore!' roared the cloaked figure.

'No!' shouted Sammy, hoping he sounded a hundred times braver than he felt. 'It's not here. Leave us alone.'

'Very well,' the cloaked figure smiled, showing very white teeth against the jet black cape. 'You will perish here, never to be found.' The cloaked figure raised his cloaked hand and the cavern shook.

'You will perish!' shouted the cloaked figure and then with a flash he vanished in an eruption of golden mist.

'Teleport!' shouted Sammy. 'The Shape are here!'

'We can't teleport,' squealed Dixie. 'The rubies are activating.'

Sammy froze with fear. Above him, to the side of him and deep below him, the cavern was exploding in a vibrant crimson fog that was burning his eyelids. The heat was unbearable and it felt like he was being burnt alive.

'I can't move!' shrieked Dixie. 'Help!'

Sammy picked himself up and grabbing Dixie by the wrist and Darius by the shoulder, he yelled at the top of his voice, 'Oasis Café! Oasis Café! Oasis Café!'

CHAPTER 26

OASIS CAFÉ

The chamber under the Great Pyramid, burning with the extreme heat from the rubies, dissolved from sight and was swiftly replaced with a tremendous splash as Sammy, Dixie and Darius plummeted into the deep end of the pool at the Oasis Café.

Struggling for breath, Sammy kicked to the surface. He bobbed his head out of the water and the first thing he saw was Dixie. She was in tears with bright, bloodshot eyes.

'I thought I was going to die,' Dixie wept, splashing water over her face.

'Me too,' whispered Sammy, unconsciously drawing her close.

'Me three,' moaned Darius. 'Hey, you're not getting mushy are you?'

'No way!' Dixie giggled, unravelling her ponytail and hoisting her rucksack out of the water. 'Shall we get out? It's dark and cold.'

'Pyramid time,' muttered Darius. 'It must be nearly midnight.'

'Having an evening swim are we?'

Sammy looked up. Dr Shivers was standing on the bridge across the pool that joined the sunbeds to the pool bar. He did not look happy at all.

Dr Shivers waved his arm vigorously and motioned for them to get out of the pool, stepping back as Darius splashed water near him.

'You'll have to put up with the run down barracks at the end of the pyramids,' said Dr Shivers. 'Everyone else has booked into the hotels. Oh, and I'll have the diamond pin as well please,' he added smugly. 'It seems that you didn't need it after all.'

'We've got these,' said Dixie, digging the golden VIP tickets from Antonio out of her rucksack. She thrust them at Dr Shivers. 'We're staying at Hotel de la Pyramid.'

Dr Shivers scowled. 'You should lose stars,' he said, his voice softening, 'but arriving soaking wet at the most prestigious hotel at the Land of the Pharaohs should be sufficient embarrassment and a fitting punishment, so, be on your way.'

Sammy dragged himself up on to the bridge checking he had both his staff and his rucksack. He took out the dragon shaped pin with the tiny diamond eyes and handed it to Dr Shivers.

Dr Shivers smiled at him and took the pin. 'Have fun,' he whispered and marched off.

'I hate him for standing there like that,' grumbled Darius. 'He could have helped us get out of the water.'

'What's he doing out so late?' asked Dixie.

'Do you reckon he knew we've been inside the Great Pyramid?' asked Sammy. 'Why else would he want the diamond Dragon Minder pin back?'

'I don't know,' said Dixie. 'One thing we do know for sure is that the Angel of 'El Horidore isn't in the Great

Pyramid any more.'

'If it ever was,' said Darius. 'Did you see the size of those rubies in the chamber. I bet that's where Sir Ragnarok gets the rubies we were given in our second year from. He probably takes tiny chippings out of the giant cave.'

'Perhaps that's why Sir Ragnarok said for us not to bother looking there,' said Sammy as they started to walk back to Hotel de la Pyramid. 'If he gets rubies for Dragamas every year he would know for certain there's nothing in the cavern under the Great Pyramid any more.'

'He's very lucky he never got stuck in there,' snapped Dixie. 'Do you reckon the man from the Shape is still in there? Did he get trapped by the ruby mist?'

'No,' said Sammy. 'He teleported. But we should have told Dr Shivers about him.'

'Dr Shivers would have gone mad if he knew we'd been in the Great Pyramid,' said Darius.

'He'd probably have locked us in that ruby cave himself,' added Dixie, pushing open the small gold gate that led to Hotel de la Pyramid.

They walked through the exotic garden with palm trees and brightly coloured flowers, up the pebble path to the grand pillared entrance with the gold and white front door.

Sammy remembered the last time he had arrived here. It had also been late at night and he had been covered in mud and blood. This time, he was drenched with water.

'Hope we're not too late,' said Sammy as he pushed open the smart front door of Antonio's hotel.

'Tickets please,' said a small voice from inside. 'You can't come in this late without a ticket.'

Dixie handed over the three golden passes.

'Oooh, VIPs are we?' said the voice.

The door swung wide open, revealing a wizened old

woman with silvery grey hair tied on top of her head in a plaited crown. She was wearing a smart white shirt buttoned to the top of her neck, with a gold blazer and a gold necklace with lots of small silver keys dangling down.

Sammy noticed she wore large gold earrings and lots of gold rings on all of her fingers. The woman was sitting on a black leather chair at a plush mahogany reception desk. She looked up as Sammy, Dixie and Darius walked in.

'Good evening young sirs and...oooh...a troll,' said the silvery grey haired woman.

'Have you got a problem with that?' Dixie glared at the woman and Sammy knew how much she hated people drawing attention to her bright green hair and troll heritage.

'Ooh no, just that it's quite a novelty in these parts,' said the silvery grey haired woman. 'The last green haired girl I saw was at the Floating Circus a few years ago. She bought a pair of dragon toenail clippers from my grandson if I remember.'

'That was Dixie,' said Darius enthusiastically. 'She cut Sammy's arm and saved our school, Dragamas.'

The woman frowned. 'What on earth did you want to do that for? I would have been grateful if my old school had shut down. Nasty place it was. Young people aren't what they used to be. Now where did I put that key?'

'Is it one of the ones around your neck?' said Sammy, spotting the small silver keys attached to her necklace.

'Yes! There it is, around my neck, I'd lose my head if it wasn't tied on! You're in room number one.'

After a wheezy bout of infectious laughter, the old lady unhooked one of the silver keys and handed it to Darius.

'It's a room with three beds and a dividing partition for the young lady, unless you're...'

'We're not,' said Sammy hastily setting the record straight, as Darius got the giggles.

'Oh and Happy Birthday Sammy,' the old woman smiled broadly at Sammy. 'Mr Antonio Havercastle asked me to prepare this for you to eat. It would be best to eat it in your rooms now that I have cleared the dining tables, but enjoy it none the less.'

The old lady reached in behind her desk and withdrew three silver platters piled high with what looked like dark brown lumpy gravy and three sets of silver knives and silver forks.

'Don't drip it on my carpets,' she chuckled as they made their way up the stairs.

Darius scooped up one of the brown lumps with his hand. He shovelled it into his mouth.

'Yuck! It's camel stew,' said Darius, spitting out the tough meat in disgust.

CHAPTER 27

ROOM NUMBER ONE

Antonio and Vigor's hotel was very upmarket with gold swirls on the white marble floor. In the large hallway, two enormous sparkling teardrop chandeliers were suspended from the ceiling on thick gold chains.

The walls were lined with thick gold wallpaper with large mirrors reflecting the light from the chandeliers in many dazzling rainbows that danced around the room.

A wide staircase was in the middle of the hallway with a thick gold carpet with gold bars on each step. At the edge of the stairs, there were gold banisters and a gold hand rail.

After fifteen steps, the staircase split into two branches, leading to the left and to the right. There was a small gold banistered balcony walkway that led to more stairs and the bedrooms on the first floor.

Sammy felt guilty as they squelched up the stairs leaving a watery trail behind them. Up and up they went looking for VIP room number one.

At each floor they stopped and checked the doors to find out the room numbers. Sammy noticed the hotel room numbering seemed to start with high numbers on the lower floors and descend into smaller numbers the higher they climbed.

On the very top floor, they walked up and down the corridor looking for their room. There were two normal sized doors with the number two and the number three written in gold numbers. There was also a smaller door that looked as though it might be a laundry cupboard.

'Shall we knock on one of these doors?' asked Darius. 'Maybe there's someone inside who can help us find our room?'

Sammy shook his head. 'Let's keep looking. It must be here somewhere.'

After searching the entire length of the corridor, they started poking and prodding the walls in case there was a secret passage.

Eventually, Sammy, Dixie and Darius returned to what they had previously dismissed as a laundry cupboard door.

Sammy bent down and saw that the door had a number one written in small red beads just above the handle. There was a small silver lock next to the red beads.

'It's here,' said Sammy. 'The door was here all along.'

'No wonder we missed it,' said Darius. 'It's a bit out of place.'

'That's exactly why we should have seen it,' said Dixie. 'Come on Sammy, open the door.'

Sammy pushed the silver key into the silver lock. The key made a quiet clicking sound and the door swung open revealing a dark passage.

'Fire,' whispered Dixie holding out her staff. 'I'm not walking down there in the dark.'

A small orange flame appeared at the end of her staff and she stepped forward into the passage.

Darius pushed ahead. He turned on his torch and the

beam lit up the whole of the passage.

'It's just another dead end,' said Sammy, seeing the gold wallpapered wall illuminated in the beam of light from Darius's torch. The door clicked shut behind them and the passage jolted.

'It's not a dead end. We're in a lift,' exclaimed Darius. 'We're going up. We'll probably end up on the roof!'

The lift stopped after a few seconds. The door opened and Sammy gasped. The lift had stopped outside a glittering door embedded with thousands of shards of beautiful red rubies decorating it from top to bottom.

'This door must've cost a bomb,' said Darius.

'Two bombs,' agreed Sammy, checking that the rubies were dull and not about to activate and trap them again. 'Do you reckon we have to knock?'

Before Dixie or Darius could answer, the ruby door swung open. Sammy went inside first. He noticed that he stepped over an iron grill shaped mat that reminded him of the cattle grid back at Dragamas that shielded the school from anyone who wasn't connected with dragons from seeing inside.

Before he saw the whole room, Sammy knew his mouth was hanging wide open. It was so luxurious, like no room he had ever been in before. The room easily extended the length of the whole hotel and was decked from floor to ceiling in gold and sparkling jewels.

Closest to Sammy were three large white leather sofas facing a coffee table made of a sheet of thin glass resting on the point of a knee-high, hand-crafted stone pyramid.

Paintings of pyramids and exotic palm trees hung from the walls. In between the paintings were the skulls of camels and sand cats mounted on wooden plaques.

Across the farthest wall, were rows upon rows of books, scrolls and tapestries stacked high on wooden bookshelves.

The lighting in the room impressed Sammy the most. There was a giant chandelier hanging from the ceiling in the middle of the room. It was identical to the chandeliers in the downstairs reception hallway. It spouted hundreds of beads of multi coloured light in a waterfall effect, dripping rainbows of colour throughout the room.

'Wow!' said Darius after a long pause. 'This is beautiful.'

'Dr Shivers was right,' whispered Dixie. 'My Mum would have so much to say about me turning up here soaking wet from landing in the Oasis pool.'

'Then it is just as well that she isn't here,' came Antonio's voice from somewhere in the room.

Although Sammy couldn't see Antonio, he guessed the voice came from somewhere near one of the cream leather sofas.

Sammy stepped forward and suddenly he could see both Antonio and Vigor sprawled out on the sofas. They were each holding a full glass of bubbling amber champagne. Dixie and Darius stepped into the room next to Sammy.

'Look!' hissed Dixie pointing to their feet. 'You can't see Antonio or Vigor unless you're over the grill.'

'Like the garden at Dragamas,' said Darius. 'That's awesome. I want one of those grills for my room at home.'

'Me too,' grinned Sammy. 'My Mum would freak out if I started to move things and she couldn't see me.'

'Poltergeists,' said Dixie. She walked into the room and sat next to Antonio on one of the cream leather sofas. 'Hi Antonio! Thank you for having us to stay here.'

'Hello Dixie,' Antonio smiled, showing a couple of gold teeth. 'I was expecting you a little earlier, no doubt you have had an adventurous afternoon.'

Antonio looked at the silver dishes they were carrying and shook his head. 'I wouldn't eat the stew if I was you. It was not one of Vigor's best creations. Very lumpy.'

Vigor rolled his eyes at Antonio. 'Cooking is not my strength,' he laughed heartily, showing his gold tooth.

'We went inside the Great Pyramid,' said Darius flopping himself down on the third white leather sofa.

'Then the Shape turned up,' added Dixie. 'But thanks to Sammy we got away.'

'Did you teleport?' enquired Antonio. 'That is one of Sir Ragnarok's little jokes. Anyone who teleports in the Land of the Pharaohs ends up in the Oasis pool at my café.'

'But I asked to go there,' said Sammy. 'When I teleported, that was where I wanted to go. The Oasis Café. That's where we ended up. I didn't mean to land in the pool though.'

'Why choose the Oasis Café when you could have chosen to end up anywhere in the Land of the Pharaohs?' asked Antonio. 'Would it not have been easier to teleport here? You could have arrived at Hotel de la Pyramid. It's simple. You were obviously influenced by the great Sir Ragnarok. Mind control,' Antonio sniggered.

'Mind control?' asked Sammy.

Antonio nodded. 'You should know better than to disobey Sir Ragnarok's instructions. He did not want you to go into the Great Pyramid so your punishment was to land in my Oasis pool. Now, there are clean towels in your rooms and feel free to take a hot shower or have a soak in a nice bubble bath.'

'Thank you,' said Sammy. He had never wanted to curl up in a warm bed more than any other time in his entire life.

'Before you go to bed, we must wish our special guest a very happy birthday,' said Antonio. He prodded Vigor who had already curled up and closed his eyes.

Vigor awoke with a start. 'Yes Antonio,' said Vigor and he tapped the table firmly with the palm of his hand.

Three crystal champagne glasses appeared on the glass topped table. Vigor poured three glasses of the amber champagne he and Antonio had been drinking.

'It's non-alcoholic,' said Vigor, passing the glasses to Sammy, Dixie and Darius. He raised his glass. 'Happy thirteenth birthday Sammy! It all starts now!'

Sammy sipped the amber champagne slowly. The cool liquid tasted of orange and pineapple juice and was very refreshing.

'Happy birthday Sammy,' said Dixie, raising her glass and taking a small sip.

'Happy birthday Sammy,' said Darius, downing his amber champagne in one gulp. 'Can we get ready for bed? I'm exhausted.'

Sammy smiled and followed Darius into the bedroom they were sharing. Dixie went into the room next door. Sammy heard the lightswitch go on and he knew Dixie would be sleeping with the light on.

'What do you think Vigor meant when he said it all starts now?' Sammy asked Darius, as he put his jeans and tshirt over a radiator to dry. Luckily the waterproof seal on his rucksack had protected his books, spare clothes and pyjamas, which were completely dry.

'Maybe Vigor had one too many glasses of his amber champagne?' grinned Darius. 'Did you see he switched the bottles? I bet their glasses had alcohol in them.'

Sammy settled into the deep four poster bed drawing the purple silk duvet up to his chin. Despite Darius's comments, he couldn't help thinking back to the time at Dragamas where Dr Shivers had informed him that very bad things would happen from the day of his thirteenth birthday.

Sammy woke up hours later to the warm smell of toast wafting near him and a knocking at the door.

'Breakfast in bed Sammy?'

Sammy looked up. Antonio was standing in the doorway holding a monstrous platter of alternating brown and white toast in the shape of camels and two large pots, one containing yellow curls of creamy butter and the other filled to the brim with strawberry jam.

'I made the toast,' said Antonio. 'Vigor hasn't done anything, except for buying the butter and strawberry jam in the market.'

Sammy sat up, making room for the plate. He smoothed the purple silk duvet and rested the platter of toast up against his knees.

'Did you know that your parents knew about the room under the pyramid?' asked Antonio, perching himself on the end of Sammy's bed. He helped himself to a slice of white camel bread and lathered it with butter and jam.

Sammy shook his head. 'Not really.'

'The cavern with the rubies was built by King Serberon himself,' said Antonio. 'Sir Ragnarok always said it must have been the most secure prison ever created and therefore it would be suitable for housing such a dangerous item. Even the Snorgcadell, before General Aldebaran was elected, agreed the Angel of 'El Horidore would be safe there. Now, I have something to tell you that must be kept so secret that you must guard it with your life. Can you do that for me?'

'Please can you tell it to all of us?' asked Sammy, taking a bite of camel toast and strawberry jam. 'Dixie will kill me if she misses out.'

'Very well,' said Antonio, 'I will tell all three of you. After you finish your toast, get dressed and enjoy the morning as you wish. I shall ask Vigor to look after the Oasis Café for me this afternoon. He can't be there before this afternoon as he is expecting a delivery of new camel blankets from New Grande this morning and I need to give him warning that I may be some time. With three of you knowing what I will tell you, I am sure there will be three times as many questions.'

Antonio finished his camel toast and left Sammy and Darius with the platter.

'What do you reckon he can tell us?' demanded Darius, helping himself to five slices of the camel shaped toast. 'So what if your parents knew the Angel of 'El Horidore was hidden in the Great Pyramid.'

'Let's wait for him to tell us,' said Sammy. 'He didn't say any more than I've already told you.'

'Which is nothing,' grumbled Darius. He got dressed and picked up his toiletry bag. 'How long to you reckon Dixie's going to be in the bathroom?'

While they waited for Dixie to come out of the bathroom and for Antonio to return, Sammy and Darius played hide and seek in the VIP penthouse suite.

After nearly thirty games of hide and seek with Darius, Sammy felt he knew every nook and cranny, perhaps even better than Antonio or Vigor. As he discovered Darius hiding behind the bookcase for the third time, Antonio returned to the penthouse suite.

'Thank you for waiting,' Antonio puffed, holding a carrier bag from which he distributed generous portions of chips and hamburgers.

'As I was saying...' started Antonio, pausing in mid-sentence as Dixie finally walked out of the bathroom wearing a low cut silver dress and perfect make-up.

Her three hours in the bathroom explained everything. Every single strand of her bright green hair was in place. She had subtle touches of blusher on her cheeks, dark kohl around her eyes and black mascara on her usually green eyelashes.

'What do you think?' she asked, twirling around and balancing on the toes of her silver shoes.

'Beautiful,' praised Antonio. 'A metamorphosis.'

'A frog princess,' giggled Darius. 'What've you got all that on for?'

'It's for Nitron Dark,' said Dixie blushing. 'I'm going to wear it to that party he invited us to when we get back. What do you think Sammy? How do I look? Do I look ok?'

'What do you want to dress up for him for?' snapped Sammy, surprising himself.

Dixie's face cracked and she fled into the bathroom.

'Couldn't you just have said "yes"?' said Antonio, frowning at Sammy. 'Not only will it take another hour to take it off but she really wanted your opinion.'

Sammy shrugged. 'I don't care. Nitron Dark hates trolls. She shouldn't dress up for that scum.'

'Rich scum,' added Darius. 'Rich scum with a fully grown dragon.'

Contrary to Antonio's prediction, Dixie appeared in under ten minutes, without the make-up. Instead of the silver dress, she was still wearing the silver shoes but now with denim shorts and a black and silver t-shirt instead.

'Now you look good,' said Sammy, trying to apologise.

'Like you'd know anything,' retorted Dixie.

Antonio coughed nervously. 'Drinks anyone? No, ok, well please take a seat and we shall begin. Now, Sammy, you know that your parents were very close at Dragamas, inseparable almost. Your mother was the best alchemist and seer I have ever had the privilege of knowing and your father, Charles Rambles, well, he knew almost everything about gemstones. I doubt if either Dr Lithoman or Mrs Hubar could have taught him anything he didn't already know.'

Sammy exchanged an "I told you so" glance with Dixie

and Darius. He was so happy. Pride was burning absolutely red hot inside his stomach. It was amazing that his parents once knew so much about the dragon world.

'Anyhow,' continued Antonio, 'Charles and Julia both believed, or suspected, your uncle, Julia's brother, of foul play. They knew Peter Pickering had been following them when they were on Sir Ragnarok's routine missions to check on the Angel of 'El Horidore and they knew, as we all did back then, that your Uncle Peter wanted more than anything to be like his sister, your mother, who frankly beat him hands down at anything and everything. Julia was a true seer if ever there was one.'

Antonio paused for a swig of champagne straight from the bottle and leaned close to Sammy.

'Charles and Julia both believed Peter was going to join the Shape, so that he could have powers of his own.'

'Uncle Peter did join the Shape!' exclaimed Sammy. 'He led my parents to the Shape in the clearing. I saw it happen in a vision.'

'Hmm,' said Antonio. 'I wonder whose choice it was to show you a vision of that. It's not the sort of thing for young eyes.'

'Uncle Peter stood on the treestump in the clearing,' said Sammy.

'It was an initiation ceremony,' added Darius. 'That's when Sammy's parents lost their sight.'

'A sad day indeed. Now my theory is, and has always been, should anyone ask, that Charles and Julia managed to hide the Angel of 'El Horidore before they "lost their sight" as you call it.'

'Do you think my parents took the Angel of 'El Horidore away from the Land of the Pharaohs and hid it somewhere before the ceremony took place?' asked Sammy a slight pitch in his voice. 'So what you're saying is that the

Angel of 'El Horidore might be at Dragamas after all.'

Antonio put his fingers to his lips. 'I have trusted you to be discreet. Do not mention this to anyone, least of all to the Snorgcadell. Even I do not know who can be trusted.'

'You trusted us,' said Sammy. 'We will find the Angel of 'El Horidore.'

'I believe in you,' said Antonio. 'I have faith that you will find it. Now, how about enjoying yourselves before you go back to school?'

'How can we enjoy ourselves?' exclaimed Dixie. 'If we stay up here then the Shape might find the Angel of 'El Horidore at any time.'

'The Shape are following you, so you must be very vigilant,' warned Antonio. 'You may always contact me, either here, or through my older brother Andradore at the Floating Circus, or through my sister, Anastasia. She lives in the Land of Forever More.'

'Thank you,' said Sammy picking himself up from the deep white leather sofa and taking out a Gemology book from his rucksack to study. 'We'll keep searching up here so it won't look suspicious.'

CHAPTER 28

LESSONS AND CHAOS

Over the next ten days, in amongst lessons, Sammy, Dixie and Darius helped Antonio and Vigor decorate Hotel de la Pyramid from top to bottom with Christmas baubles, tons of tinsel and sparkling lanterns and fairy lights.

Sammy found it all very strange to be thinking about celebrating Christmas in the intense heat up in the Land of the Pharaohs. Far down below, Dragamas would probably be covered in the usual layer of thick white snow.

In between decorating sessions at Hotel de la Pyramid, Sammy, Dixie and Darius kept busy with their usual lessons, which remained more or less the same. The only real difference was that the lessons were taking place at the Land of the Pharaohs instead of in the castle classrooms at Dragamas.

Professor Burlay kept the students on their toes with his Astronomics lessons. The lessons took place either at dawn or at dusk at the top of each of the pyramids surrounding the Great Pyramid. Sir Ragnarok allowed the fourth and fifth year students to have their Astronomics lessons on the top of the Great Pyramid.

In one evening Astronomics lesson, Professor Burlay pointed at a very bright star above the Great Pyramid. He informed the third years that this was quite possibly the Christmas star and he told them that the summit of the Great Pyramid was where the Christmas star had first been seen.

With Sir Ragnarok's reluctant permission, Mrs Hubar had taken the third years inside the Great Pyramid to examine the intricate cluster structure that held the ruby chamber in place.

Sammy hadn't enjoyed being back in the chamber, nor the fact that Mr Synclair-Smythe had started following the third years from class to class.

One Wednesday morning, Mr Synclair-Smythe felt the full angry wrath of Mrs Hubar by his attempt to activate the rubies. She wouldn't listen to a word he said when he tried telling her he wanted the third years to have an impromptu Armoury lesson.

Mr Synclair-Smythe hadn't followed the third years after Mrs Hubar had finished shouting at him and threatening to speak with Sir Ragnarok and having him thrown out of Dragamas and the whole of the teaching profession.

Sammy noticed Professor Sanchez seemed preoccupied with something in their Alchemistry lessons. After a couple of lessons, he found out she was bothered by a rumour that her son, Simon, had asked Rachel Burns from the South house on a date and had been turned down.

Out of the familiar structure of Dragamas, the lessons soon began to deteriorate into chaos between the students and even between the teachers. Without the familiar classrooms, students turned up late, or not at all. They were missing notes and text books that had been left behind and the fifth years expressed concerns about the interruption to their education environment potentially affecting their end of year exam results.

After an explosive confrontation between Mrs Hubar and Mr Synclair-Smythe, where they both fired red sparks from the top of the pyramid and caused substantial injuries to the market stall holders, including setting fire to Vigor's rug and camel blanket stall.

Another rumour that started circulating was that Artisan Hefnew, the Lord Mayor at the Land of the Pharaohs, had personally contacted Sir Ragnarok and asked him in no uncertain terms to take all the students back to Dragamas for Christmas.

Antonio and Vigor had prepared a "goodbye" buffet in the large dining room at Hotel de la Pyramid. However, due to one of Mr Synclair-Smythe's complicated Armoury lesson overrunning, there was no time to eat it.

Sammy, Dixie and Darius crammed the food into their rucksacks and pockets in a hasty exit. They packed their belongings in record time.

'Thank you for having us to stay,' said Sammy.

'It's been great staying here,' added Dixie, heaving her food-laden rucksack over her shoulders.

Antonio beamed at Sammy, Dixie and Darius. 'You are most welcome,' he informed them. 'Remember what I said to you about the Angel of 'El Horidore.'

'You think it's at Dragamas,' said Darius, making sure none of the other students could hear him.

Antonio rested his hand on Sammy's shoulder. 'I believe you will find it,' he said confidently.

Sammy felt the pressure mounting and he nodded. There was a lump in his throat and he couldn't speak. He shook hands with Antonio and Vigor, wondering when he would see his friends again.

Sammy, Dixie and Darius were the last to leave Hotel de

la Pyramid and they waved goodbye to Antonio and Vigor. Once outside the exotic hotel garden and beyond the gate, they broke out into a run to make sure they reached the other students without appearing to be late.

Even running to the transportation pyramid, they nearly missed their slot in the lift. Professor Burlay was rounding up the third years into groups so that they could go back down to Dragamas in an orderly fashion.

'Keep up at the back,' shouted Professor Burlay.

Sammy turned around. There was no-one behind him and he guessed Professor Burlay meant him, Dixie and Darius.

Inside the transportation pyramid with the square lift to take them back to Dragamas, General Aldebaran Altair, leader of the Guardians of the Snorgcadell, was sitting at a table outside the Palm Café. He was being served a drink by a man who was dressed like a mummy and was wrapped from head to toe in linen bandages.

'That is so tacky,' said Darius as soon as he saw the mummy.

Even though Sammy had thought the idea of the staff dressing up at the café was pretty good on his first visit, he couldn't help agreeing with Darius that it was rather tacky.

He thought it was even more tacky when a small boy, accompanied by his mother, pulled at one of the mummy's bandages. The bandages unravelled and revealed a skinny white man wearing nothing but a pair of purple boxer shorts. Next to him, Gavin laughed hysterically.

The unravelled mummy man glared and shook his fist first at Gavin, then at the boy's mother. The man started shouting in a language Sammy didn't recognise and the woman and her son apologised and hurried away.

'North first,' said Professor Burlay. 'Then South, West and East last.'

Sammy shuffled forward onto the large square platform in the middle of the pyramid. He stood back as the four glass triangles covering the lift shaft opened like an envelope and the lift with Captain Firebreath came into view.

'Hullo boys and girls,' growled Captain Firebreath. 'Who's next then?'

Sammy took a large step forward. The lift platform felt solid and was a change from the sandy floor inside the pyramid. He didn't like to think of the eleven minutes and thirteen seconds journey down to the school. But he knew that was what was coming. So he set his legs wide apart for balance and braced himself for the steep descent.

Captain Firebreath waited until the last student in the group was on board the lift and cranked the lever to send them downwards.

'Righto, let's go,' growled Captain Firebreath.

Sammy found himself wondering how the dwarf was so good performing the lift journeys going repeatedly up and down between the different lands without feeling ill.

Halfway down the lift shaft, when Sammy was standing with his face squashed against the wall trying to cool down as his cheeks burned and he tried not to be sick, a gold mist enveloped the lift cavity and General Aldebaran Altair appeared.

'You started taking the students back to Dragamas too early Captain Firebreath,' said General Aldebaran Altair frowning at the flame haired dwarf. 'I had yet to give my address. I have news about the Angel of 'El Horidore.'

'They've had enough speeches,' grumbled Captain Firebreath. 'Children want to be out and about, playing games not running after some fancy goose chase.'

General Aldebaran Altair ignored Captain Firebreath and surveyed the ten students in the lift.

'The Shape are after the Angel of 'El Horidore,' said General Aldebaran Altair, giving Captain Firebreath a frosty glare. 'There will be time for fun and games when it is found.' He leaned close to Sammy, talking over Gavin's shoulder. 'I trust if you knew the whereabouts of the Angel of 'El Horidore that you would tell me?'

Sammy felt Gavin shaking behind him. Gavin, the twin who wasn't afraid of anybody was clearly scared of General Aldebaran Altair. Sammy focussed on the food in his pockets as he felt General Aldebaran Altair examine his mind, trying to penetrate his thoughts. Unsuccessfully.

'Very well. I shall return in the Spring with my comrades in the Snorgcadell,' said General Aldebaran Altair. 'Keep your ears to the ground and your eyes peeled. The Angel of 'El Horidore has to be somewhere, even if it is no longer where it should have been.' A gold mist surrounded General Aldebaran Altair and he vanished into thin air as he teleported out of the lift.

'Even if it is no longer where it should have been,' cackled Gavin. 'He's lost it! The mighty Snorgcadell General has lost the Angel of 'El Horidore!'

Captain Firebreath cranked the lift to an abrupt halt. 'And it's best it gets "unlost" if yer follow me.'

'Whatever,' laughed Gavin. 'My Mum's dragon is dead. Who cares about the other dragons now? Let the Shape do what they want.'

'You'll be humming a different tune when it's your dragon they've took,' growled Captain Firebreath.

Gavin shrugged. 'We'll see.'

Captain Firebreath shook his head and uncranked the lift plunging it into a swift steely descent.

When the lift finally stopped, Captain Firebreath turned to Sammy.

'Yer haven't changed your mind about fighting the

Shape an' all, have yer?' Captain Firebreath growled at Sammy as he left the lift and they stepped out into the Dragon's Lair. For mid-afternoon, it was cold and damp with a slight drizzle in the air.

'No,' said Sammy firmly. 'I want my parents to see dragons again and they won't be able to see dragons while the Shape are still out there.'

'I wish Gavin wouldn't go like that,' said Dixie as they reached the bottom of the stone steps. 'My Dad's out there fighting the Shape and Gavin makes it sound like my Dad is fighting for nothing and no-one wants him to bother.'

'Your Dad will come home,' said Darius. 'All the Dragon Knights will come home eventually.'

Dixie looked away. 'I know. I just have to keep hoping that he'll come back one day.'

'Do you want to play a game of Dragonball?' asked Sammy, turning up his collar to keep out the rain. 'It looks like there's a game going on over there,' he pointed towards the Dragonball pitch where some of the older students, who had already arrived back at Dragamas, had retrieved their dragons from the Dragon Chambers and were playing Dragonball in the rain.

'It's a bit different than it was here on Bonfire Night,' said Dixie dreamily, 'when Nitron Dark was here.'

'Yeah,' said Sammy.

'Sorry Sammy, I forgot that was the night your parents' house burned down,' Dixie apologised, touching Sammy's elbow.

'It's ok,' said Sammy, fighting a lump in his throat. 'I think I'll ask Professor Burlay if I can stay at Dragamas over Christmas. I don't really want to go to Switzerland when we now know the Angel of 'El Horidore is supposed to be here anyway.'

'Me too,' said Darius, slapping Sammy on the back. 'If I

go home for the holiday my Mum will only have depressing stories about all the dragons she couldn't save.'

'What about your grandparents?' asked Sammy. 'Don't you usually stay with them?'

Darius looked at the ground. 'Um, they died over the summer, that's why I was staying with my parents and my cousins. They didn't really want me there any more than I wanted to be there.'

'That's awful,' said Dixie, linking arms with Darius. 'But at least you know for certain your grandparents aren't coming back. You don't need to be awake at night wondering about it all.'

'Get lost!' shouted Darius angrily. 'You don't know what it's like.'

Darius broke away from Dixie and Sammy and ran towards the castle, his rucksack bouncing against his back as he ran through the rain.

Dixie looked at Sammy defiantly. 'It's true. I don't know if my Dad's coming back or not. I'll ask if I can stay at Dragamas for Christmas as well.'

Dixie paused for a second. 'Hang on,' she said gloomily. 'I think my Aunt Celia is coming for Christmas so I don't know if I'll be allowed to stay here. She's my Dad's sister, hairy, fat and has green teeth. He never liked her much.'

Sammy laughed. 'Darius will be ok. He should have told us about his grandparents.'

'Do you still want to play Dragonball?' asked Dixie. 'I can go and find Jock and get him to let out our dragons.'

'Absolutely!' said Sammy. 'I'll go and find Darius and meet you back here in a minute...North tower common room.'

Sammy teleported and returned to the Dragonball pitch a few minutes later with Darius, who had got over his quarrel with Dixie almost as quickly as it had started.

Dixie returned a few minutes later. She was riding on her blue-green dragon, Kiridor, and looked incredibly happy to be flying again.

Jock was riding Darius's navy dragon, Nelson, with Sammy's blue-green dragon, Kyrillan, flying behind them.

Sammy ran forward to see Kyrillan. He realised how much he had missed his dragon while they had been staying at the Land of the Pharaohs. Kyrillan seemed pleased to see him as well and knelt on the grass, waiting for Sammy to leap onto his scaly back.

Jock guided Nelson in to land on the Dragonball pitch and dismounted. He gave the harness reins to Darius.

'You can play,' said Jock. 'I haven't got a dragon any more so I'll just watch.'

Darius took the harness and leaped onto Nelson's back. He circled once around the Dragonball pitch, then flew back to where Jock was standing, looking longingly at the dragons flying in the air.

'Come on board, Jock,' said Darius, patting the empty space on Nelson's back. 'You can ride with me.'

Jock's face broke into a huge smile and he vaulted onto the navy blue dragon, tucking his knees tightly in behind Nelson's wings.

Sammy threw one of the black leather Dragonballs to Jock.

'Come on! Let's play Dragonball!' shouted Sammy.

CHAPTER 29

CHRISTMAS AT DRAGAMAS

Sammy woke early on Christmas Day. His nose was frozen and there was an icy cold wind blowing in through his bedside window. He opened his eyes and saw Darius leaping from bed to bed flinging all five tower windows open as wide as possible.

'What on earth are you doing?' asked Sammy, reaching up to close the window. 'It's freezing in here!'

'Gavin and Toby let off stink bombs,' grumbled Darius. 'They went home for Christmas five minutes ago and let off this awful stench on their way out!'

Darius picked up the remains of the stink bombs and threw them as far as possible out of the nearest window.

'They should be grateful I didn't put the empty stink bombs in their beds,' said Darius. 'Imagine that! They'd come back from the Christmas holiday and their beds would be covered in a stinky smell.'

Sammy laughed. 'That would have made the whole room stink forever!'

Darius let out an explosive giggle. 'It would have been

really funny when they came back though!'

Sammy noticed that Jock's bed was empty as well as Gavin and Toby's beds. He guessed Jock had woken up much earlier and gone down to the gemstone mines under the school to see his parents, who lived down there.

'Happy Christmas anyway!' Sammy called across the room, his breath misty in the cold air.

'Happy freezing Christmas,' said Darius grinning at him. 'Hey, guess what! I got you something this year.' Darius threw a small rugged shaped parcel at Sammy.

Sammy caught the parcel and tore open the bright green wrapping paper.

'Dragonskin gloves, cool!'

'They're specially made for holding Kyrillan's metal harness,' said Darius. 'They'll keep your hands clean too.'

'And warm,' said Sammy, trying them on. They were a perfect fit. 'Hope you like your present.' He threw Darius an identically shaped package. 'Snap!'

'Great minds,' laughed Darius, opening an identical pair of dragonskin gloves. 'Did you get them from Excelsior Sports?'

Sammy nodded. 'I think I've got another pair here from Dixie!' He unwrapped the parcel Dixie had left on his chest of drawers and took out another pair of dragonskin gloves.

'They'll be good as a spare pair,' giggled Darius. 'I gave you the gloves first, so you have to wear mine first!'

The next hour disappeared with Sammy and Darius opening the rest of the presents they'd received from parents and classmates.

Darius was particularly pleased to open a foldable metal detector he'd asked for from his parents. Even though they didn't celebrate Christmas, it seemed that this year they had been generous and sent him a number of gifts, including a woolly hat and enough chocolate to feed a small village.

Sammy unwrapped several packets of his own chocolate snowmen, chocolate reindeer, parcels of jelly fruit sweets and bizarrely, a Swiss doll, from his parents.

The doll came with a five-page letter written by Julia Rambles. The letter described the house in Switzerland in so much detail Sammy could almost imagine he was living there. She had included dozens of photographs of the Swiss house and family photos. There were lots and lots of photographs of his baby sister Eliza and the nanny who helped look after Eliza while she and his father were at work.

Sammy felt a little bit homesick as he read about how General Aldebaran Altair, who his mother called Big Al, had helped with everything to do with the fire at his uncle's house and taken care of all the paperwork for them.

Knowing how high-up General Aldebaran Altair was in the ranks of the Snorgcadell, Sammy wasn't surprised he had been able to help with what was probably a minor incident compared with the importance of finding the Angel of 'El Horidore and other Snorgcadell business.

The letter finished with a request for Sammy to telephone his parents after lunch on Christmas Day and a wadge of money, which Sammy wasn't surprised about considering his mother worked in a bank.

Sammy tucked the money into his wallet in the top drawer of his chest of drawers and had another look at the Swiss doll, which was dressed in a white shirt and red tartan pinafore dress.

'What is that?' asked Darius erupting into hysterical bouts of laughter that threatened to regurgitate his chocolate snowman breakfast.

Sammy held up the doll and shook his head. 'What am I supposed to do with this? My parents haven't got much idea, have they? Do you remember what they sent when I asked for a Dragonball set?'

Still holding his side from laughter, Darius nodded vigorously and held up a Gemology textbook and a bar of chocolate.

'Let's go down to the den and do some homework.'

Sammy laughed. He couldn't remember ever doing any sort of homework on Christmas day before. But he picked up his staff, his notebook and pens, a large handful of chocolate snowmen, his hat and scarf and followed Darius out of the castle and into the forest.

Even though the school was usually mostly empty during the holidays, Sammy found it eerie walking through the forest to the den.

He pushed the branches aside and stepped inside the den. The shimmering protection Serberon had cast was still there, but it seemed weaker, as though it would need to be redone to prevent anyone else from coming in.

'Brrr, it's so cold,' said Darius. 'Can you light a fire, Sammy?'

Sammy nodded and pointed his staff at the treestump in the middle of the den.

'Fire!' said Sammy and bright orange flames erupted from the end of his staff and settled into a warm glowing fire on the top of the treestump.

'That's better,' Darius grinned and opened his copy of "An Aeon of Amber". He flicked straight to the back of the book, where there were practice tests. 'Test me on these questions first,' said Darius, handing the textbook to Sammy.

'You probably know most of the answers already!' said Sammy.

'Probably,' said Darius, letting out an explosive giggle.

After answering all of the questions in the Gemology book twice, Sammy was exhausted and didn't want to hear any more about amber ever again.

'Is that enough questions?' asked Sammy, putting down the "An Aeon of Amber" book and wishing Ron Pirate hadn't written such a comprehensive textbook. 'Can we get some lunch?'

'Lunch?' Darius's brown eyes sparkled. 'Why didn't you say so earlier. Sir Ragnarok's doing our usual massive Christmas dinner with all the trimmings!'

'I know,' said Sammy. He laughed and packed up their things. He extinguished the fire on the treestump, which fizzled and went out without any scorch marks. 'Shall we teleport there?'

'I'd prefer to walk,' said Darius. 'My teleporting isn't as good as yours.'

'Ok,' said Sammy, stepping out of the den onto the snowy forest floor. He wrapped his scarf tightly around his neck. 'We can run to the Main Hall to keep warm!'

'Yeah!' Darius punched the air and took off at an athlete's pace.

Sammy was out of breath as he caught up with Darius at the entrance of the Main Hall. As promised, Sir Ragnarok had prepared a magnificent feast for the small number of students who were staying.

Sammy and Darius sat at the North table with Jock, his parents, Mrs Hubar and Captain Stronghammer. Halfway through the meal, Captain Firebreath joined them, bringing a pile of Christmas crackers and a large Christmas pudding.

There was no sign of Sir Ragnarok. Sammy imagined the Dragamas headmaster was tucked up in his office with Lariston, celebrating Christmas quietly by themselves.

After the meal Captain Stronghammer started singing a variety of Christmas carols rather badly out of tune and Sammy remembered he needed to telephone his parents.

He excused himself from the party and made his way

outside and over to the Gymnasium to make the long distance telephone call.

It was only when he got to the Gymnasium foyer entrance that he wondered why he hadn't teleported.

Mr Ockay was in the foyer sitting at his desk watching a Dragonball match on his small television.

'Hello Sammy,' said Mr Ockay. 'You'll be wanting the telephone to speak with your parents I presume.'

Sammy nodded and held out some coins. Mr Ockay waved Sammy's hand away.

'Telephoning your parents on Christmas Day is most important Sammy Rambles,' said Mr Ockay, waggling his finger at Sammy. 'This telephone call is going on the Dragamas telephone bill.'

'Thank you,' said Sammy, handing Mr Ockay a small piece of paper. 'Here's their number.'

Mr Ockay punched in the numbers and there was a slow crunching as the telephone made the connection. Then a slow dial tone that went on and on. Sammy was worried he'd made a wasted journey.

Then just as he was about to hang up, Julia Rambles answered the telephone in Switzerland.

'Hello Sammy! Merry Christmas!' said Julia, then in a muffled voice, Sammy heard her calling, 'Charles, Sammy's on the phone.'

Sammy felt his eyes prickle with a wave of unexpected homesick tears.

'Hi Mum. Hi Dad. Happy Christmas!' said Sammy, his voice choking. 'Thank you for my presents.'

'You're welcome Sammy. Have you had a nice day? We've had a delicious Christmas lunch and Eliza has eaten a whole roast potato...'

Sammy only registered half of the conversation. He was answering on auto-pilot. It was so nice to hear his parents' voices after everything that had happened.

'...and we are going to be seeing Big Al for drinks at a New Year's Eve party,' finished Julia. 'Isn't that exciting!'

Sammy nodded, then said "yes" as he remembered they couldn't see him. Hearing General Aldebaran Altair's name reminded him of the Angel of 'El Horidore and it was on the tip of his tongue to ask his mother about it. Then he heard his sister crying at the other end of the telephone.

'Eliza needs changing,' said Julia. 'I'd better go. You can talk to your father for a bit if you like...oh, actually, I'm sorry honey, he's just taken a call from a client. We'd better go, but call us anytime Sammy. Bye honey. See you soon.'

'Bye Mum,' said Sammy. He hung up the telephone and stood still for a whole minute before turning around and making his way back slowly through the snow to the castle.

CHAPTER 30

ON WITH THE QUEST

The Christmas holiday disappeared almost as soon as it had arrived. December turned into January and the weather became much milder.

The scattering of snow that lay on the floor melted from everywhere, except where a few snowflakes were caught in the shadows under some of the rhododendron bushes in the castle grounds.

The excitement of Sir Ragnarok's Christmas Day feast was quickly forgotten as the Dragamas students who had gone home, returned to school as usual.

Sammy and Darius were down by the school entrance waiting for their third year classmates to be dropped off in the layby opposite the gates.

Captain Stronghammer and Captain Firebreath were there to help with students' suitcases and their dragons.

'There's Dixie's car!' shouted Sammy as Sylvia Deane's rickety blue Land Rover hurtled down the lane towards them kicking up a cloud of dust behind it.

The Land Rover screeched to a halt in the layby. The

rear door with the spare tyre attached to the back swung open and Serberon leaped out, followed by Mikhael and Jason.

'Hello Dragamas! We're back!' shouted Serberon, punching the air with his fist. 'Hi Dukey and Firey! Give us a hand with our cases please!'

The two dwarves scuttled across the lane. Mikhael and Jason heaved the four suitcases out of the Land Rover and helped the dwarves carry them over to the school gates.

'Come on Dixie!' shouted Serberon. 'Or are you still sulking?'

'She's sulking,' said Jason, his ponytail swinging as he laughed. 'Just because of Aunt Celia.'

'I am not!' came Dixie's voice from the other side of the car. The passenger door swung open and Dixie stepped down. 'She's just a grumpy old troll!' Dixie slammed the door shut. 'I am not sulking!'

'Didn't give you a Christmas present as good as the ones we got, did she?' said Mikhael, ruffling his sister's hair.

'Stop doing that!' said Dixie. 'You know I don't like it.'

Sylvia Deane wound down the driver's side window. 'Stop fighting please,' she called out of the window. 'Is everybody out? Good! Work hard! Behave yourselves and I'll see you soon.'

Sylvia Deane wound the window back up to the top and with a final wave, she spun the Land Rover around in a neat three point turn and drove off at top speed back the way she had come from.

As the dust settled, Sammy greeted Dixie with a hug. Serberon, Jason and Mikhael appeared to have gone down the Shute with the suitcases and were nowhere in sight.

'So you didn't get a Christmas present from Aunt Celia?' asked Sammy, grinning at Dixie.

Dixie laughed. 'No! She hates girl trolls.'

'Really?' asked Darius. 'Surely she must have been a girl troll herself at some point?'

'I know,' said Dixie. 'Never mind. Anyway, how was your Christmas holiday? Did you like the dragonskin gloves I got you?'

Sammy caught Darius's eye and they both fell about laughing.

'What?' demanded Dixie. 'What's so funny?'

'We all gave each other dragonskin gloves,' said Sammy. 'Darius wants me to wear his first!'

'Hah!' snorted Dixie. 'We'll see about that!'

'Come on,' said Darius, poking Dixie in the ribs. 'Let's go to the den and get some studying done before dinner.'

Dixie nodded. 'We need to figure out how to find the Angel of 'El Horidore as well.'

Leaving Captain Stronghammer and Captain Firebreath at the school gates, Sammy, Dixie and Darius ran to the clearing in the forest.

The den was exactly how they had left it, although the protective sapphire bubble Serberon had created around the den was considerably paler than before.

'The magic is weakening,' said Dixie, running her hand over the bubble.

Sammy squeezed past her and sat on one of the fluffy green cushions he and Darius had borrowed from the North tower common room. Darius flopped down beside him and got a notepad and a packet of pencil crayons out of his jeans pocket.

While Sammy and Darius sat on the green cushions, plotting maps and diagrams where the Angel of 'El Horidor could be hidden, Dixie paced around the den, rubbing her hands and stamping her feet every so often to keep warm.

Using coloured pencils and a ruler, Darius drew the

intricate maps of the school and the surrounding area with the same precision he always used to create his gemology diagrams, which always scored top marks.

Darius was officially the best in the class at Gemology and surprisingly also at Alchemistry, although even Darius himself didn't know why.

'What do you think of my map?' asked Darius, holding up his notebook. 'It's only a rough drawing, but it shows the school and the places we've already searched for the Angel of 'El Horidore.'

Dixie looked at the map with approval. 'It's really good,' she said. 'There are still lots of places to look.'

'Thanks,' said Darius, snapping the notebook shut. 'Shall we go back to the North tower? I want to revise some Alchemistry as we've got that test coming up.'

'The test is tomorrow,' said Dixie. 'Professor Sanchez wants us to turn a ball of wire into a ball of gold.'

'How do you know?' demanded Darius.

'Simon Sanchez and Amos Leech were talking about it before the Christmas holiday,' said Dixie. 'It should be fairly easy.'

'Easy!' spluttered Darius. 'Have you got any idea how it's done?'

'No,' said Dixie. 'Have you?'

'I've got no idea!' said Darius. 'Why do you think I want to revise?'

Sammy held his hands up to keep the peace. 'Let's go back to the castle and have a look in the Alchemistry book. Or we can always go to the Library and ask Mrs Skoob if she's got anything that can help.'

'Like a miracle,' muttered Darius, stomping off towards the castle.

Dixie and Sammy scurried after him and they met Tom Sweep the school caretaker in the castle courtyard. Tom

Sweep was showing a dwarf that Sammy didn't recognise, but looked familiar, into the caretaker's office.

The evening passed in a blur of revision with Darius acting as the teacher and testing Sammy and Dixie on everything they knew about the theory of alchemy.

Even with the last minute extra practice, Professor Sanchez's Alchemistry test was extremely difficult. When the third years arrived in the Alchemistry classroom they found Professor Sanchez sitting at her desk and that her desk was covered with dozens of balls made from dull coloured wire. Each ball of wire was the size and shape of a tennis ball.

Professor Sanchez waited for all of the students to sit down. She waited a little longer until she had their full attention and then held up one of the balls of grey wire.

'Take the wire and use your mind,' said Professor Sanchez. 'I want you to turn the wire into something made of gold, silver or bronze,' she added, expertly turning her ball of dull grey coloured wire into molten gold liquid.

Professor Sanchez raised her staff and, without touching the bubbling, boiling, hot liquid, she moulded it into the shape of a dragon and then back into the ball of grey wire.

'It is easy,' said Professor Sanchez, transporting forty balls of grey wire through the air and dropping a ball onto the desk in front of each student. 'Use your mind and your staff and let me see what you can create.'

Despite complaining bitterly about having to take the test, Darius, to his surprise, successfully turned his ball of wire exactly into separate thirds of the three metals they had been asked to create.

'Look at this!' shouted Darius, pointing at the three piles of gold, silver and bronze on his desk. 'I've done it!'

Professor Sanchez raced across to the desk Darius was sharing with Sammy and Dixie and examined the materials.

'This is perfect!' beamed Professor Sanchez. 'Not even Sammy or my son Simon has achieved this.'

'Can I keep it?' asked Darius, looking hopefully at the shiny metals.

Professor Sanchez laughed and turned the piles of precious metals back into one large ball of steel. 'Now you may keep it,' she chuckled. 'I will award your house some stars instead.'

With a flick of her staff, Professor Sanchez awarded North twenty-one stars, seven stars for each metal Darius had created.

Sammy watched as the golden stars flew out of the classroom window and floated across the courtyard towards the Main Hall. He knew they would attach themselves to the giant North noticeboard which collected all the stars. The stars were house points that counted towards which house would win the end of year trophy.

Disappointingly, neither Sammy nor Dixie turned their grey wire into anything more exciting than a ball of wool.

Dixie's wool had come out bright green, exactly the same colour as her hair and at the end of the Alchemistry lesson, she promptly took it to the school postbox to send to her mother as a peace offering for upsetting her Aunt Celia during the Christmas holiday.

While Dixie was busy finding an envelope for the wool, Sammy explored some more of the school grounds with Darius and Jock.

Halfway on their way towards the Dragonball pitch, Darius announced he had brought the pocket sized metal detector, he had been given at Christmas.

He strapped the device to his ankle and they walked the entire length and breadth of the Dragonball pitch, making sure they stayed some distance away from Tom Sweep, who was mowing the pitch into neat stripes on his ride-on lawnmower.

Sammy, Darius and Jock walked behind the lawnmower, listening for a high pitched "beep".

After finding nothing more than a broken hairslide and a fifty pence piece, Darius had thrown the metal detector on the ground and stamped on it.

'Detect that!' Darius had shouted as the metal detector shattered into hundreds of pieces. Then he had bent down to pick up every single tiny shard so they wouldn't hurt any dragon's feet.

Later that evening, Sammy crawled under his comfy green duvet and ran his fingers over the maps of Dragamas that Darius had drawn.

As scientific and precise as ever, Darius had divided each map into square segments and he had numbered each segment using a thin black pen, in exactly the same way as he labelled his detailed Gemology diagrams.

Sammy ran his fingers over the grooves in the map. Earlier that evening, they had already eliminated the large segments containing the Gymnasium and Dragonball pitch.

The Gymnasium was a fairly modern building which didn't appear in the "Shaping the Future of Dragons" painting of Dragamas in the lower corridor. Although the grassy pitch had always been there, the Gymnasium would have been built after the time Sammy's parents would have been at Dragamas.

Sammy smiled as he remembered walking around the school grounds. He rested his head on his pillow and closed his eyes.

He awake lay in bed for a few minutes, wondering where on earth his parents would have thought would be safe enough to store the Angel of 'El Horidore. It was such an important item to guard and make sure the Shape would never find it.

It crossed his mind to search in the Teachers' Garden, which was protected by the small cattle grill and needed a password to get inside. He scribbled that idea down on a piece of paper beside his bed.

Then before he could write down any more ideas, Sammy fell fast asleep and while he slept, he dreamed of finding the half-moon shaped Angel whistle and presenting it to Sir Ragnarok in the middle of a school assembly.

CHAPTER 31

THE ANGEL IS FOUND

A few weeks later, Sammy sneezed and woke suddenly as a feather landed on his nose. He jerked his eyes open and found Gavin was standing at the end of his bed.

The dark haired twin was shaking a pillow so hard that the feathers exploded out of the green cover. Small white feathers from the pillowcase were flying everywhere around the room and landing all over the floor.

'Give it back!' Sammy heard Darius shout.

'Shh,' cackled Gavin. 'Sammy's asleep.'

'I don't care! Give it back!'

'I'm not asleep any more,' said Sammy, grinning and pushing Gavin aside. 'What's going on?'

'He's awake!' yelled Gavin. 'Sammy, you're on my team, us against Daz and Jock, Toby's out...' Gavin paused mid-sentence. 'Hey, what's that you've got there?'

Sammy looked at his chest of drawers. Gavin leaped off his bed and snatched up the pieces of paper.

'What's this?' demanded Gavin.

'It's nothing,' said Sammy, snatching the paper back out

of Gavin's hands. 'Nothing at all.'

'It doesn't look like nothing,' retorted Gavin.

Darius pushed his head around the curtain. He spotted the paper with his diagrams and came to Sammy's rescue.

'It's nothing for you to worry about Gavin,' said Darius. 'Mind your own business.'

'You keeping secrets?' Gavin flung the curtain rattling on its rings at Darius. 'Did you know about this?' he glared at Jock.

Jock took one look at the paper and shook his head. 'Looks like a map of the school. I'm going to check on the dragons. If you see Naomi, tell her that's where I'm going.'

'I'm keeping this map, or whatever it is,' said Gavin and he threw the broken pillow to Darius where it promptly exploded in a cloud of feathers in his face and snatched the paper back out of Sammy's hands. 'I want to find some secret passages.'

'It's not...' started Sammy, pausing as he received a warning glance from Darius, 'um, yeah, we've found loads of passages. You can borrow it if you like.'

'I'm going to keep it,' laughed Gavin. 'Me and Toby, we'll find them all.'

'We know where we've already been,' said Darius, winking at Sammy. 'You keep the map.'

'Losers.' Gavin made an "L" sign over his forehead and hitched his rucksack over his shoulder. He marched out of the tower room, clomping down the stairs.

'General Aldebaran Altair will be here this morning,' said Darius bending down to scoop up the feathers and stuffing them back into the pillowcase. 'It's the first day of Spring, remember.'

Sammy nodded. 'I think we should tell him that my parents may have brought the Angel of 'El Horidore back here to Dragamas. Obviously it was stored in the Great

Pyramid at the Land of the Pharaohs at one time. Then my parents must have moved it out of the ruby cave and brought it back to Dragamas.'

'Maybe we should tell him about it,' agreed Darius. 'We definitely have to find the Angel of 'El Horidore before the Shape find it. You can tell General Aldebaran Altair. It's about your parents after all.'

'Ok,' said Sammy, bending down to find a matching pair of socks from under his bed. He dressed at top speed and followed Darius downstairs for breakfast.

In the Main Hall, General Aldebaran Altair had taken Sir Ragnarok's chair at the head of the teachers' table. He was wearing his silver armour breastplate and chainmail and had rested his silver visored helmet on the table by his breakfast plate.

Sir Ragnarok was sitting on General Aldebaran Altair's right. He appeared to be distracted and was pulling his long grey beard into twists and plaits.

When the Main Hall was full and the students were sitting at their house tables, Sir Ragnarok stood up.

'Good morning Dragamas!'

'Good morning Sir Ragnarok,' the students chorused back to him.

'Students of Dragamas, I am pleased to present General Altair of the Snorgcadell to you this morning. He has some very good news about the Angel of 'El Horidore that we have been seeking.'

General Altair stood up stretching his hands in front of him. He was taller than Sammy remembered.

'Thank you Sir Ragnarok,' said General Altair. 'The Snorgcadell received some extremely reliable information that the Angel whistle created by King Serberon's dwarves as a wedding present to his wife, Queen Helena Horidore, has been found. I am delighted to inform you all that the

Angel of 'El Horidore is now finally within our grasp,' General Altair finished dramatically.

There was a gasp from every student sitting at the house tables. No one moved and everyone's attention was firmly focussed on the General of the Snorgcadell in his shining metal armour.

'Dragamas students have given us key information,' continued General Altair. 'Those who found it, please stand up now and come to the front of the hall.'

There was a shuffle among the fifth years at the North table and Serberon, Mikhael and Jason stood up and marched to the front table with broad smiles.

'My brothers found it?' muttered Dixie. 'No way.'

'This can't be happening,' whispered Sammy. 'Antonio said my parents brought it here. They can't have found it.'

'Shh,' snapped Gavin, picking up the salt and pepper shakers and tapping them together on the table. 'I want to know where the stupid thing was.'

Serberon, Mikhael and Jason stood at the teachers' table and General Altair leaned over to the brothers.

'I present you with the Cross of Bravery,' said General Altair. 'Usually this medal is bestowed...' he swung the first cross around Jason's neck, '...on individuals who show bravery, courage and convictions...' he hung the second cross around Mikhael's neck.

Sammy scratched the back of his hands in anger and clenched his fists. 'It's a fake, it's a fake. They haven't found it, they can't have found it,' he projected in General Altair's direction.

'...against overwhelming odds and great adversity,' continued General Altair. 'Finding the Angel, despite the "ease" at which you modestly claim, you three have shown true courage against our common adversary. The Shape.' Aldebaran swung the third cross over Serberon's neck.

'The future of dragons is safe!' he roared holding up a half moon shaped whistle made of pure gold.

Unable to take any more, Sammy stood up. 'It's a fake!' he shouted. 'Blow the whistle. That Angel is a fake!'

The whole school turned around and stared at the third year North table.

Gavin tugged at Sammy's jumper. 'You'll lose us stars you stupid idiot,' hissed Gavin.

General Altair turned from Serberon, Mikhael and Jason to face Sammy, his face black with rage. He stormed up to the third year North table stopping within three inches of Sammy's face. Everyone held their breath.

'I have been studying this item for longer than you have been alive!' thundered General Altair. 'Do you not think I can recognise it? Do not think for one moment you can tell me how to do my job. Insolence!'

'It's true,' Sammy shook, gripping the edge of his chair for support. He looked General Altair in the eye. 'That Angel is fake,' he stammered.

'You'll be telling me next if I blow it then no dragons will come here?' sneered General Altair. 'Your Uncle Peter Pickering would love that. Did he put you up to this charade?'

Sammy stared. 'No,' he whispered. How could General Altair think that he would do something like that. Up in the Land of the Pharaohs, Antonio Havercastle had been so sure it would be him, Sammy Rambles, who would find the Angel of 'El Horidore.

'Then we have a problem,' General Altair shouted and Sammy felt his cheeks burn with embarrassment. 'If the Angel is fake and it is blown, no dragons will come. Yet, if it is real, and my suspicion is that it is real, else I would not have awarded three Crosses for Bravery just now, then by blowing it all dragons living and dead will fly to this hall, converging for the Shape to conduct the worst massacre of dragons where all the dragons in the world will die.'

If the ground had caved into the bottom of the earth Sammy would have been grateful to be out of General Altair's tortuous stare and his voice thundering through the hall and out into the corridors. He was grateful to see that Sir Ragnarok had stepped up to the North house third year table and was resting his weathered hand upon General Altair's shoulders.

'Everyone is entitled to their opinion,' soothed Sir Ragnarok. 'We have all put equal effort into the search. Particularly with your parents being who they are, Sammy, I can understand why you care more than the other students. I believe you have even been told that your parents will regain their sight of dragons by rebuilding the Stone Cross with draconite.'

'It's a fake,' whispered Sammy. 'It has to be a fake. Antonio said my parents…'

'Oh-ho,' snarled General Altair, 'your parents' friend is in on things. No doubt using my own son, Commander Altair, as a pawn.'

Out of the corner of his eye, Sammy was grateful to see Dr Shivers, Professor Sanchez and Professor Burlay helping to usher all of the students out of the Main Hall and off to their lessons.

Sammy lurched forward as Serberon, Mikhael and Jason walked past his chair, shunting into him and whispering "green eyes", that Sammy knew from Dixie meant jealousy in troll-speak.

'I'm not,' he mumbled, knowing how much it looked like he was.

'You just wanted another Cross for Bravery,' hissed Toby as he left arm in arm with Gavin.

Even Dixie had her green eyes wide open in shock as

she walked quickly past his chair with Professor Burlay and Milly. She mouthed "good luck" to him and then was gone.

'You do realise when the Stone Cross is built with draconite that all dragons will have been killed by the Shape,' asked General Altair. 'How would your parents see dragons then? There would be no dragons to see!'

Sammy's heart fell into his shoes. He hadn't thought of that. He shook his head angrily and wiped his eyes with the back of his hand.

'Someone has fed you poppycock. I am sorry for you.' General Altair laid his hand on Sammy's shoulder.

Sammy looked up into General Altair's blue eyes with a jolt. 'You believe me,' he whispered, his forehead burning as General Altair projected his agreement.

General Altair nodded solemnly. 'There are people here at the school who are passing information to the Shape. We had to let the Shape know we think we've found the Angel of 'El Horidore. We hope they will reveal themselves. My son, Commander Altair will take this fake Angel to Silverdale where the Shape cannot follow.'

Sammy's head spun. 'You made me do this? You made me look stupid in front of everyone in the whole school?'

General Altair nodded. 'My son, Orion, is a good man. You would have been wise to trust him and told me what Antonio told you sooner, but I suspect Antonio would have advised against it.'

'After Charles and Julia, your parents, left Antonio's Hotel de la Pyramid all those years ago, for a moment we believed they were part of the Shape,' added Sir Ragnarok. 'I personally advised both Andradore and Antonio to exercise caution when speaking of the Angel of 'El Horidore and as a result it has made them both rather guarded.'

'We discussed the small possibility of you accusing us

that this whistle was a fake,' said General Altair kindly, 'but we assumed you would have been more discrete. However, as it happens, I am pleased with the results of this morning. Eliza Elungwen was a teacher here so there is no reason to presume there are not more Dragamas staff involved.'

'It would be the perfect disguise for the Shape to be within my staff. Imagine the knowledge they would have about our dragons. They could even control the birth of our dragons,' added Sir Ragnarok.

'So do you know where all the dragons are living?' asked Sammy.

'Yes Sammy, and we also know to whom they belong,' said General Altair. 'We know exactly how many dragons there are in the world and we know where they are. This would be valuable information for the Shape indeed.'

'So, your son, Orion Altair, isn't in the Shape?' asked Sammy.

'A likely story,' scoffed General Altair. 'He will return as Commander of the Guardians of the Snorgcadell when the real Angel of 'El Horidore is found.'

'Are you saying that Angel you're holding isn't real after all?' asked Sammy.

'Questions, questions! It's as real as those fake medals I gave out,' General Altair put the half moon shaped device to his lips and he blew into the whistle until his cheeks puffed to their capacity.

No sound came out and General Altair smiled and tucked the fake gold whistle safely into his pocket. 'This whistle won't call any dragon, ever. Take that I did not trust you as a privilege not a defeat. You may be the closest asset we have to the Shape on our side and I do not wish to put you in more danger.'

'Trust me,' said Sir Ragnarok, 'Dr Shivers and Professor Sanchez made that gold whistle for me this morning out of a ball of grey wire. It is an exact replica of the Angel of 'El Horidore on page two hundred and thirty four of your Dragon Studies textbook.'

Sammy nodded thoughtfully. 'So, I have to tell everyone this Angel is real, but I can keep on looking for the real one.'

'Please do,' said General Altair, smiling at Sammy, his blue eyes sparkling and serious. 'We must all keep on looking. Promise me you will contact me, or Orion, or Sir Ragnarok when you have found it.' General Altair gave Sammy a small black business card with white writing.

'Ok,' Sammy turned over the business card, which had the words "General Aldebaran Altair" on the front and a twenty digit telephone number on the back.

'We believe it will be you who will find it, Sammy,' said Sir Ragnarok. 'We will protect you where we can.'

General Aldebaran swept his charcoal grey cape around his shoulders. 'I hope to return when you have good news old friend.' He shook Sir Ragnarok's hand and they saluted each other, raising their right hand with the palm upwards.

A cloud of golden mist swept through the Main Hall and both General Altair and Sir Ragnarok vanished.

CHAPTER 32

RETRIBUTIONS

Sammy surveyed the Main Hall, the empty tables, the quietness without any students talking, shouting or running around. He remembered he had forgotten to say to General Altair that the real Angel of 'El Horidore was probably here at Dragamas.

In the far corner of the hall, Tom Sweep was brushing breakfast crumbs into a bright yellow dustpan. Captain Firebreath was talking to Mrs Hubar who was helping him stack the dirty dishes into enormous piles, ready to take to the Dragamas kitchen for washing.

They stopped talking when Sammy walked past and he made a lonely journey up to the North tower. He wasn't surprised to see Darius sitting on the bed tucking Sammy's torn duvet and ragged books and photos into some kind of order.

'They trashed your stuff,' said Darius. 'Me and Jock we held most of them off. It was Serberon and Jason mainly. I gave Mikhael a big thump and he couldn't get up for ages.'

Sammy looked at the mess. Even Gavin and Toby's

areas had been trampled on. Darius had a cut on his forehead and a bruised eye.

'They said they'd kill your dragon for saying the Angel they found was fake,' said Darius. 'That's where they went but I don't think they'll be allowed in.'

'Their crosses are fake too,' Sammy grinned. 'Leave the mess. We can sort it out later. Thanks for sticking up for me. Shall we go down to the Dragon Chambers?'

'Jock teleported there,' puffed Darius, sprinting down the spiral stone staircase after Sammy. 'He'll see his Dad down there. Captain Stronghammer will sort out Serberon, Mikhael and Jason. Don't worry Sammy. Kyrillan will be ok.'

Sammy resisted the urge to teleport and scrambled down the corridor to the radiator which concealed the North entrance to the Dragon Chambers.

Darius banged on the radiator with his fist. 'Let us in!' he shouted through the metal.

'Who's there?' demanded a female voice.

'Naomi, it's us!' shouted Darius. 'Me and Sammy.'

'Come down!'

The radiator swung open and Sammy and Darius made their way down the narrow steps.

Dixie, Jock and Naomi were hunched behind a large green dragon pointing their staffs forward. Sammy noticed Naomi grinning when she saw Darius.

'Serberon has been here,' said Dixie. 'They found out their Crosses for Bravery are fakes. Guess how!'

'They tried to fuse them into dragon scales but ended up burning them,' laughed Jock. 'They don't know nothing about dragons, even less than you Sammy,' Jock grinned.

'My Cross for Bravery will turn into a dragon scale?' asked Sammy. 'How does it do that? Why would you want to do that anyway?'

'Duh,' said Jock. 'Everyone knows that!'

'I didn't,' said Darius. 'Prove it! Get your Cross for Bravery Sammy.'

Jock looked at Sammy with respect. 'What did you do to get your Cross for Bravery?'

'He saved the school, identified Dr Lithoman as the "E" in the Shape and he stopped a poisoned lion from dying,' said Dixie proudly. 'Sammy helped get the money to pay the ransom so Dragamas didn't have to close.'

'Nice,' said Jock. 'I nicked mine from my grandfather. He took it from his grandfather who was there when the Stone Cross was built by his grandfather,' said Jock, equally proudly. 'Let's have your Cross a second and I'll show you how to do it.'

Sammy swung the silver grey cross over his head. He felt a bit ashamed when he wore it. Almost as if he couldn't be brave and strong without it, even though it had been given as a reward for already being brave.

'Wow!' breathed Jock. 'It's so cool!'

Sammy watched as Jock ran his hand to the centre of the Celtic style cross with the wheel head containing "X" shape of the crossed bars in the middle. He clicked the central ridge. The cross melted like liquid mercury and turned into a golden dragon scale.

'Cool huh,' said Jock. 'My gramps showed me this, it's a trick used by people who wear it as a disguise.'

'It's a bit girly,' said Darius flatly. 'Blue-green would suit you better Sammy!'

'Blue-green, that's like Kyrillan's scales.' said Jock and he ran his hand back over the golden scale so that it turned back into the Celtic cross.

'And Kiridor's scales,' said Dixie.

'Show me how to do that,' said Sammy. 'Do I just run my hand over...'

Sammy's eyes widened as the Celtic cross vanished and was replaced by a golden scale in the palm of his hand.

'You did it!' laughed Jock. 'Took me ages. You must have dragon blood!'

Sammy stared at the golden dragon scale in his hand.

'No wonder the Shape are after you,' grinned Darius. 'You've got dragon blood!'

Talking about the Shape sobered Sammy instantly and he remembered how important it was to defeat the Shape.

'What's our first lesson?' he asked changing the subject.

'Armoury's first,' said Darius holding up his timetable.

'Mr Synclair-Smythe,' spat Jock. 'I hate him so much and I wish Commander Altair would come back.'

'He will return,' said Sammy, picking up his staff and assembling it with the three gemstones shining at the top, his onyx, ruby and amber gemstones representing his first, second and third years at Dragamas.

Even though they ran from the Dragon Chamber to the Armoury room, they were late for the start of the lesson and Mr Synclair-Smythe greeted them with a frosty glare.

As usual, Mr Synclair-Smythe was wearing his green and grey tartan suit. He was examining a gold pocket watch attached on a gold chain clipped to the breast pocket of his tartan jacket.

'You're late,' barked Mr Synclair-Smythe, tapping the pocket watch. 'You are five minutes late. What do we do with people who arrive five minutes late?'

Mr Synclair-Smythe surveyed the students at their desks in the classroom. He ran his hand through his thick grey hair and stared at them.

'What do we do?' repeated Mr Synclair-Smythe.

'They lose stars,' shouted Gavin, almost leaping out of his chair in his haste to answer the question.

'Correct,' beamed Mr Synclair-Smythe. 'Two stars for

you Gavin. Jolly good! Well done boy! Samuel, Darius, Jock, Naomi and Dixie, you will lose one star each.'

'Great,' grumbled Jock as he nudged Sammy towards the remaining empty seats in the front row.

'Now that you have finally arrived, extremely late I must add, I was in the middle of explaining...'

'Rubies!' shouted Gavin. 'You were telling us about rubies and how to stop yourself getting frozen.'

'Correct Gavin,' said Mr Synclair-Smythe. 'Take another two stars! Perhaps we should have a demonstration. What do you think?'

Without any warning, Mr Synclair-Smythe raised his staff above his head. The ruby gemstone at the end of his staff glowed crimson.

'This is so boring, I could do it standing on my head,' moaned Jock as a breeze of red mist descended on the classroom. 'I've been able to do this stuff since I was four.'

In Sammy's opinion, it was lucky Mr Synclair-Smythe hadn't overheard since he was the sort of teacher who would relish the opportunity to watch Jock make a fool of himself. There was no love lost between himself and Mr Synclair-Smythe but with Jock there had been growing animosity against Mr Synclair-Smythe who never missed the opportunity to remind Jock that his dragon was dead.

'Try to move yourselves around the classroom,' said Mr Synclair-Smythe. 'If you can resist the power of the ruby then I will award you a gold star.'

Like Jock, Sammy found he was strong enough to repel the red mist and he walked almost normally around the desks and the frozen bodies of some of his classmates.

Darius was moving very slowly but Dixie kept up with Sammy and Jock. As Mr Synclair-Smythe slowly reduced the red mist, she started skipping and she danced her way back to her seat.

'Very good,' said Mr Synclair-Smythe. 'I will award every student a gold star. None of you have failed completely.'

When his movement had fully returned to normal, Gavin jumped up and down on his chair.

'Gold star! Gold star!' shouted Gavin, punching the air.

Sammy was grateful when the bell rang for Gemology and then again for lunch and once more to start an exciting afternoon playing Dragonball.

Mr Cross had an unusually energetic lesson planned where, instead of pairing the houses North and South versus East and West, he pitted the four houses free-for-all against each other.

Sammy realised how much he had missed Kyrillan over the winter when they had been to the Land of the Pharaohs. He loved the rush of the wind in his face as he flew on Kyrillan's back, swooping up and down the Dragonball pitch. Every time he scored a goal, he took Kyrillan up and around in a giant loop the loop to celebrate.

Sammy noticed that apart from Dixie, Darius and Jock very few North classmates passed him the ball and even classmates from the other houses stayed as far away as possible.

Gavin broke it to him in the showers with an arrogant grin saying they had put Sammy in Coventry for acting up in front of General Altair. Although Sammy desperately wanted to explain the situation about how the Angel was a fake, he had assured General Aldebaran Altair that he would act along with the story.

When Sammy didn't retaliate, Gavin merely laughed and pushed him aside.

CHAPTER 33

SCARS AND KISSES

Two days later, Sammy, Dixie, Darius and Jock were sitting on the green cushions inside the den. The sapphire protection could only just be seen on the perimeter.

The blue protection was much weaker than when it was new. But it still prevented anyone from coming in and that was just the way they liked it.

'It doesn't matter that I was right about the Angel being fake, does it?' asked Sammy.

Darius shook his head. 'Gavin's an idiot. He can't see past his Mum's dragon dying to see that the Shape must be stopped.'

'Sometimes I think "so what" too,' added Dixie. 'More Dragon Knights are back, but my Dad isn't. One way or another, if the Shape win, or we win, I want him to come back home.'

'We have to win,' said Jock. 'Otherwise my Dad will be out of a job. If there are no dragons then there will be no Dragamas. He'll be unemployed and we'll have to move on somewhere else again.'

Sammy nodded, he knew how much Dragamas meant to Jock, and to himself. There was no way he would have wanted to go back to the school at Ratisbury. The Rat Catchers would have moved on to the secondary school now but they would probably still be nasty bullies.

'I guess there's not much demand for mining dwarves who look after dragons,' said Dixie. 'Or trolls for that matter.'

'Or Healers,' added Darius. 'My parents would be out of a job too and all my studing so I can become a qualified Healer would be completely wasted.'

'Exactly,' said Jock. 'That's why we have to win. How are we doing with the search? Sammy, have you got the map of the school?'

Sammy nodded and pulled the piece of paper with the gridlines out of its hiding place inside his "An Aeon of Amber" Gemology textbook.

After Gavin had snatched the map and scrumpled it up into a ball, he had thrown it out of the window. Darius had found it in the castle courtyard in amongst a pile of leaves.

'Word is,' said Jock, leaning close to the treestump they used as a makeshift table, 'Mrs Grock's husband is coming back permanently.'

'I know him,' whispered Dixie. 'He served with my Dad. We have to and see Mrs Grock. Maybe he's already here and knows about my Dad!'

Jock stretched. 'You go and see Mrs Grock. I'm meeting Naomi at five o'clock to check on the dragons. Dragon Minder duties,' he added self-importantly.

Darius stood up to let Jock out of the den. 'Can you give her this?'

Sammy saw a small white envelope change hands.

'What's that?' asked Sammy.

'Nothing,' Darius shuffled with the maps on the

treestump. 'Nothing for you to worry about.'

Sammy grinned at Dixie.

'It's nothing at all,' protested Darius, as Dixie started laughing.

'It's a love letter,' teased Dixie. 'You're asking her out on a date!'

Darius went beetroot red. 'It's nothing like that!' he said, but neither Sammy or Dixie believed him.

Sammy smoothed out the map of Dragamas. 'There's still plenty of places to look for the Angel of 'El Horidore.'

Darius pointed to a blob near the edge. 'I'll look round the Dragon's Lair. Sammy, you take Mrs Grock's house and Dixie…'

'I'll do the classrooms,' interrupted Dixie, 'and the Girls' Towers. I think I can go in the North, South, East and West towers, if I pretend I'm a Dragon Minder.'

'I'll ask Naomi to do the towers,' said Darius. 'She's a real Dragon Minder this year.'

'Fine,' Dixie shrugged. 'If you think you can trust her.'

'Hey,' interrupted Sammy, breaking up the fight. 'That's settled. I'll search at Mrs Grock's house. I can just say I want to see at my parents' dragons.'

'Actually, I'll ask Naomi to help search the Dragon's Lair,' said Darius blushing again.

'Seems you've got a shadow,' muttered Dixie. 'Fine, I'll ask Milly to help search the classrooms. She gets away with anything so it won't be a problem getting into the towers. She'll probably want to search the Boys' Towers as well.'

'The more eyes the better,' said Sammy, relieved when both Dixie and Darius agreed. He wasn't altogether happy about involving more people but Dixie and Darius insisted.

'I'll find Naomi and start now.' Darius slicked his hair with spit and straightened his shirt.

Dixie grinned broadly when Darius had gone. 'There's

something going on there,' she giggled.

Sammy shook his head despairingly and checked his watch. 'There should be time to go and look at Mrs Grock's house before tea.'

'I'll come,' said Dixie at once. 'I can ask her about my Dad.'

The den shimmered as they left. They knew the protective bubble Serberon had cast wouldn't last forever.

'That'll need re-doing before the end of the year,' said Dixie. 'It's wearing off and people will be able to come in if we're not careful.'

Sammy nodded. 'It's been a good place to hang out.'

'We just need the blue stones we get next year to create the protection to cover it. Or I can ask Serberon...'

Sammy shook his head. 'Serberon's not speaking to me. Besides, he won't be here,' said Sammy holding open Mrs Grock's front gate, 'he'll be at college in September.'

'I know that stupid,' said Dixie. 'He'll have to do it before he goes.'

Dixie rapped on Mrs Grock's green front door, leaning up to look through the peep hole, even though it only let people inside see who was outside.

After a moment's wait, Commander Altair opened the door, his staff in his hand, the crystals pointed towards them.

'Oh, it's you,' said Commander Altair, lowering his staff. 'Come in, quickly please.' He barely left them time to walk over the threshold, before slamming the door shut.

'Your dragons are downstairs Sammy,' said Commander Altair. 'Be quick tonight please. We are expecting someone.'

Sammy felt nervous in Commander Altair's presence. He no longer seemed the ordinary Armoury teacher they once knew. Something in the way he ran his long fingers down his wooden staff seemed ominous and almost foreboding.

'Um, maybe we could come back,' said Sammy.

Dixie pushed Sammy towards the store room. 'We'll be quick,' she promised, flashing a smile at Commander Altair.

Commander Altair nodded. 'Your Mum says she's sending those things you asked for. I didn't ask what they were. Just make sure you keep yourself out of trouble.'

Dixie grinned. 'It's just girl stuff. Come on Sammy! Hurry up!'

Inside the store room, Sammy thought the shelves seemed to be fuller than ever. They were stacked high with large sacks of hycorn for the extra dragons living under Mrs Grock's house. Sammy picked up a steel bucket and shovelled the white grains out of one of the open sacks into the bucket with his hands.

'This hycorn stinks,' said Sammy, grinning at Dixie.

Dixie laughed. 'You should try living at my house. When my Dad was there, he had a huge green and brown dragon that could eat all of the sacks of hycorn in here and still beat Nitron Dark at Dragonball! We had so much dragon food Dad used to sell it to the Snorgcadell, that's how I know Commander Altair so well. He's been coming round our house since before I was born.'

Sammy grinned as Dixie paused for breath. 'Sounds really cool. Wish my parents did the...what?'

'Your parents probably did come round to my house!' squealed Dixie, hoisting open the trapdoor and exposing the stairs down to the underground room. 'Think about it. If they were Dragon Knights, they would have.'

'They are Dragon Knights,' corrected Sammy, not daring to tell Dixie about the knot in his stomach or the lump in his throat.

'They'll see dragons again,' puffed Dixie, slamming the

trapdoor open against the store room wall. 'Come on!'

Sammy lit a fire and dangled it ahead of Dixie as she marched down the steps.

In the underground chamber, the six adult dragons, Cyngard, Jovah, Paprika, Mrs Grock's purple dragon, Professor Burlay's dragon and Commander Altair's dragon, were coiled head to tail in a clockwise circle. Cyngard opened a coal black eye when Sammy stood in the chamber.

'They look in really good condition,' said Dixie.

Sammy nodded. 'They won't want to leave in the Summer.'

He scattered some of the hycorn in front of Paprika who turned her nose up at it hurrumphing and snorting, belching thick black clouds of smoke. She ate a handful of grains and closed her eyes. Within two seconds she was snoring gently.

'Oooh, they've already been fed young Dragon Knight,' called Mrs Grock, an imposing shadow at the top of the steps. 'Don't give them any more, they canna take it.'

'They get really bad indigestion,' explained Dixie. 'We did it to Dad's dragon as a joke once and it threw up right in the middle of a Snorgcadell meeting.'

'Oops,' said Sammy, wishing he didn't feel so left out. He kicked the steel bucket and stomped back up the steps unable to hear Mrs Grock trying to reassure him it was ok to feel bad that his parents couldn't see dragons..."yet" he reminded himself.

Sammy didn't notice the raised voices in Mrs Grock's living room until he was out of the store room and it was too late.

Commander Altair frowned at him and waved for him to go away.

As Sammy backed into the store room, he caught a

glimpse of the small dwarven man, no taller than Captain Stronghammer, who was standing beside Professor Burlay. The dwarf was wearing a long black cloak and he peered back at Sammy.

'Who's that?' whispered Sammy, accidentally bumping into Mrs Grock and knocking several coloured potion jars flying.

'Lucky they're plastic jars,' giggled Dixie, picking them up off the floor. 'Mrs Grock, you have to tell me about my Dad if "he's" home.'

Sammy found his head was spinning. 'Is Mr Grock back home? Is that who the man is out there?'

To his and Dixie's embarrassment, Mrs Grock sat on to the half open sack of hycorn enveloping them in a white cloud of dust.

'Aye,' Mrs Grock sobbed into a purple and white spotted handkerchief. 'My Alfie has come back here looking for re-enforcements. He wants the fifth years to be doing some volunteering. He wants some to hunt the Shape and some to hunt the Angel,' she sniffed.

'But it's good if he's home, isn't it?' asked Sammy. 'He's your husband.'

Mrs Grock sobbed louder, pulling off her bonnet and shawl. As her shawl fell down, Sammy gasped. Mrs Grock had burns and scars all down her arm from her wrist to her shoulder and under her bonnet, large tufts of grey hair were missing and she had bald patches.

'Did your husband do that?' asked Sammy, his mouth open in shock.

'I was so happy when I found John Burlay. I could put my past behind me and be happy again.' Mrs Grock blew her nose. 'What am I doing sharing my problems with you young 'uns. Forgive me. It will come right in the end.'

'Put wrongs to right,' whispered Sammy.

'Aye, that and all. Anyhow, you'd best be off. I have a lot of talking to do with my Alfie.'

'And with Professor Burlay too,' added Sammy.

'That's my business,' reproved Mrs Grock, her grey eyes twinkling. 'You can go back down the passages if you like.'

'Cool!' Dixie took control of the fire. 'When we get to the fork we just need to go down the right hand passage to get back to the castle.'

'The left fork goes to the Dragon's Lair,' said Sammy. 'Actually, we could go to the Dragon's Lair and meet Darius. What does he think he's going to find there that we haven't already found?'

'He's looking for the Angel with Naomi,' giggled Dixie.

'Ooch, young love,' chuckled Mrs Grock. 'Anyhow, I'd best get on. Alfie and I have a lot of...'

'Talking. We know,' said Dixie, stepping down into the chamber with the sleeping dragons.

As they reached the fork in the passage, Dixie stopped making Sammy bump into her.

'What?' Sammy asked crossly.

'It doesn't seem fair on Professor Burlay,' said Dixie. 'He's all right really. I know we muck about in his classes but he's a friend of Commander Altair and a good person. Why did this happen to him? Mrs Grock will go back to her husband who burns her arms and pulls out her hair. That's not right.'

Sammy shrugged. 'I don't know. Just the way it is, I suppose. Bad things happen. Like the fire at my Uncle's house.'

'Yes, but it's not right,' said Dixie. 'Do you think maybe Alfie knows something about my Dad?'

'Or something to help my parents,' added Sammy. 'Come on, it's this way.'

'I'm going to ask him tomorrow if I can,' said Dixie.

'He's bound to be staying at Mrs Grock's house now.'

'Do you reckon anyone else knows about all these passages?' asked Sammy.

'Of course they do,' said Dixie. She bent down and picked up a cigarette packet. 'Look at this! Someone's even dropped some litter down here.'

'Alfie Grock's been here,' whispered Sammy.

'How do you know?' asked Dixie reaching down.

Sammy took her hand. 'He smokes and I recognise the smell from the pyramid. Maybe he's in the Shape.'

'Unlikely,' scoffed Dixie. 'The guy who stole Mary-Beth from Serberon smoked these. It's probably him, maybe he hasn't left Dragamas. Maybe he's in the Shape too!' she giggled. 'Hey look, there's Darius over there.'

Sammy hoisted himself up out of the passage, finding they had emerged between two of the milk white "Dragon Teeth" stones guarding the mouth of the Dragon's Lair.

Below them, Darius was sitting on the bottom step up to their ledge, his face leaning close to Naomi's face. Dixie pressed close to Sammy's side, her right index finger pressed against her mouth.

'It's like this,' said Naomi. 'You turn your head to the left and put your hand...here.'

Darius leaned closer. 'Like this,' he whispered huskily.

Although it was nearly dark, Sammy saw Darius tilt his head and crash against Naomi's cheek. He let out a huge laugh sending Dixie into hysterics.

'French kissing for beginners,' giggled Dixie. 'It's in this month's SuperWoman magazine!'

'What magazine?' asked Sammy, horrified such things existed. Life had been simple with Dixie and Milly as friends but suddenly it seemed much more was expected.

In that split second, Darius had angrily flung himself away from Naomi tripping over a stone that sent him flying over backwards into a pile of leaves.

Darius rubbed his mouth. 'What are you doing here?'

'We've come to help you search for the Angel,' giggled Dixie.

'He has found her,' said Naomi, holding out her arms and pointing to herself, 'me!'

Sammy bent double with laughter.

'Darius said he wanted to find an Angel and I said I would be her. How much did you see?' Naomi held the magazine behind her back.

Sammy said "nothing" at exactly the same time Dixie said "everything" which sent Darius into one of his famous explosive giggles. Naomi slapped Darius with the magazine in disgust.

'Grow up,' she scolded, mouthing "watch it" to Dixie, who ran a pretend zip across her mouth.

'So, how much did you see?' asked Darius on the way back to the castle.

Sammy copied Dixie's zip motion with his index finger and thumb squashed together. 'Come on, it's chicken and fried potato for tea,' he grinned focussing hard on the meal so that Darius couldn't read his mind.

CHAPTER 34

STAYING FOR EASTER

A few days later, Sammy spent the entire weekend thoroughly exploring both inside Mrs Grock's house and in her garden, including inspecting the chicken run and the vegetable patch. The chickens objected to him rummaging amongst their hay bedding and started squawking and clucking very loudly.

Sam even leaned over the edge of her Wishing Well to see as far as he could down the well. This wasn't very successful as Mrs Grock came running out of her cottage to find out what on earth he was doing.

'You canna do that Sammy!' said Mrs Grock, hauling Sammy out of the well. 'And what have you done to upset all of my chickens? Be off with you young Dragon Knight. I don't know, whatever will be next?'

After being sent on his way, Sammy had explored the Dragon's Lair. He had scoured every inch inside the cavernous mouth-like entrance and checked around all of the milk white teeth stones.

During the weekend, Sammy had also visited most of

the classrooms inside the castle with Dixie, Darius and Naomi.

Darius carried his map and a list of the classrooms and as they searched through each classroom, Naomi crossed them off one by one using a thick black marker pen.

The number of places where the Angel of 'El Horidore could possibly have been hidden was gradually getting smaller and smaller.

Gavin met them coming out of the Armoury classroom.

'You're wasting your time looking in there!' Gavin sneered. 'Sir Ragnarok has already told us the Angel of 'El Horidore has been found. It's in his office.'

Sammy wasn't put off by Gavin in the slightest and between himself, Dixie, Darius and Naomi, they scoured every inch of the castle. They searched everywhere, from Dr Shivers' cold, windowless, Dragon Studies classroom in room fifty-five in the East wing, to the darkest depths of the dwarven miners' homes under the West tower.

Jock had helped distract his parents and the team of miners to give Sammy and Darius the chance to sneak into the miners' quarters and search through the rooms.

Sammy had felt a little uncomfortable entering the dwarves' homes without permission. Darius was quick to point out that the dwarves ransacked the earth for gemstones, so what they were doing didn't seem so bad.

Other than two shimmering pieces of blue-green draconite in Jock's parents' double room with ensuite bathroom, they found nothing to help with their search for the Angel of 'El Horidore.

'You've got to bear in mind that you may not find it,' said Professor Burlay calmly one Thursday afternoon as Sammy stayed behind after Astronomics for the fourth time to ask if he could search on the telescope balcony.

'I have to look everywhere,' said Sammy. 'Sir Ragnarok

said it would be me who finds it. I'm letting everyone down by not finding the real Angel of 'El Horidore.'

'Just because your parents were the last to handle the Angel, ten years before you were born!' exclaimed Professor Burlay, scratching his head in disbelief.

'Yes,' said Sammy, feeling stupid. 'If I find it, then the Shape won't kill all of the dragons.'

'Have they killed them all?' asked Professor Burlay kindly. He opened the door to the balcony and stepped outside.

Sammy looked at the floor. 'No Sir, but they are killing our dragons one by one.'

'The tide will turn in our favour,' said Professor Burlay casting a glance up to the sky. 'Look at the sky. The answers are up there.'

Sammy didn't have to look up at the sky. He already knew there were several hundred tiny red dots circling the Dragamas constellation, where the familiar North, South, East and West stars protected the dragons.

'With so many of us looking for the whistle, the Angel of 'El Horidore really has no choice but to be found,' said Professor Burlay firmly. 'The remaining question is whether it will be us who find the whistle, or the Shape.'

Sammy shook his head. 'Since General Aldebaran Altair said the Angel of 'El Horidore has been found, most people have stopped looking for it.'

'Do you think that was a mistake?' asked Professor Burlay. 'What would you have done instead?'

'I wouldn't have told everyone to stop looking for it,' said Sammy. He kicked the base of the nearest telescope in frustration.

Professor Burlay gave Sammy a disapproving look but didn't deduct any stars.

As the Easter holiday approached, Sammy grew more

and more concerned about needing to find the Angel of 'El Horidore. At breakfast one morning, he went up to the teachers' table and asked Sir Ragnarok for permission to stay at Dragamas over the Easter holiday.

'I will write to your parents,' said Sir Ragnarok. 'However, I am almost certain they will want you to visit them in Switzerland. Don't you want to see your sister and your new home?'

Sammy shook his head. 'I need to find the Angel, Sir,' he said to his headmaster. 'I can spend the whole of the summer holiday with my parents. They'll be really busy with my baby sister and their work. I want to stay here and carry on searching for the Angel of 'El Horidore. Please will you ask them for me?'

'Very well,' said Sir Ragnarok nodding his agreement. 'I am truly convinced it will be you who finds the Angel of 'El Horidore. Leave it with me and I will see what can be done for you to stay here over the holiday.'

Later that day, a long letter was written by Sir Ragnarok and sent to Sammy's parents in Switzerland. Then, a few days later, Captain Firebreath interrupted an Alchemistry lesson and called Sammy out of the classroom.

'Yer to go up to Sir Ragnarok's office,' growled Captain Firebreath. 'Telephone call for yer.'

'You may go Sammy,' said Professor Sanchez. 'You will read chapters fourteen, fifteen and sixteen and answer the questions on page two hundred and twelve as your homework from this lesson. It may come up in your exam,' she added ominously.

Escorted by Captain Firebreath, Sammy marched through the Main Hall, through the tapestry and up Sir Ragnarok's spiral staircase.

Captain Firebreath knocked importantly three times on Sir Ragnarok's office door. The door swung open and

Lariston greeted them.

'Right-o Sammy,' said Captain Firebreath. 'Here yer are.'

'Thank you,' said Sammy, watching as the flame haired dwarf clomped back down the stairs.

Lariston nudged Sammy's knee and Sammy stepped into Sir Ragnarok's office. He climbed the short flight of stairs and stepped into the circular room.

Sir Ragnarok was sitting at his desk, which was empty, except for a large red telephone. Sir Ragnarok had the handset close to his ear and was talking quietly. When Sammy arrived, he looked up and smiled.

'Here you are Sammy,' said Sir Ragnarok. 'I have your parents on the line.'

'Thank you,' said Sammy, taking the handset from his headmaster. 'Hi Mum. Hi Dad. How are you?'

Sammy spent nearly an hour on the telephone with his parents catching up on their news and telling them about his friends and his lessons.

Every so often, Sir Ragnarok would take the handset and chat with Charles and Julia, reassuring them that Sammy would be fine.

Finally, after much persuasion from Sammy and a little persuasion from Sir Ragnarok, Charles and Julia Rambles both eventually agreed that Sammy could stay at school for Easter.

Sammy felt awful knowing that he couldn't explain the real reason why he wanted to stay. He desperately wanted to tell his parents that he needed to stay at Dragamas over the holiday to keep searching for the Angel of 'El Horidore. But he knew they wouldn't know what it was, or why it mattered so much, so he said nothing about it.

It wasn't that Sammy didn't want to go to Switzerland. He was looking forward to seeing their new house and he did want to see his parents and baby Eliza.

'Yes,' Sammy told his parents. 'Of course I'll miss you until the summer holiday comes around.'

Eventually, Charles and Julia were satisfied that Sammy would be revising for his exams during the holiday and they were happy to let him study so he could achieve the best exam results as he possibly could.

'Thank you Sir Ragnarok,' said Sammy, after he put the handset back on the telephone. 'I won't let you down.'

Sir Ragnarok nodded and put the red telephone back into one of his desk drawers.

'I know you won't Sammy,' said Sir Ragnarok. 'But this quest will not be easy.'

CHAPTER 35

ALFIE GROCK AND JACOB DEANE

As it turned out, Sammy wasn't the only person who wanted to stay at Dragamas for the Easter holiday. As he finished breakfast one morning, Sammy noticed he had a shoelace undone and stopped by the teachers' table to tie it back up.

As he stooped down, he overheard Professor Burlay asking Sir Ragnarok which members of staff were on the Easter holiday staff rota to look after the students who were staying.

'The answer is "no",' said Sir Ragnarok. 'I have made out the rota so that everyone takes a fair turn. If I start making changes it will interrupt other members of staff's plans for the holiday.'

'I could swap with Professor Sanchez,' said Professor Burlay hopefully. 'She could take Simon on holiday somewhere.'

'Professor Sanchez and her husband are already taking Simon away this Easter,' said Sir Ragnarok. 'No, my mind is made up. You shall go up to the Floating Circus as usual.'

'But I have things to sort out here,' said Professor Burlay, and it sounded to Sammy almost as though his Astronomics teacher was begging the headmaster. 'I need to see Elsie. I have to sort things out with her.'

Sir Ragnarok shook his head. 'She has things of her own to resolve with Alfie Grock that would be much better accomplished with you giving her some space. She will still be here when you come back from the Floating Circus. Besides, Molly and your mother will both want to see you and I would very much like to try some of their new candyfloss. Perhaps you would be so kind as to bring some back for me?'

Professor Burlay laughed. 'The candyfloss is very good. Very well, perhaps you're right that I should give Elsie some more time. I will go up to the Floating Circus.'

'Dr Shivers will be responsible while you are away for any North boys and girls wishing to stay at school,' said Sir Ragnarok. 'He has informed me that he needs to catch up on paperwork for a meeting with the board examiner for the Dragon Studies end of year exams.'

Professor Burlay nodded. 'I must do the same.'

'You are still going to the Floating Circus,' said Sir Ragnarok kindly. 'Try and enjoy yourself, John.'

Sammy stood up and joined the procession of students leaving the Main Hall. He rather suspected Dr Shivers had other reasons for wanting to stay at the castle.

Unlike some of the other teachers, Dr Shivers had never mentioned having a partner, or a family, or indeed anything at all to suggest he had a life outside of the school.

When Sammy got to the North tower third year boys' room, everyone was packing up and getting ready to go home for the holiday. Sammy helped Darius pack up his things and went downstairs with his friends to say goodbye.

'See you Sammy!' said Darius, dancing out of the castle

courtyard arm in arm with Naomi. 'We're staying with my parents in their new minibus.'

They ran down the castle driveway, clutching their staffs and small rucksacks with holiday clothes and textbooks. Sammy ran all the way to the castle gates with them, even though he was definitely staying at Dragamas.

Sammy looked out of the shimmering gold bubble protecting the school. He saw Darius's parents' brand new minibus arrive and park in the layby opposite the school gates.

The Murphy family minibus was still painted in the bright purple, orange and lime green colours, but it seemed bigger and had a brand new registration plate.

The words "Murphy Family Dragon Healers – Looking After Your Dragons Since 1980" still appeared on the side of the minibus, but now they were printed in large white letters instead of blue.

A man got out of the minibus. He was the spitting image of Darius with short dark curly hair and dressed in dark trousers and a dark shirt. He greeted Darius and Naomi with a firm handshake and led them across the road to the minibus.

Darius dragged open the minibus door and jumped inside. He helped Naomi up the step and budged up the other passengers so they could sit together.

With hands waving out of every window, the multi-coloured minibus swept off down the country lane kicking up a cloud of dust in its wake.

Darius and Naomi were among the last to leave and Sammy felt a little bit lonely when they had gone.

Dixie and her brothers had left just after breakfast. Dixie was extremely excited about the Easter holiday, telling anyone who would listen that she was going on a skiing trip with Serberon, Mikhael and Jason as a treat before her brothers' final fifth year exams.

After Darius and Naomi had left, Sammy returned to the North tower common room and sat alone on one of the large green beanbags. He found one of the issues of Naomi's SuperWoman magazine and thumbed through it mindlessly.

Sammy grinned to himself as he read the problem pages where readers sent letters to the magazine and an agony aunt, called Aunty Susie, did her best to answer them.

In one letter, a girl named Carly had been trying to get on her dragon's back, but had tripped over a stone and fallen over in some mud in front of a boy she fancied.

In the next letter, another girl had been overheard by her brother's best friend while she was talking to her dragon egg.

Both girls wanted advice on these problems and Aunty Susie in the magazine had some very good answers that Sammy felt could be genuinely useful in the future.

What caught his eye was a feature article that could have been sent in by Gavin since it was about the death of a dragon in the family.

Sammy felt a lump in his throat as he remembered the day in the field when they had found the remains of Anita Reed's dragon.

Sammy flipped to the next page and it was some sort of fashion page that was advertising more handbags and shoes than he had seen in his entire life. He shut the magazine quickly as Jock thundered into the North tower common room.

'Just us two!' shouted Jock jumping on the sofa. 'We've got the whole castle to ourselves for two whole weeks!'

'Has everyone else gone?' asked Sammy.

Jock nodded. 'Doesn't bother me. I'm used to it with my Mum being a teacher and my Dad always working in the mines. I'm always at school but Dragamas is by far the best school I've ever been to.'

'I kind of wish I was with my parents,' said Sammy, 'but they're working and my baby sister Eliza has got a full time nanny who doesn't like boys.'

'You could teleport over there,' said Jock. 'Teleporting probably works abroad. I've never tried it though.'

'Me neither,' said Sammy, giving the matter some thought. He imagined the look on his mother's face if he was to teleport himself into their house in Switzerland.

'Oh yeah,' added Jock. 'Mum got us these Easter eggs. One's supposed to be for my sister, but she's in South and I'm not talking to her at the moment after she stirred up trouble, so I'm giving it to you instead.'

'Why is she in the South house?' asked Sammy, taking the football sized chocolate egg wrapped in red foil. 'I thought they kept families together? How come she's not in North like you?'

'Like Dixie and her brothers are all together in North?' asked Jock. 'No, what house you go into is supposed to be your destiny, you know, do great things outside of the world of man. It's in our letters.'

'Yeah,' Sammy thought back to his letter. 'My letter was at home, at my Uncle Peter's house, I mean. It got burnt.'

'That's really unlucky,' said Jock. 'Still there's no guarantee your parents were North.'

'They were in South,' said Sammy.

'You being in the North house must be Sir Ragnarok's idea then,' said Jock, grinning suddenly. 'You can reverse the polarity. South becomes North. You're going to undo all they did wrong...hey it was a joke!'

'But it makes sense.' Sammy stood up. 'I'll see you later. There's something I have to do.' He was already reaching for General Aldebaran Altair's business card, memorising the number almost before he reached the telephone in the Gymnasium.

The Gymnasium foyer was empty so Sammy let himself into the reception area. He put two silver coins into the slot on the side of the telephone and dialled the number. After just two seconds there was an answer.

'Hello? Is that General Aldebaran Altair?' asked Sammy.

'Wait there please,' commanded a male voice at the other end of the line.

Sammy waited, shifting his weight nervously from one foot to the other. Supposing he was wrong. General Altair would be very annoyed with him. Perhaps he should have gone up to see Sir Ragnarok instead.

As another voice said "hello" Sammy dropped the receiver and sprinted out of the Gymnasium and back to the castle. He bumped into a dwarf wearing blue dungarees and a white shirt on his way out of the Gymnasium foyer.

'Watch it,' growled the dwarf.

'You're Alfie Grock!' exclaimed Sammy, recognising the man. 'I saw you at Mrs Grock's house the other day.'

The dwarf eyed Sammy suspiciously. 'So what if I am?'

Sammy took a deep breath. 'Do you know anything about Dixie's Dad? Is he coming back?' he asked, feeling like he was taking a shot in the dark.

The dwarf looked up at Sammy, tucking his thumbs into his blue dungaree pockets. 'That would depend on who Dixie might be,' he growled.

'Dixie Deane,' said Sammy. 'Um, she's Jacob Deane's daughter, green hair' he added.

'Oh, Jake, yeah, he'll be back,' the dwarf laughed. 'Last I saw him, he was wanting to stay on. He wanted to find the Shape, stop them dragons dying. Left him to it I did, waste of time. I can send word if you like. Who shall I say's asking? What's yer name boy?'

'I'm Sammy Rambles,' said Sammy

'Rambles?' Alfie Grock seized Sammy's hands. 'You look a bit like him.'

'Who?' asked Sammy. 'Do I look like my Dad?'

Alfie Grock laughed. 'Nah, yer look like yer uncle, that's who. Peter Pickering was a dirty piece o' work if ever there was un, double crossing...' the dwarf paused mid flow, 'course 'e got what was coming to him, putting us up to what 'e did, letting who 'e did in my bed that North scum.'

'I'm North,' said Sammy, 'but my parents were South, but they can't see dragons anymore.'

'I know,' said Alfie Grock, flashing Sammy a gold toothed grin. 'In that case, I'll be off. Tell this Trixie, Pixie, whatshername, I used to be old Jake Deane's partner in the Snorgcadell and she has my word he'll be back,' Alfie Grock sniggered and marched into the Gymnasium muttering, 'Sammy Rambles, well I never.'

Sammy looked at his hands where Alfie Grock had touched him. They felt cold and sticky. He felt like he wanted to wash them in warm clean water.

Sammy shook himself and prepared to teleport. He needed to focus on his own task of getting to see Sir Ragnarok as quickly as possible.

'Outside Sir Ragnarok's office...please,' he added as the gold teleporting mist hung around him like a cape.

CHAPTER 36

YOU'RE ONE OF US

It took Sammy a couple of seconds, while the gold teleporting mist cleared, to realise he had just teleported himself to the top of the tower staircase outside Sir Ragnarok's wooden door at exactly the same moment that Dr Shivers was walking up the stone steps.

'Well, well, well. Good evening Sammy, what a pleasant surprise this is.' said Dr Shivers, straightening his suit jacket and stepping up to Sir Ragnarok's office door. 'Didn't Commander Altair teach you not to teleport on top of someone else?'

'I'm sorry Sir,' apologised Sammy.

Dr Shivers brushed his apology away. 'No need, I can tell you have important news for Sir Ragnarok. You may go first.'

'No, it's…' Sammy turned around and saw that Sir Ragnarok's smoke grey cat Lariston had opened the wooden office door and was staring at them both with his cool amber eyes. Lariston cocked his head, indicating for them both to follow him inside.

'It seems that we are both to go in to see Sir Ragnarok together,' said Dr Shivers gripping Sammy's shoulder.

Sammy nodded and followed his Dragon Studies teacher into Sir Ragnarok's office.

Sir Ragnarok was sitting at his desk as they walked in. He motioned for them to take a seat.

Dr Shivers took off his grey suit jacket and rested it on the arm of the purple sofa. He sat on the sofa and put his feet up on the coffee table.

Sammy noticed the bowl on the table, that usually held dozens of different coloured sweets, was unusually empty. He found himself wondering whether Sir Ragnarok had seen lots of visitors today, or perhaps the headmaster had an unusually sweet tooth and had eaten them all by himself. Dismissing these thoughts, Sammy took a deep breath.

'Sir Ragnarok,' started Sammy, 'please may I ask you a question about my parents?'

'That was one question. You mean another question I presume,' chuckled Sir Ragnarok, his blue eyes twinkling. 'A question about your parents no doubt. Have you found the real Angel of 'El Horidore?'

'No Sir, well in a way Sir,' began Sammy, trying to find the right words. 'Jock said that because my parents were South, I am North to reverse the...the...'

'Polarity,' said Dr Shivers helpfully. 'To undo what they did wrong.'

'Put wrongs to right,' added Sammy looking up at Sir Ragnarok, who had climbed on to his desk and was standing with his arms outstretched, reaching up to the top shelf on his bookcase for a large brown box.

Sir Ragnarok passed the brown box down to Sammy. It was heavy and Sammy placed the box on Sir Ragnarok's desk and held out his hand to help his headmaster back onto the floor.

Sammy peered into the box. It appeared to be full of brown leather bound books. Each book had silver numbers on the spine. Sammy guessed they were dates for annual yearbooks and that the books contained information recorded about the school and its students over the years.

'Over twenty years ago,' chuckled Sir Ragnarok, picking up one of the books. 'To think I'd be reading Sir Bonahue's notes one day.'

Sir Ragnarok picked up a large magnifying glass and hovered it over the spine of the book, reading the faded letters.

'Too early,' muttered Sir Ragnarok, 'much before their time.'

Sir Ragnarok rifled through the box and picked out another brown book. He opened the book in the centre pages.

'Ah yes, here they are,' Sir Ragnarok pointed with an orange pencil at two students on the far left of a black and white school photo. 'Julia and Charles in the South house,' said Sir Ragnarok. 'Look, there's the South emblem on her shirt pocket. Your mother was a "seer", I believe.'

'My Uncle Peter was South as well,' said Sammy, sitting down on the sofa next to Dr Shivers. 'Is that him standing behind her?'

Sir Ragnarok nodded. 'Yes, that's Peter Pickering. I had a letter from Aldebaran the other day. He tells me that the Snorgcadell believe Peter may know where the Angel of 'El Horidore was hidden.'

'Then we can find it?' asked Dr Shivers, leaning forward and mopping his forehead with a grey silk handkerchief. 'Finally perhaps we can get all this nasty business finding the Angel whistle behind us.'

'A false hope,' said Sir Ragnarok, smiling kindly. 'If Peter Pickering knew of the Angel of 'El Horidore's whereabouts, then surely he would have mentioned it to his comrades in the Shape? The whistle would have been found and the Shape would have used long before now.'

'Maybe they already know where the Angel is hidden!' exclaimed Sammy. 'Maybe that's why the Dragon Knights are returning. They have to protect the Angel of 'El Horidore because they know it's here at Dragamas.'

'A fanciful thought, that I worry to be true,' said Sir Ragnarok resignedly. 'We have searched and searched but the area is just too big and the Angel is so very small. It could be hidden under a floorboard or buried six feet underground. Although Aldebaran has not said it directly to me, I have often wondered if your parents did manage to hide it that day, before...'

'Before my uncle turned them over to the Shape,' said Sammy with venom in his voice. 'I hope he rots in the Dragon Cells.'

'Rest assured Sammy, I will tell you all as soon as there is more news,' said Sir Ragnarok calmly. 'It must be nearly dinnertime. Go and collect your lunch Sammy please. Now, Dr Shivers, what can I do for you?'

Sammy got up from the purple sofa. It was obvious his conversation with Sir Ragnarok was over. He had been told as much as he was getting told by Sir Ragnarok today.

He was worried that his uncle had managed to get word to the rest of the Shape from within the Snorgcadell and that even now, they were searching the school in the same methodical way that he was searching for the Angel of 'El Horidore with Dixie and Darius.

Despite all of the help from those who were still willing to look for the real Angel of 'El Horidore, the task of finding something so small was overwhelmingly difficult.

Also, Sammy thought, even though he had helped to identify his Gemology teacher Eliza Elungwen and his

Uncle Peter Pickering as members of the Shape, there were still three other people involved and no one knew who they were.

He knew the three remaining members of the Shape would stop at nothing to find the Angel of 'El Horidore and they would have no hesitation to use it to call all the dragons together. Then with all the dragons together, the Shape would kill them all and take the precious magic draconite stones out of the dragons' brains and use the draconite to rebuild the Stone Cross.

Lariston showed him to the door, purring gently and weaving between his legs as Sammy walked down the stone staircase and out into the Main Hall. The tapestry swung back into place and Lariston padded back up the stairs to Sir Ragnarok's office.

As hardly any students were staying for the Easter holiday, meals had to be collected from the school kitchen, which Sammy had eventually found, despite it being well hidden behind another tapestry in the Main Hall.

The tapestry was of a group of travellers sitting around a campfire. They were cooking their dinner in a black saucepan suspended over a frame of sticks. Behind the tapestry, there was a small, dark, narrow staircase leading into the kitchen.

Sammy stumbled down the rough steps, wondering why the passage was so badly lit. It wouldn't cost very much to have a couple of candles to guide the way.

He remembered the first time he had been into the school kitchen. It was an enormous stone floored room directly underneath the Main Hall.

Gigantic cookers were powered by the fifth year dragons, who took their turn in rotation to breathe fire into a pipe that fed into each of the cookers. It was in the kitchen that all the food was prepared before it was magicked onto the students' plates.

Sammy went to collect his lunch, hoping it would be something nice. As he reached the kitchen he found Captain Stronghammer was there with his wife, Mrs Hubar. They were weaving a silver mist around some freshly made sandwiches.

Sammy watched as the sandwiches seemed to melt and disappear. He guessed they were being teleported further down underground to the miners working in the jewel mines under the castle.

'Hold out yer hands,' growled Captain Stronghammer.

Sammy reached out, palms skyward, nearly dropping the huge plate of cheese and cucumber sandwiches that materialised in front of him.

'Thank you!' said Sammy, grateful for the mountain of food.

'Eat your lunch anywhere you like,' said Mrs Hubar. 'Young Jock's taking some of the dragons that have been left here over the holiday for flying practice, if you want to join him, he'd probably be glad of the company. There should be enough sandwiches for both of you.'

Sammy nodded and teleported outside with the plate of cheese and cucumber sandwiches. He found Jock on the Dragonball pitch.

Jock was riding Dixie's blue-green dragon, Kiridor, in circles, looping around the enormous Dragonball pitch with three other dragons in pursuit. Jock waved when he caught sight of Sammy.

'Get Kyrillan!' yelled Jock, throwing a small object down from ten feet in the air.

Sammy put the plate of sandwiches on one of the benches beside the Dragonball pitch. He caught the silver Dragon Minder pin and nodded. 'I'll be back in a second!' Sammy shouted and teleported himself to the entrance of the Dragon Chambers.

Outside the entrance, Sammy felt an odd sensation, like he was being watched, creeping up his spine in an icy chill. He looked around but couldn't see anyone.

Sammy clicked the Dragon Minder pin into the dragon shaped grove on the castle wall. The wall faded into the portcullis door that led down the stone ramp into the chambers. An odd orange liquid was splattered on the walls dripping down on to the path. Sammy ran forward, fearing the worst.

He burst into the Dragon Chambers and found Captain Firebreath rubbing a large grey dragon with a gigantic bath towel soaked in foul smelling soapy liquid draped across its back. Hundreds of dull grey scales littered the chamber floor.

'Got the fever this 'un has,' grumbled Captain Firebreath. 'He's losing all his scales.'

'I've come for Kyrillan, please,' said Sammy, holding his nose. The smell was unbearable but Captain Firebreath didn't seem to notice or care.

'Yer dragon is over there,' said Captain Firebreath, waggling a short soapy arm towards the darkness. 'Bin some funny goings on 'ere today.'

'Like what?' asked Sammy.

'Like that Mrs Grock's husband's bin trying to get in, 'e had some silver badge I didn't recognise, didn't let him in an 'e threw a wobbly. Chucked gunk at me castle wall, threatening like. If I didn't know better, I'd say 'e threw dragon blood at me.'

Sammy opened his eyes wide. 'Dragon blood?'

'Aye, and some Dragon Knight he'll be if it was!' growled Captain Firebreath.

Sammy reached for Kyrillan, a sudden thought striking him. 'There haven't been any more killings, have there?'

'Yer didn't hear it from me,' whispered Captain Firebreath, coming up a little close for Sammy's liking, 'but your Professor Burlay reckons there's somethin' in the stars.'

Sammy laughed. 'Professor Burlay's always saying that!'

'Just sayin' I'd watch me back, that's all. An' you didn't hear it from me if somthin' goes down,' growled Captain Firebreath, slamming the portcullis shut and almost catching Kyrillan's spiky tail in his haste to close the Dragon Chambers.

'Be back before dark,' shouted Captain Firebreath, 'and tell young Jock the same!'

Sammy leaped on to Kyrillan's back. He gripped his dragon's smooth scales with his knees and reached forward to put the harness around Kyrillan's neck. He was pleased to see Kyrillan's scales were bright and shiny, glinting the colour of mother of pearl in the sunlight.

Sammy tapped Kyrillan's flank with his heels and they set off, padding slowly at first, then faster and faster until Kyrillan's blue-green wings expanded. The webbed wings shimmered, taking the air current and with a final push from Kyrillan's front paws, they were up in the air and flying.

Sammy leaned on the harness, guiding Kyrillan to go North towards the Dragonball pitch. They flew over the castle and over the trees and swooped down to meet Jock, who was leaping in mid-air from an enormous dark green and orange dragon to a slightly smaller red dragon with gold spikes on its tail.

'Hi Jock!' shouted Sammy. 'That's really good jumping!'

'Thanks!' Jock shouted back, guiding the two dragons down to the ground. 'Why don't you have a go at some tricks as well?'

Sammy nodded, the conversation he'd had with Captain

Firebreath at the front of his mind.

'Do you know Alfie Grock, Mrs Grock's husband?' asked Sammy. 'He's back and has been trying to get into the Dragon Chambers. Captain Firebreath just told me.'

Jock took some treats out of his pocket and held them towards the red dragon.

'Here you go Sennen,' said Jock, lifting his hand towards the dragon's mouth.

The red dragon edged over and nuzzled his palm, taking the multi-coloured pellets Jock offered.

'Maybe I do, maybe I don't,' said Jock. 'You tell me what you know first.'

Sammy scratched his head, wondering where to start. 'Ok, we know he's Mrs Grock's husband. He's a Dragon Knight and he went away a few years ago with Dixie's Dad to fight against the Shape.'

Jock pocketed the treats and climbed on to the large orange dragon. He took off and circled Sammy and Kyrillan about ten feet above their heads.

'That's unlikely,' Jock shouted down. 'Alfie Grock is a dwarf. He hates trolls. He would have hated being partnered with Dixie's Dad. You've seen what the rest of Dixie's family look like. Her Dad is probably the ugliest of trolls you'll ever meet!'

Sammy laughed, picturing what Jacob Deane might look like. Perhaps an older version of Serberon, Mikhael and Jason with green hair, hook nose, towering over everyone.

'My Dad reckons all Dragon Knights are a waste of time!' shouted Jock, taking the orange dragon up and over in a dramatic loop the loop.

'My parents were Dragon Knights!' shouted Sammy, urging Kyrillan back into the air.

'Yeah, they "were" Dragon Knights!' yelled Jock. 'They're not Dragon Knights any more. I bet they were glad to lose the ability to see dragons. They have as much chance of finding the Angel of 'El Horidore as us now! Here, catch this!'

'Hey!' Sammy caught the ball Jock lobbed at him.

'What?' Jock grinned. 'It doesn't matter who your parents are or who they were. It doesn't stop us being good Dragon Knights. If I didn't know better, I'd say you were born on a dragon's back. You're as dragonish as me! You're one of the dragon folk. You're one of us!'

'One of us,' repeated Sammy, smiling broadly. He threw the ball back to Jock and did a loop the loop, his cheeks pink with more than just the biting wind in his face.

CHAPTER 37

ANCIENT AMBER MAGIC

After two weeks of spending every moment of daylight outside on the Dragonball pitch, Sammy felt as though he knew each and every dragon that had stayed at the school for the holiday by name, shape and colour.

During the Easter holiday, Sammy and Jock had taken all of the dragons out of the Dragon Chambers on to the Dragonball pitch to exercise them and to improve their flying abilities.

For Sammy, the best part of staying at school was spending time with his parents' dragons and his uncle's dragon, Cyngard, Jovah and Paprika. As far as he knew, he was the only student to be looking after three adult dragons. It was quite a responsibility.

The adult dragons were much easier to ride. This was because they had already been trained how to fly and they knew exactly what was expected of them.

Even so, Sammy found he had new muscles on the inside of his thighs and on his forearms from holding the harnesses.

In particular, his uncle's dragon, Paprika, was extremely strong-willed and stubborn. It took all of Sammy's strength to guide her and stop her wanting to fly out of the school grounds. He guessed she was looking for his uncle, but it would have been a disaster if she had escaped.

With Jock's help, Sammy learnt over a hundred Dragonball manoeuvres and, his personal favourite, how to ride bareback without using a saddle, then stand up and leap from one dragon to another in mid-air. It wasn't as easy as it looked.

One sunny morning, Jock arranged for fifteen dragons to stand in a neat line about six feet apart. At his command, the dragons flew up into the air, keeping their positions and hovering at about twenty feet high in the air. One of the dragons in the middle of the line started blowing smoke rings, which made it difficult to see where to land.

As Sammy jumped bravely from dragon to dragon, he wondered whether Nitron Dark would be impressed with his new skills. He also wondered whether sportsmaster Mr Cross would be impressed and pick him and Jock for the school Dragonball team.

Sammy couldn't remember if there were any rules about whether you were allowed to change from one dragon to another in mid-air during a match. It hadn't come up in any of their lessons, but perhaps, Sammy thought, it was a little bit advanced for some of the third year students, some of whom were still struggling to ride their dragons at all.

He didn't have long to wait for the answer to this question as Dixie, Darius and the rest of the Dragamas students who had gone home for the Easter holiday arrived back at the school.

The North students piled into the common room, flinging their rucksacks onto the study tables and sitting down on chairs and beanbags to catch up on the gossip.

Dixie and her brothers were buzzing with excitement about their skiing holiday.

'It was amazing, Sammy,' said Dixie, her green eyes shining. 'We were skiing, sledging, ice skating, everything!'

'It sounds great,' said Sammy, noticing Dixie had a few more freckles on her nose and wondering if his parents' house in Switzerland was anywhere near where Dixie had stayed. If it was, then perhaps his parents' house would be up in the snowy mountains and he could learn to ski and sledge and ice skate as well.

'You'd love it, Sammy,' said Dixie. 'Jason was the best at skiing, then me, then Serberon and Mikhael was rubbish.'

'I was not!' said Mikhael, ruffling Dixie's hair. 'I just needed more time to practice.'

'I've got a question about Dragonball,' said Sammy, changing the subject. 'Are you allowed to jump from one dragon to another dragon during a match?'

Dixie scratched her head. 'I guess so,' she said. 'I don't think it's ever happened in a match before. Usually the players stay on their own dragons.'

'Unless their dragon gets injured,' said Serberon. 'Then they're allowed to change to a different dragon.'

'Or, if a player gets injured then another player can ride their dragon,' added Mikael.

'I can't really see the point of changing dragons in a match,' said Dixie. 'Why would you want to do that anyway'

Sammy shrugged. 'I don't know. Jock showed me how to do it while you were away skiing.'

'Why don't you ask Mr Cross in our next Sports lesson?' asked Darius. 'He used to play Dragonball and Firesticks professionally. He'll know the rules inside out.'

Sammy nodded. He had checked his timetable earlier in the morning and knew that the third years had a Sports lesson straight after lunch.

After gorging themselves on too many fish fingers, peas, carrots and mashed potato, the third years ran to fetch their sports clothes and raced to the Gymnasium to change for Dragonball.

Mr Cross met the third year students in the Gymnasium foyer. His assistant, Mr Ockay, was sitting at the reception desk reading a copy of The Metro newspaper and drinking a mug of steaming hot chocolate that smelt delicious.

The biscuit tin Mr Ockay used to collect the watches, bracelets, necklaces and earrings belonging to the students was at the very end of his desk. Mr Ockay waved towards the tin without looking up. He had a pen in his hand and was deeply engrossed in doing the crossword.

'I hope you didn't eat too many Easter eggs during the holiday,' said Mr Cross.

'Me and Toby ate ten Easter eggs each!' shouted Gavin. 'We had chocolate for breakfast, dinner and tea!'

Mr Cross laughed. 'Well I hope it doesn't affect your game Gavin. I don't want to have any unfit players on my Dragamas Dragonball team.'

Gavin grinned at Mr Cross. 'No way, Sir. Me and Toby are well fit!'

Everyone laughed and went outside to where Jock, Naomi and the other Dragon Minders were waiting with the forty dragons.

Sammy was exhausted at the end of the lesson. They had spent two hours flying all the way around the Dragonball pitch in clockwise circles, then anticlockwise circles.

During the lesson, Mr Cross taught the third years several new manoeuvres he said they could use to create an attacking formation. Then he switched to teaching defensive formations he promised would help the team to prevent a large percentage of balls getting past the row of defenders and reaching the goalkeeper.

It was only in the last half an hour of the lesson that Mr Cross allowed them to play a game. While they played, Mr Cross was writing furiously on his clipboard, taking notes about which players were playing well and which players would be good enough to represent Dragamas in friendly matches for league teams to practice with.

Sammy was back on speaking terms with Gavin and Toby after he showed them how to do some of the new Dragonball manoeuvres he had learnt.

'Show us how it's done again!' yelled Gavin from across the pitch.

Mr Cross blew his whistle violently. 'No more! I have chosen my team for the friendly matches. There's no need to show off. We're going to give the Nitromen a run for their money! Game on!'

Eventually, Mr Cross blew his whistle in three short sharp bursts to signify the end of the game. Sammy was glad to jump off Kyrillan, take a shower and go back to the castle with the rest of the third years for their Astronomics lesson with Professor Burlay.

Up in room thirty-seven, Sammy, Dixie and Darius took their usual seat in the back row by the window. In the high ceilinged room, the large windows offered the perfect view of the castle grounds if the lesson was dull.

Professor Burlay spent most of the Astronomics lesson staring further into space and studying coloured spheres on his desk. Whilst most of the class had been satisfied that the Angel of 'El Horidore had been found and was now safe, Sammy knew Professor Burlay was using the spheres to try to predict the location of the real Angel whistle.

'It's almost as if the Angel of 'El Horidore has somehow been re-hidden,' Professor Burlay announced in the middle of a test on the planets' orbits. 'It is almost as if it has been protected by deep magic.'

No one looked up or acknowledged him. It was almost as though nobody except Sammy and his close friends actually cared any more.

In Armoury, Mr Synclair-Smythe also seemed to have lost interest in the search for the Angel of 'El Horidore. Every Wednesday, he had a copy of "The Metro" on his desk. The newspaper was always open on the jobs pages and the positions he was interested in applying for were circled several times in thick red pen.

It was now common knowledge that having been reinstated in the Snorgcadell, Commander Altair would definitely be returning to his post of Armoury teacher in September. As a consequence, and not that anyone really minded, it was clear that Mr Synclair-Smythe would be made redundant.

In the evenings, Sammy went over his notes with Dixie and Darius in preparation of the exams. In every spare moment, to Darius's despair, he went over and over their map of the school and all the places they had searched.

Just as Sammy was at his wits end thinking where on earth the Angel of 'El Horidore might be, Dr Shivers called him back at the end of a long dull Dragon Studies theory lesson about the types of food a fully grown dragon should eat in order to stay healthy and have shiny scales.

Dr Shivers checked that Darius, who was last to leave the classroom, was out of sight before he closed the windowless charred door and leaned uncomfortably close.

'I hear you're still looking for 'El Horidore's Angel whistle, when those around you have given up?' said Dr Shivers in a low voice.

Sammy nodded.

'I believe it will be you who finds it,' whispered Dr

Shivers.

Sammy rolled his eyes. 'So what? Sir Ragnarok says I will find it, but I can't remember anything, I can't see into the past to find out where my parents put it.'

'What if you could see into the future, Sammy? What if you could see exactly where you will find the Angel?' Dr Shivers chuckled. 'Would you allow me to help you? I can help you see things as they might become?'

In his head, the voice of reason begged Sammy to shake his head, "you'll manage to find it yourself" it told him, but instead, Sammy scratched his head and asked Dr Shivers what would need to be done.

'What indeed,' Dr Shivers smiled. 'Ancient magic must be invoked. Bring your dragon to me this evening.'

'Here?' interrupted Sammy.

'Right here,' said Dr Shivers conclusively. 'All will be revealed.'

'What time?' asked Sammy.

'Whenever you can fetch your dragon and meet us. We will be waiting,' said Dr Shivers.

His head spinning, Sammy left the Dragon Studies classroom and found Dixie and Darius in the castle courtyard. They were walking towards the den and Sammy ran to catch them up.

'Dr Shivers wants me to meet him tonight,' said Sammy. 'With Kyrillan. He wants me to try some ancient magic to try and see where the Angel of 'El Horidore is hidden.'

Dixie frowned. 'You need to be careful with ancient magic,' she warned. 'It can be really dangerous.'

Darius nodded. 'I'll have to cancel meeting Naomi to see this,' he grumbled. 'She's learning to play the flute. I said I'd meet her after she's finished practicing.'

Sammy rolled his eyes. 'The flute?'

'Better be good,' grumbled Darius as Sammy whisked

them under the protected opening to the den. The protective bubble around the den was fading to a pale blue shimmer but they were still hidden from sight.

'That'll need to be done again,' said Dixie, holding up a green nail varnish.

Sammy thought privately that she seemed to be painting more varnish on the treestump she was resting against than actually on her fingernails.

'We can do it ourselves next year,' said Darius. 'As soon as we get our sapphires we can create the protective bubbles.'

'I can't wait,' said Dixie. 'I'm looking forward to sealing up my room to keep my brothers out. At Christmas...'

'We know,' grinned Sammy, 'they came in and hid all of your presents.'

'I'll do it to them when I get my sapphire gemstone,' said Dixie. 'We've only got onyx, ruby and amber so far.'

At Sir Ragnarok's instruction, everyone in the third year and above at Dragamas received a piece of amber and everyone's amber had fossilised bugs inside. Tiny flecks of the remains of ants and creepy crawlies that had once been climbing trees were frozen in the yellow sap, hundreds and hundreds of years ago.

'We haven't done much with the amber, have we?' said Sammy, pulling the yellow gemstone away from the cluster of gems at the end of his staff. 'Woah there,' he blinked and looked again. 'Look at this,' Sammy held up the gemstone. It had turned a murky grey.

When he had last looked closely at the amber gemstone, he had been able to see right through it as if looking at something through yellow cellophane or through yellow tinted sunglasses, but now it had turned a dark grey, almost black.

'You use amber to see the future,' said Dixie. 'If you

hold it up to the light, you're supposed to be able to see things. You probably need magic eyes for that,' Dixie added gloomily. 'I've tried often enough.'

'I'm disappointed with mine too,' said Darius. 'My Mum sometimes uses her amber a bit like a timer so she knows when tea's ready. Or if they're trying to heal a dragon, they can use the amber to work out if it will be ok.'

'Dr Shivers wants me to read the future,' blurted out Sammy.

'What!' shrieked Dixie, dropping the green nail polish on to the leafy floor.

'Are you absolutely sure he said that?' asked Darius, looking very serious. 'It's worse than teleporting. You've really got to know what you're doing. It's very dangerous.'

'You said "no", didn't you?' asked Dixie abandoning her green varnish. 'Tell me you said "no". It's incredibly dangerous.'

'No,' said Sammy.

'Good,' Dixie relaxed and smiled. 'Wait, do you mean no to saying no, or no you said yes?'

'Yep,' said Sammy, grinning at her.

'You said "yes"?' shrieked Dixie, standing up and shaking her head. 'You can't do it!'

Sammy nodded, secretly impressed by the fuss. 'I can do it and I will do it. Dr Shivers said to bring Kyrillan and come at any time.'

'Double magic,' groaned Darius. 'You'll use Kyrillan's natural power with the amber in your staff. If Dr Shivers joins in, it'll be triple magic. Who knows what you'll see.'

Dixie looked keenly at Sammy. 'If you really are going to do it, will you try and see my Dad for me?'

'I don't even know if I can do...' faltered Sammy staring into Dixie's mesmerising green eyes, '...I'll see.'

CHAPTER 38

BY THE POWER OF

Sammy struggled to find inspiration to write anything sensible for his Astronomics essay homework. He was planning to write it and then go to see Dr Shivers. But it seemed that the whole of the North tower had heard about his meeting and were offering him advice. Even Serberon joined in. He gave Sammy a rusty amulet that was supposed to shield the bearer from any unpleasant visions.

Sammy finally broke away at half past eight with Dixie, Jock and Darius. They teleported into the North corridor, where they hid behind a long green velvet curtain shielding a draughty window until it was silent and all footsteps had gone past.

When they whisked the green curtain aside, Sammy took the green-eyed Dragon Minder pin from Jock and inserted it into the groove in the radiator to open the secret passage.

They collected a stubborn Kyrillan from next to the food bath where Sammy's reluctant dragon stopped eating hot oats, stomped his large feet and puffed blinding smoke rings around the chambers.

This caused a huge chain reaction as the other dragons reacted angrily to the disturbance and started blowing thick grey smoke rings of their own.

'Thanks Jock,' whispered Sammy, gratefully handing back the Dragon Minder pin.

'Anytime,' whispered Jock. 'I'll distract my Dad, you three come over with Kyrillan when I'm outside his office.'

Dixie nodded, stroking Kyrillan's nose. Sammy found he was angry at Kyrillan for stopping stamping and blowing smoke rings at Dixie's light touch. He cheered himself up with the prospect of seeing the future. At least he had been chosen and not Dixie for this special task.

They crept past Captain Stronghammer's office where Jock was swigging cider behind his father's back. He waved as Sammy ducked under the portcullis followed closely by Dixie and Darius.

'I'll see you later,' Darius apologised and coughed nervously as they got outside.

'What?' exclaimed Sammy. 'I thought you were coming as well...oh, I see,' he finished, as Naomi Fairweather stepped out from behind the rhododendron bush.

Naomi was wearing a low cut pale pink vest top and dark blue skinny jeans. Her hair was unusually perfectly coiffed and plaited in cornrows away from her face, which Sammy noticed, was covered in an extraordinary amount of makeup.

'You're late,' Naomi scolded reaching for Darius's hand.

'Bye Daz,' grinned Dixie.

'Unbelievable!' moaned Sammy watching them go. 'He's the best with crystals, I thought he was coming too.'

'Aren't I good enough?' asked Dixie, one hand on her hip.

'Uh, sure, it's just...' started Sammy.

'I think Dr Shivers wants you to go alone anyway,' said

Dixie, turning on her heels and stomping back into the castle at record speed.

'No wait!' started Sammy, torn between chasing after Dixie to apologise and asking her to come with him and not losing sight of Kyrillan.

His shimmering blue-green dragon had got bored of waiting and was following fireflies in the direction of the Dragon Chambers. At any minute, Sammy expected to see Captain Stronghammer open the portcullis and stop him from going to meet Dr Shivers.

'Ug!' Sammy threw his hands up in despair and set off after his dragon. 'Kyrillan! Wait! We have to go to Dragon Studies.'

Sammy reached for Kyrillan's scaly neck and leapt on to his dragon's back.

'East Corridor!' Sammy shouted and grinned as the gold mist enveloped him. He reappeared moments later in the dark East corridor outside of room fifty-five, the familiar Dragon Studies classroom.

In the East corridor, the walls were made of bare stone with black scorch marks here and there where misbehaving dragons had left their mark like graffiti.

Tiny windows with no glass let in the smallest shafts of light and underfoot, there was no carpet, simply the solid grey flagstones, some of which were burnt or broken, or both.

'Good evening,' a cool voice called out of the darkness and Dr Shivers appeared.

The Dragon Studies teacher was wearing a rich maroon velvet robe that covered him from the neck downwards, tied at the waist by a silver cord. The velvet was the colour of dried blood. Sammy found it dark and slightly menacing.

Professor Sanchez was standing next to Dr Shivers and she was also dressed from head to toe in the same dark blood maroon velvet material. Her robe had a hood that was spread around her shoulders like a scarf. Her robe was tied at the waist with a similar silver cord.

In Professor Sanchez's right hand, she held her staff with the multi-coloured crystals at the top. In her left hand she was holding a third maroon robe and two pieces of silver cord, one much longer than the other, which she passed to Sammy.

Sammy took the maroon robe out of Professor Sanchez's hands and found it was thick, heavy velvet in the shape of a rectangular sheet. At the top, there was a large hole for his head to go through and two smaller holes for his arms.

'And one for Kyrillan,' said Dr Shivers, holding out a much larger maroon robe that was the size of a large tent.

Sammy dismounted and put the blood coloured robe over his head. He slotted his arms through the narrow side holes and tied the silver cord around his waist.

Next, he draped the second robe over Kyrillan. It was the perfect fit over his dragon's scaly back and Sammy tied the robe in place using the longer silver cord.

Professor Sanchez nodded her approval. 'Come,' she beckoned. 'Come and see what we have to show you.'

With some apprehension and feeling cold prickles at the back of his neck, Sammy stepped forward through the doorway and into the dimly lit classroom.

All of the ancient wooden desks in the Dragon Studies classroom had been pushed to the edge of the room. They were also draped in more of the maroon velvet material.

Sammy found himself thinking it was like stepping inside a dragon's brain.

'Good,' beamed Professor Sanchez. 'You are focussed already.'

'We would like you to try to see the future with this,'

said Dr Shivers, the corners of his mouth twisting upwards as he passed a handful of silver to Sammy.

'It is one of the most precious Dragon Minder pins,' said Professor Sanchez. 'It is one of the two Dragon Minder pins held by the head boy and girl that allows access to any area of the school...any area you want to go into,' she added.

Sammy rolled the Dragon Minder pin over in his hands, smoothing his fingers over the cold silver. He recognised it straightaway. This Dragon Minder pin was the same Dragon Minder pin he had been in possession of earlier in the school year. It had two perfectly formed eyes made of diamonds that glinted at him, as if they were daring him to use their power.

'Why me?' whispered Sammy, aware Professor Sanchez was staring anxiously at him.

Professor Sanchez sighed. 'We have chosen you because my son, Simon, has tried and he has failed. Everyone believes it will be you who finds the real Angel of 'El Horidore. We believe you will need this when it shows itself to you.'

'Your parents were head boy and head girl in their fifth and final year at Dragamas,' said Dr Shivers. 'It stands to reason they would have tried to use the power within their Dragon Minder pins at the last possible moment before their capture.'

Professor Sanchez raised her staff and pointed the crystals towards the floor. Without her saying any words, a small fire appeared on the maroon velvet covering the floor beneath their feet.

Sammy leaned forward, holding his hand with the diamond eyed Dragon Minder pin outstretched. The flames were warm on his fingers but they did not burn him or ignite the velvet.

'Do you see anything yet?' asked Professor Sanchez casting more flames into the centre of the room. 'Point your amber crystal towards the fire.'

She turned her staff towards the lightswitch by the door. With a single green spark, she turned out the electric lights, plunging the classroom into a layer of eerie shadows that danced on the walls.

Dr Shivers started walking anti-clockwise around the fire. Professor Sanchez followed him, murmuring quietly under her breath.

Sammy caught fractions of the words as he held tightly to Kyrillan, pointing his amber towards the fire as Professor Sanchez had instructed. He wished Darius hadn't gone off on his date with Naomi and he wished he hadn't fallen out with Dixie right before coming to the Dragon Studies classroom.

He drew a little inner strength from the Celtic cross for bravery around his neck, a little comfort from Serberon's amulet on his wrist and finally reminded himself that he still had his staff clenched in his right hand.

'By the power of East and Air,' chanted Professor Sanchez swaying around the fire.

The flames turned bright yellow and fizzed upwards creating tiny yellow sparks.

'By the power of South and Fire,' Dr Shivers joined in and the flames turned red. 'Come on Sammy,' hissed Dr Shivers, 'you have seen the way this works.'

'By the power of West and Water,' said Professor Sanchez and this time the fire turned blue with tiny jets of sapphire coloured sparks appearing in the blue flames.

'By the power of North and Earth!' finished Dr Shivers, leaving Sammy transfixed, holding Kyrillan for his life, his knees shaking and the world changing around him.

In the corner of his eye, Sammy saw the flames blaze

emerald green, then they returned to bright orange. The orange flames rose high up towards the ceiling, giving off a burning heat searing through the maroon velvet robes.

The heat penetrated through the robes into Sammy's skin. His forehead was dripping with sweat and his hands were gripping tightly to Kyrillan and to Serberon's amulet for protection. Bravely, Sammy looked into the fire.

His vision was blurred but he was aware that he was no longer standing on the maroon robes spread out on the Dragon Studies classroom floor. His feet were on soft green grass in what looked like the woodland bordering the castle.

'What do you see?' hissed a voice in his right ear.

Professor Sanchez was standing beside him. 'We are in the clearing in the woods. We are where your parents lost their ability to see dragons. Look! They will be here soon.'

Sammy forced his eyes to open wider. The amber on the end of his staff was glowing. He could see the tree stump. He could see the cloaked figures. Then the pain hit him like a bullet in the back of his neck.

As Sammy fell backwards, he saw his father, aged fifteen, holding a gold, half-moon shaped whistle, inlaid with tiny sparkling shards. In the vision, Charles Rambles kicked the Angel of 'El Horidore towards the treestump.

Suddenly the vision was broken. The fire in the Dragon Studies classroom came crashing down onto the floor and went out instantly. Sammy's amber gemstone flew off the end of his staff and crashed onto the floor. He heard it crack into pieces.

'What is going on here?' a voice roared, the sound both distant and fierce.

Sammy opened his eyes and saw two blurred maroon shapes moving in front of him.

'Out! Both of you!' roared the voice. 'Get out!'

'Hello?' Sammy found his voice faint and weak.

Strong hands gripped his shoulders. 'Sammy! Tell me you're all right? Can you see?'

'Commander Altair? Is that you?' asked Sammy, his eyes slowly adapting and returning to normal. He saw his sandy haired Armoury teacher standing in front of him along with General Aldebaran Altair and Sir Ragnarok.

'We're here,' said General Aldebaran Altair in a very deep and grim voice. 'I believe we have come just in time. Orion, make sure the boy can see his dragon.'

'My dragon?' said Sammy, his voice high pitched and he was suddenly panicking. 'Where's my dragon? Where's Kyrillan gone?'

Sammy felt himself being shaken vigorously. 'Tell me you can see me!' said Commander Altair.

Sammy nodded. 'It's a bit blurry, but I can see you.'

'And Kyrillan?' asked Commander Altair. 'Can you see your dragon?'

Sammy scratched his head. 'I was holding him. We were by the treestump. Yes, there he is,' said Sammy, pointing towards his dragon. 'Ugh,' Sammy winced as Commander Altair clapped him hard on the shoulder.

'He can see his dragon,' said Commander Altair triumphantly. 'I told you Father. Sammy is capable of more than you expected. He is not like his parents who lost their sight of dragons many years ago.'

General Aldebaran Altair looked down at Sammy and Sammy saw himself reflected in General Aldebaran Altair's shiny silver breastplate.

General Aldebaran Altair grabbed Sammy's wrist, looking at Serberon's amulet in surprise and disbelief.

'What were you hoping this plastic would achieve?' General Aldebaran Altair demanded. 'You are young and foolish, dabbling in things you can neither comprehend, nor understand.'

Sammy stared at the charred amulet Serberon had given him. It was just plastic, another fake red herring from Dixie's brother. The amulet was a gimmick, a toy trying to make him braver than he felt.

'But I saw it!' breathed Sammy rubbing his shoulder which was sore from Commander Altair's grip. 'My father had the Angel of 'El Horidore. He definitely had it. It was in his hand. Then, then, he kicked it in...oooh.'

'What?' demanded General Aldebaran Altair.

'It's in our den,' Sammy whispered.

'Poppycock,' growled General Aldebaran Altair. 'I see why you hung up on me when you made your silly telephone call in the Gymnasium. You were wasting my time then and you are wasting my time now. Orion insisted I came here, but my time has been severely wasted if you think a boy in the third year could weave a magic so strong he could hide an ancient treasure that has been lost for many years. Goodbye!'

General Aldebaran Altair vanished in a thick cloud of silver mist that made Sammy choke. When the mist cleared, Sammy found he was light headed and angry.

'I know you'll find it,' Commander Altair tried to reassure him. 'We must all keep looking.'

'Fine,' snapped Sammy, clutching Commander Altair's arm as he felt dizzy standing up. 'I'll show everyone.'

'You do that,' Commander Altair smiled. 'Sir Ragnarok and I will put Kyrillan back into the Dragon Chambers. In the meantime, keep practicing your Armoury. I have a feeling you'll need all your skills before I officially return in September.'

'Fine,' said Sammy, putting the diamond eyed Dragon Minder pin in his pocket. 'North Tower.'

'North Tower, third floor, boy's tower, Sammy, be

specific, Sammy,' said Commander Altair.

'I'll walk,' snapped Sammy, wrenching himself away from Commander Altair's steely grip.

CHAPTER 39

THE GEMOLOGY EXAM

In the North tower, things didn't improve when Darius asked Sammy how he had got on using his amber to see the future, then burst out laughing hysterically when Sammy explained that his amber gemstone had cracked and broken into two pieces.

'You're not as good as you think,' sneered Gavin.

'It's advanced magic,' said Sammy. 'It's way beyond anything you could do.'

'Beyond even you!' retorted Gavin.

'Shut it,' moaned Toby, 'look at all the revision we're supposed to have done.'

'You should work much harder in lessons,' said Darius grinning as he held up pages of perfectly neat notes.

'Swot,' grinned Toby. 'Are you ready Sammy?'

'Ready for what?' asked Sammy, spinning out of his daydream. 'I saw the Angel of 'El Horidore. The real Angel of 'El Horidore.'

'We know,' giggled Darius. 'Your Dad kicked it and it's probably been found by dwarfs, the thieves.'

'Oi!' grinned Jock. 'Actually, it's a good point. I'll ask my Dad. Wait there...oi!'

Sammy looked up, his roommates were frozen stiff and a dusty red haze hung in the air.

'You're still not affected Sammy,' said Dr Shivers, smiling broadly in his gaunt face. 'Now please tell me, what did you see?'

'He kicked it away,' said Sammy. 'My Dad kicked the Angel of 'El Horidore away from the Shape.'

'I see,' said Dr Shivers. 'I shall ask Mrs Grock's husband to keep an eye out when he does his weeding. Now bed! All of you!'

'He's locked us in!' said Sammy looking despairingly at the oil slick wrapped around the door and five windows.

'I'll...fix...it,' said Jock, moving slowly and pointing his staff upwards. 'Darn...it...that...ruby...potion...was...strong.'

'Sammy...wasn't...affected,' said Darius proudly.

'Good...for...Sammy,' growled Gavin.

'Ooh er, touchy,' sniggered Jock shaking himself as the potion weakened. 'I guess I'll have to ask my Dad how to destroy the sapphire protection he used to lock us in here tomorrow.'

'Or your Mummy in Gemology. She found you another dragon egg yet? No? Some good she is,' sneered Gavin.

'Sticks 'n' stones,' laughed Jock pulling his curtain tightly, 'with sticks and stones I'll break your bones. Night Sammy! Night Daz!'

Only a few hours later, Sammy checked his wristwatch. The dial showed six am. It was too late to sleep and too early to get up. The oil slick sealing them into the tower dormitory had gone and they were free to come and go again.

Sammy sat up in bed and pulled some of his Gemology worksheets towards him, thinking he'd try a couple of practice questions before the exam.

The next thing he knew was the curtains being whipped aside and Darius grinning from ear to ear looking at him.

'It's another practical exam! We get to use our amber gemstones! Mrs Hubar wants us to find the Angel of 'El Horidore using amber to see where it is!' shouted Darius.

'But I already know where it is,' said Sammy. 'If I'm ever going to get the chance to go to the den and look.'

'That's where it "was", about twenty years ago!' cackled Gavin. 'It's long gone!'

'What if it isn't,' said Jock. 'Let's go and look for it!'

The tower door opened and Professor Burlay marched in. He was wearing his usual grey pinstripe suit with his usual crisp white shirt, but his pale green tie was unusually flipped over his left shoulder, as though he had been running. He looked rather windswept with his light brown hair askew.

'Morning boys,' he blustered, 'you've got Gemology, then Armoury this afternoon. Then Astronomics and Alchemistry tomorrow. Only a few more days and then you can all go home for the summer holidays.'

'We know!' shouted Gavin throwing his Gemology book at Toby.

'Life doesn't get any easier as you get older,' snapped Professor Burlay. 'You have to take some punches. Sometimes you have to take the rough with the smooth.'

'All good things come to an end,' added Jock helpfully.

'Quite,' said Professor Burlay adjusting his tie back into position. 'Now, please go down to the Main Hall, Mrs Hubar has prepared an examination for the whole school to take together. She says it will prevent cheating,' he added with a sideways glance at Sammy.

'All of us?' asked Darius. 'Where on earth are we going to sit?'

Professor Burlay shrugged. 'That's not my problem. I suggest you get yourselves dressed quickly and go down to the Main Hall and you'll find out soon enough.' The Astronomics teacher turned on his heels and marched down the stone stairs.

'What's wrong with him?' demanded Gavin.

'Lovesick,' said Darius, his eyes wide and dreamy.

Sammy knew Darius was preoccupied thinking about Naomi Fairweather. He thought Darius was a bit lovesick as well as Professor Burlay.

'Come on!' shouted Sammy, throwing his pillow across the room at Jock. 'Let's hurry up and see what your Mum wants us to do in this exam.'

Jock grinned and tapped his nose. 'I know exactly what's coming up in this exam,' he said, throwing the pillow straight back at Sammy. 'Good luck,' he added. 'You'll need it.'

Downstairs in the Main Hall, the students filed into the empty room. The house tables had been pushed back against the walls as if the room was to be used for an indoor Firesticks lesson. Jock's mum, Mrs Hubar was standing at the front of the room, her hands on her hips.

'Standing only please,' barked Mrs Hubar. 'This exam will be slightly different. I have devised a practical exam for the fifth, fourth and third years who will attempt to see where the Angel of 'El Horidore has been hidden. First and second years observe and take notes. Your marks will be based on your success. Are you ready?'

As the whole school chanted a resounding "yes", Mrs Hubar switched out the lights and drew the curtains. Amelia Hodge in the first year caused a scare by lighting a fire to see her notes.

Sammy raised the broken pieces of Amber on his staff thinking how much of a waste of time it was to see something he already knew where it was, or at least where it had been, in a vision of something that had happened around twenty years ago.

'Good, good!' shrieked Mrs Hubar as a boy from the front row produced a grey cloud with four people walking down an empty street. 'More!'

On command, Sammy found his broken amber glowed a pale yellow and he dragged his own cloud of smoke up above the heads of everyone in the room.

Aware that most people were looking at him, Sammy tried to bring the cloud into focus. With extreme effort, the cloud went from being fuzzy and blurry to a crystal clear picture.

The cloud above Sammy's head was filled suddenly with a television style broadcast of his parents sitting around a breakfast table. Eliza was in her high chair gurgling over a bowl of what looked like porridge. With a pudgy hand, she picked up a handful of soggy porridge and she flung it their father, hitting Charles Rambles squarely on the nose.

Snickers came from the second years but Mrs Hubar was not deterred and she ran through the students to Sammy.

'More! More!' squealed Mrs Hubar. 'Do your parents discuss the whereabouts of the Angel of 'El Horidore?'

Mrs Hubar rested her hand on Sammy's and it was as if she had turned up the volume on a television as Charles Rambles stood up, his chair creaking, surveying the mess on his face in the back of his spoon.

'Could do with a staff to sort this out eh?' he laughed. 'Your brother used to do this too!'

Next to him, Gavin nudged Sammy. 'That's awesome!'

'Just need to take her to Sarah's,' added Julia. 'I hope Sammy's ok. He'll be sitting his exams now, poor little darling. We'll have to sort something out as a treat for him.

He asked for a Dragonball set for his birthday. Do you remember we couldn't get it for him because we didn't know what it was?'

'Dragon nonsense,' retorted Charles, 'get him some stocks and shares or something worthwhile. It will be an investment for his future.'

'Honey, we do know what a Dragonball set is now...' said Julia Rambles, wiping the porridge off Charles's face. 'If Sammy hasn't already got one then we could get him one. We'll just have to ask him which shop it comes from...'

'Keep going!' laughed Mrs Hubar. 'Perhaps they will reveal secrets!'

Sammy grimaced. He felt violated. Mrs Hubar held his wrist in an iron vice. He was grateful to see out of the corner of his eye, Dixie and Darius usher back some of his classmates. The less they saw of his private life the better.

'Big Al says Dragonball is a game Sammy plays at school,' said Julia. 'He says Sammy is quite good at it.'

The remaining students laughed out loud. Other students had managed to create similar clouds and were laughing amongst themselves at the scenes they had conjured up.

'Relax Sammy,' whispered Mrs Hubar. 'You must sift the wheat from the chaff. When you use amber, you must decipher exactly what is real in the images you see. You must compare what is real with the things you imagine to be true and also the things that you might wish to be true. If you can do this successfully, then you will be a true seer.'

'I've seen enough, thank you,' said Sammy firmly. He wrenched his wrist away from Mrs Hubar. 'I don't want to see any more of this.'

'Of course,' soothed Mrs Hubar. 'A round of applause for Sammy Rambles. He has passed his Gemology exam.'

Everyone clapped and Sammy made his way out of the Main Hall fighting back tears. It wasn't fair of Mrs Hubar to pick on him. He felt torn in two, wanting to stay with his friends and wanting his parents to come back.

He didn't notice where he was going and walked slap bang into Alfie Grock who eyeballed him.

'Hear you knows where this Angel of 'El Horidore is,' growled Alfie Grock pulling out a smoking pipe. 'Want some?' he wheezed. 'You going to tell us where it is?

Sammy shook his head. 'No thanks,' he muttered stalking off towards the den to catch up on some Armoury and Astronomics revision.

Despite his good intentions to study, Sammy ended up searching in the grass outside the den on his hands and knees. He was desperate to try and find the Angel of 'El Horidore in the precious few minutes alone that he had.

CHAPTER 40

THE ARMOURY EXAM

When he returned to the castle, Sammy met Dixie and Darius and they ushered him back into the Main Hall for their next exam.

'Jock said Mr Synclair-Smythe is doing the same exam we did for Commander Altair last year,' said Dixie.

'He couldn't think up anything original,' added Darius. 'We just have to stand in the Main Hall while he blasts red mist using his ruby at us...'

'...and whoever gets out first gets 100%,' finished Dixie. 'We did really well at it last year, remember.'

Sammy nodded. He touched the ruby gemstone on the end of his staff, wondering if it was in the rules of the exam to create his own red mist and fire it straight back at Mr Synclair-Smythe.

With just forty third year students returning to the Main Hall to take the next exam, the room seemed much bigger. When everyone had arrived, Mr Synclair-Smythe held up his staff and pointed it at the sea of students in front of him.

A pale pink haze emanated from the end of his staff, growing darker and darker until it was red as blood. The red mist grew into a large red curtain wafting towards the students and slowing them down to a standstill.

Sammy felt it begin to take effect. His feet felt like lead and he had trouble breathing. He could still see and he looked around to see how everyone else was doing.

Simon Sanchez was already taking giant steps in slow motion towards the door.

'You may start!' shouted Mr Synclair-Smythe from the other side of the red mist. 'Make your way to the exit and you will earn your percentage score which will be your exam result. Remember, only one student can score 100%, one student can score 99% and so on. When we reach 80%, the rest of the class will fail. Half the class will fail this exam!' Mr Synclair-Smythe shouted the last words with dramatic effect and the students heard him laugh out loud.

Sammy remembered this all too well and he made a real effort to lift his left foot off the floor. It might as well have been superglued to the floor. His foot was so heavy it could have been made of concrete. He tried to lift his right foot instead and made small progress tiptoeing towards the door. Every movement was difficult and took a lot of concentration.

About ten minutes later, Sammy felt a shove in his stomach as he followed Simon Sanchez out of the Main Hall. Dixie was really close behind them until she stopped for a split second as well, then carried on through the double doors and out of the hall.

'100% Simon Sanchez,' called Mr Synclair-Smythe. '99% to Samuel Rambles. 98% to Dixie Deane.'

Dixie gave Sammy a dirty look. 'You pushed me back so you could come second,' she said.

'I didn't,' said Sammy. 'I wouldn't do that. I got pushed

back as well.'

'It was me,' said Simon Sanchez, grinning at them both. 'I pushed you both back just enough so I came first. My mother will be so proud of me getting the top marks.'

'Who cares what Professor Sanchez thinks anyway?' said Dixie, shrugging her shoulders.

Despite Dixie trying to act cool, Sammy knew that she would have liked to come first in the Armoury exam and have been able to tell both her mother and Commander Altair that she had been the best in the class.

On their way back to the North House common room, Sammy kept glancing out of the tall castle windows. High above the school, he could see the Dragamas constellation and the mass of red dots around the Dragamas stars. It reminded him that Professor Burlay had been dropping hints that there was an extremely strong possibility that the constellation would come up in some of the questions in the Astronomics exam.

'There is such a thing as too much revision,' teased Professor Burlay at teatime. 'Sometimes what we want most is closer than we think.'

Sammy felt the diamond-eyed dragon pin in his pocket. He had taken to carrying it as a talisman that had proved as effective as his cross when calming him in preparation for the exams.

Dixie seemed distant at tea until Sammy overheard her explaining to Milly that it was only because it was her brothers' last term at Dragamas and they would be at Kings College next year.

'You've still got us,' said Sammy, trying to cheer her up, 'and your Dad's coming home soon.'

'Maybe,' snapped Dixie. 'I spoke with Mrs Grock's husband, Alfie Grock, earlier and he didn't seem too sure what has happened to my Dad when I asked him earlier.'

'He doesn't like trolls,' said Jock. 'He probably wishes they were all dead.'

Sammy winced, knowing what Dixie's reaction would be to anyone who criticised her family being related to trolls.

Dixie looked at Jock and sighed. 'Well, at least I've got my tickets to the Nitromen to look forward to.'

'They don't like trolls either,' said Gavin. 'Still at least we like you, don't we Sammy?'

'Uh,' Sammy felt like he couldn't just say "yes", otherwise Gavin would tease him about him fancying Dixie again.

'Well? Do you?' snapped Dixie, her bright green eyes blazing. 'Don't bother, I know where I'm not wanted. I'll see you later.'

'Oooh,' giggled Darius.

'Couldn't you have just said "yes"?' demanded Naomi. 'And stop laughing Darius.'

'Oooh,' giggled Darius. 'Ow!' he squealed, as he got a sharp slap on his arm from Naomi. 'I'm sorry! Honest!'

Darius was led away from the dinner tables by an angry Naomi to a round of applause from Gavin, Toby and Jock.

'Come on, let's leave her and Darius to sort themselves out,' grinned Jock. 'Show me this den of yours, we'll see if we can find the Angel.'

'We'll come!' shouted Gavin, cramming as many of the chocolate bars and cheese and biscuits from dessert into his pockets until they were bursting. 'Come on Toby! Come on Milly!'

Even though he had spent time scouring every leaf inside the den, Sammy was pleased when Gavin asked permission to come into the personal space he, Dixie and Darius had created with Serberon's help.

Darius and Naomi turned up an hour later arm in arm and carrying two bottles of cola to drink.

'You need to fix this,' said Naomi, pointing to where the pale blue halo that had surrounded the den had now evaporated altogether, 'anyone could get in now!'

Sammy sat on the treestump taking his turn to swig from the cola bottle. As he sipped the fizzy drink, he rested his hand on the treestump. It felt peculiar, almost like a groove under his fingers, a queer shaped ridge that he thought he recognised. He stood up suddenly, spilling the drink.

'Watch it Sammy!' giggled Gavin.

'He's got ants in his pants,' said Darius, frowning. 'Sammy's wasted the cola.'

'It's here!' yelled Sammy. 'The Angel of 'El Horidore is here! It's got to be here!'

Darius stared blankly.

'What do you mean it's here?' asked Milly, flicking her hair over her shoulder.

'Look!' Sammy pointed to the dragon shaped groove. 'I bet there's a hiding place right here!'

Jock and Naomi fought to insert their minder pins into the hole in the bark.

'Mine's too small,' groaned Jock. 'We need Largo Oil.'

'Let me try,' shrieked Naomi. 'I'm a Dragon Minder too.'

Naomi pushed past Jock and thrust her emerald eyed Dragon Minder pin towards the dragon shaped groove. Nothing happened, even though she twisted and turned the Dragon Minder pin this way, then that way.

'Let me try with your Dragon Minder pin, Naomi. You're probably doing it wrong,' said Jock, trying to take the Dragon Minder pin out of her hands.

'Wait a minute,' said Sammy as they stepped back defeated. 'Let me try.'

'But you're not a Dragon Minder this year. You haven't

got a Dragon Minder pin,' said Naomi, her dark brown eyes wide as Sammy reached deep into his jeans pocket.

'I'm not a Dragon Minder this year,' said Sammy, 'but I've got this…'

Sammy pulled the silver Dragon Minder pin with the sparkling diamond eyes he had been given out of his pocket and lay it on the palm of his hand.

'Ooh,' said Milly. 'Sammy's got a Dragon Minder pin.'

'It's bigger than ours,' whispered Jock. 'Try it! It has to fit.'

Sammy bent down and knelt on the mossy floor. His hands were shaking. Sweat was building into tiny beads on his forehead and he could feel his heart pounding in his chest. He pressed the warm metal into the soft bark.

The Dragon Minder pin clicked neatly into the dragon shaped groove in the treestump.

'Yes!' shouted Sammy. 'It fits!'

Everyone crowded around and Sammy lifted open the top of the treestump. It felt like he was about to open a long lost treasure chest. It creaked open to reveal a small compartment hidden inside the top of the treestump.

Sammy reached inside the hand-sized compartment and his fingers closed around something solid. He held his breath as he brought his hand back out into the open.

'Wow!' breathed Dixie. 'Sammy, you've found the long lost Angel of 'El Horidore.'

'It's here,' whispered Sammy. 'The Angel of 'El Horidore is really here.'

CHAPTER 41

THE ANGEL OF 'EL HORIDORE

Sammy stopped breathing as he held shining arc. It was beautiful, a gold half-moon shaped harmonica encrusted with tiny shards of blue-green draconite. On the inner curve, tiny pin prick holes led inside the device ready to be breathed into. One single breath would play the sound that would call all dragons, living or dead, to this exact location.

'Let me look at it,' said Naomi, leaning forwards.

'No,' Jock shielded her away from Sammy. 'Sammy found it. He has to take it to Sir Ragnarok. No-one can touch it. It's too powerful.'

'Do you think I'd use it?' demanded Naomi.

'Let her see it,' said Darius rolling his eyes. 'What harm can it do to look at it?'

'No!' shouted Jock. 'Everyone get away! Stay back!'

Sammy held the Angel of 'El Horidore, his heart racing as Naomi, restrained somewhat by Darius leapt forward screeching to hold it. He ducked away and the treestump lid fell back into place, narrowly missing his fingers.

'We don't want to stay back,' said Toby, linking arms

with Gavin as they edged closer to the Angel. 'Let us look.'

'Stay back,' echoed Sammy stepping up on to the treestump he held the Angel of 'El Horidore in both hands close to his chest.

'Let's see it Sammy, please, pretty please,' said Milly, 'before you take it to Sir Ragnarok.'

'Yeah, let's see it,' said Gavin. 'We all want to see it!'

As they drew together in a circle around Sammy, Naomi screamed. Someone was there.

'Give it to me,' said a familiar voice. 'Or I'll kill her.'

Sammy swung round, a thick lump forming in his throat. Even before he saw the dwarf, Sammy recognised his voice. It was Alfie Grock, Mrs Grock's husband, who had taken the role of the new school gardener and regularly patrolled the grounds. He was holding Dixie at knifepoint.

'No,' whispered Sammy. 'Please let her go.'

'Give it to me,' said Alfie Grock in a low deep voice. 'Give me the Angel of 'El Horidore or I will kill your friend. Your magic is weak. Anyone can enter your pathetic den. Didn't you know that?'

'Don't do it Sammy,' said Dixie huskily. 'Don't give it to him.'

Sammy froze, ten million thoughts zapping through his mind. His eyes were fixed on the knife at Dixie's neck.

'Give me the Angel of 'El Horidore, or she dies,' snarled Alfie Grock. 'You're running out of time...'

'Give it to him,' whispered Milly.

'Do it,' hissed Gavin.

'He'll call all the dragons,' said Toby.

'Don't do it,' said Dixie. She was shaking, green tears trailing from her eyes as Alfie Grock held her tighter making her gasp.

'Three...two...' hissed Alfie Grock holding the knife with the sharp point ready to plunge into Dixie's neck.

'No! Wait!' yelled Sammy jumping down from the treestump. This was his chance to save Dixie from the Shape like she had for him. "Show no fear and they dissolve" he had once been told, but something in his head told him Alfie Grock wasn't going anywhere.

'Take it,' whispered Sammy, holding out his hand with the glowing half-moon shaped Angel whistle.

'Yeah, take it,' echoed Darius. 'Give us Dixie back.'

'What do you care about her?' demanded Naomi. 'Aren't I supposed to be your girlfriend?'

'That's just a fake whistle,' added Jock stepping forward, his arms folded. 'Some Dragon Knight you are if you can't tell a fake from the real thing.'

Alfie Grock laughed cruelly. 'You are ironic boy. If only you knew how I have searched long and hard for this. See how she glows, how she longs to call her brethren to her side, my princess.'

Alfie Grock flicked his wrist and drew a thin line of blood across Dixie's cheek. Dixie whimpered as the knife touched her but she stayed strong.

'Don't do it Sammy,' said Dixie resolutely. 'Don't give it to him.'

Alfie Grock put his free hand over Dixie's mouth. 'You, boy,' Alfie Grock turned to Sammy. 'This is what your Uncle Peter Pickering wanted. He was in the Shape, just like me.'

'It was what my parents tried to protect,' said Sammy. 'You'll never have it!'

'I'll get Sir Ragnarok,' shouted Gavin running towards the den entrance.

Alfie Grock smote him to the ground with the dull side of his knife. Gavin fell like a ton of bricks, crumpling onto the floor.

'Tackle him,' said Naomi, freezing on the spot as Alfie

Grock pulled a large ruby gemstone out of his pocket.

'Did you foresee this Sammy Rambles?' Alfie Grock spat on the ground. 'Did you? Now, tell me what happens next? Do you give me the Angel of 'El Horidore, or does your ugly troll girlfriend die like her Daddy?'

'I'll do it,' whispered Sammy. 'The Angel for Dixie.'

'No,' screamed Dixie and hers was the only voice left in the den.

Jock, Darius, Naomi, Milly, Gavin and Toby were frozen, their eyes darting wildly, held solid and still by the powerful ruby magic.

'I have to do this,' said Sammy.

He held out his hand, palm skyward. The golden half-moon shaped whistle was a dead weight in his hand, almost as though it didn't want to be offered to the Shape.

'My princess, I have found you,' cooed Alfie, taking the whistle in his thick, rough, stubby hands and kissing the device with his thick, rough lips. 'Now shall we see if it will be me, Alfie Agrock, who will make you work? Is there dragon blood in my veins?'

Sammy stood still. 'Give me Dixie, Mr Grock, I gave you what you asked for.'

'My real name is Mr Agrock,' said Alfie. 'You should have known that us dwarves have real names and names we use in public. This is a bitter lesson for you my young Dragon Knight friend, for you will not get what you asked for. No you most certainly will not.'

Sammy felt his mouth drop open. Flashbacks of being in Sir Ragnarok's office with the dwarven ex-Gemology teacher, Professor Margarite Lithoman, whose real name turned out to be Eliza Elungwen, swam between his eyes.

'Alfie Agrock. You're the A in the Shape,' whispered Sammy. 'It's been you all along. The mug with the initials "AA" in the tunnel that didn't belong to Commander

Altair. It was you up in the Land of Darkness. You've been following me. You wanted me to find the Angel of 'El Horidore for you.'

The dwarf laughed. 'Well done Sammy Rambles. You're not as stupid as you look.'

Sammy felt his blood boil. He was furious and he stepped forward towards the dwarf, his fist raised.

Before he could get anywhere close, Alfie Agrock raised the gold whistle triumphantly above his head. He lowered it to his thick lips and blew hard into the Angel whistle.

There was a pause, then a sweet music filled the air, wailing high then low, like the noise Kyrillan sometimes made when he was asleep. It rose louder and louder until the sound was all around them.

'My princess, they will come!' Alfie Agrock laughed and held Dixie tightly to his chest. 'Now we will be invincible! We will bring everyone together for the feasting. What a joyful day this will be. It will go down in history!'

Sammy looked up in horror as Alfie Agrock threw the Angel of 'El Horidore at his feet and weaved a thick fog in the fragile walls of the den. With an almighty explosion, the tree walls burst apart with flames shooting high into the forest above.

Sammy knelt on the earth, reaching for Darius and Naomi, Milly and the others. The explosion had knocked them over and he dragged them one by one out into the open.

As he pulled Jock, feet first, out of where the den doorway had been, he saw two pairs of shoes stretching up into long black capes and the concerned faces of Sir Ragnarok and Commander Altair.

'My father is on his way,' said Commander Altair, brushing the fog away with an emerald green stone flashing at the end of his staff.

Sir Ragnarok waved a handful of rubies at the frozen bodies to bring them back to life and reached for Sammy's shoulder. He held up a familiar circle of gold that Sammy recognised as Sir Ragnarok's Directometer.

'You saw it all,' stammered Sammy. 'You saw everything that just happened. Why did he do that? Why did he blow the whistle?'

'You did what you thought best,' said Sir Ragnarok. 'No-one could have asked you for anymore.'

Sammy bent down and picked up the golden whistle that was the Angel of 'El Horidore and handed it to Sir Ragnarok.

'Was this the real Angel of 'El Horidore, made by King Serberon's dwarves, Sir?' asked Sammy quietly. 'Is it the real Angel whistle that my parents had before my Uncle Peter turned them in to the Shape. Was it this Angel they had before they lost their powers and they lost their ability to see dragons?'

Sir Ragnarok nodded sombrely. 'This Angel whistle is as real as you or I. Many years ago, your father kicked it along with his diamond eyed head boy Dragon Minder pin into this very treestump and the two sealed together. It is a very clever trick I have seen only once before where it has been possible to make solid matter pass through solid matter.'

Commander Altair nodded. 'It's hugely advanced magic. I would suspect that the Angel of 'El Horidore has magic of its own which helped your father that day.'

'You knew where it was?' asked Sammy, looking at his headmaster. 'If you knew, why didn't you get it yourself?'

Sir Ragnarok smiled. 'Oh yes Sammy, I have known it's whereabouts for some time now, but with your clever magic seal I have been unable to retrieve it. Quite handy you'll agree, since the Shape have not been able to get inside either,' he chuckled. 'Quite inconvenient when you think this tree stump leads to the house next to your Uncle Peter's house, an old apothecary hiding all kinds of poisons in its time that they have previously made considerable use of the premises.'

'The other trapdoor in the tunnel,' whispered Sammy.

'Indeed. Now is everybody accounted for?' asked Sir Ragnarok. 'I can see Milly, Naomi, Darius, Jock, Gavin and Toby. The effect of the ruby will wear off soon enough.'

'Where's Dixie?' asked Sammy anxiously. He looked around the debris of the den, moving sticks and checking the piles of leaves. 'She was right here,' he whispered.

There was a long pause and they searched the clearing, checking under the each end every one of the den branches and in the surrounding bushes.

Eventually Commander Altair shook his head. 'I can't see her. Everyone else is here. Alfie Agrock must have taken her.'

'What for?' demanded Sammy, throwing down one of the branches he had picked up. 'He got what he wanted.'

'You may have saved her life,' Commander Altair smiled grimly.

Sammy read between the lines, tears falling unasked from his eyes. 'I've killed all the dragons in the world, haven't I. They'll be murdered as soon as they get here.'

'We will do what we can,' said Sir Ragnarok. 'Things tomorrow may not be as bad as they seem today.'

'Wise words,' agreed Commander Altair. 'We must trust that Dixie will be returned safely.'

'What do we do now?' asked Sammy fiercely rubbing his eyes.

'Go home.' said Sir Ragnarok flatly. 'It is all we can do for now.'

Sammy's eyes widened as the truth dawned on him. Whether he had blown the Angel whistle himself or not, he, Sammy Rambles, was the person who was responsible for calling all dragons, living and dead to Dragamas.

In moments they would be arriving and there was nothing he, nor anybody else could do to prevent it.

The End.

Sammy Rambles and the Fires of Karmandor

J T SCOTT

"I'm sorry Sammy, there is no way to tell where she went."

Sammy stared bleakly. It had been a tense summer after the climatic events at the end of the summer term. He had known Sir Ragnarok, Headmaster of Dragamas, for nearly four years and not once had he seen him this pale, this tired, or this angry.

"There is no way to tell where she went," repeated Sir Ragnarok.

Tying the past and present together Sammy needs to find his friend and uncover her link to the ancient Queen Karmandor. Sammy must use all his skills to attempt a daring rescue whilst staying on top of his schoolwork and celebrating a wedding.

As the legend of Karmandor comes true, it begins the systematic destruction of everything Sammy cares about in the dragon world. He finds himself yet again in the hands of the Shape and almost powerless to do anything about it.

www.sammyrambles.com

Sammy Rambles
and the
Knights of the Stone Cross

J T SCOTT

Bringing everyone together one last time, Sammy's final year at Dragamas sees him fight his fiercest battle yet.

Can he find the last member of the Shape?

Can he free Karmandor?

Will he escape with his life?

www.sammyrambles.com

Made in the USA
Charleston, SC
18 November 2016